CAMPUS COLA

CAMPUS COLA

N. Sampath Kumar

Rupa & Co

Published 2011 by
Rupa Publications India Pvt. Ltd.
7/16, Ansari Road, Daryaganj,
New Delhi 110 002

Sales Centres:

Allahabad Bengaluru Chennai
Hyderabad Jaipur Kathmandu
Kolkata Mumbai

Printed at Repro Knowledgecast Limited, Thane

To my dear mom and dad,
for standing in for God;
and to all my gurus,
for standing by me;
and to all my friends,
for letting me be;
and above all to you,
for reading the new

Contents

Acknowledgements   *ix*
Author's Note   *xi*
Statutory Warnings   *xiii*
Prologue   *xv*

1. Confusion, Fatty Decides, Escape from Delhi   1

2. Defcoms, Ragging, First Fiasco, Our Gang   11

3. Escape from Defcoms, North Campus, Mehrauli Party   22

4. Love Guru, Good and Bad Seniors, First Socials   39

5. The Ecstasies, Maniacs Cry Foul, First Date   56

6. Jilted, Sunk by ABBA, Suspense of ABBA   72

7. Road Trip, Taming of Gattu, Return to Square One   88

8. No Mercy, No Lust, No Kiss   106

9. First Strike, Rahul Attack, the Trick, the Blush   121

10. A Simple Plan, Greedy Encore, Zeno Girls   146

11. The Results, the Monarchs, the Rave   168

12. The Dare, Proxy Trouble, Inquiry, Pure Blackmail   178

13. Bluff Master, Mess Committee, Cryptic, Gattu's Logic   196

14. The Foreigners, the Boycott, the Guilt, the Learning   216

15. Bum Chums, Tulip Terraces, Lighthouse   234

16. The Change, the Harassment, the Postponement   252

17. The Bulldozer, the Shock, the Rumblings   267

18. The Mother of All Strikes   282

19. The Aftermath, the Case, the Houdini, the End   311

20. The Vodka, the Journey, God, the Games   319

Epilogue   336

Glossary   341

Acknowledgements

Krishna, Supreme Magician, Godhead.
Kapish G. Mehra, publisher nonpareil.
Sumana Ahom, editor par excellence.
Rupa's entire team, industrious folks.
Natz, thought-sharpener extraordinaire.
Maddy, Venky, family tree, mind vitamins.
B, O, K, SAV, SP, my lights, love pools.
Maya, bosom buddy, eternal sorceress.
Bhagavad Gita and *Bhagavatam*, gurus.
India, my first love, my home, my pride.
Zzzzzz, 'ideator', original thinker, guide.
Pals, oceanic hearts, sounding boards.
My mom, angelic lifeline, divine miracle.
Dear departed dad, pure soul, devotee.
Me, humble, infallible, *soi-disant* brainiac.
God, the only competition I will ever have.

Author's Note

Dear Beloved Reader,

Hi! They call me Sam when they are in a good mood – which is not often. Mostly they use nasty terms for me that would make a fish market blush. Anyway, let's coolly move on.

When I sat down to pen this campus story that actually never happened many moons ago, I thought about you – what style you'd like; whether or not you'd like cuss words; why you'd want to fork out precious money picking up this one instead of spending it on intellectual activities like watching high IQ item numbers in cinema halls full of low life...

Then I said eff it! (That 'eff' stands for 'forget', you one-track mind!)

'Just write for yourself, Sam,' I told myself, 'if someone buys it, then it is their problem and momentary lapse of reason...'

Anyway, after a week of self-motivational talks I said eff off to my chatterbox cerebrum too. (This time around, your slang-loving mind is right about that 'eff' thing though.)

So I decided to let my heart and 60-wpm-fingers do the talking instead. (Wpm = words per minute, in case you are from Burundi or Botswana or both.)

Hence, this novel has *soul*. Read it with yours.

Maybe you'll enjoy it – unless you carry some congenital Anti-Fun Gene or something.

Btw, this phenomenal (and at times, not so phenomenal) work of fiction comes with a money-back guarantee if you don't like what follows—*provided* I become richer than our global village's kompootur-savvy sarpanch, Shri Bhillu Ghates, lol...

Cheers! Have fun, take care, and God bless ☺

Yours *sincerely*,
Sam

P.S. Methinks there will only be four reactions to this novel though: (a) It's cool (if you are a warm, friendly, happy-go-lucky, intelligent kid between 6 and 60); (b) It's lousy (if you are a grouchy, cantankerous 61-year-old suffering from chronic acidity); (c) It's chilled out, folks! (if you are hip and happening); and (d) I just love Sam! (if you are Sam).

Statutory Warnings

Children below sixty are advised parental guidance.

Children above sixty are advised to adopt some parents.

Heart patients will die laughing.

Folks who fall in love will be considered heart patients.

All those who pursue medicine do so at their own risk.

All those who don't join medical school are wimps who take no risks.

Anyone who doesn't laugh will be honoured in tomorrow's obituary.

Anyone who laughs will pay an entertainment tax to the author or to the government – whosoever is more powerful by the time this hits the stands.

Those who take these warnings seriously will be forced to join kindergarten.

Prologue

Now. 0310 HRS. 11 December 2008.

𝒯HEY SAY THE CLOSEST THINGS TO A MAN'S HEART ARE: (a) His mum during childhood; (b) His woman during adulthood; and (c) His bank balance during hunchback-hood. I haven't the foggiest idea which chronological category I fit into right now as the only thing that sets my pulse racing these days is trouncing my remote opponent on Yahoo! Chess. Apart from that, there's nothing else that makes me happy.

I log in daily and dive right into an online chess room called Frog Pond because that's precisely how I am feeling nowadays—like the proverbial croaker thirsting for the magical damsel's kiss which will transform him into a charming prince—and generally live on the hope that something miraculous awaits me just round the corner.

You will surely agree that depression makes you believe in anything, even fairy tales and miracles. Well, since miracles are in short supply these days, at least in Thane—which is a stone's throw from South Bombay, provided you can chuck a stone to a teeny-weeny distance of some forty-odd km—online chess is the best way to dawdle away the ten to twelve waking hours that you *must* kill intellectually day after day just to remain sane and keep your mind off nauseating thought patterns.

Like: Don't you know all females are the type of spiders or scorpions that eat or sting the mate after mating?/Arachnophobia should mean fear of females, no? – hasn't the dictionary got it all wrong?/Didn't I warn you that all girls are just LPG cylinders rolling from one needy customer to another?/You are finished man finished, a spent force, a born loser, and a gone case, what use life?

Repetitively nauseating, isn't it?

Neither reefers nor Old Monk rum help drown the mad voices that are churning my gut, numbing my heart, and systematically crippling my self-confidence, self-esteem, self-worth or self-*whatever's-left-of-me*.

I'd love to jump out of my body, mind, heart and all, but haven't mastered that voodoo art yet.

Only Yahoo! Chess helps, especially when I am winning. Anti-depressants don't. 1. e4 e5. If I'm on a winning streak I continue playing and write happily between moves. 2. Nf3 Nc6. If I'm on a losing streak I continue playing and write sadly between moves. So, that's my life these days, and these days are nothing to write home about.

Last week my shrink said I'd get over this phase very pretty soon. I asked her how soon was *very pretty soon*. She said as soon as I accepted the fact that life dishes out numbing experiences to steel us enough so we can easily face more numbing experiences in the near future, which in turn will help us absorb even more numbing experiences on our immune chin in the distant future.

How very reassuring! I'm almost beginning to fall in love with *numbing experiences* and thanking them for being so very considerate, and for taking such a personal interest in making me stronger and stronger and stronger, hah, and how I wish they were persons I could hug and kiss and marry because we are bonding so very well. 3. Bc4 Bc5.

I walked out of her clinic feeling so low and abysmal that I thought I ought to be decompressed when I surfaced back into life.

'Life is nothing but a series of *numb*———>*number*———>*numbest* experiences strung together till Death,' my shrink had droned on.

I swear on Lord Vishnu's cosmic-fury-fuelled, raging, golden, serrated *Sudharshan Chakra* that I'd have sued her for leaving me more depressed than ever before had I not been so sapped and drained by the sessions, both mentally and monetarily.

The only thing I'm sure is going to happen very pretty soon is the very pretty murder of a very pretty shrink. 4. d3 black out! Dammit! Another power cut! Thane is the worst place in the world to tide over your blues in.

'Why the hell don't you get the UPS repaired, you dimwit?' I scream.

'Get a life, man, or get yourself a laptop, but I guess you're too broke and broken-hearted to do that…dude, stop sulking like a horny whore in a monastery…and count your blessings that at least I have a PC,' guffaws a distant voice from the bedroom that belongs to Paddy, my flatmate-cum-nephew-cum-confidant.

'Shut up and don't act cute. Don't forget how you wailed like a wimp when Suzy dumped you in Delhi,' I say.

'It's three in the morning and you better grab some shut-eye. Psychologists say one gets the most romantic dreams at four in the morning. Mostly wet. Reality bites, dream excites,' he says, dodging my barb, and laughs the laughter of sadists thrilled to bits by their catty rhymes.

'Bastard!' I scream, and sail into the kitchen to get some candles.

'Ditto,' he retorts. 'And get me a Coke while you are at it – and resist the temptation of making faces with the candlelight held in front of your face. Don't reflect horror in the bathroom mirror and frighten yourself to sleep and suffer nightmares and wake me up…'

'Shutthafuckup! Did you get Maggi and Knorr soup?' I ask.

'Ya, but I guess the cylinder's empty, hook up the spare, no mushrooms for me though, just onions and some potato…'

'Buzz off! If you want Maggi, you come and make it,' I say grouchily, and light up a cigarette with the candle that has just been lit with the cigarette lighter. It's fun lighting up a ciggie with a freshly-lit candle. The smell of melting, crackling, vaporising paraffin wax combined with nicotine is a heady combination and guarantees a double high. Try it sometime and please don't tell the Health Minister I told you so.

Chess. Cooking. Chronicling. That's all it takes to give the dipping mood the anti-gravity lift-off. Either I am playing or cooking or writing these days since I am economically inactive and can't concentrate on my work as a Creative Director in my medium-sized ad agency. Why, you ask? I'll give you four reasons. 1) Because you have to be happy to be creative, and I am anything but happy. 2) Because Tanu aka Tanuja Mistry dumped me last month for a hotshot hunk, and gave me the blues. 3) Because my boss wants me to 'take a break and recharge'. 4) None of your meddlesome business. (Okay, okay, sorry about the last one. Blame the outburst on melancholy.)

So, Paddy has invited me over to his place and promptly employed me as his flunkey, which is not a bad thing considering that all I have to do is walk his dog, Zorro; man his kitchen; and entertain his girlfriend, Neelu, with vulgar jokes and French fries, when she shacks up with us during some weekends.

At forty-three, I guess it's okay to be dumped by a nineteen-something, nubile girl who fell for you after watching *Nishabd*—a Bollywood movie starring a nymphet who falls for a cradle-snatching sexagenarian (pun not intended)—and wooed, courted, proposed and mated you for a torrid seven months.

Then she went and watched mushy old teenybopper-loved classics like *Grease*, *Grease II*, and *The Blue Lagoon*, and decided that youthful oestrogen deserves equally youthful testosterone. So, she dumped a zero-pack fatso already half his way into his grave and made this book happen. Sigh.

I should have seen it all coming and saved my ego by dumping her *before* she dumped me, but then, dude, I didn't see it all coming.

So then, there she is: cuddling a wannabe actor; and here I am: cooking for my nephew.

Life's unjust and unfair, and I wish to grab Life by the scruff of its neck and screw its trip, but how the hell do you go about doing that to Life? Any ideas?

I wouldn't have been feeling this way if Ranju were alive.

Ah, Ranju. My human sunrise. My friendly goddess. My wife. My life. We'd got married a week before my twenty-ninth birthday anniversary; and she'd died a month after my thirtieth. That's when I slipped into a major depression which has become as permanent a part of me as my semi-Tamil accent. It's been a tad more than thirteen years since Ranju left me and I don't think I can ever get over her. I'm a loyal lover, no? Clap for me please.

Well, that's my story till now, but who the hell wants to be in the *now*?

Let's walk down the staircase of time – into the *then*; the salad days; the happiest years of my life.

If you're wondering who is Ranju and how we got together, I invite you into the monsoon of 1985. Come, be a part of my life at Defcoms, Bangalore, where it all began…

I

Confusion, Fatty Decides, Escape from Delhi

Then. July through August 1985.

THEY SAY ONLY THREE KINDS OF PEOPLE JOIN DEFCOMS, Bangalore: (a) Those who are looking for a secure career as a doctor in one of the Indian armed forces; (b) Those who are looking to pay out and work later as a civilian doctor; and (c) Those who don't know what they are looking for.

I belonged to the third category.

That's not *entirely* true though. I had just graduated with a dumb B.Sc. degree in Botany from Hans Raj College, Delhi; and the main reasons that had driven me towards the course were three: (a) I could be part of the North Campus cool scene for a while; (b) I could hit on my classmate, Vishaka, a ravishing bomb from my school who had joined the same course; and (c) I could just get some stupid degree and join a newspaper later. I knew what I was looking for then and I called them the three 'F's – Fun, Frolic, Freedom. Let me tell you, it was pretty difficult to add the world-famous fourth F to that list. (Yes, the one that rhymes with 'luck', because the only things that ever got laid regularly in my life were dinner plates on the dining table – well, at least that was my situation till I got married; and after my wife died and I reached the magical age of forty-two, I met that nineteen-something bitch called Tanu who dumped me as if I were an over-burnt, barbecued potato, *after* using me like a sex toy-cum-teddy bear for a while. Well, given my size and shape now, that teddy bear analogy is both metaphorically and physiologically true, I guess.)

Anyway, so there I was, gawkily manoeuvring an age when you are battling pimples and hormones, while also trying to desperately find the three 'F's wherever you could. You'd agree that only life-denying nerds cared for the three 'R's – Reading, 'Riting, 'Rithmetic. All such depraved souls usually joined IIT (India's best engineering college, which is also your visa to MIT or Caltech). Or, they went to AIIMS (India's best medical school, which is your passport to superstardom status in the marriage market). Or, they joined Defcoms (India's most disciplined medical school, which is your business class travel ticket to prestigious patriotism); or, some such huge institution which designed huge entrance exams that hugely taxed your confidence levels and sent you huge rejection letters saying how hugely brainless you were. I got rejected eighteen times by twenty-three different exams. How, you ask? Since that doesn't add up? You sure are smart, buddy. Well, I bunked five exams, heehee, and while my parents thought I was taking medical entrance exams, I was actually taking acting lessons from Richard Burton and screaming lessons from Bruce Lee and shooting lessons from Clint Eastwood, either at a seedy theatre or at a friend's place, thanks to the National VHS recorders that had just made their appearance in India.

I'm sure you have rightly guessed by now that I wasn't the studious type, and I'd just taken any medical entrance exam that came my way for a lark. In fact, I took them just to please my folks so that they could flaunt the fact on their filter coffee circuit that their son was not idling away his life, but was fruitfully involved in noble pastimes like getting rejected by med schools.

Whether I ever got through or not was never an issue, at least not at home. Dad always said that one was allowed to fail provided the failure was not due to lack of attempt. I was always pretty impressed with his wisdom and his ability to pack profound intelligence within the space of a few crisp words. Pity, I never inherited his intellectual genes though; or, for the record, his wit, grit and knowledge. All I had done was flip through *Rajhans Guide* for a week before any entrance exam; otherwise, my only preparation consisted of reading Agatha Christie and Alistair MacLean.

So, when I got through the Defcoms entrance test, and was also allotted Bangalore, it came as a nasty surprise to me and a huge relief for my folks. (Defcoms was located at three places: Allahabad, Bangalore and Calcutta. If you got into the Bangalore Defcoms you were lucky because that was the only co-ed college of its kind. Allahabad and Calcutta only absorbed male candidates. Who'd like monasteries, dude?) Everyone's son or daughter was either trying to get into IIT or into a medical college, and anyone who wasn't trying to cerebrally bulldoze their way into either of these destinations was thought to be suffering from incurable dementia or insanity or both. There ought to have been a law against peer pressure. There wasn't.

Anyway, that was the general trend in our Tam-Brahm circles. So, there I was: getting flattened like a pancake because all our family friends kept pressuring me to join Defcoms 'to just check things out', as they put it.

Dad said if I didn't feel up to it I could quit anytime and he'd fork out the ninety-five grand which was the bond amount. You needed to cough this up if you quit midway or decided not to join the armed forces upon completion of your MBBS course. (The latter scenario was most likely in my case, considering that I loved regimentation as much as Jughead loved fasting; or as much as Bush loved Iraq. That was in 1985. Today, I'm told the payout amount is a king's ransom or close to what Somali pirates are demanding. Same thing.)

I was confused. And, Karol Bagh was a wrong place to be confused in. I could bump into numberless uncles, aunties and well-wishers who'd only push me into it unthinkingly.

So I decided to take a walk into Pusa Institute with my closest buddy and batchmate, Fatty. He had decided to do M.Sc. and I had had enough of Botany.

In fact, I was so tired of Botany that I could not bear to look at vegetables for a while. I even hated trees and anything green. Reminds me of a quote I had read somewhere: 'I am not a vegetarian because I love animals; I am a vegetarian because I just *hate* plants.' The course had sickened me to the gills and I wondered what was driving him to do M.Sc. in Botany.

'Well, I plan to join the National Institute of Immunology,' he said.

'Hell. Research. Staying cooped up in a lab all day long – I'll go crazy, man, if I do that.'

'Ya, but I'm a different kettle of fish altogether. As you can see, I'm a bit of the antisocial types. I like to keep away from people and this will be the perfect cover for the rest of my life,' he said.

'Sure, but what the hell should I do, buddy? My life seems like a rudderless ship. My brain is as decisive as an Ethiopian refugee at a buffet. And there's so much pressure to get a darned groovy professional degree from all quarters. Wish I hadn't got through – then things would've been simpler. My mind is spinning like those roulette wheels we see in James Bond movies...'

Fatty remained silent. That's one thing I liked about him. He was the kind that listened, absorbed, and never interrupted. He was the perfect sounding board and I'd told him many times that he'd make a great shrink.

I rambled on and on, and on the return journey we walked into West Patel Nagar market and polished off three plates of *gol gappa* (*paani puri*, if you are from Bombay). The gol gappa spiced up my confusion.

'Do you think I should just toss up a coin or something?' I asked.

'You know your problem...?' he said.

'Ya, I don't know what I want from life.'

'No, nobody does actually – at least not at our age. We just gravitate to whatever and try to convince ourselves later that we were right.'

'Then what's my problem?'

'You think too much. There are too many ifs and buts and what-ifs happening in you. You need to flow with the flow. You need to follow your heart, but you keep relying on your mind instead.'

'My heart's divided too.'

'No, the heart's *never* divided. The mind is. You *think* your heart's divided. Tell me, what do you *love* the most in life?'

'Hmmm...Novels, girls, Billy Joel, ABBA, Wham, *aloo paranthas*, *rajma chawal, gaajar halwa...*'

'Stop being superficial, I mean deeply,' he said, interrupting me uncharacteristically.

'Well, you expect me to say freedom, independence—that sort of thing?'

'Exactly. You've often cribbed about how stifled you feel and how you'd like to fly out of the cage. *The bird that never tries never flies*, to quote you.'

'Ya, freedom would be most welcome.'

'Then this is the perfect opportunity. Bangalore. Miles away from home. New life, new friends, new hope, and new freedom. Even new loves, who knows?'

'And what if I don't like it there—you know I've never stayed in a hostel before—and what if I don't want to join the army later?'

'Shit. Again "what-ifs" are grabbing you. Then, you can pay out. Simple. I'm sure your dad can afford it.'

So the decision was made for me by Fatty.

◇

I went home and announced that I had decided to join Defcoms.

Dad was happy that his son would become a 'noble' doctor (though I wasn't too sure if I'd be able to live up to that adjective in the coming years). Mom was happy too, but was becoming quite misty-eyed thinking about all the years of separation she'd have to endure. My confused cardiac climate was so foggy that I didn't even know if I was happily sad or sadly happy.

They say when you take a decision it beautifully integrates your being. You are supposed to feel de-burdened and de-cluttered and refreshed. They also say that decisiveness makes you feel as light as a *roomali roti* and that gravity has no effect on your consciousness after that.

They are absolutely wrong.

I was nervous as hell (what if this was going to be the *'wrongest'* decision of my life?) and the nervousness must have weighed a few tonnes.

Just as I was about to sit for dinner, the phone rang. Dad picked it up and said there was some girl on the line.

'Hello,' I said.

'Hi, it's me – recognise me?'

I wondered what kick people got out of making you play guessing games and ending up feeling sad that your guess turned out to be wrong.

'Ya, of course I do. Parveen Babi, isn't it?'

'Shut up. It's Mandira Dhillon,' said an unfamiliar voice.

I became miffed that an unfamiliar voice had asked me to shut up and asked rather sharply, 'Mandira...Dhillon...you sure you've dialled the right number?'

'Of course, Hari, I have. You even forgot my name, *huhn*? I saw your number in the newspaper. How sad *I* couldn't make it to Defcoms. But congratulations, anyway...'

'Thanks...ohhh sorry...it's youuu...' I said, recalling who she was.

We had a long convo on how she should've listened to me, etc.

Flashback: I met Mandira Dhillon at Army Public School the day we both were taking the Defcoms entrance test. We'd got into a casual discussion on how to tackle the questions and I discovered that her dad was an Air Commodore. She was accompanied by a very eager mother and a burly batman who kept asking me to help her. He kept forcing me actually.

She was sitting bang in front of me (she had arranged that) and when the test began, the invigilator—I think he was a Squadron Leader—walked up to me, wished me all the best, and said Mandira and I could discuss the answers if we so desired. I had no such desire but she pleaded with me to help her.

I said okay, we'll tackle the intelligence test first, and then proceed to Psychology, General Knowledge, English, Biology, Chemistry and Physics MCQs. She nodded assent at the strategy. After a while, we compared answers and then she didn't nod assent regarding my logic on quite a few. I was mildly irked that (a) she thought I was wrong and (b) she thought so with the kind of confidence that can get your goat. So, I just asked her to copy from my answer sheet, jokingly assuring her that that was the only way she'd get through, but she was one of those headstrong girls (I guess all those with an armed forces background are) and muddled along through the rest of the questions on her own. And, she didn't make it as I had so chillingly mock-predicted. End of flashback.

She wanted me to meet her at Connaught Place, so we decided to chin-wag a bit over a pizza at Nirula's the next day.

She was late. I hate it when someone doesn't respect your sense of time. You can steal my money, my books, my girls, even my good luck talismans, that's okay by me, but you can't steal my time – that's too precious. I was angry but she was looking so damn low that I let it pass.

'I should've listened to you…shit, we both would've joined together…me and my stupid ego…' she wailed as she sat down.

'Ya, but it's cool. We win some, lose some. You can always try next year, *yaar*,' I consoled her.

'No, I won't. Mom says I should get married and there's this guy from US who wants to marry me.'

'Hey, you can't be serious! How old are you? Eighteen?'

'Yup, close.'

'Aren't you a li'l too young to get married now? I mean there's so much to life, so much to do, before you take this once-in-a-lifetime decision. Think it over, only fools rush in…'

'Ya, I thought it over. Perhaps I'll study there or start working or something,' she said, whipping out from her handbag a small photograph of a bespectacled, nerdy guy propped up against a red sports car. (What a typical, garish way of fishing for compliments and/or girls looking for NRI grooms, yuck!) 'He's a brilliant IITian working with MIT. Perhaps we'll have a long engagement. You like him?'

'Hey, this guy looks the professor types – I dunno, it's your decision. Who knows, maybe you guys are made for each other, maybe not. Anyway, you should just follow your heart,' I said, plagiarising Fatty.

'If I do that, then I'll have to go with you.'

I sputtered out the fresh lime ice cream soda as she said that, and there was an awkward pause between us which was filled with mouthfuls of pizza.

What can you say to someone who was so obviously in love with you and looked so down and out as if a lifelong dream had just been nuked? You can't say anything. You can just make polite convo and ask them to move on.

Pity, she was so pretty, pleasant and friendly. She wasn't a bomb, but it would've been great to be with her. Perhaps I should've forced her to listen to me at the test. I felt guilty and wanted to gather her in my arms but didn't.

She wished to go for a movie, and though I hated to disappoint her, I really had lots of stuff to do back home, so I promised her that we'd surely grab a flick some other day.

'Can you at least come with me to Palika Bazaar? I need to pick up some stuff,' she said, and I had no choice but to play along for a while.

Perhaps she was testing me with the marriage bit, I don't know. Girls sometimes do that to see how you'll react, and if you register disappointment, then they know you are interested in them. If you remain poker-faced or say congratulations, then they know they have to try their romantic luck elsewhere.

Anyway, I was too full of myself to feel any deep emotion for anyone else, romantic or otherwise. So, we just exchanged addresses after she was through with her shopping and promised to keep in touch and never did.

But I still think of Mandira Dhillon on many days and hope she is doing well, wherever she is. Prayers bridge people, as Rammy would have said. (You'll meet my guru later as we chug along.)

God only knows why so many people come to see you off as if you are going on Apollo 13 to the moon. Seven uncles, sixteen aunties, eight cousins, twenty friends, five colleagues from Dad's bank, us three, and scores of other passengers with *their* parents, uncles, aunties, cousins, friends and *their dad's* colleagues dotted the chockablock concourse at New Delhi railway station.

Surely the Indian Railways makes more money through sales of platform coupons than those of journey tickets, I thought.

And you had to wish everyone goodbye and listen to the usual crazy advice like 'don't trust anyone' and 'don't fall into bad company' and 'don't do anything that will shame the honour of the family' and 'don't forget us', etc.

Nearly everyone wailed saying they loved me so very much and I was wondering if love-suffocation was precisely what I was escaping from. There are times when you don't want *anyone to love you or to care about you* – all the attention can be so very stifling.

I kept telling myself that I had to put up with them for just a wee bit longer, but the CinemaScope smile I had put on was burning my cheeks and killing all ideas of social grace. Politeness can be so very painful.

Their questions were rapping on my brain like woodpeckers and making it look like shredded cottage cheese. Have you taken extra woollens? Have you taken your certificates? Have you taken the first-aid kit? Have you taken our telephone numbers? Have you taken the savouries we brought for you? I wouldn't have been surprised if they had asked me: Have you taken yourself?

I sprained my tongue saying 'yes' seventy-six times.

Mom didn't say *anything*. She was choked with emotion and fear and was silently praying to all the gods worth praying to – which, I am told is close to 330 million, according to the celestial census figure recorded in the Indian Demigods Database. I wasn't the emotional kind—in fact, I felt sentiments were inversely proportional to one's intelligence—so I guess you could say I had close to zero EQ (at least at that time).

Finally and thankfully, the train blew its whistle and we escaped. But not before doing the final courteous thing of standing at the doorway, and waving and waving and waving to everyone rooted to the platform or running with the train, till they all became unrecognisable specks on the sooty horizon.

2

Defcoms, Ragging,
First Fiasco, Our Gang

Then. August through September 1985.

YOU GET OFF AT BANGALORE RAILWAY STATION. YOU SEE A
board saying National Hotel. You check in. Then what do you do
when you discover that it's a hub of shady and seamy activities? You
say it's okay, we are going to be here only for a day or two, so it
doesn't really matter.

Then you take an autorickshaw to Hosur Road. The driver is
talkative. He reminds you of magpies. Or, of yourself, hah! He tells
you everything you don't want to know about him, his family, his silly
in-laws, even his gonorrhoea that got cured at Defcoms OPD.

But you are too happy to ask him to shut up. You enjoy the ride.
You see a hoarding inviting you to the Bangalore race course and
the energy of the photogenic Arab stallions is infectious. You think
about your grandpa and how he had squandered his wealth on one
of these some three decades ago.

Then you ask for directions to Bangalore Military School as you
pretend to halt for tea to make sure the driver isn't cheating you.
Then you alight, bang opposite a massive colonial building with the
Indian flag decorating its colossal dome and fluttering majestically

in the breeze. You are reminded of British architects and Rashtrapati Bhavan which you had visited a year ago to meet the First Lady, along with your mom and her music group.

You see Defence College of Medical Sciences written in big brass letters. You feel proud. Your dad feels proud. You decide to join the Indian army one day. You walk the walk of a winner. Your dad walks the walk of a winner's dad.

Everything about Defcoms is grand and sublime. The place pulsates with importance. The human robots are going about their work with determined discipline. The air crackles with military precision. The drizzle-kissed atmosphere glows with respect and honour. The winds continue to caress the Indian tricolour patriotically.

You feel energised. The scene is the optical equivalent of Horlicks or Boost.

You are escorted into a huge room seating about twenty-odd students. You are asked to provide your credentials and present the bond you have got typed on stamp papers.

The formalities last just three hours and then you go for a medical test.

Those guys have a long list of chronic ailments, chronic diseases, acute conditions and incurable maladies, which, if you are generously hosting, would result in your being shown the door equally generously.

Thankfully, it is discovered that the only disease you are hosting is a bloated ego. They have nothing against that. You are cleared.

You are finally and decisively in. Thank God.

Dad had left two days ago and I had checked in at the hostel. The first thing I was made to do was a cool hundred push-ups by two seniors who kept telling me that this wasn't 'ragging' – this was just 'orientation'.

But all the ragging was mostly exercise. Push-ups, pull-ups, front rolls, back rolls, frog leaps, and lots of other aerobic *asanas* – a far cry from gross ragging like dunking your head into the WC or stripping or crass ego-crunching stuff you are subjected to at other engineering and medical college campuses. You could say even the ragging at Defcoms was pretty disciplined and all.

Looking back, I think it was all a pretty nice way to begin the day. It made the adrenaline and other juices in your body pump up like crazy, made you awfully hungry, and awesomely tough. At Defcoms, you ended up feeling like a gymnast and you were ready to take part in the Olympics. You discovered how flexible your body was and how much it could take with a little bit of prodding.

So I got oriented to the entire Defcoms culture in less than two hours and felt like going and getting a whole body massage (preferably sandwich) in Pattaya. But to begin with, you had to get yourself a makeover.

First, you needed to get a 'zero cut' and look like a plucked chicken. Second, you needed to go to Brigade Road and order name tags and other *de rigueur* stuff for yourself. Third, you needed to get into a drab navy blue trouser, a white shirt, a drab navy blue tie and a pair of black boots – all of which made you look like a steward from a glitzy restaurant. (I lied that I hadn't picked up the regulation gear yet as that would give me a few more days in my casual wear – which were called civvies, short for civilian dress. I had everything ready in my suitcase actually, but why be so eager to look like a mutant penguin?)

By afternoon I bumped into an acquaintance from Hans Raj College. This guy, Sushil Solanki, was doing Chemistry at that time, and we had met each other often whenever we went to catch some sleazy movie at Amba or Palace with our respective gangs during our Delhi days.

These two movie halls were always packed with the North Campus crowd, especially during the morning shows when they religiously screened some erotic *desi* C-grade flick. You know, the kind that says *Private Secretary – Ready For Dicktations* on a titillating poster that shows a thunder thigh actress who seems to have been brought up on an exclusive diet of Amul butter and *desi ghee* and dubious family morals.

Sushil now wanted to be called Solly though—he felt that was pretty hep and all—and I didn't mind as long as I had the company of a fellow Delhiite.

So, off we went to Brigade Road after dodging a few seniors. We were reliving our Delhi days over a bottle of soya milk and a greasy hamburger at a roadside stall when we spotted a few freshers in blues and whites. Our official joining date was two days later so we were still sporting long hair and wearing jeans and T-shirts.

I swear, it was Solly's idea. He said since we were looking like seniors, it would be fun to rib these freshers a bit. Actually I never liked the idea of ragging anyone and said let's not try anything funny, but even as I was trying to dissuade him, he walked up to the freshers and stood arms akimbo in front of them.

'Aha, freshies huhn, ready to join Defcoms?' asked Solly.

'Yes, sir,' chorused three squeaky voices.

'Do you know which batch we're from?' he asked, pointing me out as well.

I walked up to them.

'No, sir,' said the squeaky voices.

'Uniform batch,' said Solly, and they stiffened like starched shirts. Uniform batch was the senior-most at that time and was pretty notorious when it came to ragging, sorry, orientation.

Anyway, he just ordered them around, gave them some money, asked them to get us some coconut macaroons and ice cream, and made them sing his favourite song: *Zindagi Kaisi Hai Paheli* from Rajesh Khanna's *Anand*.

'Okay, let's move,' I said, nudging Solly, careful not to reveal our names.

But Solly was having fun and even a gigantic earth mover wouldn't have budged him an inch. He kept ribbing them with GK questions and told them that they were really dumb and he wondered how they had got through at all. I'd given up and was just standing quietly.

Then Solly made the biggest mistake. *Saala* idiot!

'Chill, guys, we were just joking,' he said, and laughed out loud. 'We're also freshers—my name is Sushil Solanki—you can call me Solly; and my friend here is Hari Iyengar – you can call him Hucky.'

The three squeaky voices laughed and said 'good joke' and we all shook hands and went our separate ways.

After they left, I gave him a piece of my mind.

'You brainless baboon! What was the need to tell them our names, sister-fucker?' I screamed.

'So what? A bit of *tafri* is always good for health,' he said. (Tafri = Hindi slang for idle fun.)

'Pigeon-fucker, if they rat on us, we've had it. We'll get mothered!'

'Nothing will happen. You vegetarians are just cowards – always worrying and shitting bricks. Solly says nothing will happen. Stay cool,' he said in a tone that reminded me of gang-lords. And, even of grandpa.

◇

Evening. 7 p.m. My room was 6 Top 1. Solly was camping in 6 Top 3. This meant we shared the same floor monitor. As we pushed open the gate to our floor, Solly and I froze.

A welcome party of twenty-odd seniors was waiting for us, along with our floor monitor, a bull called Ranjit Narang aka Rana, the Horrible. He looked like a butcher awaiting his prized lambs.

Nobody spoke. Not a word was said. The three squeaky voices were standing next to Rana. He just signalled with his hands, asking us to start. So, we started.

We front-rolled the entire length of the corridor about ten times. We back-rolled about ten times. Then we did fifty push-ups. Then we managed fifty pull-ups.

Someone gave us water. My eyes were too fuzzy to focus. I just took a few niggardly sips – you don't guzzle water when you are really thirsty. You just wet your lips and parched tongue – I had learned that from a western: in fact, from Eli Wallach in *The Good, the Bad and the Ugly*.

Refreshed.

Then we simulated a medical chair. I have to tell you about this. You had to pretend you were sitting erect on an imaginary chair, making an exact right angle at your knees, with your arms stretched out in front of you for balance. Your thighs would be parallel to the floor; your erect spine would be perpendicular to the floor; and your mind would be wishing your body were somewhere else.

Painful five minutes. More water.

Then we did the dead man's fall. Ten times. Want to hear about it or are you feeling queasy already? Let's run through it quickly. That was simple really. You had to imagine you were a corpse and fall flat on your chest, while also making sure you didn't smash your nose. You did this safely by breaking the fall at the nth second with your nimble palms which took your entire body weight in a way you never thought possible.

More water. In fact, lots of more water. We were given the cold shower treatment for about fifteen minutes.

All topped off with *murga* or rooster. This entailed sitting on your haunches; sliding your hands under your thighs; holding your left ear with your right hand fingers; and vice versa; and bobbing up and down till your face became red with the sudden rush of blood corpuscles and embarrassment.

Then Rana spoke.

'Did these two rag you on Brigade Road?' he asked the three squeaky voices.

'Yes, sir!' they squeaked.

'Did they finally tell you guys that they're actually your batchmates?'

'Yes, sir!'

'So they finally spoke the truth, didn't they? If they hadn't told you their names, you wouldn't have been able to squeal against them, right?'

'Yes, sir!'

I shot an 'I told you so' look at Solly. He looked away.

'And after they got their zero cut, you wouldn't have been able to recognise them either, right?'

'Yes, sir!'

'So you agree that here are two truthful young gentlemen who'll actually do the Indian army proud because they have the guts for adventure *and* for speaking the truth; whereas you guys who squeal on your *own* batchmates and get them into trouble for some pretty innocent humour are a blotch on the armed forces landscape? Am I right...?'

'No, sir! Their humour wasn't innocent, sir!'

'Really? What *exactly* did they ask you to do?'

'They asked us to get them coconut macaroons and ice cream, sir! And made us sing songs too!'

'And what's so *non*-innocent about that?'

The three squeaky voices scanned their system and found no appropriate answer in their database.

'You're sister-fucking bastards! That's what you three are. Absolutely no team spirit, no batch consciousness. In our times, we used to *protect* each other. *That* was *Uniform* batch. Mr Solanki and Mr Iyengar have four times the balls compared to you guys...'

I immediately felt my crotch.

'And freshie, who do *you* think you are? Michael Jackson, huhn?' asked Rana, mock-glaring at me.

'Sir, just checking if I've grown six more marbles!' I said cheekily.

'See?' he smiled, looking at the three squeaky voices (now, epitome of silence). 'Wonderful sense of humour and great stamina too! One hour of relentless torture and he still has the spunk. They're still standing ramrod straight like *pucca* soldiers who neither fear seniors nor ragging nor truth. Typical Delhi guys. You three bastards will be my batmen from now on. You will wake me up at 4 a.m. every day and I'll ram you bastards till you get pregnant. Dismissed!'

The three squeaky voices took off like frigid mice escaping a cat on Viagra; and Rana took Solly and me to a lavish dinner at Blue Nile Restaurant on MG Road a while later.

I learned something that day. If you did anything crazy and admitted it, the world respected you. If you did nothing crazy, the world didn't even know you existed. Well, so we did many crazy things over the years.

Thanks to Solly's idea, we became quite famous in the hostel and quite pally with most seniors. That meant we got ragged the most. But after a fortnight or so, I guess the seniors got tired of us and they'd just wave us away saying 'we are looking for new murgas'.

So Solly decided to expand our sphere of influence. This guy had taken a fancy to John Travolta and *Grease* (just like Tanu, the nineteen-something bitch who'd dumped me, remember?) and wanted to float a gang like T-Birds and look cool and all.

I prided myself for being mature, low profile and understated. But Solly felt we needed to get an image makeover and announce our presence from the rooftops.

After a few days he had roped in five more guys into his fold – Mangy from Chandigarh, Rammy and Chopsy from Delhi, Dusty from 24 Paraganas (God only knows where that is! Google it if you wish to know) and Shaky from Nainital.

No book is ever complete without a physical description of the main characters; and since you hate investing time and money in incomplete books, here goes. Rammy was the shortest and the scrawniest and least impressive of our lot. But you could say that with his Harry Potteresque impish looks and horn-rimmed spectacles, he did look cute in a queer sort of way. Solly and Dusty were pretty stocky and grew thick moustaches to complement their don't-mess-with-us deadly looks. Solly was my height, about 5 feet 9 inches; and Dusty was proud to be an inch taller. Of course, Shaky was the tallest of our lot – the only six footer actually, and he walked with a bit of a tired stoop, as if regretting that he'd risen above the accepted average. Mangy and Chopsy were slightly smaller than me, if you measured them vertically, and larger than a hot-air balloon, if you measured them horizontally (okay, okay, I am definitely exaggerating that one a bit, but I must say they reminded you of pumpkins, not ladyfingers). Me? I was your average, wheatish, clean-shaven, guy-next-door kind of person. Happy? Now shall we get on with the story please?

Well, so there we were. The secret seven. Initially, that's what we thought we'd call our gang, but then it seemed pretty kiddish and very Enid Blytonish, so we all went to Brigade Road for a brainstorming session one evening.

'Our gang's name should reverberate with *hepness*...' said Solly, throwing a hep look at a cute girl who was rummaging though her purse and casting side glances at us as if we were purse-snatchers or some such lowly lifeforms.

'Yes, yes,' said Shaky. 'At Sherwood, my gang was Illusionists.'

'But we should make one rule – we all should always be together and get girls for us as soon as possible,' said Chopsy.

Six necks and six thousand hormones nodded assent.

'How about Style Gurus?' said Mangy.

'Too loud,' I said. 'It should be muted.'

'What's muted, Tam-Brahm?' asked Dusty.

'Don't you dare call me that – my name is Hucky, okay?' I said firmly.

'Ya, don't, this is the first and last time,' Rammy seconded me menacingly, since he was a fellow Tamilian.

'Okay, I won't, sorry,' said Dusty.

So we played with lots of names for our group. Mad Maxes. Funky Towners. Seven Samurais. Brave Shaves. Gold Diggers. Life Stylers. Lady Killers...

We must have run through hundreds of names. Nothing seemed apt. Nothing captured our imagination.

'What a *maal*, man,' said Solly, eyeing a fab-looking girl walking into Wonder Shoppe. She was wearing tight stone-washed jeans and a flimsy tank top that was struggling to keep her raunchy melons from spilling out.

'Ya, she's full of sperms, man, and certainly has no space for yours,' said Mangy. 'You bloody nymphomaniac!'

'*What*-maniac?' asked Solly.

'Nymphomaniac,' explained Mangy. 'That means a guy who's got an abnormally intense sexual desire. In short, a *tharki*.' (Tharki=Hindi slang for any guy with extra libido.)

'Right sentiment, Mangy, but wrong usage of word. Nymphomaniac is a *woman* who's got an abnormally intense sexual desire,' explained Shaky. 'A man with a very strong sexual desire is called a satyr – one who suffers from satyriasis.'

'Nonsense,' said Mangy.

'Bet?' challenged Shaky.

'Okay, bet – ten bucks.'

So we went to Higginbothams bookstore and browsed through a dictionary and Mangy reluctantly parted with ten bucks.

'Hey, *Maniacs* – that's a nice name,' said Chopsy.

'Maniacs?' asked Solly, looking at all of us.

'Maniacs sounds funky,' said Rammy. And, since we were all dog-tired and in no mood to rack our brains any further, we decided to freeze on that.

◇

The fresher term routine was horrible, drab, monotonous, gruelling, and impeccably designed to convert us into Japanese robots. 5 a.m. Wake up to the alarm and wake up some stupid senior who has recruited you as his batman. Prepare coffee for him in his room. 6 a.m. Get a shave, iron your clothes, get into white shorts and a white T-shirt, and gather at the parade ground next to the new Insti. 6:30 a.m. Do aerobics and parade drills for one hour. Do extra parades if you are caught bitching about seniors. 7:30 a.m. Clamber up to your floor, bathe, dress up like a mutant penguin, avoid sadistic seniors, slink into A-mess and grab a hurried breakfast of eggshells-filled crunchy omelettes. 8 a.m. Go back to your floor, gather your stuff and cycle down to the Anatomy department. 8:30 a.m. Dissect a cadaver who's lucky to be dead and pretend to browse through Cunningham's for three hours. 12:30 p.m. Cycle back to A-mess to get your hungry stomach and palate molested again. 2 p.m. Cycle back to college for Anatomy / Biochemistry / Physiology theory and / or practical classes. 4 p.m. Cycle back to the hostel. 4:30 p.m. Gather at the ground for compulsory games. 6:30 p.m. Scamper up to your room. Get ragged if you aren't good at evasive techniques. 7:30 p.m. Reach A-mess and torture your taste buds again. 8 p.m. Exit the mess and get ragged. 9 p.m. Reach your floor. Discuss the day with your floor monitor and get ragged. 10:30 p.m. Lock your floor gates and slump on your bed. 11 p.m. Wash your clothes, polish your shoes, arrange your stuff, and set the alarm for 5 a.m.

Phew! Wonder how we survived that.

The hostel was splendid though. There were seven huge blocks of four floors each on either side of a long and broad corridor; with ten single-seaters on the left and eight double-seaters on the right of each floor, provided you were facing Ugly block, which was a glitzy annexe to the boys' hostel (it had forty of the best rooms) and was hence only allotted to toppers or civilian postgraduate students.

3

Escape from Defcoms,
North Campus, Mehrauli Party

Then. September through October 1985.

THE WORST PART ABOUT ANY HOSTEL IS USUALLY ITS MESS, which, quite understandably, lives up to its dictionary definition of chaos, clutter and confusion. Defcoms had five such. Insightfully and creatively named A, B, C, D and E. A-mess served mutton and *tandoori chicken*; B-mess served much the same, plus fish. C-mess was the only one that served pork and beef; and D-mess was pure vegetarian (or 'eggetarian' if you please). E-mess served only continental stuff. To cut a long story short, the mess served everything but good food. Though there was a silver lining. You could dine in any mess, provided you informed the mess secretary about it in advance.

We freshers were supposed to dine in A-mess and the vegetarian food they doled out there was slightly tastier than salt water on Sundays. Rest of the week, salt water was tastier. I had no option but to disgrace my Tam-Brahm family tree and sink my claws and teeth into some meatballs and roast chicken at times just to stay alive. We were told that we could join D-mess only from the second term. I noticed that I was homesick not out of emotion but because of wailing taste buds. We weren't allowed to eat out either—fresher term restrictions and all that crap—so our palate continued getting gang-raped by watery *daal*, burnt rice, undercooked vegetables, and overcooked eggshells wedded to every omelette and egg *bhurji* that came our way. We were wondering whether we were in a prison or a medical college. Perhaps there wasn't much of a difference between the two, especially when you were in fresher term. 'Academic customs are infinitely more taxing than religious traditions.' Shaky had summed it up rather well once.

But life was kind at times, though not as often as you'd have wanted it to be. I had just delivered some *pav* and egg bhurji that I had got from the *distal raydi* to Manik Goyal, a senior from Wonder batch, and was gladly polishing off some of it one evening when life revealed its rarely revealed generous side.

'Do you play a bit of badminton?' he asked.

'Well, yes sir, I do. In fact, I play pretty well.'

'Great. Would you like to go to Delhi to be a batman for our guys and girls representing us at AIIMS – at their sports meet?'

That was like asking a fiercely independent zoo lion if he'd like to be released from a fiercely claustrophobic cage. I nodded so happily and vigorously that a crick deposited itself somewhere in my neck.

'And we need one more guy from your batch. Know anyone who'll make a good helper?' asked Manik.

'Hmmm...I'll find out, sir, and let you know in a while.'

'Okay, you do that and let me know soon. You're *toh pucca, na*?'

'Absolutely, sir!'

'All right, now you go and get me a packet of Monaco biscuits when you return.'

'Thank you, sir! Good day, sir!'

Remember one thing about life if at all you wish to remember anything I say. Nothing comes free – so nothing should be given free. The Maniacs had gathered at 6 top 1 as I had spread the word that I had an important announcement to make. I was grinning and happily humming a Billy Joel tune and they were wondering if I had just got laid.

'Even better,' I said. 'I am going to Delhi next week!'

'Impossible,' said Rammy

'Nobody gets leave in first term,' said Dusty.

'I do, because I'm a badminton batman.'

'*Arre*, come to the point. What has badminton got to do with this?' said Solly impatiently.

I paused for effect. Create suspense and irk the audience with the vacuum.

'*Abbe*, don't take too much *bhav* okay, tell fast,' said Chopsy.

'Okay, who'd like to go to Delhi with me?'

'Liar, first tell us who's letting *you* go to Delhi,' said Mangy.

'Well, our seniors are playing at AIIMS next week, and I get to recommend one more person as a batman. Any of you guys even *remotely* interested?'

It's fun to have six guys begging you. It's a great feeling to wield power, howsoever trivial. It's a bit like playing God. They suggested we toss up coins or select with some random chits. I said no. I had decided to auction the trip to the highest bidder.

'Bastard,' said Shaky. 'He has shown his real cunning colours. All vegetarians are chameleons. Making money from us *hahn* – what a thought!'

'Hey listen, duffer, since you're part of Maniacs I'm even considering you. Pandey is willing to give me two hundred bucks if I recommend him,' I lied. 'But obviously you guys are first choice. And, I want cash-down payment, crackling Cashews, no credit.'

Six pairs of eyes turned inwards. Six brains did some quick maths. Mess bill: ₹400. Outings: ₹200. Ciggies: ₹150. Miscellaneous: ₹150. Six amateur accountants tried to visualise their fucked bank balance.

'Okay, guys, fast – I haven't got all day.'

I was beginning to feel like an auctioneer at Sotheby's. I had picked up a *Debonair* and neatly rolled it. That would be the auction hammer. I was standing behind the study table.

'Arre, we'll have to withdraw from the bank, na? It's closed now. We can only give the money in the morning,' said Solly.

This was good. At least they had agreed to pay. I decided not to push my luck.

'Okay,' I said. 'Tomorrow morning. 10:30 sharp.'

'Done,' said Solly.

'Okay, begin the bids,' I said pompously.

'210,' said Shaky.

'215,' said Mangy.

'230,' said Dusty.

'300,' said Solly.

Five hearts skipped many beats. He had breached a financial barrier. There was a long thirty-second lull in the bids.

'300—One, 300—Two…' I began slowly and dramatically.

'310,' said Chopsy.

Solly glared at him like a wounded hyena.

'350,' said Rammy.

Solly glared at him like a wounded *and* sodomised hyena.

It was definitely hotting up between Solly and Chopsy and Rammy. The rest looked as if they had given up. Or, so I thought.

'Hey, are the train tickets free?' asked Dusty.

'Of course! The college pays for it, you moron, and interruptions during the auction proceedings will not be tolerated and you'll be disqualified if you raise any more questions…' I said mock-angrily.

'Okay, then 375,' said Dusty, and I began salivating.

'1 crore rupees!' said a frustrated Mangy, and got mothered like a deadbeat bidder.

'Disqualified,' I said grandly.

Everyone except Mangy laughed. He lit up a ciggie, angry that his undernourished bank balance wouldn't let him continue.

'375—One...' I began threateningly.

'400,' said Solly.

'425,' said Chopsy.

'475,' said Rammy.

'500,' yelled Solly.

The stunned collective silence lasted a frozen minute.

'500—One, 500—Two, 500—Three,' I shouted, and brought the *Debonair*-hammer crashing down on the study table. 'Sold!'

It seemed as if the anatomy professor's lush crowbar moustache was supporting his face – and not the other way round. It was the basic foundation upon which his small, oblong, devilish face was resting.

When he spoke, the moustache stereophonically trembled, quivered, and begged to be twanged, which he did every now and then. He was angry now and the moustache was fluttering feverishly. Solly and I couldn't hide our smiles.

'So you two have the audacity to smile?' he thundered, and we tried burying ours under a poker-faced look but didn't succeed. 'What for are you two going to Delhi?'

'To play badminton, sir!' I lied. (Obviously, I couldn't say to *help* our seniors play badminton – that would've sounded so very corny and unbelievable, like most truths usually do.)

'And badminton is more important than anatomy?'

'Both are important, sir!' I said.

'Yes, sir! All work and no play makes Jack a dull boy,' added Solly.

'Really? Is your name Jack?' asked Dr Dandapani.

'No, sir!' said Solly.

'Then the saying doesn't apply to you. And, you think you can miss dissections and clear the viva?'

'Sir,' I began, sounding like a defence counsel, 'we can always make up for lost time later. We'll only be gone for a week...'

'*A week!*' shrieked the prof, as if week meant decade. 'During my time, I didn't miss a *single* class. I maintained hundred percent attendance and got a gold medal, and that's why Dr Dandapani is mentioned in the *Gray's Anatomy!* At this rate, you guys will just fail.'

Congratulations, you should get a Nobel Prize, I wanted to say. I wondered if he'd done anything else in life other than romance cadavers.

'Sir, University exams are more than a *year* away,' said Solly, in a tone that clearly meant: 'Hey take a chill pill, dude, and stop molesting us, okay?'

'We will definitely do well in the exams, sir!' I said.

'This is over-confidence. So, you won't cancel your trip?'

We remained silent. Which *loser* would cancel a *home* visit during fresher term? Was he crazy? Who'd be willing to lose the five hundred bucks Solly had given me?

'Okay, go. But you guys will get full six months. Mark my words.'

'Thank you, sir! Good day, sir!' we said together, and rushed out for fresh air.

'Saala, Dandy – how dare he threaten us, that sadist...' started Solly.

'Forget him yaar, he's not Nostradamus, let's chill! It's holiday time!' I yelped.

'Yup, holiday time!' he screamed, echoing me.

We were on our fourth mom-made *mooli parantha* and third bowl of mom-set curd. Pure heaven. Our taste buds emerged from a deep coma, thanked us for resuscitating them, and broke into some grateful dance. Solly was staying with me at our place in Karol Bagh as his folks had left for Calcutta the previous day for some cousin's wedding. It was 7 a.m. We were due at AIIMS at 10 a.m.

'So how's the food at the hostel?' mom asked.

'Oh auntyji, it's terrib...' began Solly.

'Oh, it's *terrific* and surprisingly nice! Not as good as home, of course, but pretty good for a hostel,' I lied, cutting him short and pinching his thigh under the table, as I didn't want mom to feel sad about our daily culinary torture.

'Yes, the army always serves good food. Even Vasanthi—you know the girl who comes to learn veena—her brother's in NDA, she says the food there is excellent,' she said, seconding my blatantly dishonest opinion.

Pity, Defcoms was a far cry from NDA. I had been to Khadakwasla when I visited a cousin in Poona in the summer of 1983. His friends had invited us over on a Sunday, and their mess could definitely be given a five-star rating. Ours should have been given a kick in its butt long time ago.

Dad had gone on an official tour to Jaipur and I was missing him. He wouldn't have been sad if I had told him the truth about our regular palate-rapes, and would've said that he'd seen tougher times and sagely convinced me to count my blessings.

The phone rang.

'Hello,' I said.

'Hello, may I please speak to Hari?' asked someone.

'This is he,' I said.

'Hi Hari, Pankaj here, what's happening?' (Pankaj Malhotra was our senior from Wonder batch and the sports secretary. Surely he was calling to check if we'd be making it in time.)

'Oh hello, sir! We were just about to leave...'

'No, no, don't. Both the badminton matches are cancelled. In fact, they've given us the walkover as their champs are down with dengue. All friendly Delhi machchars are on your side, you lucky bastards!

Maybe we will just have one lame match later, and we can manage without you guys. So, you guys can *maro thand* the entire week, okay? That's why I called…' (Maro thand = Hindi slang for chill out.)

'Oh, thank you, sir! So we aren't needed?'

'No Hari, you guys just enjoy the break – having good home-made food hahn?'

'Yes, sir!'

'Bye. Have fun.'

'You too, sir! See you later. And, thanks for calling. Good day, sir!'

I was discovering that Solly was usually ruling my life those days. I wasn't always doing what I wanted to do. I was just becoming a yes-man to whatever he was saying. But it was fun, for he was as crazy as they come, and we had quite a blast actually.

Plus the great bloke had given me five hundred bucks, right? So, let's just say he had bought a slave for a few days. And, since I was feeling guilty ripping him off that way, I was just trying to make up for it by being a good sport. And, a genial host.

Solly and I were wearing blue sports T-shirts glaringly emblazoned with Defcoms in glittering, phosphorescent white. We were waiting to take a DTC bus to the North Campus to 'catch up with some friends' as Solly put it, but the real purpose of our visit was to show off that we had made it to one of India's most prestigious medical colleges.

If you took the 152 or 153 or U-Special (U stood for University) early in the morning, say at about 8 a.m. from Pusa Road, then you could bump into the most ravishing of babes.

'*Saalay*, all we have at Defcoms are crows, man! Look at this crowd! Can't Defcoms be shifted to the North Campus…?' Solly wondered, and sighed regretfully as we clambered up into the bus.

Two girls whispered 'Defcoms, Defcoms' to themselves and Solly smiled at them. They smiled back.

'*Hansi toh phasi*,' he whispered to me. (If she smiles, she gets caught in the romantic net.) As his smile widened, they widened the distance between them and us.

'Bloody bitches – first they give you the hard-on, then they play hard to get,' he fumed.

'Chill yaar, perhaps you remind them of their brothers, and unfortunately incest is not a family tradition with them…' I joked.

But Solly, in strict violation of Rammy's impeccably-laid guidelines on how to and how not to pick up girls, bridged the distance they had created with a few semi-Kangaroo hops, swaggered up to them, and in a most embarrassing manner asked them, 'Do you girls realise that we don't bite?'

The girls looked at him as if they didn't believe him. Their smiles had been replaced by repulsive frowns specially reserved for sex-starved carnivores.

I wished we were not wearing the Defcoms T-shirts as his wham-bam-thank-you-ma'am approach wasn't doing our college's image any good.

I didn't know what to do. You might have guessed by now that I am irritatingly indecisive. I am the kind of guy who, if he is witnessing a soon-to-happen murder, might not know whether to call the cops or the ambulance or the undertakers or mom. Confusion is a sign of intelligence, I have heard enlightened masters saying, and well, by that token, I could be voted the most intelligent person on the planet. I can take snap decisions where money is involved, but when it comes to non-monetary affairs, I am just not up to it. My brain has an in-built, quick-freeze mechanism, and there's no way to get it fixed.

What Solly was doing must definitely rate as eve-teasing or optical-cum-laryngeal molestation (go include that in the Indian Penal Code if you will). He wasn't pawing any of the girls yet, but the way he was going about it, he didn't seem to be too far from such an impending manoeuvre.

But not everyone was as intelligently confused as I. Two burly guys got up from their seats and accosted him. (Actually, they were sitting right atop the rug-laden engine – you know it keeps your butt pretty warmed up during pre-winters and after, and also sends a message across the bus that you are the boss. Take care and never lock horns with anyone abutting the driver in a U-Special—if at all you board one in Delhi—and you'll stay alive, healthy, and unhurt that much longer.)

'Hey despo, back off,' said Burly Guy#1, in an accent that had definitely got fermented at Khalsa College, and the girls looked endearingly at their saviour as if he were the President of Save The Maids From The Maniacs Foundation. The girls nearly melted into the arms of their knight in shining armour, and this got Solly's goat, and he stiffened defiantly like Attila the Hun.

Burly Guy # 2 didn't say anything. Dangerous. He just stare-fucked Solly, just like Bruce Lee does in all the movies having titles ending with 'Dragon'. I was sure Solly was going to get creamed, and that would mean he wouldn't treat me to the Nirula's pizza and a movie at Chanakya that he had promised earlier, and since that involved a monetary loss for me, I found myself swinging into action.

Action meant I just walked up to the two burly chaps and said, 'Chill guys, take it easy' in the most pleading and conciliatory tone I could manage. Solly threw me a dirty look which meant: 'You infernal slime, you always wriggle out of fights like a spineless vegetarian eel.' The girls must have thought pretty much the same thing for they sniggered at me, but who cared, as long as I could keep Solly and me out of harm's way.

I deftly nudged (desperately pulled?) him away from them and we got off at the next stop. There was loud laughter after someone shouted '*Defcoms* means Defence College of Maha Sissies' and some such silly expansions of the acronym as the bus began moving away.

Solly was about to chase the U-Spl and try some masochistic *dishum-dishum* stuff and I held him back with as much power as I could marshal.

'You're a pucca wimp – you'll definitely become a *General* one day, you know the scum always rises to the top!' Solly shouted hysterically.

'Thanks for the compliment, Solly. Now, shall we take another bus or would you like to go to GB Road and bang some whores there?' I asked snarkily.

'They *abused* our respectable college and you just let them *get away* with it? Unbelievable!' His veins began bulging and crawling like feverish worms on his neck. His crimson eyeballs looked as if they would pop out any moment.

'Cool down, buddy. If you slink away from a fight, you live to fight another day. Do you realise that maybe twenty to thirty guys would've ganged up against us? And if someone calls us Tatas or Birlas, we wouldn't become that. Strength means having the patience to absorb snide remarks of stupid people. Anyway, you started all this *natak*, but we aren't sissies...' I explained.

'Bullshit! *You* are the *sissy*, they meant *you* – not *me*! I never run away. *I* never will.' He kept clenching and unclenching his fists violently. The crushed atmosphere within his palms winced in pain. A few nitrogen and oxygen molecules died.

'Okay boss, you're fearless, great, fantastic, and you can single-handedly cream a bus-load of brawny guys. You're a one-man army, Solly – and I, the cowardly vegetarian slimeball, spoiled your party, happy?'

We didn't speak for a while. We lighted up our Gold Flakes and tried to cool down our battered egos. (Tobacco smoke might contain close to four thousand toxic substances, but for us smokers it functions as a gaseous coolant that softens the heart and extinguishes the adrenaline-induced fire raging within the mind.)

Ten minutes passed in nicotine-drenched silence. Buses, cars, bikes, scooters, and lovely girls must have flashed by, but we were oblivious to life and lost in our contemplative reverie. The anger was puffed away and released into the smoggy Delhi sky, and I'm sure that made the Delhi sky distinctly smoggier for decades to come.

'Sorry,' said Solly guiltily, 'I keep getting us into trouble, don't I?'

'Hey, don't be silly,' I said generously, 'that's why you're so much fun. Life would become pretty dull without your crazy recklessness.'

He patted me and treated me to piping hot coffee at a tuckshop and we were again ready to take on North Campus, if not the world. We decided to head back home to doff our Defcoms T-shirts and get into some noncommittal cool sweatshirts (you know, the kind that say *Make love—not babies, Dream big—keep sleeping, Life is a test but I didn't take very good notes* or some such show-stopping one-liners). We needed to begin afresh as our Defcoms T-shirts now seemed to be carrying the stains of rude remarks that no detergent would be able to wash off in a hurry. We even wore shades so that we won't be recognised if we ran into some of our tormentors from the bus-gang.

◇

Scrambled eggs at Stephen's. Aloo-stuffed *bhaturas* and *chole* near Kirori Mal. More coffee at Hans Raj. We were just goofing around and trying to check if we could bump into some of our old pals. We gathered from a few acquaintances of our earlier batchmates that some had joined Law, some Anthropology, some Botany, and a few had even begun working as apprentices in some industries.

It felt kind of weird. We were still receiving cheques from home and there were some of us who were already making their own money and at least supporting themselves, if not their families.

Boy, was I envious of those of us who had severed financial umbilical cords and marched on to conquer paying jobs – who cared if the pay was low or high as long as the money was truly your own.

I imagined them sniggering at me from behind their lager beer which they'd bought with their own money and calling me a parasite. Bile bubbled in my system like acid soup and the acrid fumes burned my gut and heart.

I became wistful. Self-doubt had this uncanny habit of sneaking up on me whenever I heard about (a) folks who were minting their own pennies and (b) folks who were sure they were doing the right thing.

'What's the matter...still thinking about the incident?' asked Solly.

'Arre, no yaar,' I said. 'I am just wondering why it didn't cross my head to take up some job after graduation and be financially independent. I'm thinking if I've made a mistake...'

'C'mon, dude, we're forging a great career for ourselves, don't let the workaholics bother you – we're going to be Indian army doctors, man,' he said.

'But you heard – Punter and Sidey are already earning money, dude, close to two thousand solid Cashews, and here we are, always touching our dads for cash, it's all making me feel kind of inadequate...'

'Arre, they're doing some menial work, yaar, they're not employed as hotshot managers or something. Ninety percent of the poor bastards are still studying – either for the civil services or doing post-graduation, so we're doing pretty fine, cheer up,' he said.

Cheering up involved standing outside Miranda House; ogling at the colourful crowd; and falling in love/lust every thirty seconds. We were waiting for Mini, Solly's cousin, who was in third year, and hopefully would rope in a few *maals* from her gang so we could all chill out at Batra over some mushy Hindi movie. The day wasn't going according to plan and hobnobbing with a few blind dates wouldn't hurt our system or mood too much.

Mini arrived in a short while with a giggly bunch straight out of the 'before' version of the Clearasil commercials, and since we were clearly looking for the 'after' types, we decided to give the Batra trip the pass. We just made some polite convo, drank more hot coffee (my third) at a roadside stall, burped our goodbyes saying we had lots of catching up to do, and vamoosed from the torturous spot.

What a rotten day it had turned out to be! First the fiasco on the bus; then we couldn't trace any of our common pals at the Botany or Anthropology or Law departments as all seemed to have gone on some academic excursions; and finally we ended up doing TP with some sad women from Miranda House. (TP = Teen-speak for 'timepass'.)

We didn't have the patience to test Rammy's theory that one should never refuse a girl's friendship as an ugly girl might have a beautiful friend or cousin or whatever who we could hit on later—that might be okay in the long run, but here we were looking for instant fun, and chilling out with these apology for girls just didn't add up.

'Today, our luck is practising Chinese torture on us, dude, what to do? Am really tired of what we're doing here…' sulked Solly.

'So am I. Why don't we just go to Chanakya? Been a long time.'

'Cool,' he said, and we hopped in and out of buses, and saw some stupid English flick (we walked out of it during interval actually) and became depressed as hell. Even the burgers and the ice cream soda Solly treated me to at the downstairs Nirula's couldn't wash away our crystallised-over-the-day frustration, and by the time we reached home we looked as whipped and dog-tired as slaves on ancient Roman ships. Did you ever get frustration pimples, buddy? I did. Trust me, they were more painful than acne.

Mom had stepped out for the evening, so we rented some soft porn flick from the video library run by our landlord's sons (I think it was *Lady Chatterley's Lover*), kept munching Gold 'n Crisp potato wafers, kept sipping Campa Cola, kept cursing the darned VHS cassette that was raining shards of million silvery blips every time an 'important' scene was in progress, kept cursing the 'sex maniacs who keep rewinding and re-watching and scratching all important scenes', and kept wondering if our luck had gone on a long vacation to some distant land.

◇

Our luck returned the next day from wherever it had gone to (or so we thought). Along with Fatty who returned from a botanical excursion to Manali.

'Hi guys,' he said chirpily as we guys were digging into our breakfast of vermicelli *upma*.

'Howdy Fats! Long time, man!' I said cheerily, got up and hugged him. 'So you finally got the message.'

'Yup, been out, got back pretty late last night, mum said you guys had dropped by, so how's things – hi Solanki,' said Fatty, and I noticed that his voice was more gruff than earlier and his dress sense was more snazzy. Plus he was slimmer.

'Hey, you got a new wardrobe and a dapper look...' I wondered.

'Ya, and a new girl and a brand new cold virus...' he sniffled.

'Wow! Way to go buddy – so who's the *unlucky* girl?' ribbed Solly. Trust him to come up with cutting remarks especially when he's romantically frustrated and existentially disillusioned.

'Fats, care for some upma?' I interjected, trying to downplay Solly's sarcasm. 'And who's she? You never mentioned her in any of your letters...'

'Sure, am famished, Hucks,' said Fatty laughingly, 'by the way, her name's Reshma, and yes, she is pretty unlucky – her father's a taxi driver and she had to give tuitions just to graduate from Khalsa. She's had a rough ride through life, plus she's the eldest child and all, but a swell brainy one...'

'Sorry, was just kidding, Fats – no offence meant,' said Solly guiltily. 'And call me Solly, that's my hep nick now.'

'None taken,' said Fatty sportively, 'anyway, tell me, what's happening with you guys, I'm sure you guys aren't virgins anymore…'

'Arre, we're all romantically and sexually challenged, man – we haven't been able to hook *any girl*, and we're seriously considering becoming gay,' I said, and we all burst into raucous laughter as I ladled some upma into a bowl for Fatty.

'Oh, that figures,' said Fatty sarcastically, 'I was wondering why Solly is shacking up with you…'

'Shut up, you pig, I'll kill you if you even joke about our…er…I wouldn't call it failure…let's just say girls at Defcoms are a bit like rajma, they take time to soften up…first you have to soak them overnight in some fluid conversation…but we have a plan…we call it RAPIST…' rambled Solly.

'What the hell's that?' asked Fatty, clearly intrigued.

'Rammy's Action Plan: Ingenious Seduction Techniques,' I offered. 'Fats, you must really meet this guy, Rammy, he's part of our gang, actually our brains, and he's your types, you'd love him…'

'So you guys are still at the planning stage and making acronyms when you should actually be making girls pregnant…' observed Fatty.

'Don't rub it in,' said Solly, landing a mock-sock on Fatty's jaw.

'Okay, I get the message, touchy aren't we?' observed Fatty. 'Hey, I nearly forgot, you guys want to jam out with us at a dance party, maybe you'll meet some chicks there? – Hucks, you remember Prashant…?'

'Which one? The Greek god or the African devil? And since when have *you* started partying-shartying, antisocial animal?' I said. 'This Reshma girl sure seems to have changed your personality type hahn, good anyway…'

'The devil Prashant, yaar, you know him,' said Fatty, 'and he's got this really filthy rich cousin who's throwing a bash at his Mehrauli farmhouse, Saturday night. Any Hans Raj guy or gal is definitely welcome, and now that you guys are even elite medicos…'

Mom returned from her temple visit and I decided to take the convo to the great outdoors.

'Come guys, let's grab soya milk at Ladies' Corner,' I said.

The party was a smash hit. We weren't. Everyone had come as a couple, including Fatty and Reshma who were either on the dance floor or entwined behind a shrubbery. Solly and I were the only guys who had no dates and we felt as out of place as virgins in maternity wards. Someone even assumed we were gay but didn't seem to mind our alternative lifestyle. So, we just smoked a lot, drank lots of Scotch, and sulked a lot.

The party ended at about 3 a.m. on Sunday and after dropping off Reshma at Lajpat Nagar, we went to Maurya (in Fatty's dinky Maruti) to wash down our blues over coffee. Anyway, it was a holiday for whatever it was worth, and a welcome break from the drab routine that was Defcoms, so we consoled ourselves by thinking that things could have been much worse.

4

Love Guru, Good and Bad Seniors, First Socials

Then. Late October 1985.

THE FRESHER TERM WAS THANKFULLY DRAWING TO A BACK-aching close—what with all the spine-bending, marbles-breaking exercise—and we gathered that it was almost time to celebrate our survival with a huge party. This was called 'Socials' in Defcoms lingo and that meant you could let your hair down and dance away the night at the new Insti – technically the boys' hostel canteen which doubled up as a dance floor on such crazy nights.

Fresher term restrictions had been waived off a bit (thank heavens for tender mercies) and we could stop looking like mutant penguins and even visit the girls' hostel.

The girls' hostel was about five hundred metres away and this was the night when you could fix yourself a date and hope to proudly escort a girl who didn't mind being proudly escorted by you.

The sex ratio was horrible though. For every hundred guys there were just twenty-five girls in each batch. And, since twenty of them were the kind you'd like to deport to nunneries, you were left with five girls, so the probability of you bagging a good chick for yourself was one in twenty. (Or 0.05 – if you're the IIM or GMAT kind.)

Our preparations for getting a date began early. In fact, it all began a week before the Socials when Solly and Rammy got into an intense argument.

'Listen, dude, maals don't fall for the I-am-a-Maniac routine. You need to look sober and classy...' explained Rammy, objecting to Solly's John Travolta-influenced, carefully-careless appearance, which consisted of uncombed finger-ruffled hair, a five o' clock stubble, frayed denim jeans, a fake (pink!) Crocodile T-shirt Solly had picked up from Janpath, a beige leather jacket that had gathered telltale, fading tobacco stains, a ghastly-looking cheap Aviator shades that he kept playing with like Rajnikant does to look hep, and a pair of fabulously fake (garish red!) Nike sneakers.

Top that all up with an expression that was three-fourths a smirk, one-eighth a scowl, and one-eighth a sneer, and you had what we called BTMUDC – *Bhaisaheb* Turned Mod Under Desperate Circumstances. (Or at times B stood for *Behenji* if you were referring to those nunnery-girls.)

'Nonsense, chicks are always looking for someone who's looking like this – haven't you seen any movies?' observed Solly, admiring himself in the mirror.

'Dude, you look like a slum-dweller who's trying to appear chic – in fact, you're looking like a cross between a circus clown and a colour-blind pig,' observed Rammy.

They both were sharing the same room. 6 Top 3. That was actually our *adda* – where our gang met and made all kinds of plans from 'How to win girls and influence more girls' and 'How to pass exams without studying' to 'How to set up one government for the entire world'.

'Rammy's right,' said Mangy.

'Ya? Just look at *his* wardrobe. All checked shirts and ill-fitting, tailor-fucked trousers – totally disgusting bad vegetarian taste. What does *he* know about *fashion?*' wondered Solly. There was no argument against that. Rammy's wardrobe *was* right out of *Malgudi Days* or Raj Kapoor's *Awara*, take your pick.

'Okay, you do whatever you feel like, but don't say I didn't warn you,' said Rammy.

'I won't,' said Solly as he rolled up his jacket sleeves, gave himself a final once-over, messed up a few strands that were tidying themselves up, sprayed some cheap deodorant on himself, and marched out of the room humming *Buffalo Soldier*. He was going to the girls' hostel to try his luck with Neelima, a batchmate he fancied.

We guys went to see *Ram Teri Ganga Maili* that evening at a seedy theatre called Victory and were quite happy to see Mandakini bathing under a waterfall and teaching us chest anatomy.

'So you think Neelima and Solly went out on a date?' I asked Rammy as we exited the movie hall.

'No chance. The way I analyse the scenario is thus: Solly enters the girls' hostel; Solly requests a girl to call Neelima; Girl goes and tells Neelima that some Roadside Romeo is looking for her; Neelima says she isn't well; Solly returns to the room and jerks off. When we'll ask Solly what happened, he'll say he changed his mind and decided to talk to her later.'

'You're too cynical, Rammy,' said Chopsy. 'You never know what a girl might like in a guy.'

'We'll see,' said Rammy tersely, and we reached hostel after grabbing some *paneer paranthas* and espresso coffee at Pulp Point near Brigade Road.

When we reached our adda Solly was curled under a blanket. The ash tray had fallen on the floor and the violently crushed cigarette butts carried clear signs of his frustration. Rammy seemed to be right. Otherwise Solly would've been wide awake and waiting to brag about his conquest.

Rammy shook up Solly and he woke up rather reluctantly.

'So you got the KLPD, na?' Rammy asked snarkily. (KLPD = Kaampte Langur Par Danda / A whack on your trembling joystick – if you get what I mean.)

'No yaar, she wasn't around – she'd gone out with her uncle,' lied Solly.

'Ya, ya, we met them at Pulp Point,' said Mangy, throwing a catty, all-knowing look at us. 'Stop *phaykoying* okay?' (Phaykoying = Hinglish for spinning yarns.)

'Hey, stop ribbing him guys, if you're so smart then stop *utaroing our chaddi* and tell us how to get a girl,' said Chopsy to Rammy. (Utaroing our chaddi = Hinglish for pulling down someone's shorts.)

Chopsy too had failed miserably a week ago with Grishma from X-ray batch, and had come back to the adda carrying a hangover and a hangdog look – so he could relate to and empathise with Solly's plight more than any of us. (We would discover soon that X-ray girls were less frigid than their counterparts from Yankee batch though.)

Okay, are you wondering why batches were named thus? Here's the explanation even if you aren't. Defcoms began in 1961 with Alpha batch, and since we were the twenty-fifth flock of murgas who joined in 1985, we were Yankee batch. Got the funda or have you forgotten the alphabetical sequence? Go join KG. Okay, just kidding. I know they don't teach you NATO call signs in kindergarten. At least they didn't during our time. NATO call signs are used in the armed forces, by airline pilots and sailors, to name a few professionals who use them to standardise communication. Now, even call centre executives bring them into play. Okay, let's quickly run through it; perhaps it will come in useful when everyone on your plane dies—seen the movie, *Turbulence?*—and you have to communicate with the ATC and land the plane since you are the lone survivor. Memorise it. Happy landing! Alpha. Bravo. Charlie. Delta. Echo. Foxtrot. Golf.

Hotel. India. Juliet. Kilo. Lima. Mike. November. Oscar. Papa. Quebec. Romeo. Sierra. Tango. Uniform. Victor. Whisky. X-ray. Yankee. Zulu. That's also the first twenty-six batches at Defcoms. Of course, the twenty-third batch was called Wonder batch for obvious reasons. After Zulu, we'll call the other batches Alpha 2, Bravo 2, and so on. (All the Maniacs' nicknames also ended in 'y' in honour of our batch.) End of *gyan*. Wake up, please.

We hadn't yet tried hooking any girls (well, at least not at Defcoms) and had let Solly and Chopsy test the waters first, as the saying goes. They had obviously discovered that the waters at the girls' hostel were unfriendly, unfathomable, unapproachable, and un-pataoable, if you'll allow me that term.

We all looked at Rammy as he was the brains of our gang.

'Okay Rammy,' I said. 'How the hell do we go about it here? Socials is just a week away and if none of the Maniacs has a girl by then, then we have to hang our heads and pythons in shame.'

So Rammy began. He was looking like Moses reeling off do's and don'ts from the mount. He had already coached us a bit of course, only this time around it was more detailed.

'If you guys follow what I say, then you all can have at least a chick each by the end of the week,' said Rammy.

We all cheered. If you had been in that room that evening, you'd have felt that you'd never be lonely for the rest of your life. You would've been sure that girls would begin eating out of your hands soon. You would've been grateful that you had learnt everything about hooking a girl. I can almost write an entire book based on what he said. Maybe something like *How to Hook a Girl Without Making Her Feel Like a Hooker*. (Maybe that will be my next?)

'We have gone through this before but a quick recap will help I guess. First, approach a girl like a classy human, casually and coolly – not like a salivating dog,' began Rammy.

Solly and Chopsy flinched, blanched, tried to ignore the obvious reference, and looked at each other mournfully.

'One should always be ready with some absorbing, racy opening line. Never come up with tasteless ones like: You look pretty/You seem like someone I know/What's your sun sign?/How was the anatomy test yesterday?/I heard you cook your own omelettes in the girls' hostel etcetera. The best tried and tested lines are: Hi, you look like someone who reads Wodehouse/Mind if I borrow your intelligence?/I just need your advice/I was just wondering why you look so sharp etcetera. Remember guys, if you wish to impress a girl, use words; and if you wish to impress a guy, use pictures. I hope none of us here wishes to *impress* a guy, at least not the way we wish to impress girls.'

We all laughed.

'This is what all communication gurus since the time of Stone Age Man have been saying. Of course, Stone Age Man had a simple communication tool called grisly stone club which came in pretty handy when he wished to date a Stone Age Woman, but I'm sure you've guessed by now that, unfortunately, we live in more civilised times, and our only weapon is our intellect, which, when combined with our linguistic skills, can have our woman rushing into our arms and/or beds.'

Twelve eyes and six brains were absorbing each word and idea of his as if their very survival (and prestige?) depended on it. Rammy was rarely ever interrupted by anyone when he spoke, thanks to his mesmerising voice and amazing ability to hold your attention.

'We still have a week. The best place to talk and *patao* a girl is at the canteen – at 10:30 a.m. She's tired of classes, bored, and wants some smart or casual convo, depending on her intelligence or the lack of it. Keep it low-key if it happens. Then she goes to the bank. Always keep a pen handy and hang around. She might borrow one and that's the gap you're looking for.

'See if she reads books. For instance Solly, if you noticed, Neelima was carrying Agatha Christie's *The Murder of Roger Ackroyd* last week. You could have started a brilliant convo then, that's quite a masterpiece – but what's the point, you hardly read books. See what she likes. Observe and learn. Music, movies, what? Catch her humming some tune – and you know her fave band is ABBA. Ask her if she's heard *Voulez-Vous*. If she hasn't, say you have a tape. I know you don't, so go to MG Road, buy one, and give it to her – but make sure you scratch the cover and casing a bit to make it look used. Watch her discussing how trashy Hindi movies are – so now you know she's the intellectual type and you can ask if she's seen *Butch Cassidy and the Sundance Kid*. Watch her buying stuff at the canteen. If she picks up some cheap bathing bar, you know she's the conservative type. Maybe she cooks well and you can talk about Paranthe Wali Gali at Chandni Chowk or Roshan di Kulfi at Ajmal Khan Road. If she picks up some exotic stuff, you know she's the mod types. She can't cook to save her life—or yours for that matter—and most probably reads fashion and film magazines. If she picks up any brand reflecting an Indo-Western amalgam, like shikakai shampoo, she's conservative only in public but holds liberal views in private...'

'Okay, but what if we don't get to the point of dating-shaying? – one wouldn't want to come on too strong...' said Shaky.

'I am coming to that. Don't, repeat, *don't* ask her out on a date – at least have five good convos before you even suggest going to Brigade Road or Mahima Nagar for a *bhel puri* or something. Okay, let's imagine none of you actually get to spend quality talk time with *any* chick—it's possible—then worry not. The Socials night will be a good time to hit on a chick. Don't rush, or rush slowly, as the Buddha said. Remember, this is the first Socials so they will be as awkward and appear as pussyfooted as most of us...' continued Rammy.

'What's pussyfooted?' asked Dusty.

'A pussy falling at your foot and *begging* to be banged by you,' joked Shaky.

'Shhh! Don't interrupt him guys...' said Solly, and Rammy continued.

'Pussyfooted means cautious or timid, whatever – and you can't win a girl's trust over a few jives and dance steps. That takes time. So, don't lead her into a dark corner, always talk to her in the open and under lights.

'If *she* suggests taking a walk or something, say okay. And, walk without brushing against any part of her anatomy – even by mistake.

'But don't be too eager to please either. Maintain your stand on any topic. Most girls don't like rubber-band vertebrae.

'When you close-dance, don't peer down her cleavage – instead keep looking straight into her eyes. Of course, don't overdo that bit and have her wondering if you're planning to specialise in ophthalmology or something. And, don't drink too much and slur like Keshto Mukherjee. Nurse your drinks – we can all tank up after they leave at 11 or 12, okay?' explained Rammy.

'Okay,' said Shaky. 'But what if the good chicks don't want to talk to us? What then?'

'No problem,' continued Rammy. 'All is not lost. Go for the bad chicks...'

'What the fuck,' interjected Solly, 'what's the point, man? – my python will just shrivel up into a millipede for life...'

'I've heard Rammy saying that before – to Chopsy, right?' I said. 'Cool logic, dude.'

'Ya, it is, understand the logic, Solly. Never reject a girl's friendship – howsoever ugly, silly, pimply or garish she might be, for ugly girls might still have beautiful friends or cousins or sisters or whatever. You can hit on them later. Of course, nature will present arguments against such an approach, but fight with your nature. Rome or romance isn't built in a day.

'We are gonna be here for some four years – long time...Well, one more thing...If you talk to a girl, begin a gentle argument on some point after a while...If she says you are wrong, lay a bet. But don't bet money, like Mangy. Say, "I bet you a burger / pizza that I am right." Now, whether you win or lose the bet just doesn't matter. It's a win-win situation for you all the way. If you win the bet, she takes you out; and if you lose, you get to escort her to Burger Island. Either way, a romantic outing with her is guaranteed for you…Plus always propose to a girl. There are only three things she can say: Yes, Maybe, or No. Now, Yes and Maybe are welcome events. So there is a cool 66% chance of success. What's more, a present No can become a future Yes if you persist…Romance is nothing but the art of constant persistence in the face of continuous rejection anyway…Do bear in mind that girls love guys who consider them important and worthy enough to be pursued; and hate losers who give up the pursuit after the first No…Anyway, enough for today…Who's going to give me gastronomic *guru dakshina*? Don't pretend as if you didn't understand that, you morons! All you Indians want everything free or what? Okay, I'm famished, who's treating me to aloo parantha and egg bhurji?'

'I will, *shabbaash mere laal*, thank you for the fantastic advice,' said Solly, backslapping Rammy, and we all went to the new Insti feeling gung-ho and all.

Word had spread around like bushfire that I'd got an electric heater (you know, the one with metallic coils and all which you plug in and boil milk and water on?) from home when I'd returned with Solly after braving a romantically-frustrating week in Delhi. I didn't use the heater for three weeks fearing rough treatment from seniors, but then, temptation got the better of me one day and I was found whipping up beat-coffee in my room. This wasn't allowed in fresher term. The restrictions had only been partially waived off and what I was doing wasn't included in the waiver list. You had to live a Spartan life, and living it up and indulging in banned luxuries like room-made beverages meant instant trouble and relentless ragging.

Perhaps a bit of Solly's recklessness had rubbed off on me or perhaps I was too bored to really care, whichever, but I decided to breach hostel tradition one lazy afternoon and found myself being interrogated by Walia, a hell from Uniform batch who lived in the opposite wing, in 5 top 3, and his mustard-oil-drenched room was now functioning as an interrogation-cum-torture chamber.

'Who gave you permission to get a heater and make your own coffee?' he asked, after a few jealous Yankee batchers had ratted on me. 'Hundred push-ups.'

The Samantha Fox posters he had plastered his walls with were making me pant more than normal. I wondered if her boobs entered a room five minutes before she did. When I was through with the first leg of what would surely become a ragging-marathon, Walia rephrased his question.

'So why were you flouting hostel rules?'

'Sir, because I wanted to,' I said, and was surprised at the irreverence flavouring my tone.

'Really, so you think you can do anything you feel like? Aren't you afraid of us? – we're terrors, you know.'

'No, sir, I'm not afraid.' (I gathered later that he was growing his lush beard by malingering that he was carrying a facial skin allergy that supposedly got aggravated by razor blades.)

'Aha,' he said, a sardonic smile escaping from behind his luxuriant beard, 'and why is that?'

'Sir, at the most you will rag me – and I've got used to it by now. Plus if you waste time on such trivial issues and don't study, then you're going to flunk your exams. So, it's your loss, not mine, and as far as I'm concerned, I'm just exercising more than most, and it's kinda helping me develop a sculpted body which I've always been rather too lazy to develop, so I actually want to say thank you…' I explained smilingly.

'You smart fucker!' he screamed, and then looking at his batchmate and room partner, Khanna, 'saala, this guy is psyching me, man, I hope we won't fail, bastard, I hope he doesn't have a black tongue, hundred pull-ups.'

'Wali,' said Khanna, 'remember when we cooked a boiled egg in our room during fresher term, how Foxy mothered us…?'

'Ya, you're lucky,' said Walia, looking daggers at me, 'we guys are not half as nasty as Foxy from Quebec batch. Thank your lucky stars that he's passed out. Okay, stop. Now repeat, "*Sirs, you will definitely pass all Univ exams with flying colours*" hundred times and make it sound as if you believe it.'

So I repeated the lines hundred times and both Walia and Khanna listened with their eyes closed to the motivational hypnotic metronome and looked as if they were feeling better.

'I hope you aren't cursing us secretly,' Walia said smilingly.

'Not at all, sir, I wish the best for you – in fact, for the entire Uniform batch!'

'Okay, you're our type, man, you have guts, and you have a point, we can't be wasting our time like this, and now remember one thing. Anytime you want to make coffee, just walk into our room, no need to knock or greet us, and, other than us, take whatever you want—milk powder, sugar, coffee, whatever—and make *three cups* and bring it here and help us *paaaassss*, man, we're all so fucking psyched,' Walia said good-humouredly. 'And if any fucking bastard asks you why you're using your room as a kitchen, just tell the sister-fucker that Walia sir has given you special permission, okay?'

'Okay, sir,' I said triumphantly, saluted them both, and walked out feeling hundred feet tall and two hundred feet wide.

◇

Some seniors, especially from Uniform batch, didn't like the fact that I was being given preferential treatment. One evening, one of my batchmates said that Gurmeet of Uniform batch has called me to his room, and I went to meet him.

'So freshie, fresher term is not over, okay?' observed Gurmeet.

'Yes, sir, I guess not,' I said.

'Okay, take that cloth and that mug over there and go down and wash my scooter. It's a grey Chetak and the number is…' he said, throwing instructions in a clipped tone.

'I won't, sir,' I said.

'What? You're *talking back* to me? I'll fuck your trip. Now, pick them up and go down, and that's an order!' he screamed.

I picked up the greasy rag and the mug, went back to my room, fixed a beat-coffee for myself, changed into shorts and T-shirts, and crashed like a log.

After about an hour or so, I was violently shaken awake by Rana. Gurmeet Singh was standing next to him.

'So what are you doing here?' asked Gurmeet.

'Sleeping,' I said.

'And what did I ask you to do?' screamed Gurmeet.

'I'm not here to clean scooters, sir,' I said, looking at Rana, 'if you so desire, you can rag me…'

'Okay, hundred pull-ups and hundred push-ups,' said Rana.

I finished the pull-ups, and when I was perhaps on my eightieth push-up, Gurmeet became barbaric and kicked me in the butt. I stopped the push-up, tilted my head upward, and glared at him like a tickled dragon. He was about to kick me again when Rana held him tightly, got wild, and said, 'Enough Gurmy! You aren't going to *kick my guy*. You heard him—he won't clean scooters—find some other wimp for your dirty job.'

'Balls,' said Gurmeet, '*he will* clean my scooter, he's not some maharaja, I'll see to it that he does, I'll beat him up so badly…'

'Try it,' I said looking at Gurmeet, 'and I promise to beat the shit out of you…'

'You bastard!' screamed Gurmeet, and as he began advancing towards me, Rana gave him a shove and yelled, 'Fuck off, Gurmy, if

I ever see you calling any guy from my floor again, I'll personally screw your trip!'

Rana sat down on my bed and became pensive, even as a visibly defeated Gurmeet disappeared down the corridor. Did I see a tinge of guilt and regret on Rana's face?

'I'm proud of you, buddy, and I apologise,' he said.

'It's okay, sir,' I said.

'No, it's not okay, I'm truly sorry. Kicking a freshie is just not part of Defcoms culture — I'm feeling so ashamed today. You have more strength and principles than creeps like Gurmy. I'm regretting belonging to this batch — I've never felt this way before,' he wailed.

'Sir, one bad fish doesn't make an entire pond wrong. Uniform batch is wonderful, sir. I really admire you, Walia sir, Khanna sir, Lingam sir, and many more. All of you guys are wonderful, warm, friendly, understanding and so generous. Don't let one person spoil your mood, sir, it will affect your studies…'

Rana got up from bed and hugged me like a long-lost brother.

'I promise, after today, no fucker will ever touch you,' he said, his voice choking with emotion; and his eyes misty-eyed with guilt.

I heard later in the evening that Walia, Khanna and Rana had creamed Gurmeet in his room and I thought it was pretty weird that I wasn't feeling happy about it. Anyway, after that day, nobody ragged me, and frankly, I began missing all the attention that had been accorded me earlier.

A week before the final Univ exams were about to commence for Uniform batch, I was summoned to Walia's room. I looked around and Walia was not to be seen. Instead, a clean-shaven, bespectacled guy with mowed-down hair was sitting on his bed, intently reading *Golwala*, a book of Medicine.

'Sir, where is Walia sir?' I asked.

'Hundred push-ups, you myopic cretin!' he said.

'Sir! Is that you?' I shrieked as I recognised his voice. 'What happened sir?'

'Now you convince me that I *am* indeed me – I'm suffering an identity crisis,' said Walia.

I didn't know why, but he was now clean-shaven and had even got his hair cropped real short – perhaps the tropical climate had got to him or he'd become allergic to the beard now or he was pleasing his South Indian girlfriend or whatever.

So I stood there and repeated, 'Sir, you're indeed Walia sir!' ten times, and I guess he became convinced that he was indeed he, and I made some beat-coffee and boiled eggs and chilled out for a while with him.

◇

There are only four kinds of girls, dude: the Footballs, the Tennis Balls, the Squash Balls, and the No Balls. C'mon, don't tell me that the first thing you look for in a girl is inner beauty and all that crap. Go join a monastery.

When we saw a girl, we looked at her chest first and then decided whether we wished to look at her face. Plain and simple.

We had also sub-divided girls' faces into four types: the Ecstasy, the Happiness, the Ok, and the Sadness.

The Ecstasy meant an ultra-beautiful girl you'd like to die for.

The Happiness was a beauty you'd like to meet often.

The Ok was an average babe you'd like to do timepass with.

The Sadness meant a girl you'd like to introduce to your worst enemy.

Neelima was a Football Ecstasy. Rushali was a Football Happiness. Tara was a Tennis Ball Happiness. Meena and Payal were Squash Ball Oks. The rest of the girls in our batch were Sadnesses and No Balls who were religiously avoided by our gang.

So now you know what the Maniacs meant when they used cryptic codes like FBE, FBH, TBH, SBO, etc., whenever they analysed the oomph quotient of girls.

◇

The Socials, that great make-or-break happening, that last frontier that would separate the romantic haves from the have-nots, that sociological Noah's Ark that would give sanctuary only to a few, was just twenty-four hours away. We all had splurged a small fortune on shoring up our wardrobe with new FU's jeans and Verrano T-shirts and fake Adidas sneakers. 'Look new, feel new, think new' was our collective dictum and we practised enough positive thinking to have Norman Vincent Peale beaming approvingly.

We hadn't bagged any dates to proudly escort to the Socials though—despite trying out every technique that Rammy had suggested (and then some he hadn't)—and convinced each other that we'd soon hit pay dirt on the dance floor.

6 Top 3 now carried a huge full-length mirror we had bummed from Walia, and we rehearsed everything from our walks and expressions and tones and welcome smiles to opening lines in front of it. We were confident, well-prepared, and thoroughly drunk on mutual admiration and motivational talks.

◇

Two hours to go. Does the 'D' in D-Day stand for dance, wonders Mangy. Perhaps. Who knows how words get invented and who cares? Rammy says the science of word origins is called etymology or something, but the only *science* we guys are interested in is how to improve the *chemistry* between us and some gyrating Ecstasy and how to experience some *reproductive biology*.

The loo is packed to capacity. The shaving mirrors are working overtime. Solly is shaving his armpits (he's done with his face); Chopsy is pinch-demolishing two pimples camping on his cheek and dousing the hurt with Dettol and getting more hurt; I am Listerine-ing my mouth for the fourth time and scraping off Gold Flake stains from my teeth; Shaky and Mangy are trimming their moustaches; Dusty is pruning his bushy eyebrows (it really does make him look like a dacoit from Chambal valley if he doesn't); and Rammy is giving us last-hour tips and back-thumps.

We gather at the adda. We colour-coordinate our attire and debate whether we should wear caps and optical enhancers; decide against it as the *mantra* for the evening is 'cool, muted, and formally casual'; laugh our hearts out seeing Solly slipping a condom into his wallet saying 'just in case' ('I'll tonsure my head if you get to use that tonight,' says Mangy; and Solly bets him fifty bucks that he will, and the bet is on, though reduced now to twenty bucks); reserve 6 Top 1 and 6 Top 3 as love nests if any of us became infinitely lucky; scrutinise each other for the nth time; guzzle a pint of some cheap whisky Dusty has mixed with Limca; pop mouth fresheners that Rammy is passing; high-five each other; say 'Tora! Tora! Tora!' (oh, I forgot to tell you before – 'Tiger! Tiger! Tiger!' is the motto of us Maniacs, and yes, it's borrowed from a USA/Jap movie title); take enough deep breaths to create oxygen shortage in Bangalore; and march on to the war zone to conquer some amorous hearts.

The Ahuja speakers are belting out *That's All* by Genesis, and the DJ, Rohit Verma from X-ray batch, says to me that the volume is cleverly adjusted to loud so that you get an excuse to inch closer to a girl every time you wish to say something and be heard above the din. The winking strobe lights are raining enough astral colours to give kaleidoscopes an inferiority complex. The hundred-odd guys gathered at the new Insti are in various stages of epileptic fits. The rum punch is acrid and tastes horrible. The girls present can be counted on your fingers.

Three Sadnesses. Zero Ecstasies. Zero Happinesses.

'Three girls, and all NBS,' I hear Chopsy shouting into my ears, 'man, they should make attendance compulsory for Socials.'

'It's just eight,' I say optimistically, 'they will trickle in by nine.'

There is nothing much left for us to do than guzzle rum punch and munch *samosas* and potato chips. There is no worthwhile bird in sight to try the RAPIST methods on. (Rammy's Action Plan: Ingenious Seduction Techniques, in case you've forgotten.)

By 9 p.m. the Maniacs are too sloshed to care. By 10 p.m. we are so smashed that even a few guys begin to look beautiful. By 11 p.m. we are back at our adda and pillow-suffocating Rammy who is incoherently rambling about how patience is a virtue and all that crap...

After three days, the first term was topped off with the mandatory terminal tests and we all promptly flunked them. Rammy was the only one from our gang who cleared the Anatomy viva and Mangy said that he should be fined heavily for breaking fresher term traditions.

5

The Ecstasies, Maniacs Cry Foul, First Date

Then. Early December 1985.

THE SECOND TERM HAD BEGUN AND NOW WE ALL WERE FREE to do our own thing and even join the vegetarian D-mess (only Rammy and I were part of it from our gang). This brought us closer than we were earlier and, over the days, I learned so much about life, Philosophy, Literature, Atomic physics, Palmistry, Astronomy, and even theories of intelligent design from him. The guy was a walking encyclopaedia on eclectic subjects and perhaps had four brains.

As you might have gathered by now, Rammy was the oddball among us Maniacs. He never smoked, never drank anything other than water or orange juice (the Socials night was the only exception), never abused anyone (well, at least not in Hindi, or rarely at that), never blew his fuse, never lied, never cheated; and since he was our exact opposite in close to a million ways, we all felt naturally attracted to him. We had even coined a new name for him now—Master Nevero—since he *never* did anything 'normal' and had also been unanimously acknowledged as our 'guru'. He carried the title lightly though.

He had his eccentricities, as all geniuses must have, and that made him all the more endearing. He meditated thrice a day; chanted *Hanuman Chalisa* early in the morning; bathed twice a day (our group average was twice a week; in winters it was twice a fortnight); kept to himself and read lots of highbrow literature which he used to call 'brain food'. I used to joke that his brain would one day explode due to 'over-eating'. The only similarity he and I shared was in our taste for music – we both loved Billy Joel and Jethro Tull.

Rammy now shared a room with Solly at 3 Ground 4 and we all tried our best to reside on the same floor, but it wasn't an easy thing to manage since rooms were religiously allotted by an incorruptible hostel committee. Now, 3 Ground 4 was our new adda. Whenever we needed advice or tips or consolation or money, you could find us making a beeline for Rammy.

Solly kept cribbing that he wasn't allowed to smoke or drink in the room, but also couldn't dare to part ways with Rammy because we all needed him so very much, both as a wise counsellor and as our collective anchor.

Anyway, girls were far from our minds and, frankly, we had given up any hope of snaring a few from the girls' hostel in the foreseeable future; and since we were just ten months away from the dreaded Univ exams, we decided to get down to some serious studying.

Of course, we were definitely and conveniently bunking drab classes and all. In fact, our gang took turns doing it so the rest of us could give 'proxy' for the absentees – but unfortunately it wasn't easy bunking dissections and getting away with it.

Dissections were from 2 p.m. to 4 p.m.—just after lunchtime—and Rammy was the only one among us who bunked them religiously, and he was forever explaining both to us and the Training Officer (T.O.) that ripping apart a cadaver after a detestable lunch made him feel like a cannibal. He was also hauled up by Dandy quite a few times but he just didn't seem to care – perhaps he had left it to Lord Hanuman to see him through in the Univs or was banking on his sterling performance in the fresher term anatomy viva. The rest of our gang was more diligent and only bunked theory classes.

Then we had to go for compulsory NCC training between 4 p.m. and 5 p.m. and Rammy bunked that too. The T.O. hauled him up but Rammy didn't budge a millimetre and I guess he just wrote Rammy off as a bad egg.

Well, the bad egg had influenced us too, and after a week we decided to give the NCC training the go-by. We were pulled up too, and as Rammy had advised us, we just said that we'd malinger a stomach ache or back pain or spondylitis or something if he pushed us any further, so the T.O. didn't push us on that.

Neelima was now seeing some guy from Wonder batch and Solly had given up the chase. Grishma was romancing some guy from Victory batch and Chopsy had given up on her. We all were too busy and neck deep in journals, bone sets and thick books, so all thoughts of romance had disappeared from our system as cleanly and swiftly as ice lollies would from a blast furnace.

It was 7 p.m. The squash game had dehydrated Chopsy and me beyond tolerance levels and we decided to grab some life-saving soya milk at Mahima Nagar, a small residential colony just two km from the hostel which had some neat chaat joints run by some Maharashtrian migrants who served authentic and cheap *bhel puri*, *aloo chaat*, and *paani puri*; with 'cheap' being the operative word here, so the stalls were infinitely popular with all strapped-for-cash Defcomers.

After guzzling two bottles each of the soya ambrosia and tucking away some fruit and aloo chaat, we felt sated and alive. As we were returning to the hostel, we saw three girls from X-ray batch walking in front of us – about twenty feet ahead of us, bang opposite a rundown tea shop we all used to frequent, which was insightfully and imaginatively called Tea Time.

We surveyed the trio. One Tennis Ball Happiness. One Tennis Ball Ecstasy. One Football Ecstasy. All single, and hopefully ready to mingle. Infinite luck! Shubhra Rajan. Alka Pandey. Ranjana Chawla.

As the Hindi saying goes, when God gives you something, He tears the roof and has the goodies raining on you like there's no tomorrow.

We looked at each other, too tired or too stunned to speak, and were wondering what our course of action ought to be. Rammy hadn't trained us for unexpected godsends, so we had to play this one by ear. Chopsy excitedly jerked his neck a few times pointing out the girls (you know, the way guys do when they are egging you on and forcefully begging you to rise to the occasion – pun intended), waved his eyebrows, nudged me desperately in the ribs, and became all aflutter with renewed libido.

'Cool it, dude,' I whispered, 'I am thinking.'

'Fuck thinking, man!' he said. 'This is action-time. We won't get another chance like this. Talk to them, fucker, talk to them…'

Alka had snubbed me a week ago when I had tried to talk to her as she exited the college library, and since I was still smarting from the ego-wound, I was definitely not going to speak with *her*. Plus, she was just a Tennis Ball Ecstasy. Ranjana was the Football Ecstasy and I'd definitely like to do much more than just talk to her. Shubhra seemed the *behenji* kinds who do not have a mind of their own and who will just flow with the general trend of events.

Chopsy elbowed me again and I nearly slapped him.

'Okay, I've decided…' I whispered.

'Thank God!' he said, his eyes glinting with testosterone-powered hope.

'I am not going to talk to any of them,' I said.

'Fuck, man, are you crazy? – don't you dare wimp out now…'

'No, what we'll do is simple. We'll just walk past them slowly and casually. And, we'll keep talking something to each other—let's discuss what fun we had at the Socials or something like that—so they will notice us, and then the ball is in their court.'

'What if they don't notice us?'

'They will, buddy, they will, we'll be loud enough – but they might just notice and ignore us. That means they aren't interested. And, if *they* say hi, then our game plan is working…'

'Okay, whatever we do, let's do it fast, we're close to the hostel…'

'Okay, *now*,' I said, and we began walking faster, pretending to be deeply absorbed in our full-throated discussion, and smoothly filed past the girls.

We must have gone ten feet past them, and I had nearly given up any hope of striking up a convo with them that evening, when I heard them sniggering from behind.

'So the Yankees won't talk to X-ray girls, hahn?' It was definitely Alka's voice. *Was she trying to make up for the earlier snub?*

'Maybe they're the shy kinds.' That was definitely Ranjana.

'They will,' I said confidently, turning around, 'provided hoity-toity X-ray girls don't snub them.'

'Hey, c'mon,' said Alka, remembering that evening from a week ago, 'I was just in a bad mood that day – don't take it to heart.'

'Okay, I won't, so where's the party coming from?' I said.

'Oh, we just went for some *bhel puri* – you guys look as if you're returning from the National Games,' said Ranjana.

'Squash,' said Chopsy tersely, obviously trying to impress them with our athleticism and his fake accent.

'Orange or Mango? – I think Jupiter Juice Bar gives good squash, no?' asked Shubhra, and I wondered if she was sarcastic or seriously demented.

'Shut up, silly,' said Ranjana, 'they were *playing* squash – right?'

'Yes,' I said, 'do you girls ever play any games other than snubbing guys?'

'Oh-ho, there you go again,' said Alka, 'okay, *baba*, sorry.'

'Accepted,' I said, 'hey, how about a juice at Jupiter? Shubhra's right – he does whip up excellent squash.'

They looked at each other, raised their eyebrows, giggled some secret giggle that I couldn't decipher, and nodded assent.

'Your treat,' said Ranjana.

'Of course!' said Chopsy, happily and most chivalrously.

So the five of us trooped down to have mango milkshake (what a universal favourite!) at Jupiter Juice Bar and were busy exchanging juicy gossip and come-hither looks for close to half an hour.

'So do all of you guys smoke?' asked Ranjana, and I kept eye-hinting Chopsy to keep his mind and vision off her boobs. Chopsy was pretty bad at taking eye-hints though.

'No, not all of us,' I said. 'Rammy doesn't smoke – in fact, he's a bit of a goody-goody hermit.'

'How boring,' said Alka.

'You *like* guys who smoke and drink?' asked Chopsy, trying to blow smoke rings and hoping that it would make them like us even more.

'Of course,' said Ranjana. 'They're the ones who're cool and so much more fun. I *toh* just hate the *bhaiyya* kinds.'

'How can you say that?' objected Shubhra, and I thought she and Rammy would make an ideal pair.

'Hey, you guys call yourselves Maniacs or something, right?' said Alka.

'How very observant! Dusty has etched it on all the desks in college,' I said.

'Ya, we noticed, and there's also so many hearts with arrows going through them against each of your names – you guys are masters at getting jilted, na?' teased Ranjana.

'Not always,' I said, adding a sly wink to my words, 'sometimes we're lucky – especially on Saturdays.'

Chopsy laughed loudly and said 'good one', more so to be part of the convo than for any other reason.

It was a Saturday evening, buddy, and I was back-thumping myself with an imaginary hand that all was going well, according to plan, and it definitely seemed that we had these girls literally eating (sorry, drinking) out of our hands.

'They're getting ideas!' said Shubhra, the spoilsport.

'Ya – aren't they a bit too fast!' wondered Ranjana.

'Okay, name an animal,' I said to her, masterfully deflecting our talks to more intriguing intellectual territory.

'What?!' said Alka. 'Where on earth did that come from?'

'Don't think too much, dear, just name an animal,' I persisted.

'Why?' asked Ranjana.

'Name it and I will tell you why later.'

Girls hate suspense and if you succeed in creating it, then you've won ninety percent of the romantic battle. I was sure that by the end of our juice-session I'd be a battle-scarred veteran. Great going, Hucky, said a gleeful voice from within me.

'He'll definitely pull our legs – definitely some prank, don't fall for it,' said the spoilsport.

'Ya, and you'll become taller or longer.' I laughed a laugh that weak jokes don't deserve. 'Depends on whether you're standing or lying down.'

They made wry faces and pouted and looked more beautiful.

'C'mom,' I said, 'be a sport – it's really interesting. Name an animal.'

'Hucky,' said Ranjana, and all of them cackled.

'Very funny,' I said sarcastically.

'Okay – cat,' said Alka.

'You,' I said, pretending to look causally at Ranjana.

'Hmmm...monkey.'

'Your turn, Shubhra, and don't repeat any animal.'

'Well, donkey.'

'Chopsy, remember what they said okay? All right, second and third animal, no repetitions, all say different-different animals,' I said to Alka.

'You said one animal, na?' she objected.

'C'mon, just two more – fast...'

'Hmmm...dog...and horse.'

'Your turn, Ranjana.'

'Cow...hmmm...tiger.'

'Your turn, Shubhra.'

'Elephant...and tortoise.'

'Okay, I remember. Alka said cat-dog-horse. Shubhra said donkey-elephant-tortoise. Ranjana said monkey-cow-tiger. Am I right?' said Chopsy.

'Bang on,' I said, and became silent as a morgue. I straw-sucked the last drops of my mango milkshake and looked vacantly into the distance. Sixty seconds of mango-flavoured silence passed by.

'So – what?' asked all three, almost simultaneously.

'What?' I teased them.

'What's it for?' asked Ranjana.

'Oh, I just find it cute when girls say the names of animals – just a fetish that began when I was in primary school,' I said smilingly.

'Cheapo,' said Shubhra.

'I knew it – he would come up with something stupid like this,' said Alka.

'Got you!' I said. 'Just kidding. Actually this is an ancient Chinese system of divining a personality subconsciously.'

I could hear Rammy's voice playing in my mind. ('Girls are always trying to understand themselves most of the time—that's the prime reason most guys can't figure them out—because they're riddles unto themselves and wrapped in layers of unfathomable mystery,' he had said to me once. 'If you can get a girl interested in knowing something about herself, then you get to have a good conversation with the girl.') I was sending invisible flying kisses to Rammy. The dude's theory was turning out to be right.

'Oh, really?' asked Ranjana, obviously intrigued. 'How's that?'

'Well, you said monkey-cow-tiger,' I explained, savouring the rapt attention all of them were providing me, 'so here goes. The first animal—monkey—is what *you* think you are. The second animal—cow—is what the *world* thinks you are. The third animal—tiger—is what *you really are.*'

'You mean tigress,' said Ranjana.

'Yup,' I agreed.

'Hey, what about us?' asked two voices.

'Okay, Shubhra, you think you're a donkey...'

We all laughed out loud and she squirmed and shrivelled and I felt like saying 'serves you right, spoilsport'.

'...the world thinks you're an elephant,' I continued against the backdrop of more laughter, 'and actually you're a tortoise.'

'Hey, that's cool,' said Alka, 'she does clam up often,' and I felt my face blushing, and my body began gathering goose pimples as she affectionately patted me on the shoulder.

'Ya, Alka, and you think you're a cat, the world thinks you're a dog, and actually you're a horse.'

'Cool, man, really cool,' said Ranjana, and I knew that I had won them over.

'Hey, it's getting late,' said Shubhra, 'time to head back.'

They consulted the itsy-bitsy HMT watches they were wearing (as if their collective wrists were final arbiters on life-and-death decisions) and we escorted them to the girls' hostel. Chopsy whispered 'good show' into my ear and Alka asked me what he was saying and I lied that he was wondering if we could go for an English flick playing at Rahul tomorrow. The girls shot us the kind of look you'd normally shoot at someone who coolly asks if you'd like to lose your virginity to him. Then Ranjana and Alka shot us the kind of look you'd normally shoot at someone you don't mind losing your virginity to. Shubhra looked at them aghast and I was sure she was thinking '*ooi maa*, what sluts to agree so soon'.

'What movie is playing there?' asked Ranjana.

I wanted to say who cares which movie is playing as long as we get to enjoy your company within the dark mushy confines of a theatre, but ended up saying that I didn't know. Chopsy too pleaded ignorance on the subject, and I knew that we had goofed up, especially since we had made the suggestion.

I tried salvaging the situation by saying that we'd look it up in the newspaper and let them know later.

'Okay,' said Alka, 'let's go see *Saagar* – it's playing at Neelayam.'

'Ya – nice movie,' said Chopsy.

'So Ranjana, tomorrow. *Saagar*?' I asked to confirm, as she clearly was the decision-maker for the trio.

'Sure – you guys pick us up at ten. And, it's a date.'

'Hey,' said Alka, 'how about getting your entire gang – that way we can meet all of them.'

Chopsy's jaw dropped a mile and I held mine in place by cluck-clucking that it seemed to be a swell idea. But then, I remembered Rammy and his take on girls not liking rubber-band vertebrae, so I suggested that maybe this time around we could go by ourselves, diplomatically adding that they all could always meet the rest of the Maniacs later. (Deplorably selfish, weren't we? But then, as the justification goes, everything's fair in love and hormonal war.)

'Okay,' said Ranjana, 'but don't ditch, okay?'

'Of course not!' I said. 'Chivalry isn't extinct yet.'

We saw them off at the girls' hostel and I don't remember whether we walked or hopped or floated towards our adda.

Any hostel is a close-knit community – which meant that nothing you ever did stayed private. There were prying eyes everywhere and guys residing in Ugly block were masters at surveillance techniques (legend had it that the block had gathered its name after a Mike batcher nicknamed Ugly had single-handedly bashed up three burglars trying to sneak into his room one night). Ugly blockers even had binoculars and mini-telescopes with which they monitored every activity happening across the road. And, since Jupiter Juice Bar was nestled at the far corner of the petrol bunk that was bang opposite Ugly block, and also because Ranjana was a Football Ecstasy, Chopsy and I were pretty famous by the time we reached 3 Ground 4 to provide the breaking news. Well, it wasn't exactly breaking news anymore – it was now old, stale, discussed, debated, analysed and plastered all across the fuming faces of the five Maniacs gathered at our adda.

'Hi, guys,' I said. 'Wassup?'

'*You* tell us – what *you guys* have been up to?' asked Shaky, glaring at me, and then at Chopsy.

'Nothing yaar,' said Chopsy, 'we just went to Mahima Nagar to grab some soya milk and chaat...'

'*Ya?*' wondered Solly bitterly, like a lawyer cross-examining a key witness. 'And...?'

'And what? We just happened to bump into some X-ray girls and we said hi,' I added. 'That's not a crime.'

'I guess not,' said Mangy, 'but we're told this "hi" lasted some half an hour at Jupiter...'

'Oh-ho, they were just giving us tips on how to tackle anat and physio etcetera, they wanted to give us their notes,' I lied.

'Really?' said Solly accusingly, 'I think I saw you guys laughing and joking and having fun.'

'So what, dammit!' I launched a counter-offensive, pretending to lose my cool. 'Are we staying in a Zen monastery or something and sworn to eternal celibacy and all?'

'No, but we guys were sworn to a pact and you guys broke it,' explained Rammy.

'Hey, c'mon, we know we had decided not to talk to any girls and all for a while, but it was *they* who spoke to us,' I defended.

'You could even have avoided them, stop giving *butris* okay?' said Dusty. 'These girls have been bad-mouthing us at the girls' hostel and you're shameless enough to talk to them?' (Butri = Defcoms-speak for lame, unacceptable, ill-conceived, stupid, wafer-thin excuse.)

'Okay, we spoke with them. So, what's the jury's verdict – hangman's noose, lethal injection or electric chair?' I teased.

Five pairs of accusing eyes glared at us. Five minds were wondering what should be the penalty for treason. Five hearts were jealous – I could clearly read (smell?) that.

'Listen, guys,' said Chopsy, 'they are swell girls, and this way you also will get to talk to them and hit on a few girls later – especially after we watch a movie with them tomorrow...'

'Ya, we have a double date for a movie at Neelayam...' I confirmed.

'MOOVVVVIIIIIIEEEEEE?' screamed five voices, and the wall plaster peeled off a bit and the windows rattled and we all became partially deaf for a while. It took them a minute or two to absorb the shock.

Obviously, Solly couldn't absorb it too well for he came lunging at me, held me by the scruff of my neck, and just when he was about to sock me madly on my surprisingly paralysed jaw, Chopsy did the timely reflexive thing of pulling him away. So, he socked Chopsy instead and they began punching each other like some heavyweight boxers at Madison Square Garden. It took much effort to separate them, and they were finally deposited on two different beds, and were now throwing glare-missiles at each other.

'Enough! I've had enough of this! Now we've even started fighting with each other,' said Rammy, reprimanding Solly for his violence. 'Any differences should be sorted out through mutual dialogue...'

'Fuck you and your mutual dialogue, you twerp! What do you think we are doing – sitting at the United Nations?' screamed Solly. 'These guys have betrayed our trust, these bloody slimeball bastards...'

'Okay, okay,' said Mangy, throwing an arm around Solly's shoulder, 'cool down now.'

'Fuck you all – you're all good-for-nothing jealous guys, we're *definitely* going for the movie, and balls to you, Solly,' said Chopsy, and left the room in a huff.

'I am not going, Chopsy, not like this…' I said as he stormed out, and Chopsy didn't reply.

We all sat in mournful silence for a while, and Shaky suggested we go to the new Insti to cool down. It was already 9 p.m. and we had missed dinner, so we'd do the usual thing of having aloo paranthas and egg bhurji out there. We were all sitting on the steps of the new Insti and looking at the stars and I was feeling both guilty and angry, with guilt being the more dominant emotion.

Chopsy was sitting all by himself at a distance, puffing away a ciggie like an over-worked chimney, and Solly got up and began moving towards him. Rammy held Solly, but he brushed him away, and Rammy loud-whispered something like 'don't create a scene here and have everyone laughing at us – remember, we can only fight in private'.

We were worried that Solly would begin a no-holds-barred scuffle again (Chopsy and Solly were the body-builders of our gang – both were built like oxen actually).

We saw Solly parking himself next to Chopsy, and Chopsy looked away. Then Solly put his arm around Chopsy's shoulders and must have said sorry or something similar for they both got up, tearfully hugged each other, and returned to where we were sitting and mulling over our intra-gang tiff.

'Tora, tora, tora!' screamed Dusty, and all was forgiven.

'Okay, I'm sorry,' said Solly, 'and I'm treating all of us to beer as compensation.'

'You fool,' said Chopsy, 'they've invited *all of us* for the movie…'

'REALLLYYY?' asked Solly, looking at me.

'Of course,' I lied, 'would we go all by ourselves? How could you even *imagine* something like that? We actually set up the date for all of us.'

'But you said double date,' observed Rammy judiciously.

'We were joking – okay, I'll also chip in for the beer,' said Chopsy.

'We all will, guys!' I said, happily back-thumping them both.

'Yippee!' said Mangy, 'way to go, guys, way to go.'

◇

If Ranjana and Alka were surprised to see seven guys waiting for them at 10 a.m., they didn't show it. We all were nattily attired in regulation jeans and T-shirts and shades (in fact, we were all wearing exactly the same outfit as on the Socials night) and sporting we-are-the-coolest-dudes expressions.

'Aha, seems like the entire jing-bang is here,' said Alka.

'Ya, surprise, the more the merrier, plus Chopsy and Solly are your bodyguards for the day – as you can see,' I said, playfully cupping their biceps.

The introductions were done, shy hellos were exchanged, and we were wondering who'll ride with whom on whose bike. Five bikes. Seven guys. Two girls. A better sex ratio finally. So, who was going to be the lucky one?

'Always ladies' choice,' said Chopsy, so we left it to them.

'If you guys don't mind, I'll pillion-ride with Hucky – unless *you* mind,' said Ranjana, eyeing me mischievously.

'Not at all. My pleasure,' I said happily. 'And you, Alka? Who do you trust *your* life with?'

'Hey, don't scare me okay? You guys are not on pot or something, na?' she wondered.

'Don't be silly,' said Chopsy. 'Not at this time of the day, yaar. Look at our eyes. Clear as virgin daylight.'

'So you guys do smoke pot?' asked Ranjana, nudging my elbow and pretending to be horrified.

'Who do you think we are? Mother Teresa?' I asked. 'All cool dudes smoke pot – but only in the evenings. But Rammy here—he's a saint—doesn't even smoke ciggies.'

'That's good, Rammy, keep it up,' said Ranjana patronisingly, 'don't let their horrible company spoil you.'

Rammy smiled sheepishly and nodded his head and made some incomprehensible grunting sound. I guess he was only good at the theory part of seducing girls and all – when it came to the practical part of it, he seemed to be quite a miserable dud. (Or was he just pretending to be so to have us shining that much more? I decided to check later. Come to think of it, I'd never seen Rammy speaking with *any* girl, so I made a mental note to monitor him over the days.)

'Alka, we're waiting for your carefully-considered and impeccably-weighed decision – or would you rather toss up a coin?' I asked.

'Maybe she wants to consult with her mom or an astrologer,' Ranjana ribbed her, and we all laughed.

'Shut up okay? Hmmmm…okay, Solly seems to be a good bet,' said Alka, and Solly said 'welcome, welcome' as if he'd fall apart any moment, burdened as he was by the unmanageable tonnage of unexpected happiness and bliss. How gawky could you get!

Saagar is a great movie. It teaches you a lot about unrequited love and sacrifice and all that crap. But I was hardly watching the movie. (I had already seen it with mom at Sheila in Delhi a few months ago. In fact, I'd been quite bored of all the mush, though mom had liked it.)

I was instead watching Ranjana watching the movie from the corner of my eye, and observing if she sighed during romantic scenes and if she looked at me during such times. If a girl did that, you could be hundred percent sure that she had more than just sisterly or platonic love for you. Seventeen sighs. Eight looks at me already. And, we were just reaching interval. Of course I kept count, buddy. (What else was there to do anyway?) I had arrived on the romantic horizon. Say congratulations.

Alka was sitting with Solly and Chopsy on either side of her, and they were exchanging giggles the last time I sneaked a look at them – so something good was cooking there too. Great! The Maniacs had two almost-girlfriends now. The rest of us were feeling pretty left out I guess (poor things, but who cared a damn, they were just 'pile on' bones in the double date *kebab* anyway). They were pretending to appreciate Kamal Haasan's histrionics and debating if he was hamming or over-gesturing or over-emphasising his genius or all three at times…

'Nice movie, na?' asked Ranjana to me as we exited.

'Ya, but wasn't it a bit too mushy?'

'Of course, silly,' said Alka. 'You don't like mush?'

'I prefer it happening in real life than on the screen,' I said naughtily, and the girls exchanged I-told-you-so looks or so I thought.

'Okay,' said Alka, 'this time I want to see how Chopsy rides with a girl pillion-riding him – or does he become a nervous wreck?'

Solly's face fell like a meteor but he said 'sure' and smiled graciously. Thankfully, Ranjana didn't shift loyalties, and held me more tightly than she had on the onward journey, and we all went to India Coffee House at Brigade Road for lunch.

6

Jilted, Sunk by ABBA, Suspense of ABBA

Then. Late December 1985.

THERE ARE TIMES IN LIFE WHEN YOU FEEL BLISSFUL, BLESSED, and you are almost looking at yourself with renewed vision, and pinching yourself every now and then to make sure that it's all not part of some nebulous, transient dream. There's a spring in your gait and a perpetual smile on your lips. There's always a song in your heart and a dance in your soul. Heaven pales in comparison on such days.

But life has this uncanny habit of proving some killjoy proverbs right every once in a while, perhaps to create an emotional balance and keep things on an even keel. It was a Sunday when life decided to play one of its mean tricks on me by proving an African saying right. Life informed me that nothing good lasts more than three days. Or, close to three weeks in my case.

Rammy and I were in D-mess, polishing off a heavy breakfast of omelettes and bread rolls when it all began happening.

'Hey, Hucky,' said Solly as he came rushing to our table, 'there's a call for you.'

There was just one landline phone next to the Warden's office and you needed to cover a distance of hundred metres once the relayed information reached you – and cover it real fast lest the call got disconnected by the time you reached it. I was in no mood to run or to take calls as I was feeling heavier than a pregnant hippo.

'Who's it from?' I asked.

'Who else, man?' he said, throwing a wink at Rammy.

'Ranjana?' I wondered.

'Yup,' said Solly.

'Okay,' I said, raising myself reluctantly.

I trudged as fast as my overloaded system would permit.

'Hello,' I said into the phone.

'Hi – what are you doing now?' Her voice was strangely crisp, clipped and cold.

'Nothing, was just having breakfast, why?'

'Okay, you come over after you finish it.'

'Actually I'm through – what's the matter?'

'You come, *na* – I'll tell you.'

This wasn't sounding good, dude. Her tone was almost bordering on a threat and her words lacked the earlier warmth and softness.

◇

'What's this?' she asked, flashing a cassette as I switched off the bike outside the girls' hostel. She had been waiting for me to reach and that wasn't a good sign either.

'What – it's a cassette, a TDK cassette, what about it?' I said crabbily.

'And what has it *got*?'

'Why, a magnetic tape and maybe some songs, how should I know?'

'*Your name* is written on it – and *you* don't know?' Her anger created a bit of static electricity around her.

'Ranjana, what are you talking about? And why are you sounding so upset?'

'UPSET? Upset wouldn't describe a millionth of what I am feeling right now – you BASTARD!' she yelled, slapped the cassette into my hand, turned sharply, tossed her hair angrily, contributed more to global warming than refineries, and disappeared into the girls' hostel.

Close to twenty folks had heard that. A few looked away to spare me the embarrassment. A few didn't. A few sadists scanned me like an X-ray machine. I felt as small as a Bantu tribesman at a Beverly Hills bash. I felt as low as an open manhole. I felt as insignificant as an insecure bacterium taking an IQ test. I felt my knees becoming as weak as soggy potato wafers. Then I didn't feel anything. I was so limp and zonked that a guy had to help me kick-start the bike.

◇

'What happened?' asked Rammy as I secreted the bike at the parking lot outside 1 Ground.

'Nothing,' I lied.

'You look like you just interacted with a man-raping, homosexual ghost.'

'No, I'm okay,' I moaned, and went and crashed in my room. My body and thoughts tossed and turned.

I was a mangled mind of mad questions and answers. What the hell was the matter with her? This was just a cassette of ABBA. Was she angry that it had a suggestive song titled *Honey, Honey*? No, that couldn't be. And, how had it reached her anyway? I hadn't given it to her. Perhaps one of the Maniacs had. I rolled up into a shrivelled mass (mess?). Or was she battling PMS? Perhaps. I tucked in the blanket tighter. Did you ever get sadness fever, buddy? I did. I was too tired to play the cassette. Fuck it. I tried to sleep away the sinking feeling. I didn't know how many minutes passed. I didn't even know if I was alive or dead.

'Get up,' said Solly, shaking me wildly.

'No, leave me alone.'

'What the hell,' said Shaky, 'what happened, man?'

'Why did she abuse you – that fucking bitch!' screamed Mangy.

'Don't call her that,' I said weakly.

'Listen Hucks,' said Rammy, 'tell us what happened. Why was she livid?'

'I don't know.'

'What did she *say*?' asked Solly.

'She said something about an ABBA cassette which she returned...'

'What cassette?' asked Shaky.

'It's there on the table,' I said.

'Have you played it?' asked Rammy.

'No...I mean not now,' I moaned, 'but it's just got some songs, I know, I recorded them a few months ago – was she just joking...?'

'No, man, she wasn't joking, girls don't joke while abusing, and they don't abuse while joking, they do only one thing at a time...' explained Rammy.

'*Chup kar yaar*, Rammy,' said Solly, 'stop the lecture and play the cassette. Did you give her that cassette, Hucky?'

'No.'

'Then how did your cassette reach her?' asked Shaky.

'I don't know, I thought one of you guys must have given it to her.'

And Rammy played the cassette on my hi-fi Bush compact double-deck, my prized possession which could do hi-speed dubbing from cassette to cassette, also normal speed recording from room to cassette, and which was gifted by dad on my previous birthday anniversary. Now, it would play ABBA and also shed tons of light on why an innocent harmless tape had made Ranjana fume like a steam locomotive on steroids. Hopefully.

Side A: *Honey Honey, Mamma Mia, Fernando*...

'Just keep fast-forwarding it, man...' said Solly, losing his patience.

'No, we can't, we might miss something significant,' said Rammy.

The hummable numbers were making me feel more horrible than before, and I was shrinking and shrinking and looking at Ranjana and all my old flames flashing in my mind's eye, and wondering if life was a giant vacuum cleaner that specialised in sucking out all the energy from you before catapulting you into oblivion...Is this what happened just before death?

Side A (continued):...*Waterloo, Ring Ring, SOS*...My mind involuntarily sent an SOS message to God just in case there was a God: *Help me if you are alive, you bastard! Let there be light!*

Then the cassette went blank for quite a while. Everyone listened intently and got pretty cheesed off that there was nothing to listen to. I was too tired to explain to them that I always left a recorded tape blank in the end for about five to ten minutes so that I could add other similar-sounding numbers if I ever came across them later. Anyway, we had to listen to it entirely lest we missed something.

'Nothing. Just songs and silence. What's the prob,' said Solly, 'why would she be angry about this?'

'Maybe she erased something?' observed Shaky.

'Possible,' said Mangy.

'Arre, let's check out Side B also – the only exercise you guys seem to be getting is jumping to conclusions. Always examine the *entire evidence* before you begin your stupid analyses, but then you guys hardly ever read Poirot or Holmes...' sighed Rammy as we waited for the auto-reverse function to kick in.

Side B: *Gimme, Gimme, Gimme*...

'Could she be angry about the lyrics – gimme gimme gimme a man after midnight…?' wondered Shaky.

'Possible,' said Mangy.

'Shut up, you *gobar*-brained gruds – it's more serious than that!' said Rammy. (Gobar = Cow dung. Grud= Defcoms-speak for despicably stupid, dense, pea-brained moron.)

Side B (continued): …*Voulez-Vous, Dancing Queen, Does Your Mother Know, Hasta Manana*…screech…'…fucking Socials, man, I thought at least a few Ecstasies from X-ray batch would be there, but the primitive bitches are acting pricey…' (That was Solly's voice! We all sat up. Our ears and eyes were glued to the tape.) '…shit, I wish at least Ranjana were there, it would've been nice to see her Footballs go up and down like a yo-yo…' (That was Shaky!)

Hell! So this was it!…screech…*Hasta Manana say we'll meet again, I can't do without you* …

I knew I'd never meet her again. And, I also knew that I can't do without her now.

'*Band baj gayee*, man!' said Solly. 'When did *that* get recorded?!'

'Socials night,' said Rammy, pensively raising his eyebrows like Poirot, and his pupils clearly seemed focussed on a distant and fuzzy night. 'Remember, we were in 6 Top 3…I recall hearing this that night…hmmm…one of us must have pressed the recording button accidentally…and then released it realising his mistake…anyway, we were all too smashed that night…'

'*Mar gaye yaar*,' said Shaky, 'no wonder she's boiling…'

'So what do we do now?' asked Mangy, and four heads turned towards Rammy.

'We will definitely work out something, don't worry,' said Rammy, throwing his sinewy arms around my shoulders, 'at least now we know *what* went wrong' – as if that was any help.

'Our relationship is positively ruined, fucked, buried, shit!' I groaned. 'How could *this* have happened?'

'But who the hell gave her this tape?' asked Mangy.

'If it's none of us, then it must be Chopsy or Dusty,' said Solly.

'Saala pig – must be Chopsy, he must have given it to Alka to impress her and she…' began Shaky.

'Stop witch-hunting, guys,' said Rammy, 'this is not the time for any blame game, it's nobody's fault, okay?'

'But, man, what do we do now?' asked Solly.

'Hucks, look at the plus point. *You* didn't say anything in the tape. It was just Solly and Shaky. So, you have a window, though a very small one…' Rammy tried consoling me.

'Fat lot of good *that* will do me,' I moaned.

'Okay, let's grab lunch, guys – it's close to two,' said Shaky.

'Let's eat out,' said Mangy. 'I don't feel like going to the mess. We'll chalk out some action plan over lunch…'

'Roll a joint, man,' said Solly to nobody in particular, and then looking at Shaky, 'you got stuff, dude?'

'Ya, in my room,' said Shaky, and Rammy threw a dirty, holier-than-thou look at them.

'Your brains will get chewed one day – whatever's left of it that is,' said Rammy to all of us in general.

'Hey, you got chew?' asked Mangy. (Chew = *Chillum*, a conical smoking pipe that all holy men and unholy collegians in India use to smoke weed or hashish and connect with divinity or bliss or whatever.)

'No yaar, it broke,' said Shaky, 'let's do reefers. Wait, I'll get the stuff.'

He returned with some weed wrapped in a small polythene packet and began cleaning the stuff. Solly was emptying the tobacco from a few ciggies.

'Make a nice roach, dude, don't just sit doing nothing,' Shaky told Mangy, and he began tearing one of the small visiting cards that I always kept on my study table for this purpose. (Roach replaces the ciggie filter, in case you wish to know.)

'Who scored this maal, man? It smells good,' said Solly.

'I think Dusty,' said Shaky.

'Where are they, gone again to Chopsy's LG's?' asked Mangy. (LG = Local Guardian.)

'Yup,' said Solly.

'Where is this stuff from – Ulsoor or Street?' asked Solly.

'I think it's Ulsoor stuff,' said Shaky.

'Why the hell don't you guys ever score from Anna? Krishnarajapuram maal would be even better,' said Solly, showing off his GK.

'Who'll drive down to KRP? – your *chacha*? Now, don't be greedy, count your blessings, dude,' said Shaky.

Rammy was leafing through *The Bangalore Herald* and no doubt reading some highbrow stuff. I was wondering if I could wish-kill myself.

'Play Tull, man,' said Mangy.

Living in the Past. How apt. Then *Bungle in the Jungle*. We seemed to have an amazing knack of playing numbers suited to the occasion.

Solly lit the reefer and the sweet smell of marijuana smoke seemed sickeningly nauseating (to me) and fantabulously uplifting (to them). When a smoker hates weed-smoke, you know that a smoker's mood is a dark shade of blue.

'C'mon, take a drag,' said Solly, passing the joint to me, 'it'll make you feel better.'

I took a few deep drags and certainly didn't feel better. Marijuana heightened feelings. At least that's how it was with me. If you were happy, it made you happier. If you were sad, it made you sadder. Just when I was beginning to feel as low as an earthworm practising scuba diving, Chopsy and Dusty breezed into the room.

'So you guys are chilling out without us, huhn?' said Chopsy.

'Fucker,' said Solly angrily, 'the pea-brain has finally come…'

'Hey, Solly, what's with the abuse, you stoned or what?' wondered Chopsy.

'Ya, and you should be stoned—with a few rocks—for what you have done. You gave this ABBA cassette to Alka, na?' accused Mangy, showing him the tape.

'Hmmm...I guess so...last week, why? Good she returned it, I want to record a number,' said Chopsy.

'Idiot, can't you check what's there on the tape before passing it?' said Shaky.

'Guys, you're making no sense at all,' said Dusty, and Rammy looked up from behind the newspaper, briefly explained the general trend of events that had punctuated the ghastly morning, and went back to his perusal. They didn't believe us, so the tape was played again, and I sank like a torpedoed submarine.

'Oh no!' said Chopsy.

'Holy crap!' said Dusty.

'Poor Hucky!' said Chopsy.

'Poor Hucky!' said Dusty.

'Guys, stop echoing like Thomson and Thompson twins now and make him feel even worse...hear this, guys,' said Rammy, reading something from *The Bangalore Herald* that had caught his intellectual attention. 'A king asks a Sufi saint to tell him something that will make him happy when sad; and sad when happy. And, the saint says: "This too shall pass." Good one, na?'

'Ya, good one, this too shall pass, and Ranjana will pass on to the next guy who makes a pass at her,' I said morosely.

After collectively gulping two more reefers and converting my room into a gas chamber, we all decided to go to Snehal at Mahima Nagar.

Chopsy kept saying sorry a million times as we walked the distance and had to be shut up forcibly.

Rammy observed rather philosophically that 'sorry doesn't bring a dead man alive anyway and just makes the wound sorer because apologies only help you remember the hurt that much more vividly.'

I was too emotionally drained to agree, and thankfully Solly quickly changed the subject and they all began planning for a movie to while away the evening.

◇

'Okay, gimme a pen,' said Rammy, pulling out a tissue from the glass holder.

'What for?' wondered Solly.

'Arre, we gotta make an action plan, na…' said Rammy.

None of us had a pen.

'What's wrong with you guys, didn't I tell you to always keep a pen handy?' wailed Rammy.

'Why don't you follow your own advice for a change?' observed Shaky.

'Shut up, I'm the planner – you guys ought to execute the plan. Anyway, ask the waiter for a pen,' said Rammy.

Chopsy placed our orders for grub and a pen, and we all began looking at the tissue on which Rammy was feverishly scribbling Venn diagrams, arcane symbols, slender arrows and hurried scrawls.

∞ Problem——→Girl is angry.

Ω Solution——→Girl becomes senti.

How?——→Why?←——When?

(Senti = Campus-speak for sentimental.)

'Hey, this looks good, man – pretty professional and all, you should do an MBA,' teased Mangy, but Rammy carried on untrammelled.

He closed his eyes and dug deep into his intellectual reserves. He emerged out of it after a few minutes as the waiter placed our ceramic soup bowls of one-by-two Veg Manchow and three-by-five Chicken Dumpling on the table.

'Hey, explain, na,' pleaded Solly, 'don't be so snooty.'

'Okay,' began Rammy, 'always begin at the beginning…and in the beginning was the problem…represented by alpha or infinity…same thing…'

'How can alpha and infinity mean the same thing? You aren't even stoned, dude…' said Shaky.

'He's *passively* stoned,' said Chopsy, and everyone except me laughed.

'You've ever seen a circle?' asked Rammy.

'C'mon, talk sense,' said Shaky.

'Where does a circle begin?' Rammy's gimlet eyes bored into Shaky.

'What do you mean…er…,' Shaky stammered, stalling for time, '…er…anywhere on the circle, man…'

'In other words, a circle has infinite alpha points – just like problems. It is not just the cassette that's the problem. The alpha point is elsewhere—the cassette is a mere trigger—the omega point is the solution, get it?' said Rammy, guiding us through the doodles he had drawn.

'Don't screw my trip, man,' said Shaky, 'you carry on without explanations, just tell us what to do in the end…'

'Hey, let him explain, his line of reasoning is so intelligent and so very interesting…' said Solly. (Dope always catalysed the pseudo-intellectual in him.)

'I think Hucky should just send her a nice card or something,' said Dusty.

'Shut up,' said Chopsy, 'that'll be so corny and childish…we have to do something more mature here…'

As they continued their debate, Rammy knitted his brows, sipped the soup disinterestedly, and scribbled on, clearly inspired by some inner voice.

Solve trigger first: A gun without a trigger is safe
Alpha point will take time to discover
Reach Omega point real fast
To remove a thorn, use another thorn
Eureka: Send another cassette. Simple!

'That's it!' announced Rammy, his eyes glinting like that of a mad scientist who's just stumbled upon some elusive truth, 'I know what we'll do – we'll send her another cassette!'

'Another cassette? Man, you need to come up with something better, she can't be wooed back with mushy songs anymore,' said Solly, clearly disappointed with the weak strategy.

'Who said anything about songs?' shrieked Rammy. 'Dude, assumptions are dangerous – they ruin lives. This will be like a cassette-letter, addressed to her from all of us...'

'Balls! She'll just throw it away,' said Mangy.

'No, she won't,' said Rammy, 'girls are inherently curious, and we'll record one that will make her so senti that *she will* apologise to us...and to Hucky of course...'

'Thank God I'm included in your scheme of things,' I said, obviously uninterested in this mad plan.

'Who knows, maybe it will work,' said Dusty.

'Bet? Twenty bucks. It won't,' said Mangy.

When we went back to my room Rammy began writing something feverishly and all the guys were interrupting him every now and then, asking him to change a few words here and there.

I don't know whether Rammy paid any heed to their suggestions for I was too emotionally-sapped to stay awake any longer. When I woke up after about an hour, they had prepared beat-coffee and were getting ready to record something Rammy had written.

Rammy was preparing a fresh tape for Ranjana and I saw him writing ABBA on Side A, and expanding the acronym and writing **A B**ig **B**old **A**pology on Side B of a brand new TDK cassette.

'Okay, now we record,' said Rammy excitedly, 'and I want *complete* silence and choked feelings. Give it all you got guys, and sound as senti as Rajesh Khanna in *Amar Prem*, okay? Don't sound as if you're reading from a script – make it spontaneous and...and...ya, impromptu. Sound natural, guys, just as if you are speaking to her directly. Imagine she is sitting in front of you. And please, will you stub the ciggie, Solly? No smoking while the recording is happening.'

And this is what they recorded:

Dear Ranjana,

This is Rammy. I speak for all the Maniacs right now. Sorry we are calling you dear—but you really are—because you are very dear to one of our dearest friends who, of late, has become as talkative as a coffin.

Make that as talkative as a snow-white coffin—that's how pale he is looking these days. Your anger has really improved his complexion—though we must confess that *we were* happier when *he was* darker and bubblier.

We'll come to him later. First, a few words from Solly ...

Hi, Ranjana, I hope you are still listening to us. Firstly, a big sorry for what we said and for what you heard on the tape. I was as zonked as a millipede on marijuana that night – and you know how the drunk tongue will say things that the sober heart never really means.

Anyway, sorry to have hurt you – and to have also hurt our dear friend in the process. But Ranjana, every guy in every room in every hostel speaks the same language – but I know, that's no excuse. In fact, if I were in *your* place, I'd find it very difficult to pardon *me* for what I said.

But thank God, I am not in your place, and in your place is a dear friend instead, who will always be liked and respected by all of us, both for her warmth and her generosity.

Thank you for hearing me out, Ranjana. I know you won't like to speak with me ever. So, have a great life. I will really miss our friendship. Take care.

Rammy again. Shaky would also like to say a few words, and he has promised to keep it short and sweet. Okay, delete sweet, for truth is bitter...

Hi, Ranjana. I don't seek forgiveness, because what I said on the tape doesn't *deserve* forgiveness. I know you will not like to ever talk to *me* either, and I promise, I won't bother you ever. Your anger is justified. We are not worth it, well, at least *I* am not.

But I will *still* say sorry because I mean it – though I do not wish to be forgiven. In fact, I should be punished. Words can't be withdrawn – how I wish life were a video movie and I could rewind the tape and delete a few unwanted scenes. But then, it's not, and one has to live with one's mistakes. And, I'll live to tell my tale. Of how I lost a friend I really liked and continue to like.

I will always regret what I said every waking minute, every waking hour, for I think with just twenty-four short words I lost a great buddy for a long lifetime. But thanks for the movie and the lunch – that was one of the best days of my life. How happy we were! Remember how we laughed and brought Coffee House down that day? Thanks for the laughter, Ranjana – you will always be in my prayers and my heart. Take care, buddy.

Hi, this is Rammy again. NOW, A FEW WORDS FROM THE SNOW-WHITE COFFIN ...

(Prolonged silence lasting five seconds.)

Sorry, Rammy again. Coffins don't speak, Ranjana. Especially when they are feeling real low and buried. Funny that some of them should get buried for the fault of others though.

I wish Hucky could have said a few words, but he's clammed up like a tortoise in his room; right now we are in my room as Hucky wants to be left alone – and Chopsy is joking that maybe we should try a can opener on him.

But I am sure if Hucky had spoken, he'd have just said three words to you, Ranjana. Because that's how he really feels.

That's how he *thinks* of you. He's said those words to me on many nights. And, I've always been surprised because his tone never changes. And, I've never heard them said so devotedly. In fact, I've never heard them said like this by anyone in my life. Just three words. But Ranjana, they hide three billion feelings behind them. Hucky's favourite words. In fact, Hucky's mantra these days ...

My friendly goddess.

You'll always be that to him, Ranjana. And, to all of us. Always. Take care, buddy, and a final sorry from all of us.

Hasta Manana. Or maybe you never want to meet any of us again. Understandable.

Our loss.

Our Ranjana – and how we lost her. That's how we will always think of you.

Nice title for a book, na? Or for a mushy movie? Maybe like *Saagar*?

Anyway, thanks for your time and patience, buddy. We gotta get going.

We are renting a canoe just to move within Hucky's room these days. Perhaps I should have learnt swimming. Perhaps I will. Goodbye, Ranjana, thanks for listening, and God bless!

By the way, Hucky doesn't know anything about *this* cassette – just like he didn't know anything about *that* cassette.

'Amazing, man! Superb!' said Solly as the recording session ended.

'Great job, Rammy, you sure can write, man, you write like Erich Segal...' said Shaky.

'This will work,' said Chopsy, 'hey Hucky, sounds great, doesn't it?'

'Rammy, when did I *ever* say to you that she is my friendly goddess?' I asked.

'Never, but you better start saying it *now*, if you want to woo her back. And guys, remember – Hucky has *no idea* about this cassette, okay?'

'Killer stuff, the line about three words is a masterpiece. She will expect you to come up with *I love Ranjana* and will be surprised. *My friendly goddess*—wow!—you got ten brains Rammy, way to go...' said Dusty.

'I hope this works,' said Mangy, 'I don't mind losing twenty bucks.'

'Guys, now we got to pass this on to Alka,' said Rammy, 'hmmm...who will go...Chopsy?'

'No, Rammy, you go, they feel you're the most sober of our lot anyway,' said Solly.

'Ya, you do it, Rammy – it's your brain-baby anyway,' said Chopsy.

'You mean brainchild...' said Shaky.

'Ya, ya, same thing,' said Chopsy.

'And a darned good one at that – I was in tears, man, wow, we guys should make a movie one day,' said Dusty.

'Ya, and the part where Rammy says...now a few words from the snow-white coffin...she'd expect Hucky to speak and he doesn't. *Yaaron*, that's *the* masterstroke,' said Solly.

'Okay guys,' said Rammy, 'I'll deliver it. It's five now. And, if all goes as planned, by six she will begin sobbing like Meena Kumari. Play it again, Dusty, let's hear it once more, and make a fresh tape for us, we need to keep a copy for ourselves, and dub the same on her cassette on Side B too...'

'Done, boss!' said Dusty.

7

Road Trip, Taming of Gattu, Return to Square One

Then. Late December 1985 through early January 1986.

IT WAS RAMMY'S IDEA THAT WE GUYS VANISH FOR A WHILE from the scene and only return to the hostel on New Year's Eve. So, early Monday morning, we all took off to Bellandur Lake on our bikes which were getting used to our wanderlust by now. Solly observed that the T.O. would mother us and Rammy said he'd handle it for all of us; and since we had reposed blind faith in his intellectual might and confidence-drenched convincing skills, we had all agreed to the two-day outing.

The new 'ABBA' tape had been given to Alka on Sunday evening by Rammy. The result of the mushy experiment was eagerly awaited.

'We'll return Tuesday night,' said Rammy as he opened our picnic hamper of bread and egg bhurji and a thermos flask carrying coffee. We had laid three bedspreads on the grassy ground, and the silvery-blue surface of the lake somehow reminded me of the chiffon *salwar-kameez* Ranjana was wearing when we first spoke with each other, and my mood nose-dived into a bottomless abyss.

'Wednesday – we'll be hauled up by Gattu,' said Mangy. (Gattu, or Lt. Col. Prakash Gaitonde, our Training Officer, was responsible both for our whereabouts and well-being.)

'Stop whimpering,' said Shaky, 'if Rammy says he'll handle Gattu, then God save Gattu.'

'Stop it guys, just chill out,' said Solly, readying himself to prepare reefers.

'Ya, be *cool*, remember, even Alka said we are *Made in Antarctica*...let's enjoy...you know, Bellandur Lake plays host to hundreds of migratory birds,' said Rammy, taking pics with his Kodak automatic.

'The only bird-watching I like to do is at the girls' hostel,' said Chopsy.

'Hey, Rammy, you think she must have heard the tape?' asked Dusty.

'Of course,' said Rammy, 'and if my surmise is right, she's feeling pretty guilty and is dying to bump into us...that's the reason we have vanished...absence makes the heart grow fonder...'

'Absence makes the heart go *wander*...' observed Mangy wryly.

'Make a Ganga-Jamuna,' said Chopsy to Solly, giving him a piece of hashish.

'Hey, where did you get this stuff from?' asked Solly, examining the glistening piece and smelling it and smiling approvingly.

'It's Bombay black, my cousin gave it to me last month, and I've been saving it for a special occasion...' said Chopsy.

'Bombay black contains boot polish and rat crap, it's shit stuff,' said Mangy.

'No, this one's good, here, smell it, and scratch it for me please,' said Solly, passing the piece to Mangy.

'Hmmm...it's okay, but if you can get Kashmiri or Afghani stuff...*that* hits you like a hammer...' said Mangy as he began nail-scratching the stuff.

'What's Ganga-Jamuna?' asked Dusty, and four heads turned towards him, powered by disbelief and derision, as if he had asked 'what's tobacco?'

'Man, you should be banned from our group,' said Chopsy.

'Even I know what Ganga-Jamuna is,' said Rammy, 'these idiots will mix weed with hashish...'

Solly landed a heavy pat on Rammy's back and said, 'Guru, you sure are learning a lot...'

'Knowledge always comes in useful...' said Rammy.

'So why don't you gain some *experiential* knowledge and take a few drags today?' suggested Shaky.

'No, thanks,' said Rammy, 'I don't need any *experiential knowledge* in slow suicide...'

'Hey, Hucky, say something man, stop sulking...' said Mangy.

'Leave him alone, guys, silence is a good medicine at times,' said Rammy, and thankfully they left me to my devices. For 'devices' read 'brooding like a jilted hot potato' and you have the right picture.

We chilled out the entire day out there and just smoked grass and drank some cheap beer. Chopsy had got his portable Sony tape recorder and we listened to everything from Kishore Kumar and Rafi and ABBA to Beatles on it. By noon, Mangy and Shaky were despatched to arrange lunch, and they arrived with an assortment of *maida paranthas*, *mutton biryani*, awful-smelling potato fries, and passable *sambar* rice and egg curry. But we were all (except Rammy of course) phenomenally stoned and extraordinarily hungry, so small stuff like bad taste didn't seem to make much of a difference.

Around four, Solly suggested that we could go to Madras, and Dusty said we could drive down to Mysore. Their suggestions were vetoed by Rammy who said that we were definitely going to camp at the lake for the night and maybe we could plan a road trip tomorrow.

We rode down to a seedy restaurant for dinner at around nine and everyone just settled for some bread and omelettes. We returned to Bellandur Lake and zipped ourselves in our sleeping-bags and I must confess that I slept more peacefully than I did in the room. Birds sing the best lullabies.

◇

A road trip is always a good idea. As the fresh breeze blows across your face and body, and as dollops of fresh sunbeams rain oodles of soothing warmth, all the blues you've accumulated over the days begin doing the disappearing act. I was pillion-riding Solly as he had the most comfy bike, a Bullet, and also because he had all our grass tucked into the inside pocket of his LT jacket. So, we stopped often along the Bangalore-Mysore highway and smoked weed and joked away all our recent tragic memories. Rammy had banned us from smoking joints anywhere along the way and whenever we rendezvoused with the rest of the gang at some roadside *dhaba*, we just had some tea and Gold Flakes, and neither Solly nor I removed our shades because red eyes are a dead giveaway when you are doping. Either Rammy didn't notice, or he didn't wish to disturb our peace, considering that I was slowly inching back to normalcy. Most probably the latter since Rammy's razor-sharp radar never missed a trick.

We reached Mysore at around ten in the morning. I said I knew a good place called Vrindavan where we could get a great meal of rice, authentic Mysore sambar, yummy curry, and Mysore *rasam*. But they only served food on traditional plantain leaves, I warned them.

The rest of the guys made faces at the suggestion as they were averse to South Indian food, but Rammy convinced them that one should try out the cuisine of different regions—'it broadens one's horizon and enhances one's world-view if one exposes oneself to the culinary culture of different parts of India' were his exact words—and since nobody understood what he was saying, everyone nodded in agreement.

I had visited Mysore in the early 1970s with a paternal uncle of mine who worked at Kolar Gold Fields for a while as an atomic physicist conducting experiments on neutrino particles (Rammy would've loved him had they met), so the trip brought back a whole host of soothing nostalgia gushing into my system and it made me feel that much better. The guys really liked the food at Vrindavan and thanked me for the suggestion – I felt Chopsy and Dusty were just pretending, but the rest of the guys seemed to be pretty sincere with their compliments.

'Hey, let's watch a flick, man – I think they're playing some C-grade dacoit-shacoit crap at a theatre called Shanthi, we just drove past it a while ago. Nothing like a good laugh at bad direction and clichéd acting,' said Shaky.

So we grabbed the noon show at Shanthi, a rundown theatre where even the pedestal fans weren't working, and kept passing juicy comments right through a Hindi erotica called *Chambal Chali Chaloo Chokri* (Transliteration: Chambal-towards heads cunning girl). The story revolved around a raunchy Bombay girl whose dad gets murdered by dacoits of the Ganja Guru gang on a train, so she swears revenge, reaches Chambal valley, seduces the gang members, does lots of cabaret dance, titillates everyone with her two-piece bikini act and bathing scenes, and finally sleeps with Ganja Guru, and slices his mamba and throat with a *khukhri* at the height of his orgasm.

Rammy conveniently dozed off so that his Hanuman Chalisa-powered mind would not buckle under hormonal pressure (or pleasure?).

I wondered how the Censor Board in India managed to retain its sanity after having to sit through, monitor, and certify such silly stuff. Rammy explained that 'anyone who is sane never joins the Censor Board anyway, and you can't make the already insane more insane'.

'Okay, it's time to head back, guys,' said Shaky as the movie ended.

'Hey, at least let's check out Mysore Palace, man,' said Mangy.

'No, he's right,' said Solly, 'we better get back. And anyway, I'm dying to hear what happened out there in the girls' hostel.'

'Ya, me too,' said Chopsy, 'I hope our idea has worked.'

So we drove back to Bangalore and Xerox-repeated everything we had done earlier on the return journey as well. By the time we made it to the hostel, it was close to 9 p.m.

◇

'But how can you guys just vanish without permission?' thundered Gattu at 10 a.m. on Wednesday. How predictable could he get! His huge mahogany table, which was covered with a sparkling green velvety table cloth, reverberated a bit, and the two miniature flags of India got knocked over as his heavy cholesterol-rich fists came crashing down on the table's surface with the kind of force that only heavy cholesterol-rich fists can manage to generate.

We all hung our heads in feigned shame and silence, exactly as Rammy had tutored us, and I almost heard a voice from a distant Awards ceremony saying, '…and the Oscar goes to the Maniacs'.

When Gattu saw that we were as silent as Egyptian mummies, he bubbled and boiled like fresh broth and released enough steam to power a train.

'Say something dammit! What happened? You guys just take off like some migratory birds…as if it's your father's rule…and now is there a Harrison lock on your mouth?' continued Gattu, translating Hindi sayings into English, as was his wont when he was angry.

Rammy had coached us to remain silent for the first five minutes of our interaction with Gattu. 'The idea is to tire out the enemy, absorb his verbal punches, and then, when he stops for breath, sock him one in the plexus when he is least expecting it,' Rammy had said. So, we were waiting. The five minutes were up.

'Permission to speak freely, sir,' said Rammy, in a tone that was more a command than a request.

'Uh…what…okay,' said Gattu, rather reluctantly.

Now Gattu was walking his heavy frame into intellectual quicksand territory.

If you ever gave Rammy the permission to speak freely, then Rammy could talk you into doing anything for him. Maybe you'd donate your twin kidneys or your twin corneas on the spot to him, and thank him for having been given the wonderful opportunity to be of service. Maybe you'd even vacate PoK – if you were Pakistan; and if Rammy were India. Such was Rammy's power with words. The only way to defeat Rammy was by sellotaping his mouth, and Gattu would discover this very soon.

'Sir, would you have given us the permission to go if we had asked for it?' enquired Rammy.

'What? What the hell? That…that's immaterial…' stuttered Gattu, obviously caught off-guard by the query.

'Sir, would you or wouldn't you…' continued Rammy coolly.

'Of course not!' said Gattu.

'Then you agree that the only way to go is to go *without* permission. And, if we *had sought* permission and you had denied it, sir—you yourself admit that you'd have denied it—and if we had gone despite being denied permission, then that comes under *insubordination*; whereas going without permission just comes under *gross negligence*, which is a far smaller crime according to the Code of Conduct. Gross negligence usually only invites a small fine, whereas insubordination invites rustication. So, it's far smarter to vanish, as you so aptly put it, without permission, than to vanish after being denied it. Though we're all awfully sorry to have hurt your feelings, sir, as you can see!'

We all hung our heads a tad more so Gattu could clearly see how awfully sorry we were.

'But…this…this is a totally foolish argument, what if something happens to you…what…what answer will I give to your parents?' whined Gattu, clearly gasping for words, and obviously floored by Rammy's intellectual might and remarkable sophistry.

Gattu was trying the sentimental stuff with us now, since he had gauged rightly that none of us was going to cower at his we-are-the-army bullshit. We weren't the army yet. We weren't covered by the Army Act. We were just quasi-civilian students trying desperately to look quasi-army.

'Sir, whatever happens in life happens by the will of destiny and the law of *karma*,' said Rammy, 'nobody can change that. And anyway, anything can happen to anyone anytime – but the brave ones don't live in mortal fear of an unpredictable future. The brave one just does what the brave one is born to do, irrespective of the consequences. How can our parents hold *you* responsible for anything when everything we get in this birth is due to our own past karma?'

Gattu stared mesmerised. Rammy had that silencing effect on all – call it charisma, call it animal magnetism, call it what you will, but Rammy's words could slice through a disobedient robot and take it in his control for as long as he wished to.

His words usually had a cryogenic freezing effect on his audience, irrespective of whether he was making any sense at all. And, Gattu was much weaker than a disobedient robot; and quite an impressionable audience. Gattu froze like a kulfi gone on an Arctic expedition.

'In fact, if you *grant permission* and something goes wrong, then *you will* be blamed that much more, sir,' continued Rammy. 'If you *don't grant permission* and something goes wrong, then you will have an escape route, sir. *And, it is to provide you this escape route that I decided to go without permission.* It was my idea, sir, these guys are not to blame. So, if anything does go wrong, you can always safely throw the blame on disobedient students and their flighty ways. So, it's always better to give *unofficial* verbal permission and not *official* written permission, sir...'

Rammy's words flowed so smoothly—just like Captain Cook salt—and only a feather-brained numskull would've interrupted him. There were no feather-brained numskulls in the T.O.'s room. We all felt that Rammy was sounding more like a minister advising a king than a student convincing his Training Officer.

The royalty in Gattu was clearly impressed and flattered. He smiled the smile of a satisfied Roman emperor at an impeccably-organised orgy. He grinned like a newly-wed kingfisher that has got a fish market as a dowry. He beamed like a Labrador that has inherited a juicy, bony graveyard.

He got up from behind his table, affectionately thwacked Rammy on his back, asked him to sit down—saying 'I would love to have a word with you for a while'—and dismissed us lesser mortals from his mammoth, towering presence. Gattu would have many words.

We went back to our adda (again Rammy's idea: '...don't be seen in the canteen or college on Wednesday, the idea is to starve Ranjana for a while,' he had said) and Solly observed that we were all really lucky to have a guy like Rammy with us. We all agreed and felt quite green that Solly had him as a roomie.

Rammy returned after half an hour and sank into the bed, clearly exhausted by his long-winded speech and brain-crunching schemes.

'What happened?' asked Chopsy.

'Are we going to get fined?' wondered Shaky.

'Take a wild guess,' replied Rammy.

'We are going to get a medal,' said Mangy.

'Better, we all can go anywhere, anytime, provided we inform Gattu before we do so—and if we can't, I can just call him up later—though I've been given overall responsibility for the well-being of our group...'

'Wow!' said Solly. 'This is great news, man...'

'Tora, tora, tora!' said Dusty, and even I was feeling happy.

'Any news from the girls' hostel?' asked Chopsy.

'No, I didn't ask anyone – in fact, I think I saw Alka near the bank, but I just avoided her...let them make the move, we've made ours,' said Rammy, as if life were a game of chess.

Come to think of it, perhaps it was.

◇

4 p.m. Hurried raps on my door.

'Push,' I said, looking up from the Jeffrey Archer I was reading in bed.

'Hey, get up, man!' said Chopsy, his voice trembling with excitement.

'Where's the fire?' I said lazily. 'Go do whatever you want. Count me out.'

'He won't listen like this,' said Solly, and emptied half a bottle of water on me.

'Buzz off, guys…what the hell are you doing!' I screamed as I shivered and doffed my drenched T-shirt.

'Bastard, she is waiting for you at the new Insti,' said Dusty.

'Good joke,' I said, 'clap clap.'

'You idiot – she has specially come for you, we're serious, mother promise,' said Shaky, pinching a huge chunk of his Adam's apple.

'Really?' I asked disbelievingly, since nobody pinching his Adam's apple and swearing on his mother ever told a lie.

'Ya, in fact Rammy was there at the Insti, and I think he's still there talking to Ranjana…' said Solly.

'Get ready fast,' said Chopsy.

I got ready in a trice, finger-combed my unruly hair, dabbed some Cuticura powder on my face (Solly sprayed some deodorant on me) and flew towards the new Insti. Thirty metres from my destination, I slowed down. One ought not to look too eager and desperate. Maybe she had just come to say a final goodbye – you know, some girls believed in jilting you *courteously* and all?

Ya, the guys weren't joking. She was sitting with Rammy, and he got up as I neared them, threw a mischievous wink at me, and left the scene.

'Hi! Happy New Year!' I said.

'Hi! Happy New Year!' she said. 'How've you been?'

'Good, great,' I lied.

'You don't look it,' she said.

'Oh, just got a bit of the flu,' I said, running my fingers through my three-day-old stubble.

'Stop lying okay?' she said.

'Okay, I will. I'm not feeling well. In fact, I've been feeling like a…like a…mashed potato, if you wish to know my cardiac status…'

'I am so sorry, Hucky, I shouldn't have screamed at you like that…'

'Happens, forget it, and anyway…anyone in your place would've screamed like that…'

'Still, sorry,' she said, and began sobbing, 'it wasn't your fault, how heartless of me…'

'Hey,' I said, putting my arm around her, 'it's okay…'

'How bad you must have felt…' The sobs were getting heavier. My arm wound tighter around her.

'It's okay,' I said smilingly, 'sometimes one has to feel bad to feel good – you know by contrast, today seems like heaven, Ranju…'

'You never called me that before…'

'There's always a first time for everything…you hungry?'

'Ya,' she said, wiping her moist cheeks on the sleeve of my sweatshirt.

I made a V-digital and signalled to Haluji, the canteen manager, who was always weighed down by mounting debts, defaulting debtors, and army officials who were forever complaining about lack of hygiene and presence of miniature wildlife in his kitchen. I was one of the few guys who gave him an advance and so I always received prompt service. Plus just a gesture from me was enough for him to understand whether I wanted *aloo paranthas* with omelettes, or just plain tea with biscuits, or fruit bun with a hint of butter.

'You know I missed you like crazy, where did you vanish off to…?'

'Rammy didn't tell you?'

'Just cross-checking,' she said.

'Ya? Go join Globe Detective Agency.'

'But promise that you'll never again go like this…without informing me…I was feeling so worried and guilty…'

'Arre, now will you stop whining like A.K. Hangal…?'

We spoke for about twenty minutes or so. I gathered that half the girls' hostel had heard the cassette and hence we were pretty famous there. (Which was infinitely better than notorious, right?) Nearly everyone had become misty-eyed with all the mush, if Ranju wasn't exaggerating.

This was turning out to be better than expected. This had vaulted the stock of the Maniacs on the mocktail circuit to stratospheric levels. Great. Nearly all of us could hope to snare some chicks now.

The aloo parantha and omelettes were extra-delicious, and I waved to Haluji and made a forefinger-meets-thumb circle to signal my approval. He winked and smiled and I was sure he was thinking, '…saala, he has trapped a bomb, the lucky bastard, anyway it will improve my business, lovebirds are always hungry.'

I wanted to tell him that you don't know all the pain you have to endure for a little pleasure, buddy, and when it comes to sheer return on investment, romance gives you a pretty raw deal. But would he understand that? Haluji didn't carry the kind of look that said he'd understand that. Haluji had been running the boys' hostel canteen for some ten years now. He was a portly civilian contractor and always wore a flaring white pyjama and a tent-sized kurta and a benign smile – perhaps he nursed a secret ambition of becoming a powerful MLA one day? I'd gathered one night, after Solly made him tipsy on rum punch, that his real name was Harishchandra Lingaprabhu Shetty (how we'd howled at the mention of Lingaprabhu, gosh, that translates into dick-god, heehee) and some Papa batchers had christened him Haluji. Thank goodness.

For a moment I began thinking of *sadhus* who walk the path of renunciation and wondered if they did so after getting jilted. Perhaps I'd have become a *yogi* if Ranju hadn't returned to me. Possible.

'A penny for your thoughts,' she said.

'Oh, sorry, I was just thinking of Rammy...' I lied.

'What about him?'

'Oh, you should have seen him speaking with Gattu in the morning. It was hilarious and what a class act he is...'

'You are pretty impressed with him, aren't you?'

'Ya, we all are, I wish I had Rammy's brain...'

'But you have a golden heart, Hucky, and that's what counts...'

'Cool, if you say so,' I said as we both placed our by-now empty plates on the Insti steps.

'Coffee?' I offered.

'No, enough. Okay, now you go, you're looking like Devdas,' she said, wiping her moist face on the sleeve of my sweatshirt again (this time it was the diced green chillies in the omelette that was making her sniffle), 'go get a shave, I want you looking as dapper as Gregory Peck...'

'He's ancient, how about like Richard Gere...?'

'Okay, as long as you look human,' she smiled guiltily.

'Cool, anything to please you – as they say, the way to a woman's heart is through a few shaving nicks and cuts.'

She laughed and I was reminded of Madhubala – only Madhubala didn't look half as divine.

'And I want to meet all of you – I hope Rammy has told them that,' she said.

'He must have, shall we all go to Queen's Garden?'

'Sure, you guys pick us up, I'll rope in Alka and Neha...'

'Hey, who's Neha...?'

'Neha Sareen, yaar, you don't know Neha Sareen?'

'Hmmm...your batch?'

'Yup.'

'Oh, you mean *Neharika* Sareen, ya ya, but I thought she was the behenji kinds, you know...'

'Hey,' she objected, slapping my wrist, 'don't you dare call any of us that – yes, Neha does keep to herself, but she's quite outgoing and forward-shorward, once she warms up to you...'

'Aha, I do hope she will warm up to me,' I said mischievously.

'Try it, just you try it, and you'd need a plastic surgery,' she retorted.

'Well, in that case I won't hope – maybe she can tie me a *raakhi*...'

'I'll arrange that. Anyway, now you scoot and...huh...will you guys be there by five?'

'Sure.'

'Bye, see you,' she said, and zoomed off on her moped, and I didn't take my eyes off her for a single second as she sped through the dusty distance, and then she turned left, and swam out of my sight.

'Stop dreaming, and at least blink every now and then – it's good for your eyes,' said Solly, back-thumping me. All the Maniacs suddenly appeared like termites out of woodwork. They were definitely spying on us from the stairway above the new Insti which led to the hostel library.

I got up and hugged Rammy so tightly that he was afraid I had fractured his ribs.

'It worked, man, it worked like a charm!' said Chopsy.

'Thank goodness, I feel as if a heavy container truck is off my back,' said Shaky.

'Twenty bucks?' Dusty asked Mangy.

'You had borrowed fifty bucks last week, remember? So now you owe me thirty bucks,' said Mangy.

'Hey, that's different, that's a favour. This is a winning amount. They are separate-separate things...' wailed Dusty.

'No way,' said Mangy, 'in that case you *return* the fifty bucks first, then I'll give you twenty bucks...'

'Arre, I'll return it next week, I've wired home for money...'

'No, you pay now...'

'Hey, Rammy,' whined Dusty, 'see this dopey chicken-shit is cheating…'

'I dunno, guys, it's your shit,' said Rammy, 'I'm out of it…'

'Hey, Mangy, be a sport, give him na,' said Solly.

'Okay, toss up a coin, guys…leave the decision to impartial alloy…' I said.

'Okay,' said Mangy, digging out a rupee from his pocket, 'Dusty, you call, if you get it right, you can have the twenty bucks right now…I bet you ten bucks you will lose this toss though…'

'Guys, we gotta get ready fast, make it snappy,' I said.

'Okay, bet, toss,' agreed Dusty, so Mangy tossed up the coin, and Dusty said 'Tails' and the impartial alloy swung the argument in Mangy's favour.

'Loser! Loser!' said Mangy, jumping like a horny frog, and Rammy shook his head and mumbled something like 'some mothers do raise immature intellectual pygmies' to himself, and we all gathered at the adda to get ready for the reunion with our then-angry-and-now-guilty friends from the girls' hostel.

Queen's Garden was a beautiful haunt maintained by the Government of Karnataka. It was just three km from the hostel and was a pucca paradise for lovers. Lots of foliage, trees, chirping birds, vast expanse, tons of privacy; and the place was so packed with bird-songs that it would've made a corpse feel romantic. Funny that not many used to frequent it though – suited us just fine.

We did the usual thing of ordering coffee and, apart from Ranju and me, everyone settled for burgers and sandwiches.

'So tell me,' began Alka, 'the cassette was whose idea?'

'Guess,' said Chopsy.

'Hmmm…certainly Rammy's – he's your group's brains, isn't he?' said Alka.

'I think we should call him *Raavan*ammy – he's got *ten* brains,' joked Solly.

'Good one, Solly,' said Ranju as everyone burst into uncontrollable laughter, and Solly's face became as bright as a lighthouse, and Rammy blushed like a media-shy public hero.

'Real senti hahn, I toh cried baba, listening to the tape,' said Neha.

'That was the general idea…' said Chopsy.

'So you guys planned all this hahn – you pathetic schemers!' said Ranju.

'Arre, we didn't plan or anything,' Shaky slipped in a hasty lie, 'it all happened so…so impromptu-ly, and so spontaneously and suddenly…'

'Anyway, forget it, what's important is that we all are together again,' observed Mangy.

'Ya, they spoke *ekdum* suddenly from their hearts…' said Dusty.

'Rammy, have you ever considered writing a novel – some mushy love story? You'd be pretty good at it,' said Neha, and I noticed that her eyes shone, twinkled, and danced mischievously as she surveyed him.

'Maybe it will happen one day, Neha. Maybe I can write about Ranjha aka Hucky and Heer aka Ranjana one day,' said Rammy, ribbing us.

'Oooohhhh…cooool…oooi maaa…are they in love or something?' teased Alka.

'Of course we both are in love – though not with each other,' I joked, and Ranju pouted cutely, stuck out her tongue at me, tilt-shook her head like a coy Thanjavur doll, and drowned me in the sea of sweet love.

'I hope it's not premature to ask this…Ranjana…' Rammy began hesitatingly, 'but, what exactly triggered your anger…?'

'Hey, forget it, yaar,' said Solly and Shaky almost together, 'it's all in the past.' Solly removed a greeting card he had tucked into his shirt and gave it to Ranju.

'What's this guys?' asked Mangy.

'Aha,' said Ranju, opening the envelope, 'isn't it my lucky day, what a cute card, thanks guys…'

'What have they written? – show me,' said Alka, yanking the card from Ranju's hand, and read it out to all of us.

We are true friends again

Though we gave her much pain

She chose to forgive us

Without much ado or fuss

Our sorry didn't go in vain

'Woooowww! Rammy wrote this?' wondered Ranju.

'No, our group's poet, the great Shaky,' said Solly, and Ranju shook Shaky's hand.

'Well written, dude. And, there's another limerick,' said Alka.

Thanks for your generosity

Despite our audacity

You are the one reason

That creates beautiful seasons

In our lovely, Bangalore city

'Wooooowwwww! Even better. I think I'd rather date Shaky than this bore here,' palavered Ranju, throwing a mock-scorn at me.

'Be my guest,' I said, 'I anyway want to be footloose and fancy-free.'

'Really?' asked Ranju teasingly.

'Of course,' I said, 'nothing like a limerick-writer who can also play the guitar, go for him.'

'Hey, Shaky, you play guitar?' asked Neha.

'Ya, one day we all should go to Leopard Spot and chill out,' said Chopsy.

'Hey, but why is Hucky called Hucky?' asked Neha.

'Well,' explained Shaky, 'it's an acronym actually—you know his real name is very short: Hari Ananthasesha Krishna Kumar Iyengar—so that became HAKKI, and finally Hucky...'

'Anyone care for a walk?' asked Rammy, clearly bored of our convo.

'I'll come,' said Alka, and they walked along the shrubbery, perhaps to discuss what exactly triggered Ranju's violent reaction last Sunday as Rammy wouldn't rest in peace till he discovered the 'alpha point'.

Did I see a hint of sepia green tingeing Neha's face as they walked away?

8

No Mercy, No Lust, No Kiss

Then. Mid-January through late January 1986.

RAMMY HAD FINALLY DISCOVERED THE 'ALPHA POINT' AFTER a few convos with Alka and was pretty thrilled with his investigative instincts.

It seemed that some catty girls from X-ray batch had used spiteful nicknames like 'Kama Sutra' and 'Messalina' when they saw Ranju hobnobbing with our gang and that had got her goat. (Rammy explained that Messalina was a nymphomaniac Roman empress during the times of Caligula.)

'Who said that?' asked Solly menacingly.

'Forget it, yaar,' I said. 'Forgive and forget.'

'Ya, sure, you do that, Mr Gandhi – who called her that, Rammy? *We* have a right to know,' said Shaky.

'I think Madhu, Priya and their gang...' said Rammy.

'The bloody fucking jealous bitches!' said Solly.

'The pathetic No Ball Sadnesses—those girls are so flat that you can play table tennis on their chests—don't we call them the Pointless Sisters or something?' said Shaky, and we all laughed like hyenas.

Now, we were into January and the Univ exams were just nine months away—in October—so we all paired up to do some combined study. Rammy of course didn't need to (or perhaps none dared to?) pair up for he had an incredible memory, and Chopsy wondered if the guy had a brain or a Kodak photographic film inside his head. Most probably the latter.

Our Anatomy, Physiology and Biochemistry journals were totally out-of-date and we spent the entire month just cramming and giving the journals a makeover. The weekends were the only time when we took a break, and went to watch a movie with Ranju, Alka and Neha; always topping off the evening with a dinner at India Coffee House or Snehal, not to forget rolling up some reefers and playing carrom or chess or Scrabble late into the night.

One weekend, Solly and Shaky said they had a double date; and when we made further enquiries, we were all quite angry and surprised that they planned to take Madhu and Priya out for dinner.

'Are you guys out of your *mind*?' screamed Mangy.

'Guys, if you are *that* desperate, I suggest you bang some whores,' said Chopsy.

'That's so slimy, man, how can you?' said Dusty. 'Especially when it is *their* comments that caused so much trouble…'

'Didn't you say forgive and forget?' observed Solly.

'I didn't,' Dusty shot back.

'Someone did, who said it, man?' asked Shaky.

'I did,' I said, 'cool, maybe we should actually.'

'Fuck you Hucky, and fuck you Solly, if you take out those bitches, I'm not going to share *any* of my maal with you guys…' threatened Chopsy.

'Balls! Who needs you? We can score our own grass,' said Solly, 'okay Shaky, let's get ready, man, it's time…'

'All the worst,' said Rammy sarcastically, and they both got into jeans and jackets and fake branded sneakers, threw us glaring, balls-to-you-guys looks, and took off on their bikes.

◇

When they returned at around 9 p.m., we guys had gathered at the new Insti for tea. They parked their bikes and walked up to us, and I said hi to them, while the rest of the gang pretended to give them the royal ignore.

'Great girls,' said Shaky.

'Great girls – to err is human…' said Solly.

'To forgive is divine,' said Shaky, completing the proverb.

'What a great time we had,' said Solly.

'Ya, actually they're sweethearts – everyone makes mistakes…' said Shaky.

'Shut up, you nuts, if you had a great time, you wouldn't be back so early,' said Dusty.

They both laughed and high-fived each other and looked at all of us and laughed even more. Their eyes were clear, so they obviously were not on dope. We felt that they were just laughing to rile us. We were wrong.

'So what's with the laughter,' said Chopsy, 'you traitors, you think you've done something great…?'

'April fool!' they chorused.

'It's January,' said Rammy, 'ever heard of something called calendars?'

'Cretins, we mothered them as planned, you gruds!' said Solly.

'What? What did you do? Don't tell me you did something drastic,' I said worriedly.

'Arre,' said Shaky, 'we wanted to screw their trip, and we did.'

'What, when, how?' asked Mangy.

'We took them to the Shanti Nagar Kamling…' began Solly.

'And since they also wanted to have Chinese, we said our treat…' said Shaky.

'So they nicely ordered soup and chicken and Schezwan rice…' said Solly, clutching his stomach which was getting twisted with laughter-cramps.

'And even dessert – triple sundae actually...' said Shaky, doubling up with laughter.

'So what's so funny about all this?' asked Mangy.

'Funny? He wants to know what's funny...' guffawed Solly.

'What's funny is that we made sure they weren't carrying much money when we picked them up...' said Shaky.

'We checked them by asking for change, and all they had was some hundred bucks each...' said Solly.

'Guys, get to the point,' said Chopsy, clearly irked.

'Man, the bill must have been close to seven hundred bucks...' said Shaky.

'So?' asked Dusty.

'So we excused ourselves into the loo just when we were in the middle of dessert, and here we are...' said Solly.

'And, there they are – at Kamling, explaining to the management that the prospective bill-payers have ditched them...' laughed Shaky.

'*What?*' screamed Rammy, 'don't tell me you guys *abandoned* them there...'

'Of course we did,' said Solly.

'Without footing the bill?' I asked.

'Of course, you dodo,' said Shaky, 'that was the plan.'

'Wooowww!' said Mangy, 'wonderful, guys, wonderful!'

'Ya, serves the bitches right,' seconded Chopsy.

'Tora, tora, tora!' screamed Dusty.

'Sorry, guys, to have misunderstood you,' said Chopsy.

'This is not good, guys, this is a mean thing to do,' said Rammy.

'Ya? And what they did was very Mother Teresa-ish, hahn?' asked Shaky.

'Hey, we did what we wanted to, we've been simmering for quite a few days now, and today I'm feeling totally satisfied,' said Solly.

'Ya, there's no feeling or dessert as sweet as revenge,' said Shaky.

As we were debating *The pleasure of forgiveness* vs. *The satisfaction of revenge*, Chopsy pointed out that an auto was moving towards the girls' hostel.

'That's definitely one of them,' said Solly.

'Ya, she's come to collect money,' said Shaky.

'It could be someone else,' said Mangy.

'Bet?' challenged Solly, 'fifty bucks.'

'Thirty,' said Mangy.

'Done,' said Solly.

Chopsy and Dusty were despatched to check things out, and they returned saying it was indeed Madhu who had come by auto, and the driver was waiting to take her back to Kamling, and Mangy passed thirty bucks to Solly.

'The T.O. will mother you guys tomorrow morning – make that Monday morning…' said Rammy.

'That's where *you* step in – you'll teach us how to wriggle out of the predictable predicament,' said Shaky.

'Nonsense, I'll do nothing of the sort,' said Rammy, and left in a huff, leaving behind a strange smell of disgust in his wake.

Sunday. 4 p.m. The guys were playing carrom at the adda; Rammy and Mangy were deeply engrossed in their Caro-Kann defence chess game, and I was learning the basics from them. Rammy won again and I began convincing him that he ought to help Solly and Shaky find a way to checkmate Gattu on Monday. Finally, Rammy relented and began coaching them.

'Okay, guys, remember one thing – when you set out to take Vienna, take Vienna,' he said, quoting Napoleon.

'Meaning?' asked Solly.

'Meaning, you don't apologise – you state upfront that the girls deserved the rough treatment because they gave the rough treatment to Ranjana.'

'Okay,' said Shaky.

'And as I said earlier, to convince a man, use pictures,' said Rammy, and fished out snaps of me with my jilt-stubble which he had clicked at Bellandur Lake. He selected two that looked really depressing and asked them to show these to Gattu. 'Tell him this is what their catty remarks ended up doing to our dearest friend.'

Solly and Shaky nodded like kids at a kindergarten.

'As he examines the snaps, ask him: "Sir, what will *you do* if someone calls your wife or sister Kama Sutra or Messalina?" That will clinch it...'

'Hey, can we dare do that?' wondered Shaky.

'Of course, say request permission to speak freely right at the beginning. I'll write down things for you later but practise the following: (a) Sir, girls who are friendship-destroyers are more dangerous than terrorists; (b) Sir, words are more dangerous than guns; words kill your eternal spirit, whereas guns only kill your temporary body; (c) Sir, a verbal assault scars one for life, and even Lord Krishna said in the *Gita* that for an honourable person dishonour is worse than death; (d) Sir, the tongue is used either as a weapon or a balm; and (e) If you don't believe us, ask Ranjana, sir. Get it?'

'Fantastic!' said Solly, 'I am confident that Gattu will be floored.'

'Of course he'll be – at the most he might slap a small fine to please the sobbing Pointless Sisters, that's all, but you must insist that a fine should be slapped on them too to set a precedent in the girls' hostel, okay?'

'Done, guru!' said Solly.

◇

Rammy would have put Nostradamus out of business. Not only did the ploy work on Monday morning but it also got the guys brownie points from Gattu who felt that girls were getting bitchier by the day and someone ought to teach them a lesson. Solly said Gattu stopped short of saying 'well done' and slapped a hefty fine of twenty bucks on the Pointless Sisters after Ranju sobbed copiously in front of him when reminded about their cutting remarks.

Shaky mentioned that Gattu had also told them to 'convey my regards to your guru, Ramakrishna, who coaches you so very well'.

Our T.O. was smarter than we thought, and more understanding and humane too. Appearances can be so very deceptive, as the cliché goes.

'Guys, we need to celebrate the victory,' said Mangy.

'Ya, let's go to Leopard Spot, and spend the night there, coming Saturday,' said Chopsy. (Leopard Spot was a small hillock about thirty km from the hostel and had gathered its name after someone spotted a man-eating leopard a decade ago out there, and didn't live to tell the tale. It was safer now as much of the forest cover had got burned in a forest fire a few years ago. The only carnivores that lurked out there were a few wolves and wild dogs that feared lights and bonfires.)

'Why not LBT?' asked Dusty. (LBT = Lone Banyan Tree. That was another lonesome spot some twenty km from the hostel, and you needed to climb a small incline to reach it, after you made it to a dusty path where the road ended. But it was also frequented by hooch-drinking, unruly locals.)

'No, LBT is okay for a stag party, not with girls around,' said Rammy, and his decision was always final.

'Assumptions are dangerous, dude,' said Solly, mimicking Rammy, 'how do you know the girls will agree to come?'

'It's already arranged, Alka and Neha want to go,' said Rammy.

'Yooohooo! Who you hitting on, man? Both?' asked Chopsy.

'Neither,' said Rammy. 'They are hitting on me.'

It was a night before a full moon night, so thankfully there was plenty of ambient lunar light. We had parked our bikes some five hundred metres away, and had clambered up to Leopard Spot. A part of the city flowed below us, peppered with orange and white lights. The city looked like a floating spaceship from *Star Trek*.

We were chilled to the bones (though I was thankfully basking in the warmth of love as Ranju snuggled up to me) and the guys hastily lit a bonfire.

'Did you get the popcorn and macaroons?' Mangy asked Chopsy.

'Of course – it's in my duffel bag,' said Chopsy.

'Guys, first let's get organised. Dusty, get the drinks. Chopsy, lay the bedspreads and newspapers over there. Rammy, don't just stand there admiring the scenery, okay? Organise the food, man. And, Mangy, clean the stuff, dude – you look like you could do with a smoke. Shaky, arrange the music and the emergency lights please.' Solly was shouting instructions as if he were a platoon commander. Well, you couldn't fault his organisational skills though and everyone did as directed. I noticed that he didn't give me any instructions – perhaps seeing that Ranju and I were dissolved into a surreal world of our own.

'Isn't it beautiful, guys!' said Alka as Dusty began serving drinks to all of us.

'Limca or Thums Up?' asked Dusty generally.

'Limca with gin, Thums Up with rum, you know the drill, Dusty,' said Chopsy.

Billy Joel began singing *Rosalinda's Eyes*; and Ranju looked into mine and I guess mine must have looked like that of a boy out on his first date. She said that I looked as innocent as a lamb and I asked her to slaughter me with her love.

'Thanks, guys, for inviting me. It's magical!' yelled Neha.

'Don't be silly – we should thank you actually for being a sport,' said Rammy, patting her shoulder. Did I see Alka blanch?

'Is the chew ready?' asked Solly impatiently.

'Yes boss, here, you do the honours,' said Mangy, and Solly lit up the chillum.

'Guys, you should not be smoking so much,' said Alka.

'Ya, I plan to quit – the day I get a girlfriend,' said Chopsy.

'Really?' asked Alka.

'Really,' he said.

'Okay, then I'll be your girlfriend,' she joked, and turned to look at Rammy.

Somehow we all suspected that Rammy and Alka really liked each other, but neither was admitting it openly. Solly had observed a few weeks ago (obviously in Rammy's absence) that Rammy was suffering from '*Hanuman Chalisa*-powered, confused virgin complex'. That meant your body wanted to be a Casanova, while your mind wanted to be a Vivekananda.

Perhaps Solly was right in his analysis, and on most days Rammy did try to behave like a celibate saint. He wouldn't even look at *Debonair* or *Playboy* or *Penthouse*. C'mon, that wasn't normal at our age. Though I hoped, actually for Alka's sake, that tonight would see Rammy putting an end to his self-imposed hormonal and romantic exile.

'Thanks for the offer, Alka,' said Chopsy, obviously not taking her I'll-be-your-girlfriend joke seriously.

'Behind every successful quitter is a woman, hahn, Chopsy?' said Mangy. 'Just like Farooq Shaik promised Lallan Miyan in *Chasme Buddoor*?'

'Hey lovebirds!' screamed Solly at Ranju and me. 'We also exist, okay?'

'Do you?' she asked. 'We didn't notice.'

'Ya, love is blind, go learn braille,' shouted Solly.

'Good one, Solly,' said Neha, and he smiled contentedly at her.

The guys dragged Ranju and me to where everyone was gathered—close to the bonfire—and Solly thrust the chillum into my hand. Dusty served another Limca-gin to Ranju. She looked at me enquiringly.

'Hey, go ahead – it's party-time,' I said to her as I took a deep drag of the Ganga-Jamuna, and passed it to Chopsy. He took a drag and said it's 'canned'.

'Okay, clean the pipe, dude,' ordered Solly, 'and Shaky, let's have some live music, man.'

So Shaky strummed his Yamaha guitar and we all sang *Tie a Yellow Ribbon Round the Ole Oak Tree* and *I Just Called to Say I Love You* and *Aa Dekhen Zara*, and even the usually self-absorbed Rammy seemed to be having a good time.

Rammy said that we should go easy on the chillum as nights closer to full moon nights usually triggered the kind of insanity that would be difficult to handle. Even the word 'lunatic' was etymologically linked to the word 'lunar', he added, as if we were going to cower at word origins and mumbo-jumbo stuff called scientific evidence. The girls laughed at his theories and became quite tipsy on their Limca-flavoured gins.

'Shut up, Rammy—intellect is banned tonight—anyone talking intelligently will be fined a hundred bucks,' said Mangy.

'Have a drink, Rammy, tonight's an exception,' said Chopsy.

'Yeaahh, slee evern we arl drilnking,' said Alka, obviously hoping it would melt his frigidity, and Rammy said okay, and we all cheered him on to do a bottoms-up with his glass. He actually did that and coughed and sputtered, and Alka patted him on his back. Did I see Neha blanch?

'So how did you guys get permission to spend the night out?' asked Solly of the girls.

'Oh, we jlust liedd thlat we werl going to sprend the night at Nreha's LG's – in fract herr LGs sploke to Warlden on phrone, they arl chirlled outt forlks actually…' explained Alka.

Gin was clearly adding involuntary consonants to the heavily-tipsy words rolling off her tongue. Make that 'their tongue' since the effect was universal.

'We dridn't lie,' babbled Ranju.

'Dididnr't we?' slurred Alka.

'Oph clourrse not,' giggled Ranju, 'areln't we wilth our LG—our Lurnartic Grloup—as Rammly zays?' Alcohol hadn't blunted her sense of humour though. That's a good sign if you are looking for a lifemate.

'Oh, so now we're the Lunatic Group, hahn?' laughed Rammy.

'Oph clourrsse, thlough *nice* Lurnartic Grloup,' said Alka.

'Thanks for the compliment,' said Solly, 'hey, girls, go easy on the gin...'

'You shlurt hupp hokkay – wee aaallr arl hokkay,' said Neha, and we guys had no doubt that they aaallr, sorry, all were okay.

'Zoh Rammy drear, whyy dro you hate grilrs?' asked Alka.

'Of course not, whatever gave you that impression?' wondered Rammy.

'No, we jlust ferlt it, you know...' said Ranju.

Neha looked at him as if the question would open hidden doors for her to quietly sneak in into the fortress. Alka looked at him as if the question would be met with an instant reply that he actually liked Alka and nobody else. The Maniacs looked at him hoping that there would be an emotional meltdown. But Rammy was Rammy. A wooden mannequin would've displayed more emotion.

Ranju and I were cosily quiet, especially now that she had almost drifted off on my lap, and they all seemed to have resigned to the fact that lovebirds are just silent observers and usually lost in an antisocial dream world of their own.

'No, I don't hate anyone, girls or otherwise,' began Rammy. 'In fact, hating someone is like burning your own house to kill a rat. At the same time, I can't say that I love everyone either. As far as I'm concerned (which anyway was all that he was ever concerned about) we are spiritual beings having a brief emotional experience; and one should always try and rise above mundane basic instincts to discover the infinite buried deep within all of us...'

'Fined! Three hundred bucks, that's three banned statements – continue talking at your own risk, Rammy!' screamed Mangy.

'Ya, ya, fine him, he's always giving boring gyan – keep count Mangy,' yelled Dusty.

'Youu gruys shlut upp hokay, hee's tralking zo much slense...' said Alka, happy that he was at least opening up.

'I *am* attracted to women...' continued Rammy.

'Aha, confessions of a sex-starved saint,' ribbed Solly, and turning to Shaky, 'hey, don't make the chew an *agarbatti*, man, keep passing it fast...'

'I mean I'm a man *because* I *am* attracted to women. How does a man *know* he's a man; how does a woman *know* she is a woman? Biologically speaking, you are the exact opposite of the sex you are attracted to...' explained Rammy, ignoring Solly's jibe.

'Wrong,' said Shaky 'What about homos and lesbians, dude? By your logic, homos aren't men and lesbians aren't women...'

'Not exactly, Shaky. One of them is always the dominant partner. Physically you might be a man; but psychologically and emotionally, you might be a woman. I'm also talking gender psychology here, not gender physiology alone,' observed Rammy.

'Seven hundred bucks already – and the fine meter's ticking,' yelled Mangy.

'Zo who arl you...arl you...attlracted to, Rammy?' stuttered Alka.

'Hmmm...many actually,' said Rammy hesitantly.

'Lrike?' asked Alka expectantly.

'Madhubala, Ingrid Bergman, Parveen Babi, Meenakshi Seshadri...'

'Get real, dude, she means in real life,' said Solly.

'Ya, who do you like in college?' asked Chopsy.

'C'mon, man, who do you have the hots for?' asked Dusty. 'There must be someone.'

'Well, not hots exactly, sex is a cheap animal desire, even animals have sex, but if you ask me who stirs the romantic instincts in the cauldron of my cardiac emotions...' observed Rammy.

'Fuck, man, talk English...' said Mangy sharply.

'She might not like it if I say it,' said Rammy.

'No, I dron't mlind evern iff you zay mee,' said Alka and Neha almost simultaneously, and nervously giggled their gin-giggles.

'Well, I didn't have the guts to admit it earlier, especially to myself...' said Rammy.

'Ya, but he's full of Dutch courage now...' said Solly.

'Forget it,' said Rammy.

'Hey, c'mon,' said Shaky.

'Serve the monk more Old Monk, Dusty,' said Chopsy.

'Buried secrets destroy the heart, dude, open up man,' said Shaky.

Then Rammy looked up at the sky, took a huge swig of his rum and Thums Up, coughed nervously, and for the first time in my life I saw him suffering the pangs of hesitant anxiety. That made him look all the more human and vulnerable and adorable, and I was hoping that he'd drop his guard for once and surrender to his heart. He did.

'Well,' he said, 'only if you guys promise that none here will feel hurt once I say it...'

'Of course not – what are friends for?' assured Solly.

'Stop being Alfred Hitchcock, man, say it fast,' said Shaky, and Chopsy repeated, 'Which-*cock*?', 'Hitch-*cock*!', about five times, and the guys joined him and cackled like wild geese and laughed like only stoned guys do, and they finally sobered down when Neha asked them to stop being vulgar.

'Well,' said Rammy, taking a deep breath and, looking at nobody in particular, revealed the magic name as the laughter began subsiding, 'Alka.'

Both extreme elation and extreme sadness stun you into paralysed silence. So, Alka and Neha both became as silent as gagged graveyards.

'Yipppeee!' screamed Solly.

'The goose is out!' yelled Shaky.

'Tora, tora, tora!' shouted Dusty.

Then they all looked at Alka, and she began blushing and beaming and blooming like an over-cared-for sunflower. For 'sunflower' read 'pinkish-purple petunia' for that was the colour tingeing her alcohol-dilated looks. Neha wilted like an abandoned bouquet and Chopsy looked at her adoringly, thankful that the coast seemed to be finally clear for him. (Ya, he had confessed his fatal attraction for her to me once, and none of the Maniacs knew about it. I was a safe deposit locker when it came to secrets. Still am.)

'You aarl jloking, rright?' asked Alka weakly.

'Would you rather that I was joking?' asked Rammy.

'Noo, I'd bree halppy iff you aarl not,' said Alka.

'I am serious. I've felt this way ever since we took a walk in Queen's Garden that day,' confessed Rammy.

'Crum, lerts trake anothler warlk,' she drawled, and Rammy and Alka went and sat on some boulders in the distance and were lost in trying to discuss, define, analyse, understand, and test their mutual love for each other, like all lovers do.

Ranju was zonked out on my lap and though I was desperate to get up and take a leak (alcohol is a major diuretic) I didn't feel like disturbing her (or my secure joy?) for she was looking so much like a cute trusting doll, and I asked Dusty to cover her with a woollen blanket. Chopsy asked Neha if she'd like to scan the city from a slightly higher spot, and she agreed, maybe because she wanted to move away from the bonfire which had generated more heartache than heat for her, and he happily disappeared with her into the vertical distance.

The rest of the guys were happy with their chillums and spent the night singing songs and bitching about other guys and girls...

As the misty, smoggy dawn began sneaking up on us, Solly woke up everyone who had dozed off, and we left Leopard Spot at around six in the morning, and decided to grab some English flick later in the day.

Shaky asked me if I had French-kissed Ranju yet, and I told him to mind his own business. Well, I hadn't actually, and frankly, I was feeling no lust for Ranju – only love. I couldn't feel lust when I was in love; or feel love when I was in lust, so you can say that I was pretty bad at multi-tasking.

9

First Strike, Rahul Attack, the Trick, the Blush

Then. February through April 1986.

REMEMBER THE HUGE COLONIAL BUILDING DAD AND I had alighted in front of, on our maiden visit to Bangalore? Now, that doubled up as a picnic spot after 6 p.m. Actually, it was the postgraduate wing and housed the Commandant's office. We were told we wouldn't be entering the building till we reached third MBBS. Who cared? All we were interested in was the lush lawn outside the building which we called Commy Garden, in honour of the Commandant. Every evening we converted it into a noisy area of unabashed revelry.

'Did you hear?' asked Ranju as we sank into the dewy grass.

'Heard what?' I asked.

'Arre, Wonder batch is planning a strike...' she said.

'Ya, I know,' said Rammy, 'I heard some of them discussing it at the Insti a while ago.'

'What nonsense,' said Neha, 'you can't strike at Defcoms.'

'But it's all hush-hush right now,' said Chopsy.

'Chuck it yaar,' said Solly, 'let's play Frisbee...'

'No, you guys carry on,' I said, 'but what's the strike for?'

'God only knows. We're too low in the pecking order to be let in on the politics-sholitics of it anyway,' said Shaky, and got up to join Solly and Dusty who had begun impressing the crowd with their Frisbee-chucking skills.

'Hey, where's Alka?' asked Chopsy.

'Her uncle has come to visit her, she'll join us in a while,' said Ranju.

'No wonder Rammy is sulking…' said Chopsy.

'Shut up, I'm thinking,' said Rammy.

'About what?' asked Ranju.

'The strike will just be a damp squib, these guys are just so disorganised,' he said, more to himself than to anyone in particular.

'You know Rammy, you should become a professional soothsayer. Most of what you say usually comes true,' said Ranju.

'To know the future, just look into the past,' said Rammy.

'You can read hands, no?' asked Neha.

'Ya, a bit,' he said.

'A bit? He's damn good. Rammy, stop being so modest, okay?' I said.

'Read mine na, please…' said Neha, extending her right hand as she sidled closer to Rammy.

'Hmmm…okay, show both hands,' said Rammy.

They were lost in trying to divine Neha's personality and future. Ranju and I were naturally looking at the crescent moon and the stars and wondering how many romanticists these shimmering sky-dots had inspired and blessed over the past thousands of years.

My EQ had definitely increased over the days and I had even begun dreaming dreams that I had become a father who was constantly harassed by adorable twins. I was even changing nappies in the dreams and Ranju always said that I did a better job of it than her. How very convenient.

We were officially seeing each other now, just like Rammy and Alka – only they seemed to be more of a secure couple than we were.

Perhaps we weren't as mature, for Ranju got pretty pissed off if I admired any other girl, and I got alarmingly aggressive if she spoke to any guy outside our group. Mangy (he had gone to Mysore for the day, along with his cousin) had said a week ago that Ranju and I were 'true lovers' and Rammy and Alka were 'true friends'. When I had asked him to explain, Mangy had said that 'possessiveness is the true sign of love' and 'broad-mindedness is the true sign of friendship'.

But having a steady had its plus points. You didn't waste your time in hormonal pursuits. You focussed your energies on the immediate task at hand instead. In our case, that was the second term exams when Dandy would be waiting with his tongue-whip to sadistically and generously lash out pet prophecies like 'full six months' and 'I am afraid the medical profession will be ruined by amateurs like you'.

Alka parked her moped rather hurriedly and headed straight for Rammy, pausing for a nanosecond to throw a perfunctory semi-hi in our general direction. Rammy disengaged himself from Neha and I could see Alka having a rather animated powwow with him as they began taking their to-and-fro customary walk. Of course, she couldn't be discussing his palm-reading session with Neha. I tried remote-guessing their discussion. (Curiosity was always one of my weak points, among the million others that I hosted.)

Ranju egged me on to go find out what was transpiring and I told her that Rammy hated interjections and could become silently rude if you infringed on his private space. So, we just kept looking at them and tried practising lip-reading and 'how to read a person like a book' and other crap you usually pick up from self-help books. We learned that we were pretty bad when it came to remote-assessing a conversation or a situation. Rammy was pretty good at that actually.

He could pinpoint the exact nature of a person's approach with just one glance.

In fact, I had been bowled over by his phenomenal ability to zero in on a person's agenda with uncanny accuracy some two days ago. We had just put together a makeshift bamboo chandelier consisting of three forty-watt bulbs to aid our group study session at the 3 Ground corridor, when we saw two of our batchmates, Ballu and Pips, heading for us.

'Ballu needs money, and Pips needs my anat notes,' Rammy had said.

After Ballu and Pips had left with their respective borrowings, I had asked Rammy how he managed to assess things so well.

'It's simple, Hucks. A person in need of money usually carries a should-I-ask-or-shouldn't-I-ask look mixed with urgency and anxiety. He has a slight slouch, drooping shoulders and dragging feet. His lips are curved downwards. His hands restively feel his empty pockets, hoping to magically discover a fifty-buck note buried somewhere. And, a person who wishes to borrow your study notes has a sparkle in his eyes, a determination in his gait, and a purposeful glowing expression born of academic optimism...' Rammy had explained.

'You make it sound so simple, Rammy, but I can hardly understand you and how you figure things out,' I had said admiringly.

'Sometimes, even I have difficulty understanding myself, so that makes it two of us,' he had said, laughing away my obvious adulation.

But he had that knack. Bloody gifted bastard. Bloody partial God.

◇

The new Insti wore the look of a strategic command centre bathed in hush. A few Wonder batchers were huddled together and frenetically chalking out their action plan. Rammy sipped his tea and threw a derisive look at them as if they were some delinquent kids building sand castles on the beach and convincing each other that their 'monuments' would inspire awe and reverence for generations to come. Ranju, Alka and Neha had been despatched to the girls' hostel by Rammy to gather the buzz there. The rest of our gang were still gambolling at Commy Garden.

'It seems we're boycotting the mess indefinitely,' said Pips as he sat down next to me.

'Are you crazy? What on earth for?' I asked.

'Arre, Wonder batch is going to press for free food and all – just like NDA,' said Pips.

'Really?' asked Rammy. 'Do these guys realise that we are a quasi-military institution? NDA has cadets. We are civilian students unless inducted into the armed forces…'

'Ya, ya, all that is fine, Rammy, but this will improve our mess and provide us more facilities,' said Pips.

'Nonsense, this will only result in the authorities becoming stricter with us. Nothing good will come of this, in fact we will lose the liberties we now enjoy. Nothing comes free, Pips, nothing,' said Rammy ominously.

'Anyway, we can't go to the mess…' said Pips.

'Suits me fine,' said Rammy.

After our guys returned from their game of Frisbee, we went to Pulp Point for dinner. We gathered from Ranju that all the girls had been instructed to boycott their mess too, and apart from the few who were worried about the dent this would cause in their handbags, it seemed that most girls were quite in favour of a strike.

We discussed how the boys' hostel was an amalgam of mixed reactions. The nerds were against it, and since they were a minority, their views went unheard and unheeded. The rest of the guys were either excited or afraid, with the excited ones dominating the pie chart. We Maniacs had collectively decided to just flow with the tide since our batch occupied the lowest rung on the academic ladder.

When we got back to the hostel after dinner, the new Insti was abuzz with slogan-mongers and poster-designers. It seemed the Warden and Gattu had tried to din some sense into the Wonder batch rebels who had just booed them away. Haluji was pretty happy about the turn of events as he was doing roaring business.

'*Mess bandh bilkul induffinitully,*' he beamed, and asked me if our gang would like to have some paranthas and omelettes. We declined and he happily forced us to drink the special ginger tea he had prepared to celebrate the glad tidings. 'Phree, phrum my chide,' he said, and looked as if he'd burst a vein or two due to happiness-pressure.

By 10 p.m., the girls left for their hostel. Someone hooked up a hired TV and a video at the old Insti, and a noisy group of some fifty-odd Wonder batchers began watching Amitabh Bachchan's *Zanjeer*. A few wanted to play some English flick and the video jockey placated them by saying that he'd keep alternating between Hindi and English flicks all night long. A few backpackers took off on their bikes, perhaps to Mysore or Madras.

The strike had officially begun. All of us were asked not to go to college till further notice by the General Secretary, Swapnil Makhija, who made a full-throated appeal for five minutes – as if we had any choice in the matter. If you violated any of the popular diktats issued by seniors or even your fellow batchmates, you'd be declared an outcaste who deserved to be thoroughly and collectively oppressed. So none tried violating hostel protocol or hurriedly-issued briefs – there were no Jonathan Livingston Seagulls around. (Actually someone *will* dare to swim against the stream later in our story, some two-odd years later, and perhaps we have already bumped into him many times? Keep guessing who. I bet you five hundred bucks you won't guess right. Okay, make that fifty bucks, since I'm pretty tight these days.)

We decided not to go anywhere as the past few weeks had seen us splurging on movies and drinks and dinner like there was no tomorrow; so we would need to conserve as much financial energy as possible.

Solly and Dusty were both big fans of Amitabh Bachchan, and were grabbing *Zanjeer* for perhaps 'the tenth or eleventh time'—by their own proud admission. Rammy commented that 'ninety-nine per cent of humans are just mindless hero-worshippers, so this planet is doomed'. The rest of us retired to the adda and spent the night playing Scrabble.

We woke up rather late the next day and since Haluji was suddenly catering to an unmanageable throng, we had to grab breakfast at the distal raydi. Even that was crowded, so Rammy said that we ought to go to Southern Lunch Home at Jaya Nagar for our meals till we were allowed to dine in the mess.

The corridor walls throughout the hostel were plastered with posters, graffiti and cartoons either ridiculing the system or inspiring us guys to raise our voice and fight for our rights.

The GS and a small party of self-styled representatives had gone to meet the Dean to try and work out an amicable settlement. They returned after about two hours and convinced us that they were ironing out the rough spots and that everything was swinging in favour of us students. They didn't reveal any details of the talks they had, so we didn't know what exactly they were talking about or even what our demands were. They promised to issue a pamphlet listing our demands by evening when we pointed out the absence of information flow.

The old Insti was still playing back-to-back video movies and was supposedly symbolising our defiance and collective angst. I was deputed as the information-gatherer for the Maniacs.

Rammy and Shaky just kept playing chess at the adda for most part of the day. Dusty and Chopsy had gone to Chopsy's LG's.

Mangy hadn't returned yet from Mysore (perhaps he had received the news there and decided to extend his stay?).

Solly was exploiting the opportunity and new-found student unity to the hilt by jamming with a few Wonder batchers who became pretty pally with him as they had got whiff of the fact that he could source and score the best grass in town. So, you could say he was now part of a new 'joint family' within the hostel community.

Frankly, I was enjoying the break in routine and Ranju and I spent a helluva lot of quality time with each other, seriously discussing if we wished to join the army or pay out at the end of our academic tenure.

As she began convincing me that a career in the armed forces was a more secure option, Solly brought a handwritten copy of the proposed demands-pamphlet, pulled me stealthily into a shady corner at the new Insti, and proudly displayed the hastily-scrawled text to me.

'Go show this to Rammy. Get back to me if there are any corrections. This is what Wonder batchers are planning to distribute by evening, but don't tell anyone you know about it...' he whispered, as if he were sharing a state secret, and got back to his newfound friends who were looking at me as if they were assessing my trustworthiness.

I excused myself from Ranju's advice-marathon (gosh, how irksomely patronising she could get) and rushed to the adda.

Rammy frowned as he scanned the smudged sheet.

Demands of Students' Union, Defcoms, Bangalore

1. Free boarding at the mess and improved facilities.
2. Free books and monthly stipend for miscelaneous purposes.
3. Reduction of the bond amount and option for Short Service Commission in the armed forces for at least 25 gentlemen students.

4. Better-equipped library.
5. Increase in railway concession.
6. Increase in vacation period from the present 25 days to 45 days.
7. Better hostel facilities, new hostel recommended.
8. Subsidised loans for procuring two-wheelers from army canteen.
9. No uniforms on Fridays and Saturdays.

Signed,
General Secretary,
On behalf of STUD.

'Any corrections to be made, Rammy?' I asked.

'Just one. Miscellaneous is spelt wrong—add another "l",' he said.

'So what do you think of it?' asked Shaky.

'Nothing,' said Rammy.

'Nothing?' I wondered. 'You've no opinion about it?'

'None whatsoever,' said Rammy, and moved his bishop to b5.

'But I thought you were always against uniforms – I thought you'd like that part,' I said.

'Listen Hucks,' said Rammy, not looking up from the chessboard, 'like I said earlier, nothing good is gonna come out of all this. For most people it's just a *tamasha*, a way to steal a few holidays, and trust me, once this fizzles out we're all in for some pretty troubled times.'

'But Rammy,' began Shaky, 'surely the authorities can't brush aside the desires of six hundred students...'

'The authorities are far smarter than you guys think, Shaky, and you better concentrate on the knight on g5—a triple fork awaits you, and you're definitely losing the b4 pawn in two moves,' said Rammy, and that shut up Shaky as he screwed up his eyes and focussed hard to manoeuvre his pieces out of the tight spot.

'Okay, guys, see you later, I gotta rush this to Solly,' I said, and went in search of the 'joint family'.

Solly was at 5 Top 10 with a few Wonder batchers who were listening to *Dum Maro Dum* and giving karaoke company to Zeenat Aman. (Watch *Hare Rama Hare Krishna* if you haven't already – that's the only Dev Anand flick I ever liked. It's quite a cult movie actually, though it does drag at times.) I gave him the pamphlet copy.

'So what did Rammy say about it?' asked Solly.

'He said it's excellent, concise and well-drafted,' I lied, and the four Wonder batchers gathered in the room smiled contentedly, imagining Rammy's supposed approval of the text. The entire hostel knew that Rammy was a bit of a wunderkind and getting a nod of approval from him was the intellectual equivalent of an orgasm for any draft writer. 'Only one thing, he said miscellaneous is spelt wrong, that's all, it needs an extra "l".'

'Aha, yes,' said Teji, Wonder batch's official writer, looking at the pamphlet, 'one should get all stuff proof-read by Rammy from now on. Tell him I said thanks.'

'I will, Teji,' I said, 'okay I gotta go now, Ranju must be waiting…'

'Hey, take a drag, man, this is cool Kashmiri stuff,' said Solly, tempting me with a reefer, but I declined it as I was in no mood to smoke with his new gang. Pot should only be smoked with one's closest friends, and I wasn't going to change that rule for anyone.

'Saala CKG, okay, go,' said Solly sharply. (CKG = Chokri ka ghada. That means 'girl's donkey', in case your Hindi is rusty. Rammy had mentioned once that it could also stand for Chokri ka God, adding that one should take it as a compliment if someone described you thus.) So I smiled at the compliment and rushed to the new Insti.

◇

Ranju and I were returning from Queen's Garden at six in the evening when we saw them. A phalanx of about thirty bikers from the hostel was excitedly whizzing down Hosur Road and screaming '*batch panga*' at the top of its voice. (Batch panga = Defcoms' war cry which meant that we were strategically deploying ourselves to wreak havoc somewhere.)

A huge group of two-hundred-odd students from all batches was gathered at the new Insti and frenetically preparing to join the murderous phalanx. A few bikes and scooters were creating more noise than cement mixers. Haluji was joyously distributing empty bottles of Thums Up and Campa Cola, even tea glasses, and fist-pumping the air and inspiring everyone to go and reduce Rahul cinema to rubble. I was sure Haluji would've gladly supplied a few dynamite sticks to the demolition team if he could. We discovered that the collective aggression was the direct fallout of a matinee trip to Rahul led by some X-ray batchers. They had got into a fight with a few black marketeers, snatched their tickets, refused to pay them more money than was printed on the tickets, and ended up getting thrashed in the process.

Everyone knew how the theatre management was always hand in glove with the blackies, so we had officially declared war on the cartel and the venue. Mangy was back from Mysore and he said that he had returned earlier than planned as he didn't want to miss all the action – and there was plenty of that happening now. We cheered him for his great sense of timing. Rammy refused to go with us as he was a bit of a Gandhian and fanatically against any 'hooliganism', so we didn't press him.

'Come back alive, all of you,' screamed Alka as we took off, 'we don't have enough money to organise a mass funeral!'

'Don't say inauspicious things, you fool!' said Ranju to her.

All of us were carrying duffel bags packed with enough empty bottles to start a Cola factory. Someone advised us that we could pick up more weapons along the way from some *kabaadi-wallah*.

'Tora, tora, tora!' screamed Dusty. How very apt.

The six of us rode to Rahul as fast as we could, and happily helped our seniors demolish as much of the cinema hall as was possible with our amateurish arsenal. Two pot-bellied cops watched the melee from across the road. The theatre management had given up all hope of timely intervention by government agencies. For 'government agencies' read two outlandishly outnumbered spectator cops munching masala vada and refusing to interfere in 'army matter' and you have the right picture. So, the management had just pulled down the metal grille to prevent any forcible entry into the theatre.

It was a crazy free-for-all, and I guess we all got bored breaking the same ticket windows and smashing the same glass doors after some twenty minutes. Breakable items are so very finite; and violence so very infinite. Mathematical mismatches made life so very dull, buddy. After a while, our collective adrenaline and testosterone levels began settling down, and since there was nothing much left to be smashed at the theatre, we all decided to head back to the hostel.

The next day was a Sunday. We all were chilling out at the new Insti, exchanging notes on our assault on Rahul the previous evening, and congratulating each other on the tumult and damage we had caused, and laughing at the heavy dose of fear we had injected into the management's heart. The newspapers even carried a brief report on our derring-do and we were pretty happy that Defcoms had become a household name in Bangalore, though it was not very flattering to note that the headlines said: *An army of rowdies* and *Does Dr stand for Destroyer?* But who cared, negative publicity was better than no publicity, right? Now all we needed to do was to have the top brass at the college trembling at our collective invincibility.

'Isn't that the Dean's car?' asked Chopsy, pointing at a distant green Ambassador snaking its way towards us.

'Oh, ya, that's definitely General Thakur,' said Rammy, 'unless it's his wife coming over to drink Haluji's kerosene-flavoured tea.'

A few guys from X-ray batch began shouting 'Mean Dean', 'Mean Dean', and were immediately shushed by a few Wonder batchers. Decorum was the recommended procedure when you were trying to negotiate with the top brass.

The Ambassador parked next to the old Insti and Major General Surinder Thakur alighted from it. He was dressed in an embroidered beige *kurta-pyjama* (perhaps he wore it at his son's wedding the previous month?) and was beaming cheerily as if all of us had won some international intercollegiate event that had made the college proud. Nearly everyone began milling around him and Rammy mentioned that 'surely he will die of asphyxiation or carbon dioxide poisoning'.

'So what movie are you guys watching?' asked the General in his booming baritone.

Nearly all guys got up from their seats as he entered the old Insti-cum-makeshift movie hall.

'Sir, it's an English movie called *It's a Mad Mad Mad Mad World*,' said Niranjan Gupta, the video jockey from X-ray batch.

'How very appropriate for the occasion,' said the General, and everyone laughed nervously. 'Don't you guys watch any Hindi movies? Be Indian, buy Indian, watch Indian?'

'We are alternating between Hindi and English, sir!' said Niranjan, and pulling a chair, 'please sit down, sir!'

'Wonderful. I have a video cassette of *Mother India*, lovely movie, have you seen that?' asked the General, clearly trying to sound chummy with his well-rehearsed, I-am-your-kind-of-guy routine, and plonked himself into a comfy cane chair.

'No, sir,' said Swapnil Makhija (the GS, remember?), eager to join the conversation, 'is it interesting?'

'Oh, it's hajjar great, Swapnil, you guys must see it today, I'll give you the cassette – you know I had a crush on Nargis during my younger days, but don't you guys mention it to my wife and wreck my marriage,' said the General light-heartedly.

'Smooth operator,' whispered Rammy into my ear, 'just watch, he's going to sweet-talk everybody. Wonder what he's doing in the army – this guy should have been in politics.'

'Would you like to have some tea or coffee, sir?' asked Swapnil.

'Sure, thanks, and please ask them not to add sugar – would love to have some strong coffee. Does the canteen serve you guys good stuff?'

The General was trying to use slangs and hostel lingo and making desperate efforts to prove that he was on our side, that he spoke our kind of language, and thought our kind of thoughts.

'Not always, sir,' said Niranjan, 'that's one of our demands – to have our own subsidised wet canteen in the hostel.'

'Yes, Niranjan, I've read your demands. All very reasonable, I must say,' said Gen. Thakur. 'In fact, I've spoken with some IAS officers in the Ministry and they have promised to give it *serious consideration.*'

Consideration, I'd later learn, was one of the most dangerous words that could be used by authorities. It could mean any of the following: (a) We have to tolerate your request till we find ways to rusticate you; (b) We'll make you wait so much that cobwebs will begin growing in your brain; (c) We have placed you under surveillance and are thinking up ways to silence you; (d) We think you are as important as a termite in a walnut tree, though we'd never give you that impression; and (e) What we say in the army when we actually want to laugh and say 'fuck off'.

The students cheered stupidly and lustily as the General began sipping his sugarless coffee. Rammy said that he was playing to the gallery and didn't mean a word of what he said. (Rammy mentioned something about eye movement and the General's hand language – all of which I was too dense to understand anyway.)

'So, sir, we can hope to get all our demands approved?' asked Swapnil.

'Of course,' said the General, 'I am here to help you. In fact, most of it was already in the pipeline, I had initiated it, but you know the bloody Ministry guys, red tape and all, and they're slower than snails on sedatives...'

The fools laughed again. We didn't.

'My only request is you guys rejoin college, how long can we keep boycotting classes? Sooner or later, we have to revert to normalcy,' continued the General, happy to see that most students were lapping up what he was saying.

'Sir, we will rejoin only when we have a written assurance from you regarding our demands,' said Niranjan firmly, and looked at us for appreciation. So, we appreciated by nodding our heads vigorously.

'Niranjan, even if I give a written assurance, it won't hold much water. You know we have to respect certain institutions and procedures evolved over time for our own good; though you guys do have my *verbal assurance* that I'll personally try to action all your reasonable demands. Ultimately the decision rests with the Health Ministry – it's their call. I can only recommend the changes that you demand, and I will...' said the General.

Niranjan and Swapnil looked at Rammy for support, so did we, as everyone knew that Rammy could floor anyone he desired to floor. But Rammy kept mum.

'Sir, some second termers have a few questions,' said Swapnil, nudging Rammy to speak.

'Sir, may I have permission to speak freely, sir?' asked Rammy of the General. I marvelled at the way Rammy maintained a neutral tone that was neither overly submissive nor unduly aggressive. In fact, his voice carried the magnetic flavour of a professional negotiator who had honed his skills at corporate boardrooms where he had specialised and excelled in mergers and acquisitions.

'Of course, go ahead, shoot, but only with words, okay?' laughed the General.

'Sir, when everything is going to be decided by the Health Ministry, what exactly is the purpose of *our* conversation?' Rammy asked coolly.

The logic hit the General like a sledgehammer. Rammy might as well have asked, 'Sir, what the hell are you doing here?' The effect wouldn't have been any different, unless the General was accustomed to whipping out a revolver and shooting anyone who was blatantly impolite.

'Ah…er…well…exactly that,' stuttered the General, clearly fumbling for words and trying to carve an intelligent reply, 'to precisely discuss that…that everything will only be decided by the Health Ministry…'

'So wouldn't it be better for us to speak with the decision-*makers* directly and not with the decision-*recommenders*, sir?' asked Rammy, and quite a few guys began whispering among themselves that he was making more sense than Niranjan or Swapnil. They didn't mind the observation. In fact, they seemed happy that they had relayed the conversational baton to Rammy.

Rammy had taken the wind out of the General's sails. Just when the General thought that he'd mesmerised everyone with his charisma and faked chumminess, Rammy had thrown the spanner in the diplomatic works. A hint of a frown crossed the General's face, but the seasoned veteran quickly replaced it with a sly smile.

'Of course, why don't you guys draft an official letter, I'll forward it to the Ministry, adding a few recommendations from my side. Perhaps we can even sit and draft it together…what's your name?'

'Ramakrishna Iyer, sir,' said Rammy. 'No sir, I meant why take a long-winded approach?'

'Meaning?' asked the General.

'I mean perhaps Swapnil and a few others could fix an appointment with the Ministry officials when they come next time…' suggested Rammy.

'It's not that easy,' said the General sharply, clearly irked by Rammy's bravado, even as he quickly corrected his tone and slipped again into a smoother gear, 'I wish it were, but we have to go through the proper channels of communication...'

'Sir, I was wondering if we could directly write to the Health Ministry...' said Rammy.

'And bypass the chain of command?' asked the General.

'Yes, sir,' said Rammy.

'It's not possible, my dear friend, unless you go through the proper channels, you're not going to be heard there. They receive millions of letters every day which end up in the wastepaper basket. You have a better chance if we team up on this,' said the General.

'Maybe if *you* were to send the letter on our behalf...' said Rammy.

'That's exactly what I am saying. That we should sit together and draft a letter,' smiled the General.

'So you are saying unless *you* recommend it, our demands will go unheeded...?' asked Rammy.

'Exactly!' said the General.

'And to be heard, we have to end the strike,' said Rammy.

'Exactly. But I am not blackmailing you guys. All I am saying is take a mature view of things. Do raise demands, and we will consider it. By the way, what happened at Rahul?' said the General, looking at Niranjan.

'Sir, a few X-ray batchers had a fight with the blackies—the guys who sell tickets in black, sir—and one thing led to another, and they beat up our guys...' explained Niranjan.

'Are our guys okay?' asked the General, sounding genuinely concerned.

'Yes, sir, just some minor injuries...' said Niranjan.

'And so you devils went and blasted the theatre,' said the General laughingly.

'Yes, sir!' chorused a few.

'Well done, that's the spirit, one should always fight against injustice, but remember to take me into confidence before you venture into civilian areas to settle scores next time; I'll send a Shaktiman truck full of bloodthirsty *jawans* with you...' said the General encouragingly.

'Thank you, sir,' said Niranjan.

'Okay, so it's a deal? We end the strike?' asked the General.

'Sure, sir,' said Niranjan, and looked questioningly at Swapnil.

'Absolutely, sir,' said Swapnil.

From defiant rebels to servile yes-men in twenty minutes flat. The General had enough skills to convert Frankenstein into Mother Teresa. But then, perhaps we didn't have much of a choice in the matter, and I wondered if Rammy had deliberately walked into the General's carefully-laid conversational trap to put an end to the meaningless tamasha as Rammy wasn't in favour of it anyway.

The General signalled his uniformed chauffeur to get a manila folder from his green Ambassador and the chauffeur hurriedly brought a thick file.

Rammy whispered to me that the General didn't believe a word of whatever he had said regarding considering our demands. I asked him how he was so sure, and Rammy said that the General's right eyelid twitches whenever he lies.

The General thumbed through the folder, took out an envelope, opened it with a flourish, flashed it as you'd flash three aces at a game of *teen-patti* (Indian poker), and showed us a rather official-looking letter.

'I was saving the best for the last, this arrived a week ago, even *before* you guys went on strike,' he said smilingly.

The letter was from the Ministry of Health. It was dated a week ago, so he had received it even before the strike began. Unless the Ministry had *back-dated* the letter at his request and sent it *after* the strike began. Possible. (All three Defcoms were run by the Health Ministry guys. We called them the Hellmints. Every once in a while, a few bespectacled safari-clad bureaucrats came from Delhi on 'surprise visits' to check things, and we were always given an advance warning to keep the hostel and ourselves spruced up. The quality of food touched stratospheric heights at such times though, so we were happy if the Hellmints arrived. We gathered from the official grapevine that the Ministry of Defence and the Ministry of Science & Technology had tried to take over the administration of Defcoms some years ago, but the Hellmints were a smarter lot and had prevented the coup. Well, enough of boring gyan. Let's get back to the sly General and the official letter.)

'Congratulations!' said the General. 'As I said I had already initiated much of what you guys have asked for – the government has sanctioned each student a mess stipend of forty rupees per day and a study stipend of thirty rupees per day…'

'Hooorrrraaaaay!' many students cheered.

'It gets better,' continued the General. 'All of you are entitled to travel II tier AC from the next vacation onward, and you will also get twenty rupees per day for miscellaneous expenses. But I hope you won't blow it on cigarettes and drinks.'

Rammy whispered to me that obviously our authorities didn't want to give the impression that they were buckling under student pressure, and were now smartly taking the credit for the new sops extended by the government.

'Sir, fantastic, sir!' said Niranjan. 'This is wonderful news!'

'Sir, you were just teasing us for the past twenty minutes…' said Swapnil.

'Why, only you guys can have fun, huhn?' asked the General smilingly. 'Happy?'

'Thank you, sir,' said Niranjan. 'We are positively delighted and eternally grateful to you, sir.'

'You are welcome,' said the General, 'actually we were just processing the letter and I was trying to get more details from them before I announced it. I was planning to officially announce it tomorrow, but then, all's well that ends well. Have fun! *Jai Hind!*'

He bade us goodbye, commanded us to show up in college the next day, gained close to two hundred fans, and triumphantly disappeared into his green Ambassador.

'So he was acting all along, his entire conversation was make-believe, mere drama,' I said to Rammy.

'Ya,' said Rammy.

'You read him wrong, huhn?' I said accusingly.

'He's a seasoned actor and in all probability a great poker player – no wonder he's become a Major General. I'm sure he's one of the youngest Major Generals in DMC,' said Rammy. (DMC = Defence Medical Corps.)

'So you finally met your match,' I said.

'Absolutely,' agreed Rammy, 'he deserves an Oscar, especially for the part when he stuttered and pretended to be fumbling for words as I began quizzing him. And, I was thinking how smart I was.'

'What about the twitch – that was also part of the act?' I asked.

'Ya, he's a class act. The twitch wasn't involuntary. It was masterfully executed to throw us off the scent. Phew! He has out-foxed us.'

'So can we trust him?'

'Obviously not. What a dumb question!'

'But he showed us the letter, na?'

'The letter's true. We'll get all the facilities, and of course they will also extract their pound of flesh. But if I were you, I'd trust General Thakur a tad less than Jack the Ripper and a fraction more than The Boston Strangler.'

'Logic?'

'Never trust an actor or a politician, Hucks, and you'll never be disappointed with humans or human nature. They both function by their hidden agendas. To them success is more important than the path towards success.'

'Ends justify the means kind of thing...'

'Ya, I've a nagging feeling we're just guinea pigs in some secret army experiment on *field behaviour and manipulated psychology of medicos*. I won't be surprised if we guys are on hidden surveillance cameras day in and day out from now on.'

'Shit, we even smoke pot! Hey, don't scare me, man!'

'Who do you think I am – Ramsay Brothers?'

◇

The second term exams were a fortnight away. Rammy had recorded his notes on cassettes and kept listening to them on his Sony Walkman (even when he was asleep!) and kept staring at the biochemistry flow charts stuck on all the walls in his room all day long. The rest of us hadn't covered more than ten per cent of the syllabus.

We stayed awake the entire night and tried to cram as much as possible. I hadn't met Ranju for days and had only bumped into her at the college canteen once. At least my priorities were clear.

The toughest to tackle were the bone sets. For once, I was cursing Lord Brahma for having created a human body that had 206 bones on an average. (One counting method listed the number as 208, if you considered the central breast-bone, sternum, to be three bones actually. Anyway, let's steer clear of depressing details.)

Now, thanks to Brahma's generous distribution of bones to our body, we had to try and understand most of them, with all the muscle attachments on each and grapple with other mind-bending technicalities.

That wasn't all. Brahma had also blessed the human body with numberless organs and most of these would be neatly displayed on various tables to fox your random access memory and shatter your confidence in your academic potential.

Plus you had the biochemistry and physiology stuff because Brahma also loved biochemical reactions, enzymes, hormones and all, and was a genius who designed complicated architecture.

Surely, simplicity wasn't Brahma's trademark, and you and I had to suffer for that. Life was tough. (So if you are happily flipping these pages because you don't like to leaf through text books for fourteen hours a day, then I'd seriously ask you to chuck any dreams you might have of becoming a medical doctor. Forget MBBS, it's too laborious and tortuous, and is an academic journey best left for the studious nerds to undertake. Wish them well and take a detour. Life comes with billions of rainbow possibilities, so don't wear blinkers and get into the medical grind unless you are an academic horse. Don't say later that I didn't warn you.)

◇

'Aha,' said Dandy, 'so how was the badminton trip?'

Darned vindictive bastard with the darned solid memory, I thought. All the sweat pores on my body became more dynamic than normal. There were close to sixty different bones on the table. I didn't even recognise many of them. I thought about Mandira Dhillon (remember the girl who didn't make it to Defcoms?) and felt like sending her a card saying, 'You are luckier than you think, hell is a bone-filled stink.'

'I asked you a question,' reminded Dandy.

'Huh, what, sir?'

'How was the badminton trip?'

'Good, sir.'

'Let's see if play has reduced Jack's dullness.'

I wished to tell him that it was Solly who'd made that statement to him many moons ago, but remained silent. I stared at the table blankly.

He pointed at a bone with his aluminium ruler and, in an extra-sweet tone, said, 'Please pick it up.'

I picked it up.

'Where would you find this in your body?'

'Heel, sir. It's the calcaneum – the bone that makes our heel.'

'Good. Now show me its anatomical position.' (Translation: What is its normal position when you are standing?)

'Sure, sir,' I said, and balanced the calcaneum on my trembling palm.

'You are sure that's the anatomical position of the calcaneum?'

'Yes, sir.'

'Very good. Now go and teach something new to Dr Pandit and Dr Vimala and Dr Bhasin. Tell them this is the anatomical position of the calcaneum.'

So I carried it to the tables where the other profs were grilling other poor Yankee batchers and did as instructed and all the profs laughed uproariously.

I returned to Dandy's table, sat down, and found myself spreading like a punctured balloon. The steel stool felt colder than earlier. My ego-veins were reaching bursting point. You could have written an obituary for my self-pride. My face must have been redder than an overworked *tandoor*.

'I told you – full six months, my friend, full six months,' Dandy said cheerfully. 'It's upside-down, you have placed the calcaneum upside-down!'

Rammy was standing just ten feet from the table, awaiting his turn, and I would have loved to hug and kiss him on the spot for what he said, but that would have only made matters worse.

'Sir, he's showing the anatomical position of the calcaneum when he's doing *sirshasana*, when he's standing on his head practising yoga...'

'You come here,' said Dandy to Rammy, and looking dismissively at me, 'and you can go.'

'Yes, sir?' enquired Rammy.

I went and stood a few feet away, camouflaging myself behind a pillar, and tried to grab as much of Rammy's performance as possible from the corner of my eye. This wasn't allowed (you had to leave the hall when you were through) but who cared? I had clearly flunked and Dandy couldn't flunk me anymore. Earlier, at the soft parts table, I had thought the shrivelled uterus was a tongue. (Rammy later said it was a common mistake students made and we should identify it rightly by checking the two fallopian tubes at the top. I had already made many common mistakes like that.)

'Pick up the lumbar vertebra. L-5,' said Dandy to him.

Rammy picked up the L-5 in five seconds flat. Dandy was surprised. Normally students struggled for at least three minutes in trying to differentiate between the five lumbar vertebrae, L-1, L-2, L-3, L-4, and L-5, which form your lower back.

Dandy asked him many trick questions and Rammy answered them all like a trained robot. Dandy smiled. I had never seen the grouchy prof smile like that before and that should rate as Rammy's greatest victory in college.

'Pick up the sacrum,' said Dandy. Rammy picked it up. (The L-5 sits on the sacrum, the bone resting slightly above the centre of your bums.)

Dandy asked *two* questions. Rammy answered *all ten* of them. Dandy looked up surprised. Rammy smiled.

'But you seldom attend dissections and tutorials!' wondered Dandy.

'Yes, sir,' said Rammy. 'Just goes to prove that one can learn a lot from books and the notes of seniors in the privacy of one's room.'

'Yes, yes, but not all can do that.'

'I agree, sir.'

'Well done anyway. Try to make it to classes too – at times.'

'I'll try to, sir, though I can't promise. Good day, sir.'

End of Rammy's viva. Touché.

Ranju was angry that I had flunked all the theory and practical tests. Alka was happy that Rammy had cleared them all.

'You better study, okay, next term,' said Ranju.

'Shut up. Change the topic, don't eat my head now,' I said.

'Look, I'm telling for your own good, look at Rammy...'

'Now don't sound like my mother, and stop comparing apples with oranges. Rammy is in a different league altogether. He's super-human.'

'Okay, then what about Chopsy and Dusty? They have passed at least in bio and physio theory. You've flunked all. ALL!'

'They carried *farras*.' (Farras = Small chits you carried into exam halls with a few holy mantras written on them for good luck. Some of the mantras could be decoded into answers for exam questions. Just kidding, farras are chits you copied from, period.)

'Look, I'm not asking you to cheat. I'm happy you didn't carry farras...'

'Ranju, enough. *Que sera sera*, what will be will be. I'll take life as it comes, stop spoiling my mood now.'

'Okay, bye,' she said coldly.

'Bye,' I said equally coldly.

10

A Simple Plan, Greedy Encore, Zeno Girls

Then. June through August 1986.

WE WERE CLEARLY BORED. THERE WASN'T MUCH ACTION happening when the third term began. Everyone had buried their heads in books. Rammy was psyching us as usual with his prodigious memory. The profs were conducting extra tutorials. The atmosphere was nauseatingly reverberating with biochemistry equations, physiology fundas, and anatomy tongue-twisters. We studied for a month or so and then decided to take a break. We needed it badly.

Solly felt we had to surpass ourselves this time and do something really *bindaas* that we could joyously recount to our grandchildren in the years to come.

Naturally, Rammy wasn't involved in our scheme of things for he had become an antisocial hermit.

So we six were getting really stoned on Friday evening and thinking up what to do to enliven the weekend and carry memory mementoes into the future.

Shaky came up with the idea actually. It was really outlandish and we were doubtful whether we could pull it off, and Mangy said that impossible was a word that existed only in the dictionary of fools. (Have we heard that one before or am I suffering déjà vu? Never mind.)

Chopsy seconded him and said if we planned it impeccably then this should rate as one of the greatest adventures of our college life. Dusty was as usual screaming 'Tora, tora, tora!' every time anyone said anything encouraging.

Shaky said that the plan could only be executed after three or four days as there was lots of preparing to do. A plan of this magnitude required meticulous analysis and crisp execution. It also involved a bit of training, voice modulation, acting and all. We were totally into it. Wild schemes have this uncanny knack of exciting your intellect and revving up your brash side.

The plan was simple. There was a four-star hotel called Quadrant International (we called it Q-Eye) that had come up at Race Course Road some ten months ago. Shaky's uncle was a Vice-President with Techtronix Corporation, a fledgling but rich computer firm based in New York, and he used to stay at this hotel whenever he came from US on an official trip to Bangalore – about once every three months.

A few other senior Techtronix executives from their branch office in Delhi also used to stay at Q-Eye whenever they flew into Bangalore and the hotel staffers were always happy to receive them as Techtronix guys were a cash-rich regular clientele. Hence they wouldn't even ask for any advance.

So Solly was going to pretend to be a Techtronix guy, in fact a General Manager (International Operations), check in at a hotel room, treat us all to a lavish dinner seasoned with drinks, request the steward to bill it all to the room account, and coolly exit a while later. Simple.

The plan:

1. Saturday. 11 a.m. We gave instructions to get a few business cards printed for Solly from a seedy printer near Indira Nagar,

asking him to copy the details from a Techtronix card that Shaky provided as the template. The printer said it would take him two days to get it right. We were in no hurry. He'd deliver twenty glitzy business cards by Monday morning. Cool, we said. Cost: ₹150.

2. Saturday. 3 p.m. Shaky made a few calls to the Techtronix office in Delhi (from Chopsy's LG's – they had gone to Madras). He said he was calling from Q-Eye to confirm if they needed any reservations for their guys this week. They said no – most of the senior guys had gone to US and wouldn't be back before August end. Shaky enquired about some executives, gleaned some valuable information, and hung up. Shaky knew that his uncle was only returning in September. We were in the second week of July. Great. Cost: Zilch.

3. Saturday. 5 p.m. We bought a blue shirt for Solly (he already had the drab navy blue trouser and black shoes from the fresher term, remember?) to be embroidered with the Techtronix logo, which is what all Techtronix guys wore as part of their corporate branding exercise. Cost: ₹350 + ₹55.

4. Saturday. 6:30 p.m. We bought a nice dark brown executive leather bag from a shop dealing in used luggage. Cost: ₹375.

5. Monday. 11 a.m. Dusty and Chopsy were despatched to the airport to wait outside the arrival lounge and request some passengers for their baggage tags. If anyone raised their eyebrows, they'd say they needed it for a college project. They got ten of them. Cost: Zilch. (Of course fuel expenses never count.)

6. Monday. 11:30 a.m. I called up Q-Eye to ask if a Mr Ranjan Lamba was expected to check in on Wednesday, as we had something important to discuss. The receptionist said no. I asked her to relay the message that I am Mr Vikas Khosla, a General Manager from Grindlays Bank, Bombay, on a two-day visit to Bangalore, and we wished to meet him in the evening if he did check in. I added that we had discovered that Mr Lamba was

holidaying in Kashmir when we called up the Techtronix Delhi office, and someone there informed us that maybe he'd come to Bangalore this week for a conference. The girl was extra-polite and happy to be speaking with a GM, and even said 'I hope you'll stay at Quadrant sometime sir, and it'd be a pleasure to serve you', adding that she'd definitely relay the message to Mr Lamba if and when he checked in.

7. Monday. 11:45 a.m. Shaky despatched Mangy to collect Solly's business card, or rather Mr Ranjan Lamba's business card, heehee. Mangy asked Shaky if the Q-Eye girl would call up Techtronix guys in Delhi, and Shaky said that (a) she wouldn't call as they were regular clients and (b) even if she did make a confirmation call, it wouldn't make much of a difference because there was really a Mr Ranjan Lamba who was presently vacationing in Kashmir, along with his secretary, and that was the main reason why this name was chosen for Solly, so both parties would just become confused, and the matter would end there. Plus 'since Hucky has already called up Q-Eye to confirm Lamba's holiday in Kashmir, it would all sound genuine'. Cool.

8. Monday. 1 p.m. Shaky called up Q-Eye, pretending to be a PR executive from Techtronix Delhi, and made a reservation for Mr Ranjan Lamba for Tuesday evening. The receptionist hadn't called up Delhi (as Mangy had feared) and Shaky told her that Mr Lamba was reaching Bangalore on Tuesday to oversee a business matter of grave importance. She cheerily said a Mr Khosla had called earlier and wished to meet Mr Lamba, and Shaky said that Mr Khosla was one of the head honchos of Grindlays Bank, Bombay, and promised to get her their business too. That made her happy. After he hung up, Shaky said she didn't sound suspicious, and we wouldn't need to abort the mission. Super. Cost: Zilch.

9. Monday. 4 p.m. Full dress rehearsal at Chopsy's LG's. We had their bungalow's guesthouse with us for a week. Their two servants

had also gone to Madras with them. Bless them all. So, we six had gathered there. Solly's Techtronix business card looked impressive. It said Ranjan Lamba, General Manger (International Operations). The seedy printer had done a great job. Money's worth. Mangy was touching up Solly's sideburns with a diluted solution of the Kores white eraser ink that typists used. A bit of grey on the sideburns and moustache would add a touch of authenticity to the act. Dusty asked Solly to try on a zero-power spectacles. Solly slipped into the blue Techtronix shirt, dark navy blue trouser and black boots, topped off the get-up with a blue blazer we had borrowed from a senior, and definitely looked like a successful GM of a successful computer company.

10. Monday. 4:20 p.m. Shaky began his coaching class.

Shaky (playing receptionist): Yes, sir, how may I help you?
Solly (smiling pleasantly): I believe you have a reservation for Ranjan Lamba (flashing his Techtronix business card).
Shaky: Yes, sir! Welcome to Quadrant, Mr Lamba! We have booked you into the executive suite. Room 502, sir. Hope you'll have a pleasant stay.
Solly: Oh, thank you! That's a great room, I've heard my VP saying. He stays here whenever he comes from US. By the way, I might have a few visitors coming from Grindlays Bank later in the evening...
Shaky: Oh, sorry sir, forgot to tell you, a Mr Vikas Khosla had called earlier and wanted to meet you...
Solly: Oh, yes, Vikas is a GM with Grindlays Bank...my secretary mentioned that they had tried reaching our Delhi office...but I was holidaying in Kashmir then...did Vikas leave a number...?
Shaky: Am afraid not, sir!
Solly: Never mind, and thank you! Am sure he will call again. Could you send a nice hot coffee and some cheese sandwiches to my room in a while, am famished!

Shaky: Sure, sir!

Solly: Thank you…(Dusty, the bellboy, carried Solly's leather bag and Solly tipped him ten bucks just outside Room #502, or next to the fireplace, heehee.)

Shaky: (Trrrring, trrring) Hello? Welcome to Quadrant International, how may I help you?

Me: Hello there, I'm Vikas Khosla calling from Grindlays Bank…just calling to ask if Mr Ranjan Lamba of Techtronix has…

Shaky: Oh, yes sir! Mr Khosla! Mr Lamba just checked in an hour ago. In fact, he said you'd call, let me put you through to him…

Me: Thanks.

Solly: ('Trrring trrring') Hello…

Shaky: Sir! Mr Vikas Khosla from Grindlays Bank is on the line, sir, shall I…?

Solly: Aha, great, put him through…

Me: Hi Ranjan, how are you?

Solly: Great Vikas, just great! What's up? You guys are bagging all the juicy projects…

Me: Ya, life's good, Ranjan, and must say you guys have done a swell job computerising our Bombay office, they're truly impressed…

Solly: Thanks, hey Vikas, how about meeting up for dinner…?

Me: Of course, will eight be fine by you?

Solly: Great, see you at eight. And, why don't you get…Deepak and Kapil too…we could discuss our Bangalore systems overhaul and all…

Me: Sure, I will. In fact, they're looking forward to meeting you…

Solly: Super. See you later, Vikas…bye…

Me: See you at eight, Ranjan…bye…

'Well done, guys,' said Shaky, looking at Solly and me. 'That sounded real genuine. And, remember, there's just an odd chance that the receptionist might listen in, so keep it *exactly* like that. Okay, quick recap. Solly checks in at Q-Eye at 5 p.m. tomorrow. Hucky calls at 6 p.m. I don't even want you guys calling each other by your real names till then. Use only your fictitious names from now on so you can get into the skin of the characters.'

We all nodded agreement.

'At eight, Hucky from Grindlays Bank, along with Mangy and Chopsy will check in. Hucky will ask the receptionist to inform Solly of their arrival, while they wait at the lobby, and Solly will come down from his room and take them to Sidewalk – that's the bar-cum-restaurant at Q-Eye. Remember, don't drink too much, and order Scotch on the rocks. That's what high-flying executives have. I'll kill you guys if you ask for soda or Thums Up. Max two pegs each before we order dinner…' Shaky continued instructing us.

'Hey, make it three pegs at least, dude, let's milk them…' said Chopsy.

'Shut up, Chopsy. Greed ruins plans. Just do as I say…Where was I? Yes, then, at around 8:20 p.m., Dusty and me will enter Sidewalk, take a table, and pretend to bump into you guys. Solly will invite us over to his table, saying loudly to Hucky that "these guys are my good friends from Hindustan Lever", and will introduce us two to you three at Solly's table. By 9 p.m., we all finish our drinks and order soup and dinner. Our convo will be a bit of business, some cricket, and holidays in Bangkok and Australia. I have written the details here and you all better read it. By 10 p.m., we order dessert. By 10:20 p.m., Solly will signal to the steward to bill it all to Room # 502, or whatever room they allot him, and leave tips on the table – make it ten per cent of the bill. By 10:30 p.m., we will begin exiting. First to leave will be Dusty and me. Then Hucky and Mangy and Chopsy will bid their goodbyes to Solly near the reception. Solly will begin seeing them off. Hucky will say "we are planning to take a small postprandial walk" and ask Solly to join them. Solly will say okay. And, we all will vanish from the spot by 10:40 max. Get it?'

'Tora, tora, tora!' screamed Dusty.

'Shut up! And don't you dare write something stupid like "Maniacs were here" on the table or in the loo – you can't put it past him you know, his childish creativity will help them nab us...' said Shaky.

We all laughed and Dusty made faces at us. We were gung-ho and ready to mulct Q-Eye. Wish us luck!

Tuesday. 10 a.m.

We were all memorising our fictitious names and touristy details about Bangkok and Australia from the photocopies that Shaky had typed and distributed, and were being quizzed by him.

```
Sushil  Solanki    Solly   = Ranjan  Lamba
Hari  Iyengar      Hucky   = Vikas  Khosla
Manjeet  Ahuja     Mangy   = Deepak  Mishra
Arun  Chopra       Chopsy  = Kapil  Mathur
Nirmal  Shekhar    Shaky   = Dheeraj  Makhija
Dinesh  Rastogi    Dusty   = Prakash  Nikunj
```

For the next two hours we were talking to each other using our pseudonyms and discussing business economics, computer systems and bank parlance. After that we grabbed a quick packed lunch of *biryani* and *raita*, and rehearsed our walks, expressions, accents, and went through the plan details with a fine toothcomb. If you had stumbled upon the scene, you'd have thought we were planning a bank robbery. We hadn't prepared so diligently even for our exams. By 1 p.m., we were in a state of excited readiness.

Then Shaky asked us all to grab a disco nap. 'It's good to take rest before a major stress-inducing activity as it sharpens your brain. Prakash Nikunj, set the alarm for three please,' he said.

'Hey, I'm not feeling sleepy now,' said Mangy.

'Ya, ditto,' said Chopsy.

'Never mind, then just lie down and don't talk,' said Shaky.

'Hey, I was just wondering, why is tips called tips?' I asked.

'What tips?' asked Dusty as he set the alarm for three.

'Arre, the tips you pay to the waiter, yaar,' I said.

'Does it matter?' asked Shaky, clearly irked.

'If you don't know, just say you don't know...' I retorted.

'Hey guys, let's grab some sleep as Shaky has decided, okay?' said Solly.

'TIPS is an acronym for *To Insure Prompt Service*,' said Shaky.

'Really? That's interesting. Or are you making it up?' I asked.

'Shut up and lie down quietly! Nobody talks for the next two hours!' screamed Shaky, and we all clammed up like tortoises receiving a scolding.

◇

4 p.m. Solly was ready. The leather bag carried a nice Indian Airlines tag and lots of old clothes and newspapers, heehee. Shaky would drop him off five km from Q-Eye. Solly would take a taxi from there.

5 p.m. We were getting ready. Mangy was greying up Shaky and me. Kores eraser ink *zindabad*! We both would wear formal shirts and trousers. Dusty, Chopsy and Mangy would wear formal trousers and semi-casual half-sleeve shirts.

6 p.m. I called up Q-Eye, asked for Ranjan Lamba, and the receptionist put me through to him. We had a convo exactly as we had rehearsed.

7:40 p.m. We all parked our bikes four km from Q-Eye, just outside a shopping mall. Mangy, Chopsy and I took a taxi. Shaky and Dusty waited there for a while.

8:05 p.m. We were at the Q-Eye lobby. I was talking to the receptionist. She was a bomb, and I kept whispering to the guys to keep their minds on the task at hand. She looked as if she was enjoying being ogled at. Solly arrived in five minutes and we entered Sidewalk as planned.

8:15 p.m. We ordered Scotch on the rocks and heavy starters consisting of *sheek kebabs*, cauliflower *pakoras* and grilled *paneer*.

8:40 p.m. Shaky and Dusty were about to sit two tables away, when Solly spotted them. 'Hey, Dheeraj, howdy man!' he shouted cheerily across the table. 'Hey, Ranjan, what a pleasant surprise!' said Shaky, pretending astonishment, as he and Dusty began walking to our table, 'funny bumping into you here!' Solly asked them to join us and they did. We all introduced ourselves, began discussing business economics, Bangkok and Australia, nursed our Scotch on the rocks, and placed our order for soup and dinner.

10:10 p.m. We were bursting at the seams. I had had a pure vegetarian dinner of *kulchas, naans, aloo gobi, rajma, paneer butter masala* and *pulao*. The guys had polished off *tandoori chicken, fish koliwada, butter chicken, mutton rogan josh, butter naans* and *mutton biryani*. I declined dessert, but all the other guys had fruit salads and Dusty even had space for a triple Sundae! It was now 10:40 p.m. We were running slightly behind schedule. Never mind.

10:45 p.m. Shaky and Dusty exited. Solly signalled to the steward for the bill, left a tip of ₹500 in the leather folder, and asked him to bill it to his room. The waiter agreed. (The bill: A whopping ₹6,248!)

10:50 p.m. Mangy, Chopsy and I said our goodbyes to Solly at the lobby. I asked Solly to join us for a postprandial walk, and he agreed. Solly smiled at the receptionist and asked her to have someone check the geyser connection in his room. A deft touch! As if he was going to return for a warm shower! She smiled back and said she'd get it done right away.

10:55 p.m. We four hailed a taxi.

11:15 p.m. We four rendezvoused with Shaky and Dusty outside the shopping mall where we had parked our bikes. 'Tora! Tora! Tora!'

screamed Dusty. We all high-fived and hugged each other saying, 'We pulled it off, man!'

11:45 p.m. We were back at Chopsy's LG's and nobody complained of sleeplessness.

We had finally surpassed ourselves – definitely something worth recounting to our grandchildren.

We had spent close to ₹1500 and got ₹9000 worth from Q-Eye (don't forget the room tariff). A six times return on investment was a neat business venture and it had boosted our confidence and our collective spirits. We became sure that we could pull off anything we set our minds to. Shaky said we ought to now concentrate on our studies and we knuckled down and attacked our books again with renewed vigour. A week into the process, and the adventure-bug bit us again. It was Wednesday evening. Apart from Rammy, who hardly left his room now, we six had gathered at the new Insti.

'Guys, let's do it again,' said Solly.

'Don't push your luck, dude,' warned Chopsy.

'Luck always favours the brave,' said Mangy.

'What do you say, Shaky?' I asked, clearly tempted.

'Hmmm,' contemplated Shaky, 'it's an idea…'

'Arre, let's do a repeat, man,' said Mangy.

'Obviously, the venue has to be different,' said Shaky.

'Of course,' I said.

'Count me out guys,' said Chopsy.

'Ya, me too,' said Dusty.

'Wimps,' said Mangy.

'Okay, let's do it this weekend,' said Solly.

'No, weekends are crowded – let's make it coming Tuesday,' said Shaky.

'Ya, Tuesday's our lucky day,' I said.

'Let's bleed a five star this time,' said Solly.

'How about Orchids Intercontinental at Airport Road?' I suggested.

'Sounds good to me,' said Shaky. 'Techtronix uses that too.'

◇

Friday. 4 p.m. I called up Orchids Intercontinental asking for Mr Venkat Prabhu of Techtronix. Shaky called up Techtronix Delhi and was informed that Mr Venkat Prabhu was still in US. Shaky then called up Orchids to make a reservation for Mr Prabhu for Tuesday afternoon. The receptionist was as accommodative as the one at Q-Eye. Five stars weren't doing great business and regular clients were always welcome, especially since Shaky also enquired about their corporate membership programme and all. Plus Shaky requested her not to ask for any advance from Mr Prabhu, saying a Techtronix executive would be flying in into Bangalore to settle the bill the next day. She agreed. We were ready. The adventure ball had been set in motion once again and was rolling happily. Of course, Solly had a new business card. We all had new names.

The weekend breezed past and Ranju and I went to Madras to visit my cousins. By now, my parents and our extended family knew that I had a girlfriend and the cousins I was visiting really liked her and said she wasn't 'the typical bookish kinds', meaning thereby that she wasn't dumb and vacuous.

I was happy that they approved of her and they kept teasing me that I was a beast who had bagged a beauty. That was both physically and intellectually true, I guess.

Ranju asked me if she'd have to follow drab South Indian traditions and all once we got married and I assured her that we'd lead a very cosmopolitan, very iconoclastic, and very bindaas life.

Later that night, when we walked hand in hand at Marina Beach, I felt as if I'd finally lost my virginity. No, I'm not kidding.

Don't forget that we were living in an era when even talking to the opposite gender on the telephone meant that you were a person of loose morals. There was something about that night that was so very orgasmic. And, when we sat entwined together, munching boiled peanuts and *sundal*, I felt as if we had walked down the aisle and exchanged marital vows with each other on many occasions in numberless past lifetimes. Go ahead, laugh at my primitive *janam-janam-ka-rishta* feeling, but I'm not ashamed to confess that that's exactly how I felt. My heart was so full of love for Ranju that I became afraid that it would burst. She must have felt pretty much the same thing for she hugged me and wept tears of joy. We were choked by waves upon waves of pleasurable emotions and couldn't speak at all. *Talks kill love; silence nurtures it*, Rammy would've said if he'd seen us then. Well, we nurtured our romance for some two hours as the beach sands cavorted with frisky tides; and drove back home rather reluctantly since the scene had gripped us like a giant possessive octopus. That night on the beach with Ranju was so divine, magical and blissful that I almost began believing in the existence of God...

When we returned to the hostel on Sunday evening, Shaky said that Mangy was down with flu and he wondered if we should postpone our plan. Solly would have none of it and I told Shaky that we weren't going to cancel our adventure for anyone. Chopsy and Dusty had chickened out anyway.

Another Tuesday. 4 p.m. Shaky dropped off Solly five km from Orchids Intercontinental and Solly took a taxi. 6 p.m. I called him up and we repeated our earlier convo. 8 p.m. Shaky and I reached Orchids. 8:05 p.m. We three entered Darbar – their bar-cum-restaurant. 10 p.m. We were through. Everything was working like a charm. 10:10 p.m. Solly was about to signal for the bill. Then, the shit began hitting the ceiling.

'Hey Sushil, how are you, man,' said someone, and I turned around.

'Oh...er...hi,' said Solly, to a thirty-something guy who had just exited with his girlfriend from a small Chinese restaurant, an annexe to Darbar, and, quite unfortunately, they were flowing past our table.

'So, what are you doing here, man?' asked the guy.

'Hi Anurag, just chilling out with friends,' said Solly coolly, 'meet Dharam and Vivek...Dharam, this is Anurag...my cousin's college-mate...'

We shook hands and Anurag introduced his girlfriend, a highbrow item called Smita who was so economical with her smile that I thought the government had warned her that they could slap a smile tax on her anytime. She was pretty economical with her clothes too – no wonder most textile companies were in the red, thanks to her and others of her ilk.

'I heard you've made it to Defcoms and all, congratulations!' said Anurag, and turning to Smita, 'imagine Sushil as a doctor and all, he's quite a maverick actually, and studies are greying up your hair prematurely, dude...'

Did I see the passing steward turn back sharply when Anurag said Defcoms?

'Let's ask for the bill,' said Shaky hastily to Solly.

'Okay, guys, take care, nice bumping into you,' said Anurag, and we said our goodbyes to them.

I saw the steward talking to the manager and throwing casual glances at us and the manager smiled and exited the restaurant. Solly signalled to the steward twice but he didn't respond. After about five minutes the manager walked up to our table.

'I hope you enjoyed the dinner, sir,' he said to Solly.

'Yes, it was fantastic,' said Solly.

'Would you like the bill now, or is there something else...?'

'No thanks. Just get me the bill,' said Solly.

'Shit, man,' whispered Shaky as the manager began moving away, 'where the hell did this *kebab-mein-haddi* Anurag guy land from, dude! I hope this hasn't aroused any suspicions...'

'I hope not,' said Solly.

The steward brought us the bill in a glitzy leather folder. Solly slipped in three hundred bucks and said, 'Bill it to my room.'

'I'm afraid, sir,' said the steward politely, 'that won't be possible.'

'Uh, huh – why not?' asked Solly.

'Sir, our policy is different,' said the steward.

'Hey, listen,' said Solly defiantly, 'I am staying here and this is not the first time I'm residing at a five star...'

'Sir, if you wish to, you could speak with the manager, sir, I'll get him for you,' said the steward, and left us gasping for breath.

'What do we do now!' I whispered, clearly alarmed.

'We flow,' said Shaky.

'Meaning?' asked Solly.

'Meaning we flow with our destiny,' said Shaky fatalistically.

My palms became clammy, but Solly and Shaky seemed uber cool. The manager walked up to our table again and said, 'Yes, sir, is there a billing problem?'

'Of course,' said Solly, 'why can't you bill it to my room?'

'I am sorry, sir. As you have been informed, our policy is different. So, you'll have to pay cash.'

I had a desperate desire to visit the loo. The bill was a whopping ₹3,479! We had close to ₹350 between the three of us.

'But this is preposterous – is this the kind of unfriendly service you extend to your valuable customers...?' began Shaky, and I could see two security guys in safari suits entering the restaurant and approaching our table. I was shaking like a malnourished mango leaf caught in a typhoon. Solly glared at me and I trembled even more.

'Sir, please. Let's not create a scene. I can't change company policy. Unless you don't have cash,' said the manager slyly.

'Yes, that's right. I'm waiting for the Techtronix guys to bring me cash tomorrow. You know, I had to urgently fly down from Kashmir...' lied Solly.

'Too bad, sir,' said the manager, and triumphantly whipped out Solly's business card from the inside pocket of his blazer, 'are you really Mr Venkat Prabhu from Techtronix?'

'Yes,' said Solly.

'Or are you from Defcoms?' asked the manager.

'What's that?' asked Shaky.

'Sir, Anurag and Smita, whom you just met, are personal friends. In fact, Smita is distantly related to Lt. Col. Gaitonde, your Training Officer at Defcoms. I spoke to Anurag at the lobby. Of course, discreetly, saying that you folks are regulars here and one of our most valued customers, and Anurag said that your name is Sushil. Isn't it time to own up?' said the manager.

We three stared at the manager like kids caught stealing from the cookie jar. The bastard Anurag had cooked our goose.

'I could call the cops but I don't wish to destroy your career. I have called up Lt. Col. Gaitonde instead. He's asked me to keep it all hush-hush. He'll be here in about thirty minutes. Meanwhile, make yourself comfortable. Would you like another drink?' he said sarcastically.

We remained silent and the manager left the scene. The two security guys positioned themselves close to our table, pretending to inspect the French windows behind the burgundy drapes. I sipped water. Suddenly it tasted horrible. Tons of bile gushed within my system and I felt as nauseous as a pregnant girl getting her first taste of morning sickness. Solly and Shaky were looking like frozen ice statues...

We saw Gattu entering the restaurant after what seemed an eternity. He spoke to the manager and they both approached our table.

'Good evening, sir,' said Solly as we three got up to greet him.

'Good, huhn?' said Gattu wryly. 'You guys are shameless.'

We hung our heads in shame to prove him wrong.

Gattu settled the bill and the room tariff. Eight grand in all! He drove us back to the shopping mall—where we had parked our bikes—in his rattle-trap of a Fiat. He was silent all along the way. It was killing us but we didn't speak either. 'Tomorrow morning, 9 a.m. sharp. Be at my office,' he said, and drove away fuming.

Gattu's table reverberated more than earlier because his fists had gathered more lipids over the months. He gave us a long-winded dressing down and said that he was being compassionate and not spreading the word about our 'foolish five-star feat'.

Rammy and Ranju were livid with us when they heard about the fiasco. In fact, Ranju became quite hysterical that we hadn't taken them into confidence and began wondering if she could trust my 'cheating company for a lifetime'. I kept telling her that the arrogance of youth shouldn't be interpreted as 'prone to fraud and *Shree 420* activities' but I don't think she bought the argument.

Chopsy kept saying 'I told you so' and we nearly beat him up for rubbing it in. Mangy and Dusty chose to remain silent on the subject.

By afternoon a communiqué was impaled on the notice board outside Gattu's office and at the pigeonhole in the hostel:

OFFICE OF THE TRAINING OFFICER, DEFCOMS, BANGALORE

Due to gross negligence, insubordination, lack of attendance, and indiscipline, the following three students are henceforth rusticated for a period of one month w.e.f. 30 July 1986, 0800 HRS. They will vacate their hostel rooms and report to the Training Officer on 29 August 1986, 0900 HRS.

1. Mr Nirmal Shekhar.   (DGN 3105)

2. Mr Sushil Solanki.   (DGN 3118)
3. Mr Hari Iyengar.   (DGN 3016)
Any further breach of discipline will invite rustication for
six months.

Signed,
Lt. Col. Prakash Gaitonde
(On behalf of Dean, Defcoms, Bangalore)

'Zeno Commune is spread over some twenty acres, and run by
Master Zeno, a teacher of Zen Buddhism,' informed the pamphlet,
and promised 'complete relaxation of body, mind, heart and soul'.
Precisely what we all needed but we were wary that it could be just
another pseudo-spiritual business.

I was looking out the window of our apartment and thinking of
Ranju and how much she loved cuckoos. Two lovebirds perched on
the telephone wire were cooing sweet nothings to each other and I
wondered if birds also communicated love and made romantic plans
like we did – in a different kind of language comprising primal
sounds. Maybe. But then, we'd never know.

Shaky, Solly and I had taken a small flat in Indira Nagar on
rent. It was just two km from Zeno Commune, so there were lots of
foreigner babes in white robes to ogle at. We hadn't planned it that
way, and the broker (Chopsy's LGs introduced us to him actually)
had recommended that we stay in Indira Nagar. 'Verry verry good
crowd, deechent houjes and peepole,' he had said.

We had borrowed some money from Chopsy's LGs and they
had given us some cash and a cheque, along with the kind of advice
that you'd expect from middle-aged well-wishers.

We three had called up home and informed about the fiasco as
the communiqué would surely be followed by a registered despatch
from Gattu's office informing our parents of our 'extra-curricular
achievement'.

My dad was cool and said rather sagely that 'if you don't have fun at this age then when will you have fun – after you become a grandpa?' Dad also asked me to collect some money from one of his bank colleagues in Bangalore, saying he'd call him up in a brief while.

Shaky's dad was livid but promised to wire him some money too. Solly's dad had left for Singapore on some official trip, and his mom asked him to be 'careful of good-for-nothing friends'.

Anyway, things were not as bad as they had seemed earlier. In fact, things were pretty good.

We had a flat of our own; plenty of cash; and the company of lots of foreigner babes living in nearby pads. Nearly all of them were disciples of Master Zeno, or the friends of disciples, or whatever. Six or seven of them even lived in the same apartment complex as ours, and we three began wondering if 'rusticated' should actually read 'lusticated' – if at all you'd permit us to coin such a word. (Shaky said the science of coining new words is called neologism or something. He was beginning to sound more and more like Rammy.)

Solly promptly fell in love with a German babe who kept calling him Zolly. Her name was Rita Koertig, and she was sharing a flat with two other girls – a Dutch babe called Sylvia Vogel, and a Brazilian chick called Maria Borges who had actually settled in London (she'd had a whirlwind romance and a brief marriage that lasted some seven months – with a clerk working with some bank in England). They stayed two floors below us, and we became quite chummy with them. It was actually the girls who gave me the pamphlet one afternoon when I happened to say hi to them. That was two days ago.

I must say, it was so easy to talk to foreigner girls without having to pretend that you intended to be the best of friends and all that crap. All these girls were super-looking and had no hang-ups, and if you want to know their brief descriptions in the famed Maniacs' lingo, here goes. Rita and Sylvia were Football Ecstasies and Maria was a Tennis Ball Happiness. Happy?

These girls were so chilled-out, warm, friendly and easy-going, dude, that we actually ended up radiating platonic feelings for them. (Well, at least I did.) If we ever walked into their flat and they were in their undergarments or something, hell didn't break loose. They'd just smile and ask us if we were going to 'molest violently' or 'rape gently'. In fact, we three would become embarrassed and apologise for the intrusion. They had a wonderful sense of humour and were so full of life, love and laughter.

'Why don't you guys visit the commune tomorrow?' asked Rita on a Saturday evening as she began whistling up some omelettes and potato wedges in their flat. 'There will be a good Sunday crowd, you'll have fun.'

'Hey, we aren't interested in meditation-sheditation bullshit,' said Solly.

'Zolly, it's not just about meditation. You can just chill out. Just think of it as a tourist spot,' she said.

'Anyway, what exactly happens there?' I asked.

'Well, lots of things,' said Rita, 'music, dance…'

'Even sex,' said Sylvia, and giggled uncontrollably. '*Tantra.*'

'Don't scare away the virgins, dear,' said Maria laughingly.

'Hey, we aren't inexperienced virgins…' lied Solly.

'Prove it,' said Rita, and laughed.

'What?' asked Solly.

'You heard me – prove it, Zolly,' she said.

'Hey, how can I prove I'm *not* a virgin?' he asked.

'If you *was not*, you'd know how,' said Rita.

Touché.

'Okay, Rita, you win. What do you do in Germany?' I said.

'Me? I work as waitress in restaurant. Earlier, I was clerk with bank. Sometimes, I work as travel guide…' said Rita.

'Ya, she's quite multi-dimensional and all that – she can even burn omelettes in sixteen different ways…' said Sylvia, sniffing the air.

'Oh shit! Omelette…' said Rita, and rushed to the kitchen to douse the faint burning smell wafting from the pan.

'So you guys are going to join the army as doctors…?' asked Maria.

'We don't know – yet undecided,' said Shaky.

'Hmmm…Zeno says any army is for the mindless few who can't live without taking instructions from others…' observed Maria.

'Maybe,' said Solly, 'but you guys take instructions from Zeno, don't you?'

'We guess so,' said Sylvia.

'Then you're as mindless as army guys. Everyone takes instructions from someone. A few admit it; most don't,' said Solly, defending army culture.

'Ya,' I seconded him, 'if we didn't take instructions, we won't learn anything – car driving, swimming, cycling, you name it…'

'Sylvi!' screamed Rita from the kitchen, 'where the hell is the cheese?'

'In the shelf next to the marmalade jar,' said Sylvia.

'How many times I told you to not keep cheese there – direct sunlight will ruin it…' shouted Rita, and emerged from the kitchen holding a huge plate that carried the fluffiest omelettes I'd ever seen. She placed them on the table, along with a bottle of Kissan ketchup, and Maria began feeding bread slices into the Murphy pop-up toaster.

'Sylvi, go and stir the wedges, don't just laze around,' said Maria.

'Shall we be of some help?' asked Shaky.

'Ya – eat all this and compliment me on my cooking skills,' said Rita.

Friendliness destroys lust. Plus all the girls were five or six years older than us, and remained the kind of protective angels that you'd expect 'people on the path' to be. Master Zeno was surely churning out hearts brimming with compassion, love and empathy.

Since our final Univ exams were slated for October, we guys had got a few books with us, and were leafing through them every now and then. Throughout our stay, the girls kept insisting that we ought to visit the commune someday and we kept telling them that we were just not up to it. Perhaps we guys were afraid of getting influenced by spiritual mumbo-jumbo stuff, as Shaky put it. Plus we were definitely not going to get into the mandatory 'white nighties' you had to wear if you wished to enter the commune.

The rest of the Maniacs had not been informed that we were shacking up at a flat coincidentally called New Nirvana. (Wasn't that exactly what Zeno's disciples were attempting?) I had lied to our gang that I was going to Madras to spend time with my cousins; and Shaky and Solly had fibbed that they were going home. If we hadn't lied, our guys would've wasted their time and visited us often and we didn't want to feel guilty about eroding their study time, especially since the make-or-break Univ exams were just round the corner. (Only Chopsy's LGs knew and we had sworn them to secrecy.)

We chilled out at New Nirvana for close to a month and the three girls took excellent care of us. For the first time in our lives we guys discovered that 'a girl who happens to be a friend is a far greater support system than a girlfriend'. Solly's line actually.

Contrary to popular misconceptions regarding foreigner babes, these girls didn't smoke pot or drink alcohol, and (wonder of wonders!) even we remained sober during our entire one-month stay at New Nirvana. The only thing we smoked was tobacco – and that too only when the girls weren't around. Shaky commented that the apartment ought to be renamed 'New Leaf' since that's what our lives had turned out to be.

I I

The Results, the Monarchs, the Rave

Then. September through December 1986.

T HE PRELIMS WERE SLATED FOR THE SECOND WEEK OF
September, and were supposed to be academic indicators for how
you'd fare in the final Univ exams that would begin in the middle of
October. More. The prelims would decide whether you'd be allowed
to take the Univ exams in the first place.

Defcoms had a simple unofficial rule. If your prelims aggregate
and your attendance put together touched 100 %, then you wouldn't
be detained from appearing for the Univ exams. For instance, your
attendance could be a woeful 40 %. So, you needed to score at least
60% in the prelims to be allowed to sit for the Univ exams. (The
Univ guys insisted on 85% attendance – the bastards.)

We had a week to try and score more than 45% in the prelims, so
we kept cramming as much as we could, and were busy memorising
all the mnemonics (memory aids) that Rammy had created. We all
displayed the kind of uncharacteristic diligence that engulfs you when
you are shit-scared of flunking and repeating your papers.

Dusty and Chopsy had prepared enough farras to fill a small
library, but the rest of us were not prepared to take such risks, and
decided to rely on our marijuana-filled grey cells instead.

The prelims were over in just three days (I guess we all did reasonably okay, with Rammy of course saying that he had smoothly and effortlessly cruised through all the vivas), and we all were awaiting the results that were to be declared soon. Along with the detention list, so hold your breath and keep your fingers crossed.

The prelims results were put up at the pigeonhole on a Friday evening, and thankfully, we all had scored more than 45%, and since our attendance was close to 55%, none of the six normal Maniacs were detained.

Rammy scored a mind-blowing 67% in the prelims! His attendance was just 40%. That, after the number of 'proxies' we all had given him, imagine! Anyway, he wasn't detained either. I thought that he was making an academic lifestyle statement and sending a veiled message to the college authorities that attendance norms should be done away with, since 'drab lectures and classes only boosted the ego of the lecturers and did no good in real time'. But of course his message wouldn't make any difference since our authorities were pretty good at mouthing clichés like 'exceptions only prove the rule; and rules can't be changed to benefit exceptions'.

Now, we had a month to try and sail through first MBBS.

All of us had now set up base camp at the adda and we were cramming for at least sixteen to eighteen hours every day. We hardly slept. Rammy knew nearly everything that was to be known and Shaky joked that 'we could throw away all our books and just keep discussing things with the human encyclopaedia'. Rammy just kept listening to his study tapes and referred to some notes every once in a while. He even had time to play chess (with a Univ champ from X-ray batch) and also read Archie and Commando comics! The nerve! But I guess he could do as he pleased as no exam system could block his entry into second MBBS – irrespective of whether he studied or not now.

No, I wasn't jealous of Rammy. Genius should be admired; not envied – especially when the genius was so very helpful.

Rammy had put up a hand-drawn poster at the adda (he had said that mocking the system is the best stress-buster) with Dennis the Menace sulking behind a study table and saying, 'Examinations are formidable affairs even to the best-prepared, for the greatest fool can ask more questions than the wisest man can answer.'

When I mentioned that that was a great line, Rammy said it wasn't his original thought, adding that I should be applauding Charles Caleb Colton instead for having said something so profound. But it was so very true. It's so easy to ask questions and so very difficult to provide answers. I remembered standing at the balcony of our Bombay apartment when I was a child, and how I'd asked dad about the stars and the moon, and how dad had dodged most of my questions. I thought it was quite funny that I still didn't know the answers to the questions I had asked him then; and wondered if our examiners would take sadistic delight in tormenting us (like I had tormented dad) or be paragons of compassion because they had read the Buddha's *Dhammapada* a week before. How I wished all examiners would be diehard Buddhists who had pledged not to cause intellectual injury or academic hurt. But then, wishes are horses that will never fly. Torture was a week away. So, I shrugged off silly thoughts and focussed my mind on the biochemistry flow charts Rammy had put up. Carbohydrate, protein, fatty acid and water metabolism mocked my retention potential and I kept staring at the charts, hoping that all the formulae would, by osmosis, get automatically absorbed into my system. But then, life hardly listens to the weak voice of hope.

Rammy helped us all with the bone sets and the anatomy tutorial stuff, saying that 'teaching is learning twice'. Solly was going crazy and said that the system should be sued for 'youth abuse'. Dusty and Chopsy were busy making thirty farras per day and Shaky joked that they would need to hire a Tempo to cart all the chits to the venue on examination day. Mangy and Solly were given the task of preparing reefers and we smoked joints in metered doses to stay cool and soothe our frayed nerves.

The torture week travelled at supersonic speed. There were no breaks. Anatomy, Physiology, and Biochemistry theory travelled bumper to bumper from Monday through Wednesday. Ditto the vivas. They sliced through Thursday, Friday and Saturday. We didn't know how we survived the continuous KO punches. But survive we did. On Saturday evening, we took our first relaxed breath in months. For 'breath' read 'tonnes of hashish smoke' and you have the right picture. As usual, Chopsy had reserved the best for the last, and thankfully, he had scored some cool Kashmiri stuff this time.

We got up pretty late on Sunday and the girls wanted to go for a movie, and we grabbed a re-run of *Where Eagles Dare* at Rahul. Over dinner (as usual at India Coffee House) we told the guys that we had actually stayed at New Nirvana during our rustication period, and the guys blew their top. They'd have throttled us for having lied to them if we weren't at a public place when we made the confession. Ranju didn't speak with me for close to two hours.

On Monday, we all left for our respective homes to enjoy a well-deserved vacation.

I couldn't enjoy the vacation like I thought I would. My mind was either on Ranju or on the results. Ranju called me long distance from Ahmedabad on Saturday evenings and I began missing her even more.

Rammy, Chopsy, and Solly dropped by on many days and we chilled out watching movies or shopping at Janpath and Palika Bazaar. We went to North Campus once and looked up our old pals from Hans Raj. They all seemed to be unsure about their careers, including Punter and Sidey who were working as apprentices at Marvel Steel Company and earning three thousand solid Cashews per month (they both looked pretty frazzled when they came to meet us late one evening), and I was quite happy that they all were insecure, unhappy, and looked as lost as drifters. Solly was right: we were forging a great career for ourselves and I was joyous that I had a sense of direction finally.

Thankfully, the vacation was about to end soon, and we were all eager to return to Bangalore as the suspense regarding our impending results was killing us.

Taking an exam is just like proposing to a girl. You hate it when she dilly-dallies, and hems and haws, when all you want to hear is a firm yes or no. You pop the question and you want a quick response, either positive or negative. Exams are no different. You toss off some answers and you want a swift result, either heart-warming or heart-numbing. Suspense can be as irritating as the itch at the roof of your palate where your tongue can't reach to scratch it out.

We had called up the Defcoms office and were told that the results would be announced in three days. We took the next available train out of Delhi.

They say some animals see life mostly in black and white. My vision was no different that evening. Life was colourless. The results had been announced an hour ago. The Maniacs had gathered at the new Insti. Haluji was tut-tutting, handing out ginger tea and biscuits, and saying that life is a struggle anyway. Rammy had flunked! Imagine, Rammy of all people! Anatomy theory, actually. Shaky and Dusty had passed! The rest of us had flunked an assortment of theories and vivas. Tell you the truth, we weren't sad about *our* results. We were happy to have cleared at least a few. But when we thought about Rammy, and the efforts he had put in, and the kind of stuff he knew, and the way he had helped us all, our collective mood was getting sucked into a depressive void.

'What the hell, man,' screamed Dusty, 'I can't believe it! How can Master Nevero flunk! Shit! And to think *I* have made it!'

Shaky was inconsolable. 'I don't deserve to pass, dude, in fact I guess I've only passed because of *your* coaching skills,' he said, throwing his trembling arm around Rammy.

'It's okay, Shaky, happens – only goes to prove that life doesn't come with a guarantee card,' said Rammy coolly, consoling Shaky. (Shouldn't it have been the other way round?)

'The system sucks, man,' said Solly, 'surely you'll get through after reval.' (Reval = Short for reevaluation. For a small outlay, the Univ guys would pretend to reassess your answer sheet, and say sorry a month later.)

'Don't bet on it,' said Rammy. 'Statistics show that only 0.2% lucky bastards have ever got through after reval.'

'Hey, don't lose hope, dude,' said Mangy, 'you better apply for reval.'

'Being realistic is far more intelligent than being optimistic,' said Rammy. 'And who knows, maybe the universe has a hidden purpose...'

'Fuck your philosophy,' said Chopsy, 'balls to the system, man, even *I* have cleared Anat theory...'

'Chopsy, brooding never helps. Let's put all this past us, chill out, and get ready for the April repeat, okay?' said Rammy.

'How can you be so cool, dude?' wondered Solly.

'What do you expect me to do?' said Rammy. 'One should take life as it comes, try one's best, and let things unfold as they will. No point losing one's cool over temporary events. And, by the way, it's not the end of the world, Solly.'

'Okay, forget it,' said Solly, 'as Rammy says, let's just chill. Shall we grab a movie or smoke...?'

'Junk the movie, let Shaky and Dusty treat us to dinner,' I said.

'Ya, let's celebrate their success, guys!' said Rammy generously.

◇

Anyway, we'd now be called the Monarchs. If you flunked once at Defcoms and you got the 'full six months' that Dandy was always predicting (may a billion blistering barnacles infest his black tongue, as Captain Haddock would have said), then you were called the Monarch batch. If you flunked once more, then you became a Maharaja. They said Monarchs had more fun than the regulars, and we weren't going to change time-honoured tradition.

After about a week of mourning, we were all apparently back to normal, and ready to paint the town red. Mangy had to leave by afternoon to meet his folks who were transiting through Madras en route to Tirupati. He was pretty cheesed off that they had forced him to seek Lord Vishnu's blessings and asked him to accompany them on the pilgrimage, since he had flunked so miserably.

Dusty and Chopsy had, as usual, decided to shack up with Chopsy's LGs for a few days. Ranju and Alka were only expected a week later, and we weren't too keen to stay on at the hostel. We needed a change, to change the backdrop of our fatigued minds, and Solly suggested that we meet up with Rita and gang at what we now began calling the 'Zeno zone'. Even Rammy seemed to be interested in going to Indira Nagar, as he was pretty clued-up regarding Zen philosophy and all the spiritual bullshit stuff. So, we decided to pay the girls a surprise visit on a Tuesday morning. We carried Black Forest pastries (their favourite) sourced from a four star hotel to celebrate the glad news that Shaky had cleared.

We parked our bikes outside New Nirvana and ascended the stairs.

'Wow, great crowd, man!' said Mangy, rather loudly. He had decided to chill out for a while before embarking on the 'boring pilgrimage', and he ogled wide-eyed at a few foreigner babes surfing along the road in silky white robes. 'Wish I had been rusticated along with you guys!'

'Shut up,' said Shaky, 'we have a great reputation here, don't destroy it.'

Solly rapped on their door (which now carried a small mug shot of a bearded Zeno deep in meditation) and Rita opened it after some five minutes. She looked positively zonked – surely she'd had a late night and very little sleep.

'Surprise!' said Solly smilingly.

'Zoolllllyyyy!' she screamed, wiping the sleep from her tired eyes, and hugged him hard. 'Where have you guys been?'

Maria and Sylvia came rushing from their rooms, hearing his name, and embraced Shaky and me. The girls looked as tired and sapped as Rita.

'Welcome, welcome,' said Rita, inviting us all in, and Mangy looked at the girls as if they were species from an altogether different dimension. Or perhaps his hormones were getting envious that we were being hugged by two Ecstasies and a Happiness early in the morning. Rammy didn't betray any expression or emotion. So very typical.

'Weren't we wondering where these guys had vanished off to only yesterday evening?' Sylvia said to Maria.

'Ya,' said Maria, and to me, 'so how was your exams and all?'

'Flunked,' I said, 'though Shaky has passed…'

'Congrats, Shaky,' said Rita, 'and what about Zolly…'

'Ditto as Hucky,' he said.

'Never mind,' said Rita, wrapping him up again, 'better luck next time.'

'So this is the famous Maniacs gang…' said Maria, throwing a wide smile at Mangy and Rammy.

I introduced them and asked the girls to dig into the Black Forest pastries. Sylvia said it would have been more apt if we'd brought it the previous day, as they'd been celebrating Zeno's birthday anniversary late into the night.

No wonder their eyes were bleary and their faces all puffed up. But that only made them look more human and beautiful. I said sorry that we had barged in like that, and Maria slapped my wrist asking me not to sound 'so idiotically formal'.

Rammy began leafing through a glitzy pamphlet from the commune and Rita was happy that someone seemed to be interested in Master Zeno and his mystical work and all. She brought him lots of books and magazines on Zeno and his philosophy, and Rammy began reading them as if he were sitting at a public library. After about five minutes, he became totally oblivious to our presence, and was lost in the mumbo-jumbo stuff. The bookish boor!

'But why is Shaky looking out of sorts – not well, Shaky?' enquired Sylvia.

'Arre, he is sad that Rammy has flunked. Rammy is our guru and an encyclopaedia – I don't think we have got over the fact that...' I said.

'Ya,' said Solly, 'he knows so much, and he just kept studying so hard...'

'I thought as much, he looks the studious types,' said Maria, throwing a wink in Rammy's direction, 'he's got down to studying again.'

Rammy didn't look up from a book titled *Life's a Strange Game: Winners Lose, Losers Win* and Rita shushed us and asked us not to disturb him. Was she dreaming of attracting a potential disciple into the commune?

Rita made coffee and berated Sylvia for not stocking up bread and eggs. We offered to treat them to a South Indian breakfast of idli and *vada sambar* at the nearby Udipi joint but the girls said they were too tired to step out. So, the five of us trooped down to the local grocer's to pick up the stuff and also give them some private time to freshen themselves up.

After we returned, Rita rustled up the fluffiest cheese omelettes in the world (how consistent she was with that) and we played cards and Scrabble for a while. Post pasta lunch and siesta, Maria woke us all up and poured gallons of herbal tea into ceramic bowls and asked us to sip it the 'Zen way'.

Mangy left saying he was getting late, and Maria said that all of us could go to a rave party in the evening which was being organised by some of her 'boho friends from Brazil' at a distant farmhouse on the Bangalore-Madras highway. Shaky said he was too tried to drive down; Rammy was naturally uninterested; but Solly and I were game. Rita decided to stay back to give company to Shaky and Rammy, so we escorted Sylvia and Maria to the venue at about 8 p.m. It took us a good hour and a half to reach the sprawling farmhouse and dissolve into the psychedelic world of trance music at the rave party. I imbibed so much alcohol and LSD that the world looked like a rainbow for close to a week after that.

12

The Dare, Proxy Trouble, Inquiry, Pure Blackmail

Then. June through November 1987.

THE NEW INSTI WAS FULL OF CELEBRATING MONARCHS. YES, we all had cleared first MBBS in the second attempt. Say congrats! Almost everyone was smashed; and we were stoned. That's when the argument began.

Like any typical hostel, Defcoms had many gangs.

The Death Riders gang, arch rivals of the Maniacs, was full of Dutch courage. We called those eight guys *Yamadhoots* because they all rode Yamaha 350 bikes. Perhaps they usually thought that they were riding fighter jets, for they would keep vroom-vrooming their engines to create mini-earthquakes and dust storms wherever they went. Now, they were practising their pet hobby: Maniacs-bashing. They were flavouring their tirade with enough regional abuses to make a fish market blush. So, either this was going to evolve into a full-fledged drunken brawl or into a full-throated stoned scuffle. (All inter-gang fights could be traced back to liquor/drugs.)

'Ignore them, Rammy, let's go,' I said, nudging him.

'Ya, ya, buzz off, you cowards,' said Death Rider # 3.

'What's your definition of bravery, Montu?' asked Rammy of Death Rider # 1. 'Getting sloshed, and stinking like a gutter, and hurling racist abuses?'

'Okay, if you are *that* brave, prove it,' said Death Rider # 2.

'Done. Name the task,' challenged Rammy.

'You'll chicken out, forget it, even we three couldn't manage to do it together,' said Death Rider # 3. 'What Death Riders can't do, nobody can do.'

'Try me,' said Rammy.

An eerie silence bathed the Christian graveyard that was situated three km from the hostel. Occasionally, the silence was broken by the chirrups of insomniac crickets. A few bats turned on their sonar navigation gear and practised midnight sorties. It was pitch dark. The distant tombstones glistened ever so slightly under the extremely slender slice of a just-born moon covered by dense clouds. It seemed as if a few ghosts would arise anytime for their nocturnal walks. All of which made us infinitely nervous.

An electric wave of cold fear rippled down my spine. Even the Death Riders were feeling uncomfortable. Their false sense of bravado seemed to have deserted them. The graveyard was really huge. We were standing a safe distance from the rickety wooden gate. There was no guard in sight. There were no road lights. There were no bike lights either. (The Death Riders had prohibited us from switching on the headlights of our bikes saying it would boost Rammy's confidence.)

The dare was simple. Rammy had to walk two hundred metres into the heart-stopping darkness, reach the end of the graveyard, stay there for some five minutes, and try to return intact if he survived the journey. And all this just to prove that the Maniacs weren't cowards.

Perhaps the Death Riders were right after all, for my heart was thumping like a hysterical drum. I whispered to Rammy that we could call off the challenge even now. He asked me to shut up. Shaky passed a pocket torch to Rammy and the Death Riders objected saying no luminous accessories were allowed.

'Fair enough, anyway I wouldn't need a torch. This is going to be fun. Okay, you guys wait here, while I take a walk and befriend a few ghosts. I'm sure they'll be more intellectually evolved than you cretins,' said Rammy, and began walking into the graveyard as if he were taking a stroll down the beach.

'No, no, wait, Rammy – let him take the torch, guys,' said the intelligent Death Rider # 2. 'Otherwise how will he indicate that he has reached the far end of the grave? It's so dark anyway. What if he goes just ten or twenty feet and returns after fifteen minutes? And Rammy, you lose if you light the torch midway, okay? When you reach the far end, *then* blink it thrice. And also sit on the far wall.'

'Ok,' said Rammy, and Shaky passed him the torch.

Rammy must have gone some thirty feet or so when we lost sight of him. I felt as if I'd fall apart any moment. Mangy and Shaky had both broken into a cold sweat. The rest of the Maniacs were not with us, but I was sure they would've felt pretty much the same emotions. The Death Riders began whispering among themselves that they hoped nothing crazy would happen to Rammy as we could all get into trouble for 'abetment to suicide'. I thought again of the earlier rustication notice and shuddered a secret shudder. One minute.

Everyone was trying to put on a brave front. Nobody was succeeding. Our eyes were trained on our wrists. Raw fear slows down the pace of time. We kept consulting the radium dials of our watches every thirty seconds or so. It didn't help. The collective anxiety was so palpable and fragile that you could have cut it with a dull feather. I wished we'd prevented Rammy from getting involved in this mad dare. Two minutes.

I just kept staring and staring into the dark distance and prayed to unseen forces to protect Rammy from all harm. We were as silent as wax statues at Tussauds. Five minutes.

Was it two owls sitting on the tree or was it two arboreal ghosts wearing yellow optical enhancers? Was I getting fear fever? I felt my neck with the back of my hand. Cold as frozen food. Seven minutes.

Shaky and Mangy were shuffling and transferring their nervous weight from one foot to the other. I took deep breaths and rubbed my palms to generate some heat to neutralise the psychological cold wave that had gripped me. Nine minutes.

The Death Riders began tittering among themselves. More bats. More sorties. Perhaps Rammy's walk had energised them. Ten minutes.

Then we stepped back alarmed as a weird bodiless face became aglow at the far end. Torch light from the distance! Three blinks! Then we realised that Rammy was shining the torchlight on his face to prove that he was sitting on the far wall.

We cheered! The Maniacs back-thumped each other. The Death Riders looked defeated. My heartbeat was returning to normal. If Rammy had won half the battle, you could be sure he'd win the entire war.

'You cowards,' said Mangy to the Death Riders, 'see he's made it!'

'Ya,' said Shaky, 'he has done alone what you three couldn't do together last week. That proves all Maniacs are brave.'

But I felt Shaky's logic was skewed. This only proved that Rammy was brave. This didn't prove that all Maniacs were brave. Please examine the following, and you don't need to be a postgraduate student of logic to understand how stupid the Death Riders were to accept what Shaky said.

a) Rammy is brave.

b) Rammy is a Maniac.

c) Hence, *all* Maniacs are brave.

(Correct logic: *Some* Maniacs are brave. Even more correct logic: *At least one* Maniac is brave.)

Examine another to understand how faulty Shaky's line of reasoning was.

a) Hucky is a doctor.

b) Hucky is a man.

c) Hence, *all* men are doctors.

(Correct logic: *Some* men are doctors. Even more correct logic: *At least one* man is a doctor.)

But why get into syllogisms now? It was time to cream the brash, foul-mouthed Death Riders gang. Who cared if we did it illogically? At least the Maniacs and their fans back at the hostel would have something to cheer about. The Death Riders were always getting on our case anyway. Fifteen minutes. Rammy should be back any moment now.

Tell you the truth, I'd been a nervous wreck just minutes ago. I'd felt this kind of fear only once – when a caged tiger had leapt at me at the Delhi zoo, and I must have been about nine-years-old at that time.

Call me a coward (why be angry about the truth?) but I wouldn't have ventured into this eerie graveyard even if you'd given me a billion dollars. What use is a billion dollars to a man dying of cardiac arrest? Seventeen minutes had passed by.

'*Bachao, bachao!*' screamed a high-pitched voice and thundered towards us from behind the rickety gate. It was wrapped in a black shroud and a black monkey cap and it went and gathered Death Rider # 1 in its arms.

'*Eaaaaarrrrrgggggghhhhhhhhh!*' screamed Death Rider # 1, and we all ran.

'Gotcha! You gruds!' shouted Rammy from behind us, and laughed loudly.

'You bastard!' I said, running towards him, and hugged him.

'You sure scared us, dude!' said Shaky. 'Where did you get the shroud?'

'It was lying next to the wall, along with the cap. Perhaps belongs to the guard,' explained Rammy as he threw both on the rickety gate.

'Okay, so you did it. Good,' said Death Rider # 2, trying to sound gracious and all.

'Get the champagne tomorrow – as promised,' said Rammy to him.

'Good show, Rammy,' I said as he pillion-rode me back to the hostel. 'You are fearless, dude!'

'Hucks, tell you the truth, I was uber-scared. I just kept chanting Hanuman Chalisa all the way,' he said candidly.

'Really?' I asked, thoroughly surprised.

'Nobody can be 100% fearless, Hucks. Courage doesn't mean *absence* of fear. Courage means *mastery* over fear.'

'Your line?'

'I don't know. I've read so much that I get all mixed-up. Maybe it's original. Maybe not. I think I read it somewhere. Does it matter?'

'No,' I said, my admiration for him increasing because of his unabashed candour.

◇

Fourth term was the most chilled-out time we ever had. Hardly anyone attended classes. So, 'proxies' were the norm. The trouble began on a Tuesday morning. (Funny that Tuesdays were turning out to be so eventful for us Maniacs – 'I should get that numerologically assessed sometime', I told myself a day later.)

We had gone to the Chest and Heart Institute next to the Army Hospital to attend some clinics. Mangy gave a 'proxy' for Rammy at the end of the lecture, and Shilpa objected. The lecturer hauled up Mangy and marked him absent too. We were returning to the hostel by the college bus when Solly confronted Shilpa.

'Why on earth did you do that, Shilpa?' he asked.

'Why? Are we fools to attend? – and someone can sit in the hostel and easily get attendance…?' she said.

'What's *your* problem? It's none of *your business*,' said Solly.

He was right. How the hell did it matter to her? That was the chief problem with petty-minded folks. They wouldn't help you – and would even prevent others from helping you. (This is a disease that's not going to vanish from existence in a hurry; unless such petty-minded folks become extinct. It would be an existential boon if that happens. Let's keep praying.)

'*It is* my business,' she said.

'Fuck you,' said Solly. 'On second thoughts, who'd want to fuck a bitch like you? Not even a sex-starved mongrel would want to fuck you.'

'Don't abuse, *you bastard*,' she said, contradicting herself.

Then Solly slapped her real hard. She burst into copious tears and all the other girls swung to her support. Solly said that he'd screw their trips; and Mangy and I had to hold him back to prevent mass rape. That wouldn't have looked good on Solly's resume, right? (Imagine your resume saying 'mass rape and molestation' against co-curricular.) Solly was shaking like an earthquake.

By afternoon, Gattu had hauled up Solly, and promised him a six-month rustication for having breached discipline again. When we reached the adda, Rammy told us that he'd find a way to bail out Solly. We had our doubts. This was a cut-and-dried case of assault and battery.

After lunch, Rammy and I went for the Microbiology practicals. Shilpa was sitting across the table (her left cheek was still red) and Rammy and I were discussing that girls seemed to have no batch spirit. Tara poked her nose into our convo and passed some catty comments.

'Excuse me,' said Rammy, 'this is a private conversation happening. You aren't included.'

'I have a right to…' she began.

'Tara, you have a right to join a circus as a clown – you'd do a good job of it,' said Rammy.

'Don't talk to me like that,' she said, 'you don't know what I can do…' she threatened.

'Shut up, you grud! What can you do? You can go and wail to your idiotic boyfriends from Wonder batch – that's all you can do,' said Rammy.

Tara immediately got up and left the class, pretending to have developed a sudden headache. After the practicals ended at 4 p.m., Rammy suggested that we go to the college canteen for tea.

'I think Lokesh will be waiting for me there,' said Rammy.

Lokesh Saha was Tara's boyfriend from Wonder batch. He had four other cronies and they all used to hang out together on most days, along with Tara. Surely she'd go and wear her heart on her sleeve and they'd get provoked. We were munching samosas and sipping tea. If Rammy's predictions ever went off target, you could consider *that* an event as rare as a cosmic shower. Was Rammy subconsciously willing the future to happen as he desired? After about five minutes, Lokesh walked up to our table.

'We need to talk,' he said to Rammy.

'Talk,' said Rammy tersely.

'Come outside,' said Lokesh.

'Okay,' said Rammy, and they both exited the canteen. Rammy asked me to stay put, and I saw Tara plonking herself at the last table. I looked out the window and Rammy and Lokesh were speaking animatedly with each other. After a brief while, Lokesh finger-pointed Rammy, and Rammy returned the favour with some uncharacteristic fist-clenching stuff, said something to him, and joined me. Lokesh went and sat with Tara.

'What was the jerk saying?' I asked.

'Saala idiot. He asked me to apologise to her or face the consequences.'

'What did you tell him? Tell me your exact words.'

'I said back off or I'll bash you up in front of her, right here, and you'll feel raped, you eunuch. If you're man enough, fight now, and don't get your wimpy gang later.'

'Good show. Let's go now and check up on Solly.'

'This won't end here, Hucks. We'll be at the OAT in the evening. I guess this grud will bring his cronies then.' (OAT = Open Air Theatre.)

'Cool. We'll be ready for them.'

'Don't tell anyone about this.'

'Okay.'

Defcoms screened four movies every week at the OAT in the evenings. Mondays and Tuesdays were reserved for Hindi movies. Thursdays and Fridays were reserved for English flicks. We used to have lots of fun passing juicy comments and ribbing quite a few hamming actors and actresses. (They'd have died of shame if they'd heard us.) But ribbing the audience was more fun. Once, we pulled a fast one on a Wonder batcher called Sajjan Singh who'd sat next to us on a Thursday.

Rammy said this guy was always trying to act hep, pretending to follow all the heavily-accented American dialogues and stuff (when we couldn't collectively grab more than 60% of what most Hollywood actors and actresses were saying). Rammy asked us to giggle and laugh at some inconsequential dialogues, so we giggled and laughed every now and then, as if it were a laugh-a-minute conversational comedy, and Sajjan did the same to keep pace, and laughed whenever we did, lest we think that he couldn't understand the dialogues, and we kept howling at his stupidity throughout the movie.

When the movie ended, Rammy told him that we were just pulling his leg; that we couldn't understand half the dialogues being said on screen; that there had been nothing to laugh about actually; and Sajjan got pretty cheesed off with us for having caught him pretending, and never sat with us after that evening. Sajjan was one of Lokesh's sidekicks and Rammy was sure that he'd be eager to get even with him.

The Maniacs had dispersed for the evening, and Rammy and I were the only ones from our gang at the OAT at 7 p.m. I think they were playing a come-insult-my-intelligence Hindi movie called *Kaala King Kobra*. Halfway into the movie, a scrawny Wonder batcher called Pratap tapped Rammy from behind, saying some guys were waiting outside to meet him.

'The gruds have come, Hucks,' said Rammy.

'I'll come with you,' I said.

'No, you stay here. Come out after two minutes. And, rev up the bike and keep it ready for a quick getaway,' he said.

Surely, Rammy had chalked out a plan.

When I exited after two minutes and revved up the bike, I saw Rammy breaking free from Lokesh and his cronies who'd *gheraoed* him.

'I'll get you *hijras* fucked! Just wait and watch, you bastards!' screamed Rammy, and they began running after him, and I manoeuvred the bike expertly, reached him in time as he ran along the road, and he jumped onto the backseat, and we staged an escape from the barbaric bunch with the kind of clinical precision that would've done professional bank robbers proud. A few guys exiting the OAT had witnessed the drama unfolding in real time. (*Kaala King Kobra* was passé and lacklustre. There was more action happening in real life.) I turned back to see that Lokesh and gang were also revving up their bikes and scooting away from the spot, obviously to avoid being recognised by the witnesses.

'Drive to the Dean's house,' said Rammy coolly.

I parked the bike outside the General's house. The security guard asked us the purpose of our visit. We gave him our DGNs (Defcoms

Graduate Numbers) and our names, and said we wished to speak with the General immediately.

Lilting strains of Sai Baba *bhajans* were coming from the General's living room. We waited for about three minutes. The security guard returned and said rather harshly that the General had asked us to meet him at the Dean's office tomorrow, as he was busy now.

'Okay, it's time to jolt the General,' said Rammy.

'What do you want to do now?' I asked.

'Let's go to the police chowky,' he said.

'Police *chowky*? What for?' I asked, thoroughly surprised.

'To order Mysore *masala dosa* and vada sambar,' he said, majorly irritated by my query.

So we went to the police chowky close to the hostel and lodged an FIR against Lokesh Saha and his four cronies.

When we returned to the adda, all the other Maniacs, along with many Yankee batchers and X-ray batchers had gathered there. They were waiting for us, ready with hockey sticks and all.

'What the hell are you guys planning, you idiots...?' said Rammy.

'We'll *band bajao* their trips, the bastards, how dare they touch you!' screamed Solly.

'Tora! Tora! Tora!' yelled Dusty.

'Ya, Rammy,' said an X-ray batcher, 'they ought to be taught a lesson.'

'Hey, let's not do any planning here – word will spread around. Let's go to the proximal raydi,' said Shaky.

'Don't be childish, Chittu,' said Rammy to the X-ray batcher as our revenge-thirsty gang swaggered towards the raydi.

'You mean we'll let them get away with it?' asked Chopsy.

'Listen, guys, we are thirty-strong now. They are five. We can cream them. No problem. But what will happen *after* that? All of us will get rusticated,' said Rammy.

'Point,' said Mangy.

'I'm just coming from the Dean's house, he refused to meet me, so I've lodged an FIR,' said Rammy.

'So? Hey, there's a small bruise on your temple, man,' said Solly.

'That's okay,' said Rammy, 'Lokesh socked one on me…'

'Listen, Rammy, I agree about us not doing anything directly – but you better make this a medico-legal case,' said Chittu.

'Ya, Rammy,' suggested another X-ray batcher, 'just start retching in the MI room, and they'll have to place you under observation for 24 hours suspecting brain injury…' (MI room = Medical Inspection room.)

'Hey, that's a neat idea,' said Dusty, 'that'll rattle Tara's slaves.'

'Ya,' said Chittu, 'and Hucky, you go with him…'

'But how will he vomit in the MI room?' I asked.

'Arre, stupid, take lot of salt with you, and Rammy, you eat it two minutes before you enter the MI room,' said Chittu.

Rammy liked the idea and promptly vomited in the MI room. Two seniors from Victory batch were stationed there on MI duty, and they knew Rammy from fresher term, so they happily made out a medico-legal case against Lokesh and gang. Rammy was sent for a head X-ray and placed under twenty-four-hour observation at the Command Hospital ICU.

We spread the word in the hostel that Rammy was critically wounded and the docs were suspecting internal cerebral haemorrhage.

I gathered that Lokesh and gang began shitting bricks when they heard that. Good.

I was acting as Rammy's minder. Gattu came to meet Rammy at 11 p.m. and promised strict action against the 'mafia dons'. Rammy told him that if he didn't take decisive action, then he'd move the court, as he'd already complained to the cops.

The cops came to the hostel for their routine enquiry in the morning but Lokesh and gang had vanished by then.

When I went back to look up Rammy at the ICU, Tongu of Wonder batch had come to meet him. Tongu threatened him by saying that Froster of Uniform batch had asked him to withdraw the FIR, adding that otherwise they'd make his life miserable at the hostel. Rammy retorted by saying that now Froster and Tongu would also be dragged to the court for 'criminal intimidation'. I could see that Rammy was really taking the bull by its horns and he meant business. Good.

By afternoon, Froster came to meet Rammy, enquired after his health, and said that there had been a miscommunication.

'I'm with you Rammy, all the way,' said Froster. Obviously Rammy's counter-threat had worked.

Thursday morning. Rammy was discharged. The Dean sent word that he wished to meet us both. When we entered his room, General Thakur was pacing his lair, smoking chocolate-flavoured tobacco from an expensive-looking pipe. The aroma and smoke smelled divine and inviting; so I greedily and shamelessly passive-inhaled quite a bit of it.

'Yes, gentlemen, sit down,' said the General.

'It's okay, sir,' said Rammy, and we kept standing.

'So why did you lodge an FIR and all? What are we here for, Ramakrishna?' asked the General.

'Sir, we had come to your house just five minutes after the incident. But we were shown the door. The gate actually, in our case,' said Rammy.

'Oh, I thought that—what's the guy?—ya, I thought that you were Sushil Solanki, and that you'd slapped that Shilpa girl in the morning. I didn't know it was you,' said the General.

'I am sorry that you felt I was someone else, sir. However, you could still have had the basic courtesy of meeting a student who's come to meet you, sir,' said Rammy.

I stiffened. Nobody spoke to a General that way. Evidently, the General wasn't used to being reprimanded thus either. He took a few deep drags of the burning tobacco, struck a matchstick and created a mini-inferno in his pipe. Was it symbolic of his seething rage?

'Hmmm,' said the General. 'So what's your plan?'

'None whatsoever,' said Rammy. 'I'll play it by ear.'

'I hear you're threatening legal action,' said General Thakur.

'Informing, sir, not threatening, there's a world of difference...'

'Well, this could affect *your* career, you know...'

'I'm not going to join the army, sir.'

'What?'

'You heard me. I'm not going to join the army. You guys are protecting Lokesh because his father is a Brigadier. I know it. And, I come from a civilian background. Do you seriously think I'm going to join such a biased group? Never. So, don't give me *bullshit* about this affecting my career and all, sir,' said Rammy.

'Language, my dear friend,' warned the General.

'Language reflects our state of mind, sir. And right now, my state of mind is *pretty fucked*. And, I'm not sorry about my language, so I won't be apologetic about it. You should be pulling them up, but you're talking as if *I'm* the culprit. I think you've forgotten that I'm the *victim* here. And, since I know that you'll bullshit me, I'll drag them to court. They aren't getting away with this. Any senior at Defcoms thinks it's his fundamental right to rag or bash up a junior. I haven't ragged a single junior till date, and I never will. Neither will I gang up against juniors. Are you going to initiate action against them? Or are you going to let them go scot-free because Lokesh's dad, *Brigadier Saha*, was your junior at Mahatma Gandhi Medical College?'

'How do you know about Brigadier Saha and me...?'

'Research, sir – do a complete background check before you engage an adversary. It's a cardinal rule of engagement, sir.'

'I'm not your adversary...'

'Prove it, sir.'

'How?'

'Rusticate Lokesh and gang for six months. They deserve it.'

'But the Court of Inquiry will decide that...'

'C'mon, sir, I'm not green behind the ears, the COI is just a formality. The buck stops at *your* office. They'll only recommend the extent of punitive action. It is up to you to take a decision. I know the drill, sir.'

'Okay, if I rusticate them for two months, then will you withdraw the FIR?'

'Six months.'

'But Ramakrishna, they're in their final term. We're in July. Six months would mean they will fall back in their career...'

'That's their problem, sir, not mine.'

'You're taking a rigid stance...'

'And you're taking a conveniently flexible stance to benefit them.'

'Let me see what I can...'

'No, sir, you don't call the shots here. *I do.* Plus there will be absolutely no punishment for Sushil Solanki...'

'That's not possible! He slapped a girl, dammit!'

'She *deserved* it. He slapped her *after* she called him a bastard. *After* Manjeet Ahuja marked my proxy at CHI and she interfered...'

'How can you justify proxies?'

'Sir, have you never given or got proxies during *your* college days?'

'Hmmmm...well...'

'Thanks for admitting it, sir. Plus the attendance norms are stupid. I nearly topped in prelims with just 40% attendance. Okay, I'm willing to look at things your way. Two months rustication to Lokesh and gang, as you say. Plus slap a five hundred bucks fine on each of them. Sushil Solanki gets nearly totally exonerated. We're seven guys in our gang. We'll not be detained in our second MBBS Univ exams irrespective of *our attendance* – assuming of course that you're still in office when the great detention list is put up. Shilpa gets fined hundred bucks. Sushil gets fined twenty bucks. Tara gets rusticated for one month for having instigated the guys against me. Plus she gets fined two hundred bucks. I get fined ten bucks for having called Tara a grud. I'll write down all this for you.'

'What's grud?'

'It means dense, stupid, despicable moron, sir.'

'And if I don't do as you say...?'

'Sir, he has already engaged a criminal lawyer, Shri Venkatesh Raju, who practises in the High Court and specialises in medico-legal cases,' I lied.

'You've no choice in the matter, sir. If I drag them to court, and drag them into a criminal suit, then they can kiss their career goodbye. You better decide to flow with what I'm saying if you wish to save their skin, and you better decide it fast, sir,' added Rammy.

'Ramakrishna, this is pure blackmail!'

'It is, I accept. And, by the way, even you guys blackmail us. Maintain 85% attendance or we'll detain you. That's also *pure blackmail*. So, I'm merely returning the favour. Plus assaulters deserve worse treatment actually. But perhaps I'm in a forgiving mood. So, what's your decision, sir?'

'Hmmm...you're driving a pretty hard bargain...'

'Sir, this is a simple matter, let's not waste time here. Do *exactly* as I say and I'll withdraw the FIR, it's that simple. Do I have your word of honour on this?'

'Okay, done.'

'Good day, sir!'

◇

The Court of Inquiry lasted two days. It was headed by a Brigadier, who had two Colonels as his assistants. Their task was to get to the bottom of the matter. They quizzed all those who were involved in the 'proxy incident' that began on Tuesday morning. Then they grilled Lokesh and his cronies.

Rammy asked us to just speak the truth, and we did. Of course, we didn't mention about Rammy eating salt to vomit in the MI room and all. That comes under 'suppression of facts', not under 'wilfully speaking lies'; so our conscience was clear. Just kidding – we would have lied through our teeth to get even with Lokesh and gang, but there was no need to. The truth was in our favour – that's the reason we spoke it, hah!

After the farce was over, the board outside the Dean's office and at the hostel pigeonhole carried a huge notice.

OFFICE OF THE DEAN, DEFCOMS, BANGALORE

The following students are hereby rusticated for a period of two months w.e.f. 18 July 1987, 0800 HRS, for assaulting Mr Ramakrishna Iyer (DGN 3017) on 14 July 1987, 2010 HRS, outside the Open Air Theatre. They will vacate their hostel rooms and report to the Dean on 17 September 1987, 0930 HRS. They are also each fined Rs five hundred only for their gross misdemeanour.

1. Mr Lokesh Saha   (DGN 2853)
2. Mr Ankit Thapar   (DGN 2869)
3. Mr Sajjan Singh   (DGN 2858)
4. Mr Peter D'Costa   (DGN 2764)
5. Mr Karan Patel   (DGN 2801)

The following student is hereby rusticated for a period of one month w.e.f. 18 July 1987, 0800 HRS, for instigating the said assault. She will vacate her hostel room and report to the Dean on 17 August 1987, 0945 HRS. She is fined Rs two hundred only for her gross misdemeanour.

1. Ms Tara Kulkarni   (DGN 3024)

The following student is fined Rs one hundred only for misbehaving with Mr. Sushil Solanki.

1. Ms Shilpa Kichloo   (DGN 3021)

The following student is fined Rs twenty only for misbehaving with Ms Shilpa Kichloo.

1. Mr Sushil Solanki   (DGN 3118)

The following student is fined Rs ten only for misbehaving with Ms Tara Kulkarni.

1. Mr Ramakrishna Iyer   (DGN 3017)

Failure to comply with the above order will result in automatic rustication for a further period of six months.
Signed
Maj. Gen. Surinder Thakur

◇

Rammy had indeed bailed out Solly (as he'd said he would) and also ensured that the Maniacs wouldn't be detained in second MBBS. The noose had tightened around Lokesh and gang. Serves them right, I thought. After that day, no senior could muster enough guts to bash up any junior at Defcoms. Now everyone knew that you could lodge an FIR in case someone behaved like a Neanderthal. Rammy had shown the way. He had created a safer atmosphere for all students. And, we celebrated our victory with a stag night-out at Leopard Spot.

13

Bluff Master, Mess Committee, Cryptic, Gattu's Logic

Then. January through August 1988.

RAMMY WISHED TO MEET MASTER ZENO AND RITA WAS QUITE happy about it. Rammy and I were at New Nirvana, looking at the white nighties they had bought for us, and I was joking that we'd be mistaken for spiritual ghosts. The girls kept saying that I shouldn't call it a nightie and should call it a robe instead. Zeno gave *darshans* only in the mornings, between 6 a.m. and 8 a.m., and we slipped into the regulation gear for our maiden visit to his commune.

The commune was impressive. Three white-robed monks stood at a huge purple gate flanked by cascading waterfalls. Two phenomenally huge statues of the Buddha and of another master (Sylvia pointed out that it was Lao Tzu) were sitting in a meditative posture at the entrance. I noticed that Lao Tzu had a lotus in his right hand and Rita mentioned that it symbolised the thousand-petalled lotus in all of us which bloomed when we were spiritually awakened; while the Buddha's statue symbolised the stage beyond enlightenment when we could hope to reach supreme emptiness (so he held nothing in his hand).

We walked in. Maria asked us to stand respectfully with our eyes closed in front of the two statues. For energy transfer, she said. It was all quiet, peaceful and serene. Disciples weren't allowed to speak too much once inside the commune during the early part of the day, we were told. Or you spoke in whispers if you were guiding someone or explaining esoteric meanings to visitors.

A huge pond covered with lilies and lotuses was on the right. A sprawling lawn with a few peacocks and deers was on the left. A slender bamboo bridge covered with creepers and bougainvillaea led to a large meditation hall where Zeno met with his disciples.

Rammy had got a zero cut for the occasion (I hadn't) and was looking like a monk who'd severed all social contact with the world to try and establish an eternal connection with the divine.

The get-up suited him actually, and I wondered if he'd forsake everything and join Zeno someday. You couldn't put it past him – the guy was unpredictable and already quite spiritually-inclined and all that. Perhaps all he required was a catalyst to walk the path towards enlightenment. Would Zeno provide him that?

When we entered the meditation hall, a faint fragrance of jasmine, roses and frankincense was wafting from the altar that carried a small marble statue of the Buddha. A group of fifty-odd disciples was sitting cross-legged on soft rugs and looking meditatively at the statue. They all were still, silent and serene. I looked around. Zeno wasn't to be seen. I noticed that not many Indians were to be seen at the commune either. The crowd mostly comprised foreigner babes and guys. Perhaps Indians liked loud-mouthed spiritual gurus, I thought. Zeno was quite low profile and soft spoken, I'd heard from the girls. I kept looking here and there to spot Zeno—remembering his bearded face and long mane from his mug shot—and thought that he planned to arrive late to gain more importance. It was already 6:30 a.m.

'Isn't Zeno around?' I whispered into Rita's ear.

'Shhhh!' she whispered back. 'No talking in the Buddha hall.'

Rammy had already parked himself on a rug and had closed his eyes. Meditation came naturally to him. I followed suit and lots of bikini-clad girls and even a few porn actresses flashed across my mind's eye.

I tried to shrug them away but couldn't. I placed a soft cushion on my lap for obvious reasons. Something in the air was kindling my hormones rather than any vestige of holiness left in me. I thought it'd be better if I opened my eyes and looked instead at Buddha's statue. Rammy and the girls were sitting with their eyes closed. I kept looking at Buddha and was becoming increasingly horny. I was feeling so lusty that I could have rammed a mare. A short-statured, clean-shaven monk with tonsured head (he wouldn't have been more than five feet tall) came and sat on a rug next to me. He smiled at me. Funnily enough, my libido quietened to manageable levels when he looked into my eyes. I smiled back, and closed my eyes again. I didn't know how long I sat like that. Someone tapped me on the shoulder. It was Maria.

'Zeno won't be coming,' she whispered, 'let's go to the cafeteria.'

The cafeteria had bamboo tables and chairs. The fencing around it was also of bamboo strung together with jute ropes. The roof was of much the same material, only it had lots of creepers and money plants snaking across, and when the sunbeams filtered through it and fell on the tables, it made the entire place aglow with a mellow, magical freshness. I was happy that the girls had talked me into visiting the commune. We five were sitting around a round table. The girls had ordered herbal tea and some special biscuits rich in fibre. The biscuit was tasteless; but the tea was flavoursome and invigorating. I gulped two bowls of it. The meditation session had made me incredibly thirsty. Rammy was exceptionally silent and contemplative.

The monk who'd sat next to me in the Buddha hall sat at a table beside us, and Maria went and said hi to him. They spoke for a brief while, and she invited him to join us.

'Hello,' said the diminutive monk to me as he sat down next to Rammy. 'So how do you find the commune?'

'Nice,' I said, 'though we're sad that we couldn't meet Master Zeno.'

'Never mind, maybe it's destined for later,' he said, and looking at Rammy, 'so my dear friend, how are *you*?'

'Fine,' said Rammy laconically.

'You're lost in thoughts?' asked the monk.

'Yes,' said Rammy. 'I'm thinking...what's the *purpose* of life?'

'Aha, the eternal conundrum,' said the monk, 'but does life have to have a purpose? Can't it all be purposeless?'

'Then there would be no meaning behind our existence,' said Rammy.

'What's the meaning of an apple; what's the purpose of a rose?' asked the monk.

'The first provides us food; the second, beauty,' said Rammy.

'Isn't that an egocentric notion? – to think that an apple and a rose exist for us? Man always thinks that nature was created for his benefit, and that everything revolves around him. Do you really think that apples and roses were created to provide us with food and beauty? They'd exist even if we didn't.'

'Hmmmm...now that you put it that way...it raises some fundamental questions,' said Rammy.

The girls were passive spectators listening intently to their dialogue. I thought it best that I remained silent too. Philosophy and spirituality weren't my strong points. *It is better to keep your mouth shut and be thought a fool, than to open it and remove all doubt.* That's not my line. It's a famous quote by some famous person who I can't recall now. Perhaps Abraham Lincoln, but then, I could be wrong.

'Like?' asked the monk.

'Like why do we ask why? Why don't we just exist in a state of unthinking innocence like birds and animals?' wondered Rammy.

'Because we have a mind,' said the monk.

'Why do we have a mind?' asked Rammy, and they both laughed together.

What was so funny? Did I miss the joke? Even the girls were laughing. So, I had no option but to laugh with them, though I didn't know what I was laughing about. Perhaps nobody did.

'Why do we laugh?' asked Maria.

'What's the meaning of laughter?' asked Sylvia.

'Perhaps it's all *meaningless*?' asked the monk of Rammy.

'Perhaps,' said Rammy.

'Just like a painting or a sculpture or any work of art that was created just because somebody could? Not for any particular purpose?

'It could be the same with existence. The meaninglessness of life has great significance. What is the meaning of a sunrise, sunset, or a blooming daffodil? None whatsoever. We have to give these phenomena meaning – with our keenness to appreciate beauty; and with our child-like ability to become awestruck by the magic of phenomenal creation.

'The cosmos itself is *sans* meanings. If we ever meet God, assuming there is a God of course, just in case you haven't experienced It yet, then God would become pretty stumped if we asked Him, "What is the meaning of Creation?"

'That's like asking a Van Gogh the meaning of his painting; or asking a Mozart the meaning of his symphony.

'They create because they can. The divine created because It can.

'Meanings have to be added by us; we have to enjoy the meaninglessness with eyes enthused by beauty; with ears tingling with melodies; with hearts bursting with love and laughter; with souls tap-dancing to eternal music.

'Even if a *meaning* is given, we would still ask, "What is the meaning of the meaning?", and then, "What is the meaning of the meaning of the meaning?", and this line of questioning is endless.

In logic, this is called "infinite regress". Answers breed questions, and further answers breed further questions – so existence can only be an unanswerable and unquestionable divine poem and painting and play in a state of eternal, dynamic flux. End of my *meaningless* balderdash. Have fun!' said the monk.

'An existence sans meanings?' wondered Rammy. 'Possible.'

'Okay, I have to leave now. Great talking to you,' he said to Rammy.

'Okay, thanks,' said Rammy, shaking his hand.

'And you, my dear friend, you should *meditate* more,' said the monk, looking at me. 'Hope we'll meet later.'

'What's the *meaning* of meditation?' I asked cheekily, and the monk laughed loudly and left our table.

When we headed back to New Nirvana the girls whistled up an excellent lunch of cheese macaroni, grilled sandwiches and fried rice.

'How did you find the atmosphere?' asked Rita.

'Interesting,' said Rammy. 'But whatever happened to Zeno?'

'Oh, some days he doesn't step out of his room,' said Maria, and threw a wink at Sylvia.

'You guys don't meet him often?' I asked.

'No, not often,' said Rita. 'He just asks us to meditate.'

'I wonder what his take on all this is…' wondered Rammy.

'On what?' asked Sylvia.

'Well, on existence, life, etcetera, on what we were discussing with that monk,' said Rammy.

'What do you think of that monk?' asked Maria.

'He seems peaceful. Either he has no questions. Or he has all the answers. I'm thinking if one of Zeno's disciples is so blissful, how wonderfully blissful Zeno must be,' wondered Rammy.

'He's not Zeno's disciple,' said Rita as she dumped some cheese macaroni on my plate. 'Hucky, you better eat well, okay? You're beginning to look weak these days.'

'You mean he doesn't dig Zeno's philosophy? He's just a neutral visitor?' asked Rammy.

'Rammy, he *is* Zeno,' said Rita.

'Nonsense, stop kidding me, babe,' said Rammy.

'Trust me. You spoke with Zeno himself,' said Rita.

'Shut up,' said Rammy. 'Zeno has a thick, flowing, grey beard and neck-length hair and...'

Maria and Sylvia were laughing. So was Rita.

'...unless he has cut them both and...' observed Rammy judiciously.

'Exactly!' said Rita.

'I can't believe it! That was Zeno? Is she serious?' I asked Maria.

She nodded yes. No wonder a mere glance from him had sublimated my lust. And, I could also go deep into meditation. Fancy that! We'd sat with the Master and we'd spoken to him as if he were an ordinary person. I felt guilty about the cheeky remark I had made at the fag-end of our convo.

'But he sat with us at the Buddha hall and at the cafeteria as if he's an ordinary person,' said Rammy.

'That's exactly what a Zen master is, silly. *Extraordinarily ordinary*. In fact, we aren't allowed to touch his feet or even greet him. He says he's to be treated more as an absence than a presence,' said Sylvia.

'That's why you never saw anyone wishing him or bowing to him or acknowledging his presence,' said Rita.

'But...but why did he pull this trick on us? Why didn't you guys tell us?' I asked.

'To gauge you guys. To see what work needs to be done on you. He does this rarely so you guys are fortunate,' explained Rita. 'Anyway, Masters function mysteriously, and why should we expose our Master? It's Zeno's mystical technique, and who are we to interfere in his work?'

'God, how stupid I was to think he was a mere monk,' said Rammy.

'I think he likes you, Rammy,' said Rita, 'it's not often that Zeno talks philosophy with someone. Surely he's seen something in you.'

'I wish to meet him again,' said Rammy.

'You can't for at least three months,' said Maria, 'he's leaving for Germany in the evening.'

'Anyway, at least we met Zeno,' I said.

'Ya,' said Rammy, 'he's quite something. How juvenile of me, I shook his hand as if we are pals.'

'Perhaps you are,' said Rita, 'from a previous birth?'

We were receiving all the sops as promised. We were flush with funds as our stipend and book grants were automatically deposited in our bank accounts. But as Rammy had warned us before, the authorities began tightening the screws. The Commy Garden was suddenly declared out of bounds and we couldn't picnic there in the evenings.

Ranju and Alka weren't complaining about it as they had reached third MBBS and were busy studying like crazy. Ranju's dad had promised her a trip to US (to meet her brother and a few other relatives) if she fared well, and she was trying her best to get a gold medal. So, she had made herself scarce. The only times we met was when we bumped into each other at the college canteen or at the bank, and she always seemed too absorbed in what she was planning to do at the clinics or in keeping pace with the time-table she had created for herself. I was clearly bored of her sudden dedication, but there was nothing I could do about it, so I gave her the space she wanted.

Rammy and Alka were 'drifting apart' and when I asked him what had happened, he mentioned that she was 'too materialistic and was always talking about how she'd love to have a Contessa car and designer jewellery after marriage'. I told him that this was normal with girls, and Rammy said he had serious reservations about spending the rest of his life with 'a normal girl bitten by the normal material bug'. Anyway, they weren't seeing too much of each other either. Plus Rammy was meeting up with Rita and gang at New Nirvana often, and I wondered if he was shifting cardiac loyalties to one of them. It was none of my business, so I never quizzed him about it. Or perhaps he was just interested in Zeno and his work.

'*Saala lag gayee*,' said Solly, one evening at the adda, 'do you guys know? We need to be in our rooms at 10 p.m. every night for compulsory attendance.'

'What nonsense,' said Mangy, 'who told you?'

'Arre, the GS – the notice will be put up tomorrow. And, all of us have to maintain 95% attendance in our classes.'

'Balls,' said Shaky. 'There'll be another strike.'

'Don't bet on it,' said Rammy, 'most of the guys are just sheep. I told you, the previous strike would get us into troubled times, but you guys said nothing would happen.'

'Chill, guys, the Dean has anyway promised Rammy that we guys won't have attendance problems, no?' said Chopsy.

'Ya, but only till General Thakur is the Dean – if he gets posted out, then our fortunes change with that,' said Rammy.

'Let's hope he's there till the end of our sixth term,' said Mangy.

'*Saamp hain saalay*! Now they've even increased the minimum fine to fifty rupees,' said Solly.

'Look, there's nothing we can do about all this, so let's not worry. We'll take life as it comes,' I said.

'Ya, he's right,' said Rammy, 'let's not suffer a collective panic attack.'

'Tora! Tora! Tora!' said Dusty.

'Roll a joint, man,' said Chopsy, and we smoked away our collective anxiety.

◇

The GS recommended Rammy's name for the post of D-mess committee member. Rammy was reluctant to assume responsibility and I was asked to convince him. The GS said that only Rammy could handle Sattu, an aggressive champion boxer from our batch, who was running riot in the mess. Satinder Singh, or Sattu, talked more with his triceps than with his tongue, as was the congenital habit of most brawny Northerners who hailed from the land of lasso and *lassi*. It was even rumoured that Sattu had bashed up three X-ray batchers in their room a month ago, and they hadn't complained to the Warden or to Gattu as they were ashamed to admit that they had got creamed by a junior. Sattu was the terror of Yankee batch, period. Even the Maniacs stayed away from him because Sattu's grisly expression clearly meant: 'Keep safe distance, or keep an ambulance ready for yourself.'

The waiters and the cooks were feeling pretty harassed too and many other mess members were also complaining about Sattu's autocratic ways. The mess badly needed someone to rein in Sattu, and Rammy seemed to fit the bill. I finally convinced Rammy that he ought to take up the job.

It was a Monday evening. Remember, I'd told you that on Monday and Tuesday, they screened some Hindi movie at the Open Air Theatre? The rest of the Maniacs had gone to the OAT, and Rammy and I were planning to go for a night show at Rahul – *Blame it on Rio*, in fact. On movie days, you had to grab early dinner, and the mess would be shut by 7:30 p.m. If you missed dinner, you had to make your own arrangements.

It was close to 8 p.m. Rammy and I were wolfing down egg bhurji at the proximal raydi. Sattu approached Rammy like a bull in heat advancing lustily towards an unsuspecting cow.

'I didn't get dinner at the mess,' said Sattu gruffly.

'Why?' asked Rammy. 'Did they run out of ration?'

'No.'

'Then?'

'They refused to serve me dinner.'

'What time did you go?'

'7:45.'

'Well, then they wouldn't serve you. You better make it to the mess before 7:30 on movie nights, okay?'

'Fuck you! I'll go whenever I want, and they should serve me food!'

'Sattu, I've instructed them to follow the rules exactly, they aren't going to bend it for anyone.'

But Sattu wasn't listening and he grabbed Rammy's collar. Then Rammy said something so coolly that his words and his no-nonsense, smooth tone have stayed with me forever.

'Okay, punch me, but do it fast, for we have a movie to catch. Then I'll have to go to the MI room for some first-aid treatment. That will leave me forty minutes to lodge an FIR and then reach Rahul in time for the movie. C'mon, go ahead,' said Rammy, extending his chin.

Sattu released his grip and Rammy offered to treat him to some vada sambar or dosa (Sattu was a diehard vegetarian) and Sattu said that he didn't want anyone's help.

'Okay,' said Rammy, 'if we have your esteemed permission, can we leave now?'

'You bloody slime,' said Sattu. 'You don't have the guts to fight, and you lodge FIRs...'

'Sattu, I'm here to become a doctor, not a boxer, and if you're so gutsy, why don't you try and bash up someone double your size? You pick physically weaker people to terrorise and you think you're brave? Now, buzz off! I don't have time for primitives like you!' screamed Rammy.

Sattu scrammed off without saying a word and we took off to Rahul.

◇

The Pharmacology lecture was atrociously boring. Rammy and I were sitting on the last bench, poring over the cryptic crosswords that *The Bangalore Herald* carried every day. Rammy called them 'misleading entertainment' because cryptics threw you off course most often. But they had an irrefutable logic all their own. I could barely manage to solve some simple anagrams like 'Multi-talented relatives' which was a clue for versatile.

Rammy was amazing though. He could zero in on the logic in a trice and was a big fan of Roger Squires who set the cryptic crosswords for *The Daily Telegraph* in England, and Rammy was quite miffed that we couldn't lay hands on that 'mother of all cryptics'.

But *The Bangalore Herald* wasn't a piece of cake either. And, the following seemed to have stumped even Rammy:

God abandoning shaken Shiva prior to diminutive mother rushing out of movie can be pretty curative (8)

We had been staring at the clue for the past five minutes. Thanks to Rammy, I'd become hooked to cryptic crosswords some three months ago, and it was a great way to pass time in class. As you scribbled away on the pad, the lecturer thought you were taking notes, and since you usually carried a pretty serious expression (because you weren't able to crack the clue) it seemed you were one of the studious kinds who was thoroughly interested in the side effects of penicillin and the mechanism of action of erythromycin.

The clue mocked our intelligence. We knew the second-last letter was 'n'.

'Tough, I am getting exhausted,' wrote Rammy in his scribble pad. (We called the technique scribble-talking.)

'Me too, could be medicine? That's curative, right?' I wrote in mine.

'Logic? How does it link with God, Shiva, movie, mother?'

'No idea.'

'Think. Who is Shiva?'

'Destroyer.'

'No, a word which has God in it.'

'Hey! How about demigod?'

'Wow! You are right, and we are left with demi when god leaves it! And shake it up and you have medi.'

'Bingo, so medicine is right I guess. But we have to add cine to it. How?'

'Got it! Diminutive mother is ma, and when she leaves the movie or cinema, we have cine!'

'Fantastic! Okay, let's try this 9 down.'

I stared at the clue for a while. The lecturer continued talking about new cephalosporins and fungal infections and some such crap. Poor thing, what all people have to do to earn a bit of money, I thought. I knew that I'd never become a lecturer – it's far better to die of starvation than to keep repeating the same stuff like a parrot year after year, batch after batch, shit, talk about drab robotic jobs, I reasoned.

9 down was really crazy:

Of. Of. Of. Of. Of. Of. Of. Of. Of. Of. (10)

'I got it in three seconds!' Rammy wrote.

'How? What the hell is this?'

'Think. When something gets repeated what do we call it?'

'Repetition. Hey, that's ten letters, right?'

'Ya, but your answer is wrong. Think why "of" is getting repeated. And, how would you explain this event to a child?'

'OHT,' I wrote. (OHT = Overhead transmission.)

'Okay, what is getting repeated ten times?'

'Obviously "of".'

'Good. So, you get of-ten-times.'

'Oh boy! Oftentimes! Killer clue! WOW! SUPERB!' I screamed.

No, I didn't *scribble-talk* that. I *actually* screamed! All the Monarchs turned back. The lecturer stopped his speech. Rammy glared at me.

'Get up,' said Lt. Col. Rajasekhar Sastry to me. *'What's so superb about fungal infection in one's groin?'* (So that was what he'd been talking about when I'd hollered in appreciation?)

'Errr…no…nothing sir…sorry sir…' I stuttered.

'What were you doing out there? Out with the truth,' he said.

'Sir,' said Rammy, coming to my rescue, 'we were solving the cryptic crossword.'

'Both of you?' he asked.

'Yes, sir!'

'And I'm a fool to be delivering this lecture?'

'No, sir. But we're sitting only for attendance,' I said.

'You both meet me in my room after the class,' he said, and continued the lecture.

'So you guys are addicted to cryptic crosswords?' asked Lt. Col. Sastry.

'Yes, sir,' I said. 'Though Rammy, sorry, Ramakrishna here, he's the genius, sir.'

'Aha,' said Lt. Col. Sastry, fishing out a newspaper from his desk drawer, *'Bangalore Herald?'*

'Oh, so you also solve the cryptic, sir?' asked Rammy, looking at the half-filled grid in Lt. Col. Sastry's newspaper.

'Daily, my friend, daily,' he said, 'I get bad dreams if I don't crack it.'

'Great, sir!' said Rammy.

'Okay, I'll make a deal with you guys,' said Lt. Col. Sastry, writing something in his pad, 'if you two can solve these two cryptics in the next five minutes, then I'll allow you to do as you please in my class.'

'What's it, sir?' I asked.

'Take a look,' he said.

1. Go, wolf down the earl's origin (8)
2. Short alien does about turn in fight over ancient chemical (5)

'Interesting, sir,' said Rammy.

'Okay, I'm going for a cup of coffee, and I'll be back in a while. You guys better not leave the room, okay?'

'Okay, sir,' I said as he exited the room.

'Rammy, what the hell is this?'

'Hucks, what a surprise that he's a crossword buff too.'

'Ya.'

'Let's solve the first one...'

'Okay, but what the hell does wolf down mean? Hunting?'

'No Hucks, refers to hogging, eating. Something's ringing a bell...Hmmm...name some eats, eight letters...'

'Pastries, parantha...'

'English eats...think dukes and earls...'

'Omelette...Hamburger, sorry, that's nine...Sandwich...'

'Hey, you got it! Sandwich is supposed to have been invented by one Earl of Sandwich to continue a card game uninterrupted, great, Hucks, you are good, dude!'

'Wow, so it is! So, what's the next?'

'Hmmm...think Hucks...obviously short alien is an abbreviation...what's an alien called?'

'You mean like extraterrestrial or something?'

'Lovely, it's ET...it goes backward to become TE...'

'Okay, and it goes backward in fight...what can be an ancient chemical...?'

'It's nice, I got it, think of synonyms for fight...'

'Tussle, scrap, clash, scuffle, brawl...'

'Something bigger in magnitude?'

'Combat…battle…war…'

'There, you got it…'

'Oh, ya, TE goes into war to become water…Wow! We cracked it! Yippee, we can chill out in his class…'

Lt. Col. Sastry returned in a bit and asked us if we'd been able to figure out the clues.

'No, sir,' said Rammy, smiling slyly.

'Yes, it is tough, it was first asked of me in college, and even I couldn't figure it out – so you guys get no concessions in my class, okay? You'll sit in the front row from now on…'

'Sure sir,' said Rammy smilingly, 'but only if you treat us to a *sandwich* first, and since we'd be thirsty after that, you also ought to provide us *water*…'

'You smarty!' said Lt. Col. Sastry. 'So you figured it out, huhn?'

'Yes, sir. In two minutes flat,' I lied pompously. (It had taken us four.)

'Okay,' he said. 'You guys are smarter than I thought. If you wish to, you can bunk my lectures and I'll mark you present. But don't overdo it, okay?'

'Never, sir, never,' said Rammy. 'I've a cryptic clue for you, sir.'

'Ya? Spell it out,' he said.

'I'll write it down for you sir,' said Rammy.

The tiny superintendent of police fell backward, ingesting the disturbed mixture in highly romantic zone (5)

'Interesting, interesting,' he said, staring at the paper, 'if I can't crack it by Monday, I'll pass a small bottle of Scotch to you.'

'Thanks, sir, but I don't drink,' said Rammy, and I nudged him, so he added, 'but some of my friends do…'

'So you think I won't be able to crack it?'

'No, sir, I'm sure you'll be able to,' said Rammy.

'Cool,' he said smilingly, warming up to the challenge, 'see you guys on Monday.'

'Good day, sir!' we said together, and floated out of his room, thoroughly puzzled by the fact that cryptic crosswords had, quite ironically, simply got us into direct trouble, and then solved our attendance problems instead – at least in Pharmacology lectures. In thirty minutes flat.

◇

The injection room at the OPD was teeming with patients who'd come to get their free shots. Dusty had dragged me into it, saying that I should practise delivering injections and all. He'd had a head start on us (remember, he'd cleared first MBBS six months before us?) and was supposed to be an expert at delivering injections and all by now.

He'd lined up a middle-aged guy for me to administer a Vitamin B injection to. Dusty was guiding me thorough the art of holding the syringe right, piercing the rubber cap of the ampoule, pulling in the right dosage, cleaning the patient's arm area with surgical spirit, piercing his skin and muscle, injecting an invigorating shot of Vitamin B intramuscularly, rubbing the injected area vigorously with cotton swab etcetera, saying that we'd soon proceed to the more difficult intravenous procedure.

I followed Dusty's direction and did as coached and the man said a grateful thanks. Dusty said 'well done' and I was happy that my maiden noble deed had gone on so well. Then the trouble began.

The man's skin began swelling like crazy, and I began rubbing the area vigorously, and Dusty said that I hadn't pierced the man's epidermis well and had thereby delivered a subcutaneous (just below the skin) instead of an IM (intramuscular), and the man looked worriedly at the area, and I lied that it would be okay in a while, and we scampered from the spot before the nurse could berate us. (I didn't enter the injection room for close to two years after that incident. Guilt takes time to dissolve.)

As we were riding back to the hostel, Gattu was coming from the opposite direction in his rattle-trap of a Fiat. Gosh, it used to make such an ear-tingling racket that we used to call it 'the steamroller', both in honour of its high decibel levels and the human load it carried.

The steamroller slowed down and Gattu waved us to a halt. I wondered if some nurse had complained about the injection room mishap. Hope not, I thought.

'Good afternoon, sir!' I said as I stepped off the bike.

'Good afternoon, sir!' said Dusty.

'What are you wearing?' asked Gattu, glaring at me.

'Huh? Uniform, sir,' I said, looking at my grey trouser, blue shirt, blue tie, and blue pullover. My white lab coat was slung on my shoulder, but that was allowed outside classes. What was wrong? Even the name tag and term tags were in place.

'Who gave you permission to wear a pullover?' thundered Gattu.

'Sir, I was feeling cold in the morning,' I said. (In fact, after the injection room fiasco I was feeling quite chilled with guilt and disgust.)

'It's still August,' he said.

'Sir, how does that matter?' I wondered.

'You aren't authorised to wear winter uniform in August.'

'Sir, what if I feel cold in July or even June?'

'In the army, we'll tell you *when* to feel cold. You'll wear winter uniform when we *declare* it is winter.'

'And what if I feel warm on a winter day and don't want to wear a pullover?'

'You'll still wear it. You'll wear what we ask you to wear, irrespective of the weather.'

'But this is illogical, sir.'

'The army has its own logic. Dismissed. And, I am fining you fifty rupees for flouting sartorial norms,' he said, and drove away.

'What the hell, man!' said Dusty.

'Man, I'm not joining the army,' I said. 'How can one be part of a group that dresses according to a set calendar and not according to the weather?'

'Wonder what Rammy would have to say about it,' said Dusty.

On Monday afternoon, Lt. Col. Sastry said to Rammy that he had never been to Paris, but would like to go there someday. Rammy smiled and said that he knew he'd be able to crack the cryptic. I had tried to solve it for some twenty minutes and had given up. Remember, I was still a novice when it came to chess and cryptic crossword puzzles – I was just learning the ropes from Rammy. But Lt. Col. Sastry did give a nice bottle of Scotch to Rammy, and the guys at the adda greedily guzzled the exotic elixir and emptied the bottle in just under an hour early in the evening. Of course, they did that with a little bit of timely help from yours tipsily, heehee.

The tiny superintendent of police fell backward, ingesting the disturbed mixture in highly romantic zone.

'How did he do it, Rammy?' I asked as Solly ordered Chopsy to get some more whisky from the liquor joint nearby, saying 'this hasn't even wet my throat'.

'It's easy Hucks – what's the abbreviation for superintendent of police?'

'SP?'

'Ya, tiny refers to that, and when that falls backwards, what do you get?

'PS.'

'Good.'

'Now what mixture do you ingest regularly?'

'Huh? Coffee? Tea? Smoke?'

'Close, Hucks, but what do you breathe?'

'Air.'

'Good. Now the clue says disturbed mixture, so air becomes ari...'

'Oh shit! I got it! So when ari is ingested by PS, you get Paris, which is a highly romantic zone...'

'Great job, Hucks,' said Rammy, and I felt like killing myself for not having been able to figure it out earlier.

14

The Foreigners, the Boycott, the Guilt, the Learning

Then. September through December 1988.

BEFORE YOU COULD SAY JACK ROBINSON, ANOTHER UNIV EXAM began breathing down your neck and got you into a tizzy. Rammy said that second MBBS was a joke and he'd read all the books as if they were some novels. Well, to put things in perspective, the subjects weren't all that difficult. Microbiology, Pathology, Pharmacology, and Forensic Medicine didn't require the kind of diligence or attention that you'd tried to muster during first MBBS.

Well, we had a month to try and sail through the exams, and as usual, Rammy was guiding us through the rough academic waters. (Shaky and Dusty had already cleared these six months ago, so they were also helping us.) We breezed through the exam week without any glitch and were sure that the Monarch Maniacs would clear second MBBS in the first attempt. Of course, you had the usual ATKT ('allowed to keep term' and all that compassionate crap doled out by the Univ) but hopefully we wouldn't require any of it.

Ranju and Alka appeared for their third MBBS exams and, considering that they had burnt a lot of midnight photons, you could be pretty sure that they would pass out soon. I was of course quite sad and depressed that Ranju would vanish out of my emotional radar range, and Rammy seemed unconcerned about the fact that Alka would be leaving soon. (As I said, they had drifted apart and Mangy's observation that they were just destined to be good friends was coming true after all.)

After the exams were over, Rammy and I didn't feel like going home and decided to stay back at the hostel. The rest of the guys had left for their cities, and Rammy suggested after a few days that we could rent out a room near New Nirvana and chill out at Zeno zone for a while. Maria had left for Rio (her mom was battling gallstones, we gathered) and Rita said that we could shack up with them, since they now had a spare room for a few months. Rammy offered to split the rent and all, and Sylvia got pretty miffed with him; though they allowed us to shop for groceries and stuff. Cool arrangement.

The good news was that Zeno was back and Rammy was quite excited about meeting him and discussing esoteric spiritual crap and all. I wasn't at all interested in such discussions (I wondered why people couldn't be content with their eat-drink-and-be-merry routine, but then, perhaps I was taking too simplistic a view of existential dilemmas which confronted the intellectuals among us? – thank God I wasn't one of them) though I must confess that the commune was a great place to visit, and Zeno definitely had a calming influence on one's hormone and stress levels.

Plus the commune crowd was positively great, though I hated it whenever some foreigner babes bad-mouthed India. C'mon, I had the right to say anything about my country, but I wasn't going to let foreigner babes (and white-skinned, sickeningly-perfumed, snooty folks at that) bitch about India and get away with it. I had got into an argumentative mood on many occasions and Rammy hadn't approved, saying *Athithi devo bhava*, meaning a guest is God. To hell with all that. I had asked a few foreigners at the smoking den (ya, there was a separate area at the commune to grab a ciggie) why did they fly into India if they felt it was so messy and all that, and they defended their visit by saying that 'it was one of the cheapest destinations on the tourist map which also had lots of spiritual joints and yoga spots to talk about back home.'

Most of these folks were only looking for some silly spiritual entertainment and not for any eternal truth, if such a thing existed in the first place. They spent the summers in Manali where they could score the best hashish (they called it Malana maal); winters in Goa where they sunbathed on nude beaches; autumns in Nepal; and somewhere between all that they squeezed in a few trips down South or up North. Having a Master to call your guru and all was a kind of status symbol with them—well, with at least seventy to eighty percent of them—and I wondered if a guru was the human equivalent of a picture postcard you sent back home to have your folks flaunting your 'sightseeing conquests'. A few were genuine of course, but stupid enough to madly dedicate their lives to the futile search for nirvana and all that crap; and were definitely getting pretty mind-fucked in the process. But I guess they were all having a rollicking time since the currency rate and the weak rupee ensured that their dollars and pounds and deutschemarks could guarantee the poorest foreigner the best of creature comforts. 'The flight to India, plus the boarding and lodging, was still lower than the cost of living in Germany,' someone had said.

Rammy joked that perhaps he'd quit medicine and float an ashram or something and rake in all the *moolah* that was waiting to be raked. Come to think of it, that wasn't a bad idea after all. There was no business like spiritual business (showbiz didn't even come a close second if you took into account the sheer drudgery of it); I mean, how much effort did you need to put in to teach someone to close their eyes and sit quietly? Almost zero ergs.

Rammy met Zeno in private quite a few times, and was looking all aglow with new-found peace and tranquillity. When I asked him what had transpired between them, he chose to dodge my questions. Either he felt I was too dense to understand philosophy or too superficial to be allowed into the depths of esoteric subjects. He discussed a few things with Rita and I wasn't interested in their highbrow intellectual stuff anyway. Sylvia wasn't interested either, so we just kept chilling out for a while at a few clubs and rave parties that she kept getting invited to throughout the month.

◇

The results were declared on a Monday morning and all the Monarch Maniacs had cleared second MBBS in the first attempt itself. Not surprisingly, Rammy had scored a distinction in two subjects.

Shaky and Dusty had just stepped into their eighth term (the penultimate period before they got sucked into the high-voltage grind of the final ninth term), so we weren't seeing too much of them.

A week after the results Mangy stormed into my room saying some guys were discussing that Rammy should be ousted from his post of Mess Secretary, D-mess. (Ya, he'd been promoted since he'd been managing all the chimps rather well – and even Sattu was a subdued shadow of what he'd been.) Mangy said that Sattu, Punchoo, and gang were planning to move a 'no-confidence motion' against Rammy, failing which they would threaten him to resign from the post. Sattu and Punchoo were the main conspirators who normally looked as mean as Roman senators plotting against Caesar.

'Okay,' said Rammy, when I told him about it, 'since I had refused to let them order for food in their rooms last week, they want me out.'

'So what are you going to do?' I asked.

'Wait and watch, some plans backfire,' said Rammy.

By evening, a notice was impaled at the pigeonhole. Rammy had certainly moved fast.

OFFICE OF THE RESIDENT WARDEN, DEFCOMS, BANGALORE

Due to regular complaints and conduct unbecoming of future officers, the following students are hereby shifted to E-mess w.e.f. 19 December 1988, 0800 HRS, till further notice.

1. Satinder Singh   (DGN 3110)
2. Pramod Mishra   (DGN 3039)

Signed

Lt. Col. Tarun Bhatia

'How did you manage that, Rammy, and so speedily?' I asked.

'If you can keep it to yourself...'

'Of course, tell me.'

'Well, three weeks ago, a few instant coffee bottles and butter packets were being delivered to the Warden's house late in the night, and I'd intercepted the transfer, quite by chance. Ever since, Bhatia has been pretty pally with me...'

'*Saala chor*! Why didn't you report it to the Dean?'

'Hucks, don't be stupid. If you ignore trivial issues, you can ask for favours later, like I did today.'

'When did you become a politician, Rammy?'

'To manage a mess and an unruly bunch, you have to be a bit of a Machiavellian manipulator at times.'

Gowri, a Yankee Monarch, died on a Friday evening. Her moped had been hit by a speeding car on Hosur Road and she had died of multiple head injuries. I was at the new Insti when I heard the news. Some roadside witnesses mentioned later that the car was a white Ambassador, but nobody had noted down the number. A phenomenally useless clue, since most Ambassadors were white. Rammy was meditating when I gave him the news, and he said that 'life is uncertain anyway' and went back to his meditation. I wasn't too happy with his calm indifference and walked away wondering if his heart was made of granite.

A few guys from our batch organised a condolence meeting and said that we ought to take out a scooter-and-bike procession and block Hosur Road for a while to register our protest against such lethal drivers. Some guys had gone to meet Rammy to have him participate in the protest and Rammy told them that 'you guys just want to feel important for a while; and blocking roads and disturbing traffic is a pretty primitive way of protesting.' All hell broke loose after he said that.

Rammy had already rubbed a few students the wrong way, what with his principles and all that crap, and nearly everyone became hostile towards him. 'We need to sort out this guy,' said someone. 'Ya, he thinks too much of himself,' said another.

Quite a few Yankee batchers had gathered at 4 Top to hold an emergency meeting on 'how to get even with Rammy'. No prizes for guessing that the bunch was headed by Sattu and Punchoo.

Of course, I wouldn't have been allowed to be part of that elite gathering, so I deputed Pips to find out what exactly was going on. Pips met me after about half an hour saying that they had made an action plan.

'Tell me exactly what happened, Pips,' I said.

'Arre, first Punchoo said that we should give the poor bastard the blanket treatment and Roshan said that we can't do that, since he could lodge an FIR and also get all of us rusticated since he was close to Gattu and the Warden and the Dean and all,' said Pips. (Blanket treatment meant someone would knock on your door, and when you opened it, they'd throw a huge blanket on you, wrap you up in it like you'd wrap the potato filling in your masala dosa, and beat and kick you till nobody had any energy left to beat and kick you.)

'Then?'

'Then what, then Sattu said that we will try to break him *psychologically*.'

'How?'

'Arre, everyone's going to boycott him. Nobody is allowed to talk to him or acknowledge his presence. They're going to instruct all batches regarding it, so you can be pretty sure that Rammy is going to be the loneliest soul in the hostel. And if I were you, I'd also maintain my distance from him.'

I was desperately seeking Solly, and I heard that he'd gone somewhere with Chopsy and Mangy. Perhaps they had gone to Chopsy's LG's as usual.

Shaky and Dusty were logging their attendance at the maternity ward, and I was suddenly feeling lost. When I went and conveyed the action plan to Rammy, he said, 'Balls to them, let them do whatever, I couldn't care less.'

Sattu and a few other Yankee batchers ran into me and asked me to keep away from Rammy. I didn't know what to do, so I just went to my room.

When I stepped out for dinner after an hour, I saw that the notice board at the pigeonhole was carrying some nasty posters about Rammy and some pretty lewd graffiti. All the juniors were laughing looking at the cartoons and the smart alec lines, and I was becoming pretty angry that these were the same people who used to run to Rammy for protection during their fresher term, since it was a known fact that Rammy had sworn not to rag anyone. (He didn't rag a single person in his entire tenure, and his room was usually full of juniors wanting sanctuary. Plus he used to treat all these juniors to coffee and snacks – and now these very guys were laughing and making fun of him! My opinion of human nature plummeted so phenomenally that night that I don't think it has risen ever since.)

Tell you the truth, I was scared stiff as Sattu and gang had whipped up some kind of infectious frenzy against Rammy, and I was getting paranoid that I'd also get bashed up by someone if I hung out with him. It was bad, sad, and pretty selfish of me, but I decided to keep my distance from Rammy.

Hey, hello, how can you say I was ditching him when he needed me most? There were close to five hundred people who were against him or were pretending to be; and who do you think I was? – Godzilla? So stop giving me bull – you'd have done the same thing if you were in my place.

Someone even put up a cardboard piggy bank with a poster saying, 'Donate generously to Ramakrishna Relief Fund – poor guy doesn't have enough money to fuel up his bike, so he couldn't participate in the scooter-and-bike procession.'

Many students were dropping coins into the piggy bank and I wanted to go and tell Rammy to avoid dining in the mess or walking along the corridor for a few days, but would he listen to me? Que sera sera, I said to myself, and went to D-mess. We used to sit at the last four tables, since we were the senior-most at the hostel. The waiter brought me my dinner, and Pips and Roshan came and sat next to me. Rammy entered the mess after ten minutes and Roshan said that the 'shameless wretch enters'.

All the other tables were occupied and Rammy came and sat next to me. As soon as Rammy plonked down, Roshan and Pips picked up their plates, got up from the table, and since everyone glared at me to do likewise, I whispered 'sorry' to Rammy, gathered my plate, and we all huddled together at another table. The waiters were asked to bring us the chairs from Rammy's table.

The boycott had begun. Rammy coolly ordered dinner, and the waiters threw a quizzical look at him, and a few of them sniggered behind his back as they entered the kitchen. After we finished dinner, I tailed Rammy as he exited the mess. I was a few paces behind him as he walked down the corridor to go back to his room – 5 Ground 6. I was in 5 Ground 4. Frankly, I wanted to see his reaction in the face of such collective hostility.

Rammy stopped at the pigeonhole and stood looking at the posters and graffiti for a while. Was he chuckling every now and then? Hundred pairs of eyes were trained on him. A few juniors were passing catty comments. A few Yankee batchers were openly bitching about him.

Then, everyone was taken by surprise. Rammy laughed, and addressing nobody in particular, said, 'Great cartoon—who made this?—this guy is better than R. K. Laxman, say my congratulations to him.' He also admired a few graffiti, took out his pen, and wrote a few lines of his own. The public was clearly unprepared for such a reaction and most of them became silent. And, Rammy coolly went to his room.

When I went back to my room, I saw that someone had slipped in a note under the door. 'Ask all the Maniacs to keep distance. I want all of you to join the boycott. And, that's an order – R.' I read it thrice and I knew that Rammy was just trying to make things easier for us.

Shaky and Dusty returned late in the night from the labour room, and I showed them the note, and they said that they'd just follow Rammy's instructions, though I suspected that they just wanted to take the convenient way out of all this. (Just like me, hah!)

The rest of the guys returned in the morning and Solly said that 'if this is what Rammy wants from us, then we shouldn't talk to him either – he is surely working according to a plan'.

So then, that's how it was. One man boycotted by a united bunch of nearly five hundred students – which included his core group comprising six of his closest pals. The boycott lasted some three days. The piggy bank was growing heavier. The sniggers were getting louder. The collective hostility was getting nastier.

On the second night of the boycott, Rammy removed the piggy bank from the pigeonhole, took it to his room, emptied its contents, fixed it back at the pigeonhole, and added a note saying:

Thank you all for your generous contribution to Ramakrishna Relief Fund. Rupees 138.55 has been collected so far. Surely, you guys can do better. I look forward to your continued generosity and will be eternally indebted if you could add a few notes of a slightly higher denomination – even dollars and pounds would be most welcome, if you can afford it. Counting coins is so very painful and time-consuming. May God bless you all! – Ramakrishna Iyer, 5 Ground 6.

On the third morning of the famed boycott tamasha, the breakfast tables at D-mess were agog with a strange amalgam of both success and defeat – success because all the students had united against Rammy; and defeat because it was quite evident that the plan didn't seem to be working.

'Shit, this guy is shameless,' said Roshan, 'he took the piggy bank, man, can you believe it!'

'Ya,' said Punchoo, 'he's even appreciating the cartoons and the graffiti, he even added one of his own—*You know you are famous when you dominate a conversation in your absence*—the bloody nerve!'

'Sattu is getting restless, guys,' said Pandey, 'I won't be surprised if he wallops Rammy one of these days...'

'Fuck, man, I thought this guy would break in a matter of hours...' said Roshan.

'Ya, I thought once he sees his junior friends ganging up against him, it would break his heart...' said Punchoo.

'What do we do now?' asked Roshan.

I was sitting at an adjacent table and was becoming increasingly happy seeing the collective frustration taking its toll on them. They wanted to break Rammy *psychologically* and he was definitely turning out to be too much of a tough nut to crack.

In fact, logically speaking, he was wrecking everyone *collectively*, *precisely*, and *systematically*. My regard for Rammy touched stratospheric heights.

When I went back to our floor, I saw Rammy exiting his room, wrapped only in a towel. I saw Sattu approaching him from the opposite direction and became worried thinking about the wallop stuff that Pandey had mentioned in the mess. I froze and quietly waited to grab a ringside view of the scene.

'I need to talk to you,' said Sattu, walking up to Rammy.

'What for?' asked Rammy. 'Go put up more posters...'

'I didn't put up the posters,' said Sattu.

'Well, then go and drop some coins in the piggy bank...'

'I didn't do that either...'

'Listen, Sattu, I have nothing personal against you, okay? But please, let's not kid ourselves here...'

'Rammy, we *have* to talk...' said Sattu.

'No, I don't want to talk to you,' said Rammy, and began walking towards the loo. 'And you're forgetting that you're supposed to boycott me.'

Sattu was one of those headstrong persons who just couldn't take 'no' for an answer. He held Rammy's arm and literally dragged him into the room. I could hear the bolt clicking shut inside Rammy's room, and I hurriedly went and stood outside, with my right ear pinned to the door. I wondered if Sattu would bash up Rammy.

'Okay, you want to hit me?' asked Rammy coolly. 'Go ahead, satisfy your animal instincts, since nothing worked huhn? I won't even lodge an FIR or a complaint against you, I promise. C'mon, go ahead. Hit me.' (Of course I could hear their convo from behind the closed door, dude, thanks to the cheap quality of cracked wood and the open ventilator window above. The suspense would have killed me if I hadn't eavesdropped.)

'No, no, I don't want to hit you, Rammy. In fact, I can't,' said Sattu.

'Then why are you here?'

'I just want to talk to you.'

'What about?' wondered Rammy. 'Aren't we beyond the talking stage and all?'

'No, Rammy. It's never too late to talk.'

'But what do you wish to talk about?'

'About you.'

'Huh?'

'Ya, about you,' said Sattu. 'In fact, I wanted to tell you something. It's been eating me for the past three days. You know, Rammy, I used to think that *I'm* the strongest person in the hostel – the most fearless. But these three days have made me realise that *muscles* are not strength. True strength is strength of the *mind* – and *you* have it! I don't! How could you take it! Five hundred students boycotting you! Even the juniors you helped and protected are against you! It would have broken me! But you…you…'

I heard Sattu sobbing loudly. Sattu, the terror – crying? I couldn't believe my ear! I pinned it harder against the door and my right ear lobe winced. The sobs were getting heavier. Then Rammy must have gathered Sattu in his arms or something because Sattu wailed even louder – wish I had X-ray vision like Clark Kent (okay, okay, I am just showing off my GK, I mean Superman).

'Sattu, c'mon now,' said Rammy, 'it's okay, just think of all this as a drama, as acting, it doesn't matter…'

'No…no…I'm sorry…you know…I planned to…to…break you psychologically…how cheap…' sobbed Sattu.

'Sattu, now stop it,' said Rammy, 'now you're making *me* emotional, you're a strong guy, dude, you don't know how much I enjoyed it when you single-handedly thrashed the three bastardly X-ray batchers…'

'Sorry, Rammy, really sorry…'

Did I hear Rammy sniffling slightly? Maybe! Damn the opaque door!

'Cool…friends?' asked Sattu.

'Of course,' said Rammy, 'we've been enemies for far too long, and it's getting kinda boring. And you know, Sattu, boredom is more of a torture than a boycott...'

They both laughed and decided to celebrate and attest their new-found friendship over a cup of Haluji's tea at the new Insti. (Surely, life was stranger than fiction! Sattu and Rammy—two people who couldn't stand each other for *three years*—now friends?!) I left the scene and pretended to stand casually outside my room. They emerged after about two minutes and were, quite obviously, oblivious to my presence. (Or anyone's presence, for that matter.)

When the hostel crowd saw Sattu and Rammy walking together and sitting at the new Insti like brothers who had discovered each other after a long separation that got triggered by a cruel Kumbh Mela, they began rubbing their eyes in disbelief and tearing their hair in disgust.

'Shit, man, shit!' I heard Roshan wailing as I walked to the new Insti. 'How did the slime manage *that*! It was Sattu who *initiated* the boycott!'

'Man, this bastard Rammy – he's one helluva cunning bastard, man,' said Punchoo.

You bet, I wanted to say, but didn't. Some things, like volcanic elation and oceanic admiration, are best left unexpressed.

So the boycott fizzled out because Sattu wasn't the kind of guy you could walk up to and say, 'Hey, traitor, how could you defect like this?' and hope to walk back in one piece. So, nobody said anything to Sattu and everyone started warming up to Rammy slowly and steadily. Rammy joked later that he and Sattu had actually engineered the entire action plan as he was falling short of money. (He had collected ₹212.75 from the piggy bank! Some guys had all the luck.)

Ranju's passing-out parade was a grand affair. Defcoms had created a new parade ground with shining macadam and they had even positioned an army tank, an IAF helicopter and a miniature naval destroyer at the venue to create an awe-inspiring effect. They had also placed some imposing, larger-than-life sculptures of army jawans all around. It all looked pretty impressive. Add to that the top brass with their glistening epaulets, pips, uniforms, medals and all, plus the liveried stewards who were serving Campa Cola, Rasna, samosas and pastries, and you knew that something hyper-important was happening.

She had done rather well (and yes, she'd picked up gold medals in Surgery and ENT) so you could be sure she'd leave for US before she joined the army. Ranju was going to serve the army for five years as a Short Service Commissioned officer ('my contribution to my country' she had said) and then she was planning to specialise in Ophthalmology. I was pretty sad and depressed and my mood practised deep-sea diving for quite a while.

After Ranju left, I was feeling lonely as hell, so I decided to meet Rita and Sylvia. Rammy didn't want to go and said that he needed to talk to Alka – she was joining the air force as a permanent commissioned officer. Obviously, he was going to say a courteous goodbye and explain that they were destined to be good friends and all that bull, and break Alka's heart – but who cared? I had 'my-lover-passed-out-and-left-me' troubles of my own to absorb first, tackle later, and eventually stave off – who cared about the heartaches of others if yours were more acute since they were closer home?

Rita had left for Madras with a few friends who'd come to meet her from Germany—'...maybe they will go to Mahabs and Pondicherry for the weekend,' said Sylvia—and I slumped on the settee at New Nirvana and wept like a waterfall. Sylvia gathered me in her arms, applied me to her bosom (now, now, don't you get ideas, and scandalise our platonic relationship) and petted and comforted me...

'So you're missing your girlfriend, Hucky,' she said as she cooked herbal tea and omelettes.

'Ya,' I said.

'Good, only proves that you're madly in love with her. I think it's time you met Zeno and discussed this. It was only yesterday that he was talking about love and emotions and all.'

When I entered the commune, I began feeling better. Sylvia arranged for me to meet Zeno alone in his room (only Rammy had had the privilege earlier). I removed my footwear and went and sat on a velvet rug. Zeno was writing something at his desk and didn't look up.

I looked around. There wasn't much to look at actually—Zen masters don't like clutter—save a small bookshelf close to where I was seated which had all kinds of books from Photography and Aeronautical Engineering and Architecture to modern fiction. That and the statue of the Buddha seemed to be his only possessions.

'Tea?' he asked smilingly, after some ten minutes, and I declined.

'Okay, Sylvi tells me that you're feeling pretty low, and that you're missing your girlfriend.'

'Yes, sir.'

'Call me Zeno.'

'Okay, sir...sorry...Zeno sir.'

'Is that the only thing you're feeling bad about?'

'No, I guess not. I'm feeling pretty guilty that I ditched Rammy when he needed me most.'

'Why do you feel that?'

I told him about the boycott and stuff and Zeno became pensive.

'Aha,' he said, 'so Rama can stand up to an entire hostel? Good.'

'Yes...er...Zeno, I think I should have been by his side.'

'No, you did right. Perhaps Rama didn't need your support? Perhaps he likes to leg it alone?'

'Perhaps.'

'But everything's normal now between him and the guys?'

'Yes, in fact better than normal. He's now good friends with one of his worst enemies.'

'That's life. Friends become enemies – and enemies become friends in its eternal flow. Remember, you asked me what's the meaning of meditation?'

'Yes, am sorry about it.'

'Not at all, it's a splendid question. Meditation is *acceptance*.'

'Huh?'

'Acceptance, my dear friend, acceptance of all that is. A deep let-go. Accepting all the flavours of life, without questioning why – that's meditation.'

'Okay.'

'You don't seem convinced.'

'Well, I've been trying to meditate of late and…'

'How do you meditate?'

'I…I sit cross-legged and…'

'Do you enjoy it?'

'No, it's painful.'

'Then why do you sit cross-legged?'

'Because that's how Rammy does it, that's how most people here…'

'Stop looking at people. Do what *you* enjoy doing. What do you enjoy the most?'

'These days, playing tennis, I guess.'

'Well, then that's your meditation. Learn to accept who you are. Meditation is not a *doing*. It is *being*. Doing takes effort – that's why you find it painful. Being is effortless. Just play tennis. Merge into it. Dissolve into the activity. And, stop sitting cross-legged and stop torturing yourself. Self-torture will get you nowhere.'

'Okay, and what about love?'

'What about it?'

'About…about…the way I feel and the way I miss Ranju…sorry, my girlfriend…'

'You want to know the truth?'

'Yes…Zeno…' (I was finding it difficult to call him by his name, but then, practice maketh perfect, right?)

'Accept the pain – don't run away from it. If you feel like crying, don't hold back. If you feel miserable, feel totally so. *Be* the misery. It will go, but don't try to make it go. Taste the misery deeply – it has its own beauty. Talk to Sylvi often – she's pretty balanced and all, don't you think?'

'Yes, Zeno, she is…'

'Remember, if there were no misery, we wouldn't have known what's happiness. Everything in life is complementary, made of opposites. So don't try to accept only one side of life. Accept both sides of the coin, okay?'

'Okay,' I said, and I was beginning to feel better.

'Then will come a time when there is neither bliss nor misery. But that takes time to happen, okay?'

'Sure, whatever you say, Zeno.'

'No, not whatever *I* say. Use *your* intelligence. If what I say doesn't suit you, then drop what I said, but don't drop your feelings. Remember always: Zeno could be wrong, but your intelligence and your heart can *never* be wrong.'

I fell down at his feet and he chuckled. He placed his palms on my head and I felt a mysterious wave of warm compassion sweeping across my prostrate frame. I had never felt such a deep devotion for anyone in my life, so I cried again. (In fact, I cried more than I had in Sylvia's arms.)

'Sorry,' I said, gathering myself, maybe after two minutes, 'I just…just couldn't…control myself…Zeno…'

'Tears are good, Hari. As I said, they have their own beauty. Just like misery. And, whatever happens spontaneously is also good. I'm very happy with you. It takes courage to cry. It is only the cowards who pretend to be unemotional. Okay, now you go, and send Sylvi.'

'Okay, Zeno, bye Zeno.'

'Bye.'

'And thanks for your time.'

'Thanks for coming, Hari, and just *be* yourself. And, remember, no meditation. Only tennis. Let's call it *zennis*,' he punned laughingly.

15

Bum Chums, Tulip Terraces, Lighthouse

Then. January through October 1989.

SOLLY AND CHOPSY WERE QUITE MIFFED ABOUT RAMMY'S new-found friendship with Sattu. Body-builders hate other body-builders unless they are part of the same gang – so I guess it was some kind of insecurity about who had the greater muscle mass and who deserved to be revered as the mustachioed macho man. Or, perhaps they were unhappy about the fact that Rammy kept referring to Sattu as 'the brawn with brains'. Make a person feel inadequate and you have made an enemy for a lifetime. That's an infallible theory. Try it. Never fails. You can tell a man that he's a cheat, a liar, an addict—and he might actually take it all as a compliment—but he'll hate you forever if you tell him that he's got less brains than the average brawny-guy-next-door. Solly and Chopsy couldn't swallow that.

They distanced themselves from Rammy and me, and I knew that the famed Maniacs gang, the guys who had sworn to stick with each other through thick and thin, the gang that had stayed together and played together, was pretty close to total disintegration. Rammy, as usual, was quite smug about it all and said that 'all things that begin have to meet their logical end, sooner or later'. Shaky and Dusty were busy with their studies and hardly found time to interact with us anyway. Mangy had found some new love interest (his cousin's friend) who was graduating from some weird private college called Meenakshi Shetty College for Women or something like that, and he sauntered off to meet her every afternoon or evening rather religiously. On the weekends, Mangy could just not be seen, and we assumed that he was driving down his new flame to Mysore or Madras, and generally taking her for a ride. Literally. Rammy said that Mangy changes girls as often as a traffic signal changes lights – considering that he'd dropped four girlfriends in the space of five months. Anyway, that was Mangy's problem – or that of his girls. I had stopped judging people and tried to accept them as they were, ever since that day I met Zeno in private.

Rammy was right about Sattu though. In fact, after I began interacting with Sattu I discovered that he wasn't the kind of demon and monster that everyone had made him out to be. The problem with us as a species is that we hate people we don't know, and we don't know them because we hate them – and unless the hands of fate intervene and iron out the rough spots between two persons, one is usually stuck in the vicious cycle.

And ever since the hands of fate had brought Rammy and Sattu together, they were moving around like bum chums. Sattu was actually quite sharp, intelligent, helpful and generous, and even I became pally with him. He and Rammy got along like a house on fire and they spent most nights sitting at the new Insti, drinking gallons of tea and discussing tons of esoteric stuff. I liked hanging out with them because (a) I felt safe and secure in their presence; (b) I felt I wasn't wasting my time in idle gossip; and (c) I felt I was learning things that matter – things that nobody will ever teach you in medical school (but should).

The other guys were great to chill out with, yes, no doubt about that, but if you hung out with Rammy and Sattu (how shall I put it? ya) you got the satisfying feeling that you were *evolving* and justifying your existence as a human being in the eternal scheme of things. *Nights at the New Insti.* That can make it as a separate book for the sheer volume of things they discussed. Tonight was one such night, and both Rammy and Sattu were in their element.

'You know, Rammy dear,' said Sattu, gazing at the stars, 'how many galaxies there are in our universe?'

'Close to hundred billion, I guess,' said Rammy.

'Ya, and then there are a hundred billion stars in each galaxy too,' said Sattu. 'It is estimated that the number of stars in our universe is *more* than the number of grains of sand on all the beaches of the world!'

'Wow,' I said, nearly choking on my egg bhurji, 'then aren't we a li'l too small and insignificant – and we take ourselves so seriously…?'

'Seriousness is a universal disease – do you know how long light would take to move across our galaxy, Sattu, despite travelling at a mind-boggling speed of 300,000 km per second?' asked Rammy.

'No idea, tell me…' said Sattu.

'1,00,000 years,' said Rammy.

'Wow, and there are 100 billion galaxies, wonder how big our universe is and how long light would take to traverse it…' I said.

'Nature's intelligent, Rammy, but why would an intelligent nature just create life on one planet? It seems an awful waste of space,' said Sattu.

'That's a dangerous presumption. Scientists say just by the laws of probability there ought to be at least fifty other planets in our universe with life on them,' said Rammy.

'Aha, I wonder if those species are facing the same problems as us?' wondered Sattu.

'Maybe, maybe not,' said Rammy, 'but I guess all the electrons and protons are going to be the same everywhere…'

'You know, even physicists talk like mystics these days. The electron just disappears from one orbit and reaches another, it's never found in between, nobody knows how, it's all miraculous...' said Sattu.

'Ya,' said Rammy, 'and you know though electrons and protons are evenly balanced as far as their negative and positive charges are concerned, their weights are vastly different. This difference in weight makes electrons orbit the nucleus, just like earth orbits the sun, because 99.99% of the total mass of any atom is concentrated at the nucleus. If electrons had nearly the same weight as protons and neutrons, then they all would just move around one another, and the universe and matter perhaps wouldn't exist as we know it...'

'Right, but do you know, Hucky, that the existence of solid matter is pure illusion?' asked Sattu. 'Bet you an aloo parantha you don't know why.'

'No idea, tell me why and I treat you to a parantha...' I said.

'Well, if you imagine the nucleus of an atom as a grain of rice, then the electron orbitals around it is the size of a football field! There's absolutely nothing in between, just pure space! Seen from the atomic level, things *appear* to be solid when they are just lots of empty space.'

'Amazing! No wonder most people are empty vessels,' I said, and we all laughed.

'Yup, we live in an amazing universe where everything is a mystery. You know that most things we know contract upon cooling, but there is something that has a unique property, it expands upon cooling after it touches a certain temperature...' said Sattu.

'Water?' wondered Rammy.

'Bang on. At 4 degrees Celsius and below, water begins expanding. That's the reason ice floats on water. Otherwise, lakes and oceans and seas would freeze from bottom upwards and no aquatics would be able to survive. The floating sheet of ice actually protects the lives of fishes. Isn't it amazing?'

'It is. You know, Sattu, you've seen bacteria, and they move using their flagellum...?' asked Rammy.

'Ya...' said Sattu.

'Well, I was just reading the other day that bacteria move because of a hydrogen ion pump that functions like a rotary engine and generates energy for the flagellar movement – some scientists were shown a blueprint of it and were asked if it's a good design. They said it is an engineering marvel and wondered who'd designed it, and when they were told it's already found in nature, they were pretty stunned,' said Rammy.

'You think someone *designed* all this and it didn't happen by chance?' wondered Sattu.

'How can it be *chance*? It's so precise and complex. It is an *intelligent design*, Sattu. Call it God—I guess that's just an acronym for Greatest of Designers—someone has designed all this. And, complexity of design *implies* intelligence, and an intelligent being is definitely behind this entire creation,' said Rammy.

'The sheer magnitude is amazing. Okay, Rammy, you know what happens on the sun, on which our entire planet depends for its survival?' asked Sattu.

'Ya, nuclear fusion, sun's hydrogen atoms fuse together to form helium – it's actually a huge hydrogen bomb explosion...and to burst a hydrogen bomb, we first need to generate tremendous heat by bursting an atom bomb, and the sun already has this heat...' explained Rammy.

So now you know why I liked to hang out with them. They discussed many things – from Atomic physics and Molecular biology and Astronomy and space-time-curvature and Psychology and Philosophy and politics and movies to girls. You must have heard the saying that 'small minds discuss people; mediocre minds discuss events; and great minds discuss ideas'. Well, I was happy to be with two great minds.

Of course, I was no match for their intellectual might (I didn't even know if they were right or wrong about most things they said because most things they said were clearly beyond my ken, and perhaps

I am even quoting them wrong). But it was a pleasure just listening to them and, since they weren't snooty intellectual bullies, they never made me feel out of place despite all my ignorance. Plus it was fun listening to crazy theories that life might just be a movie made by the Greatest of Directors (another acronym for God)—Rammy coined that actually—and debating if such theories were right.

Rammy also said that perhaps our entire universe just disappears and re-appears every trillionth of a second, and we will never perceive it happening because we will never know what's happening at the micro level of space-time. He said that perhaps it was God's way of saying that we live in a soap bubble. Sattu said perhaps that's what Maya is all about, for many enlightened masters keep saying that the sheer continuity is amazing and seems quite impossible.

Solly was hardly seen in the hostel or in the mess. Of course, he didn't come to classes for close to a month. I ran into him three weeks ago at the new Insti and became quite wide-eyed seeing him counting some pounds and dollars. When I asked him how he had come into all the high-value currency, he mentioned that he'd got himself a new girlfriend, a rich Dutch girl called Melissa-something.

He was looking positively unhealthy though. His hair was long and unkempt (obviously he hadn't bathed for days); his nail beds had gathered more filth and grime than a car on a Himalayan rally; his face was thinner and scrawnier; his clothes—if at all his pyjama-slacks and sleeveless vest qualified as that—were so crummy that they would have put a ragamuffin to shame; and he looked more like a punk from downtown New York than a student from a medical college. I was worried and asked him if he was on heroin or smack or crack or something, and he asked me to mind my own business.

'Listen, Solly,' I said, 'whatever it is you are into, it's not good for you, and this girl is doing you no favour by letting you be like this – is she a junkie…?'

'Fuck off, don't you dare talk about her…' he said.

'Hey, I'm telling for your own good, dude, see what you've become, I am aghast…'

'Listen, I'm telling you nicely, if I want your advice, I'll give it to you. I live the way I want to, just like you interact with the slimes you want to, okay?'

'Solly, we're friends. I'm worried for you, man…'

'No, we are not, and worry about yourself, I don't need fuck-all friends like you,' he said, and walked away.

Since Solly hadn't been seen for quite a few months and wasn't attending any classes (for once, he was pretty consistent about something) he was rusticated for a period of two months. Of course, he never saw the notice because I didn't see him for a long while after our rough conversation at the new Insti.

The hurried knocks on the door coincided with the stereophonic knuckle-raps I was drumming on my temples and I almost said 'go away' (make that 'fuck off' if you want to know the grouchy tone I would have said it in), and then I heard Sattu shouting my name, so I opened the door before Sattu could break it open.

'Are you Kumbhakarna or something – I've been knocking for ages, dear…?'

'Sorry, not too well, what happened?'

'Rammy's calling you to the Warden's office pronto, get into something decent,' said Sattu, looking at my Bermudas.

'Why, what's wrong, any trouble with the Warden?'

'No, no, Solly's mother has come over and…'

'Shit, man! *Solly's mother?*'

'Ya, you come fast – I've to go order tea and breakfast for her…'

When I reached the parents' room next to the Warden's office I saw Rammy sitting with Solly's mom, assuring her that we'd be able to trace Solly soon.

The Warden had obviously left her in Rammy's care after briefing her about Solly's consistent absence. Rammy introduced her to me, and though she was pretty distraught and all, she was still a picture of calm dignity – definitely the kind of woman who didn't let adversity colour her mood too much.

It can be pretty nerve-wracking for a parent to receive a letter saying that they suspected that their son had become a drug addict— she showed me the communiqué that had been issued by the T.O. which was followed up by a similar letter from the Warden—and I suddenly felt an uncontrollable wave of anger, and wanted to kick Solly, wherever he was.

A nasty smell of foreboding intensified inside my head. It was growing like a mushroom cloud and I instinctively shook my neck. Well, I knew where he was—he was shacking up with that Melissa-something somewhere in Jaya Nagar—but should I tell her that? Rammy asked me to spell out the truth and I told her that though I didn't have the exact address, I did have a vague idea of Solly's whereabouts. She asked me who would know and I thought about Chopsy and Mangy. I was sure Solly would've done a bit of the show-offy thing of taking them to his pad and all. I said that we'd try to get him back to the hostel, but she insisted on getting a first-hand eye-witness account of Solly and the *gori daain* (gori = white-skinned; daain = witch) and made me promise that I'd take her to his pad.

I woke up Mangy and asked for Solly's address, saying that even Rammy was pretty livid with him, and coolly lied that the Warden had promised to rusticate him if he didn't spill the beans. Mangy gave me the address and made me swear not to tell Solly about it. Two promises in the space of five minutes: one I was honour-bound to keep; the other I didn't give a rat's ass about as I felt that Mangy and Chopsy were majorly to blame for Solly's ruination.

◇

When we reached Solly's pad—it was in fact quite a nice apartment called Tulip Terraces (is this why the Dutch girl had chosen it since Tulip is the national flower of Holland?)—Rammy said he would wait downstairs since they hadn't been on talking terms for quite a while now. I suspected that Rammy feared a violent reaction from Solly. I knocked hard on the door and a bare-bodied Solly opened it after some two minutes. He was looking like a typical junkie and seemed rather shocked to see me there.

'What the hell are you doing here! Who the fuck gave you this address, you bloody swine...?'

'Why are you abusing him?' screamed his mom, swimming into his line of vision, 'I asked him to bring me here,' and Solly glared at me like a blood-thirsty hound. If nature had endowed him with poison glands he would've surely bitten me and I could've kissed my mortal coils a painful goodbye. He looked positively venomous and his glare was burning my skin.

We walked into his living room, feeling as uninvited as celibate monks at a Roman orgy, and Solly hastily kicked something under the sofa (was it a condom packet or a tampon? – either/both).

'Where *is* the *daain*?' thundered his mom.

'Mumma, how are you?'

'To hell with the pleasantries,' she said, 'where's the daain?'

'Mumma, please don't call her that...'

She slapped him so hard that I was afraid she had fractured her wrist or something. Solly stepped back, and the Melissa-something Dutch heiress emerged from her room (in a skimpy, bare-all, one-piece lingerie) asking, 'Solly darling, who the fuck are these people?'

Solly shushed her and said some foreign word (maybe Dutch for pests?) and she looked surprised. This Melissa-something defied classification or categorisation, dude. She was a Tennis Ball, yes, but I couldn't decide whether she was a Sadness or something even worse. I wondered what Solly had seen in her – or perhaps he had just seen her bank balance and decided to sacrifice aesthetics for economics. She was as tall as an electric pole; as slender; and as high-strung. She screamed something hysterically and Solly asked her to go back to her room.

'Get ready fast, we are going,' said Solly's mom to him rather commandingly.

'Mumma, give me a few days to sort things out...'

'Shut up, we leave in *five minutes*, you think you can do anything and nobody will question you...?'

'Look, mumma, I'm grown up and...'

'Ya, you've grown up into a depraved drug addict, an irresponsible bum, and a daain-worshipper, I can see that, how shameless of you, now wear something before I call up daddy and ask him to make some arrangements to forcibly drag you out...'

Solly gave in, went inside to talk to the Melissa-something electric pole, and we heard some hysterical howling for a while, which petered out into loud sniffles, and he emerged wearing pyjama-slacks and a half-sleeve vest.

'Wear something befitting a human being,' said his mom, and he hastily got into a sweatshirt thrown carelessly on a chair. 'Where's your bag?'

'Bag, mumma?'

'Bag. Your stuff, your clothes – you think you're going to come here later to collect them?'

'Mumma, please...'

'Auntyji, first let's go to the hostel and talk things out,' I said, 'we can always come back for his stuff later.'

She relented and we left the apartment, but not before the daain and Solly did some hugging-pecking-hugging stuff and his mom glared at me as if I'd known about his errant ways for a long while and had proven to be a pretty lousy friend in letting him ruin himself thus. There was nothing I could do to change that impression (well, at least not at that moment) so I absorbed her glare as stoically as I could and began walking down the stairs.

When Solly saw Rammy standing next to our bike parked outside Tulip Terraces, Solly's eyes became extra-red and glowed like a lighthouse smoking a joint. Rammy remained poker-faced and I hailed an autorickshaw for the irate mom and her junkie son.

◇

Later in the evening, Sattu and I were discussing some crazy philosophical crap with Rammy in his room when Solly barged in. He'd got a crew cut (obviously forced by his mom) and a shave. Thankfully, he was also dressed in a jeans and T-shirt (gosh, how ill-fitting his pyjama-slacks had been!) and was looking quite human and all.

'You bastard!' he yelled at Rammy, 'you engineered all this...'

'Engineered what, Solly?' asked Rammy.

'Why, you brought my mom to my pad – *saalay grud*, how could you do that?'

'Solly, now listen, all this is for your own good, we do go astray at times, that's cool, but one has to return to normalcy sooner...' said Rammy.

'Balls to you! Stop preaching to me, and don't ever interfere in my life or else I'll...' said Solly, advancing threateningly towards Rammy.

'You touch him, and I'll screw your trip,' said Sattu, and Rammy asked Sattu to cool down.

'Solly, it's not Rammy's fault, your mom insisted...' I began.

'You shut up, you shit-eating *charsi* pig,' said Solly.

'Now, now, Solly, we're your best friends,' said Rammy, and got up to throw his arm on Solly's shoulder, and Solly slapped him.

Rammy was taken aback, but quickly regained his composure, and Sattu got up menacingly, and I gestured to him to let Rammy handle this outburst.

'Okay, Solly, if hitting me makes you feel better, hit me again,' said Rammy. 'It's cool.'

'Fuck you! I don't wish to dirty my hands hitting slimeball bastards like you,' said Solly, and walked out. (Out of our lives, you can say, because we didn't see him again.)

'How the hell can he hit you, dear?' fumed Sattu. 'If you hadn't stopped me, I'd have pulverized this junkie.'

'Forget it, Sattu. Happens,' said Rammy coolly.

Solly's mom carted him away to Delhi, and Rammy received a note of thanks from her after a week in which she mentioned that they had got him admitted to a de-addiction camp, and he was apparently on the road to recovery.

Chopsy and Mangy were angry with Rammy and me as they felt that we had no business to interfere in Solly's life, and hence they stopped talking to us. So, now our group was reduced to just three people and I gathered that they used to refer to us as 'Gandhiji's three monkeys'. Rammy was pretty amused when he heard that and said it was quite a compliment actually, 'since those monkeys represent virtues and all that is valuable and desirable in human beings'.

The only time they actually spoke to us was when they both came to Rammy's room one evening carrying a foreign journal of Medicine. I was reading some newspaper article Rammy had written (ya, he had begun contributing features to *The Bangalore Herald* and *The National Chronicle* – I must say that he was a pretty good humour writer) and he was playing chess against himself.

'Hi, we've come to tell you something, Rammy,' said Mangy.

'What?' he asked, without looking up from the chessboard.

'Well, you know your problem?' said Chopsy. 'You think you're always perfectly right.'

'So?' asked Rammy.

'So, you suffer from Obsessive Compulsive Perfectomania Disorder or OCPD,' said Mangy.

'Says who?' asked Rammy.

'See, it's written by Ferguson, look here,' said Mangy, showing him some page in the journal that Rammy didn't care to look at, 'it clearly says here that such people think they are always right. It's called Ferguson's Syndrome.'

'Okay, thanks for the information,' said Rammy.

'Look, it's a disorder, you need to get yourself treated,' said Chopsy.

'Really?' asked Rammy, and I looked up amused as his tone clearly suggested that he was going to screw their trip.

'Yes, yes,' said Mangy.

'Okay, what exactly is this OCPD?' asked Rammy.

'Well, I told you – it's a psychological disorder that makes you feel that you're always right,' said Mangy.

'And who had written this?' asked Rammy.

'Ferguson, he's written it,' said Chopsy.

'And when Ferguson writes something, does he write thinking he's perfectly right or thinking he's perfectly wrong?' asked Rammy.

'What nonsense! Obviously Ferguson *knows* he's perfectly right,' said Mangy.

'Sure?' asked Rammy.

'Obviously,' said Chopsy.

'Then Ferguson suffers from this OCPD, not me, you just said that such people think they are always *perfectly right*, didn't you?' retorted Rammy.

Chopsy and Mangy looked at each other and didn't know what to say.

'Listen, you gruds,' said Rammy, 'don't try to ever get the better of your intellectual superiors. Buzz off, and don't come to my room again.'

They both left like mongrels who'd ventured into a lion's den hoping to rib the lion, only to end up discovering that lions couldn't be ribbed that easily.

◇

Rammy suddenly developed another passion. You could actually call it his maiden job. Make that *our* maiden job. One of his dad's distant relatives had read his articles in *The Bangalore Herald* and he'd lost no time in getting in touch with Rammy. He dropped him a line at the hostel – in fact, I was the one who delivered the letter to him from the pigeonhole where all letters were dutifully dropped by the postman at two in the afternoon.

Rammy said that some guy called Mr Varadarajan wanted him to work as a trainee copywriter in an ad agency he was running. The agency's name was quite catchy and all. Plus the letterhead looked positively inviting. *Lighthouse Communications*, it said, and the logo was some kind of cartoon. It showed a guy standing at the top of a lighthouse and shouting into a megaphone: Mix sound with light, to get the communication right! (The agency guys called that the tagline, I'd learn later.)

I insisted on going with Rammy the next day to this agency in Jaya Nagar and was positively impressed with the set-up. It looked more like a college canteen, what with most guys sporting ponytails and studs; and most girls dressed in mini skirts, shorts or tight jeans. The office was vibrant, colourful and buzzing with creative energy. Everyone was laughing or joking around and nobody seemed to be working. (I realised later that laughing and joking was part of the work – it was called brainstorming session.) It was all so very different from the regulated, disciplined atmosphere on our campus that I wondered if people should get paid for having fun. (Shouldn't your salary be directly proportional to the amount of misery you were forced to endure?)

The peon showed us in and Mr Varadarajan welcomed Rammy and said he was very impressed with his humour articles appearing regularly in *The Bangalore Herald*. Rammy said his best was yet to come and Mr Varadarajan asked him if he would like to work part-time in the copy department since 'someone with a twisted sense of humour always makes a great copywriter'.

Rammy said he didn't mind giving it a shot and requested that I also be allowed to be part of the 'trainee think-tank', adding that I was his sounding board and all that. I felt pretty honoured about it and Mr Varadarajan didn't seem to have any objections and said that two brilliant minds were better than one. He called in the Creative Director, a cute girl called 'Jijo' (her full name was Jagruti Joshi), and I realised later that nobody at the agency was ever called by their real names. Mr Varadarajan was 'Verry'; the accounts executive, Balaram Shetty, was 'Balsy'; and even the peon, Pandurang Acharya, was 'Panda'. Verry said that he'd decide our stipend and all over the week and promised to keep it proportionate to the quality of stuff we guys churned out.

After we wolfed down some veg puffs and guzzled two glasses of cold coffee that Panda got for us, Jijo took us to her cabin.

'So,' she said smilingly, 'congratulations, and welcome aboard the Lighthouse. Let me guide you through the basics. When we need an ad, we first give you something called a brief. And, it's not an undergarment...'

'I know,' said Rammy cheerfully, 'a brief is a synopsis of what the client wants, usually given by the accounts executive...'

'Great!' she said excitedly, 'you guys know the basics already, wonderful!' (I really knew jack shit but I happily nodded nonetheless.) 'Okay, let's rev up your grey cells. We have an anti-pimple ayurvedic tonic to try and market. First, we need to come up with some catchy name, okay? Second, we need a campaign...you know what's a campaign?'

'Ya,' said Rammy, 'a series of press ads, mostly three...'

'Wow! You've worked in an ad agency before?'

'No, Jijo, but I guess I've read a few books on advertising...'

'Super, Rammy, super, okay now you guys give it all you got, actually the presentation's in a week's time, but if we can crack something today or tomorrow, it'll be just great, okay? It's for an English-speaking audience, okay, mainly college girls and all, okay?'

'Okay, I'm on it,' said Rammy, mimicking her, and she left us at our cubicle.

It felt just great to exercise the creative side of your brain and write smart lines and all. Rammy was clearly enjoying it. Gosh, how very multi-talented he was! Did I tell you that he also used to play the harmonica rather well (how I hate it when someone calls it mouth-organ – sounds as if a slut is giving you a blow job) and he could doodle some pretty neat cartoons too?

When I'd asked him once if he was bad at anything, he'd mentioned 'cooking and cricket' – but that must have been true only because Rammy had set some pretty high standards for himself.

Rammy and I did a lot of brainstorming and drank gallons of cold coffee and ate tons of ginger biscuits (everything was on the house). By afternoon, we had come up with quite a few ideas.

Headline: Pity, I fell in love with the pimple but had to marry the entire woman.

Subhead: Here's more such lies.

Copy: Everyone loves pimples. Your boyfriend, your husband, the guy who's planning to propose to you. Why, even your would-be employer. There's nothing like a pimple to increase your attractiveness. Everyone hates clear skin. Clear skin makes you look so unreal – just like a plastic doll. It is pimples that give your beauty that rare human touch. Statistics show that nine out of ten guys just love girls with pimples.

Want to continue believing in lies? Or do you want to face some home truths?

That Cleary is the best anti-pimple tonic you can find in the market? That Cleary will make your face smooth, shiny and superbly seductive? That Cleary is what the doctor ordered for girls harassed by pimples?

Drink two spoonfuls of Cleary every day. Get drunk on compliments forever.

I suggested some alternatives for the headline: The simple truth is, a pimple is more beautiful than a dimple/Ms Beautiful Long

Hair, Ms Beautiful Lips, Ms Beautiful Smile are no match for you, because you are Ms Beautiful Pimple/A pimple is a thing of beauty and a joy forever/The simple truth: Guys love pimples. Rammy said my sarcasm was great.

Jijo came to our cubicle, took a look at our work, and said that it was pretty good for beginners, and we came up with more names for the tonic like Goldface, Beautonic, Happinezz, Happi, Lovely Lady, No More Pimples etcetera. Verry said our work was pretty mature for trainees and asked us to work on a condom account too. The condom was called 'Funky'.

Rammy came up with some ideas in a matter of minutes and I heard Jijo saying to Verry that 'this guy would be wasted as a doctor'. (Here, take a look at Rammy's ideas since we are recording all this for posterity.)

Idea # 1: Show a blackboard on which someone has written the following with chalk: What's the arithmetic of sex? Add up on bed; subtract your clothes; divide your legs; and multiply. What's the real arithmetic of sex? Funky deletes multiply.

Idea # 2: Show a bed with two bodies fully covered by a white blanket and write at the bottom: What you should be wearing when you aren't wearing anything else.

Idea # 3: Your grandpa's grandpa will never ask you to wear one. But then, your grandpa's grandpa will never ask you to sleep with your girlfriend either.

Even I came up with a few ideas, clearly inspired by Rammy's genius.

My Idea # 1: Wear it before you bare it.
My Idea # 2: Get into it. Or get ready to change diapers.
My Idea # 3: Do you want her to carry a baby or just sweet memories of the night?
My Idea # 4: Because *your* pleasure shouldn't become *her* pain.

Ya, I guess I was pretty juvenile and all that, but I had lots of fun at Lighthouse. Rammy and I became regulars out there, especially on Saturdays and Sundays. Those guys hardly ever took a break, and were always up against tight deadlines. I guess they liked the fact that there were two extra hands who were pretty good at coming up with some wild ideas. Plus they all clubbed and partied a lot, and made me feel that I was more intelligent than I thought I was, so I was quite happy to hobnob with them. Rammy even said that I tended to underestimate myself and that I was a pretty neat writer. So, I guess I kept going there with Rammy more for the ego-boost than for what was popularly known in advertising agency circles as 'creative satisfaction'. Jijo said the client had liked all of Rammy's condom ideas and they planned to carry them in a few magazines perhaps a month or two later. They even liked my condom Idea # 3 and were contemplating using my Idea # 1 as a baseline. Wow! But Rammy, as usual, expressed no emotion. The guy was neither happy nor unhappy; or perhaps he had transcended both emotions; or perhaps he was just pretending. I didn't know. Nobody did. I suspected he didn't know the state of his mind either. But me, I was happy. After a week or so, Verry decided to give Rammy a stipend of ₹600 every month; and I was promised ₹400. Good show, wasn't it?

16

The Change, the Harassment, the Postponement

Then. January through June 1990.

$\mathcal{M}$AJ. GEN. SURINDER THAKUR RETIRED AND GATTU BECAME A full Colonel and got posted to somewhere in Assam. The Warden too was bundled off to Defcoms, Allahabad, and we were seeing a change in guard. Nobody likes change—especially when you were getting along famously with the guys at the helm—and Rammy said that perhaps the Hellmints (remember the safari-clad guys from the Health Ministry?) were doing this just to begin tightening the screws.

One look at the new Dean, Maj. Gen. Yogesh Chandra Raheja, and you knew that you were looking at someone who carried DNA that had percolated from illustrious ancestors like Hitler and Mussolini. He made an I-am-here-to-make-your-life-miserable speech in the auditorium and didn't mince words as he told us that his brief was simple: '...to streamline the administration' (the faculty shuddered) and 'enforce the kind of discipline the armed forces expects' (the students shivered). He didn't say it in as many words but his scowl clearly meant that you could expect as much leniency and compassion from him as you would from a fire-breathing dragon. Rammy's prediction that 'once this fizzles out we are all in for some pretty troubled times' was about to come true. (Remember he'd said that during the strike the Wonder batch rebels had organised?)

The new Training Officer, Lt. Col. Satyapal Mishra, and the new Warden, Lt. Col. Rakesh Gupta, could have been Himmler and Goebbels in their previous births, and they kept looking approvingly at Maj. Gen. Raheja, and kept nodding their heads like ass-licking yes-men throughout his ten-minute speech (or should one rightly call it ten-minute threat?)

We were disgusted with the Dean's tone and were worried about the way he kept referring to us as 'cadets'.

'We aren't cadets, and this isn't an academy, man,' said Sattu.

'Arre, can't you understand the veiled message? He's trying to intimidate us and warn us that he means business,' said Rammy.

'So what will happen, man? This guy is worse than General Thakur,' I observed. 'General Thakur was human, dude – this guy is the devil himself.'

'He'll take everyone's trip, what else?' said Sattu wryly.

'Guys with an unhappy childhood and a sex-starved youth become sadists. I bet you folks an aloo parantha that this cuckold got married pretty late in life, tortured his wife emotionally, which drove her to infidelity, and she had a clandestine affair with his batman or some other paramour to get back at him,' said Rammy.

'Why don't you ask him, Rammy?' remarked Sattu.

'I would, if I had the guarantee that I'd get an honest answer.'

By afternoon, a huge notice was impaled upon the notice board outside the Dean's office, the Warden's office and at the pigeonhole. Our worst fears had come true.

OFFICE OF THE DEAN, DEFCOMS, BANGALORE

1. All undergraduates at Defcoms will henceforth be called Gentleman Cadet or Lady Cadet.

2. All cadets will wear their uniforms from 0800 HRS to 2200 HRS, both in the hostel and college, and when outside, on all seven days of the week.

3. All cadets will sleep from 2205 HRS to 0430 HRS, on all seven days of the week.

4. All cadets will assemble for compulsory parade at the parade ground from 0500 HRS to 0600 HRS every day, on all seven days of the week.

5. All cadets will maintain 100% attendance in all classes.

6. All cadets will report for compulsory attendance in the hostel and assemble at their floors at 2200 HRS every night, on all seven days of the week.

7. No cadet will be allowed to move out of the hostel after 1800 HRS, on all seven days of the week.

8. All cadets will air grievances (if any) through the proper channels—through the Student Liaison Officer (SLO). There will be no General Secretary (GS) and no elections. SLO will be appointed by the Dean through a selection process. The new SLO will be appointed soon.

9. No cadet from the boys' hostel will visit the girls' hostel—and vice versa.

10. Lady Cadets will not visit the boys' hostel canteen. They will visit the canteen next to the new Ophthalmology department only.

11. All cadets will assemble for compulsory games from 1700 HRS to 1800 HRS at the parade ground, on all seven days of the week.

12. Attendance is compulsory for all sports meets, competitions, debates etc organised by the college.

13. Failure to comply with any of the above will invite strict disciplinary action.

Maj. Gen. Yogesh Chandra Raheja

'Crap, man, is this a medical college or a military garrison?' asked Sattu.

'Now, it's a bit of both,' said Rammy.

Most of the Yankee Monarchs had assembled at the pigeonhole and we all were staring at the notice in complete disbelief. Oh, I forgot to tell you, the Yankee regulars had passed out in December 1989 (lucky guys). Shaky had cleared and he had paid out to try for the USMLE and migrate to America. Dusty had flunked one paper—Surgery theory—so technically he was a Yankee Monarch, though he wouldn't need to attend any classes. (Once you were allowed for the Univ exams, you didn't have to worry about attendance norms and all that crap.)

'This is crazy, man, this guy is a bully, we should sort him out,' said Punchoo.

'Give me one minute alone in a room with him…' said Sattu.

'And the Military Police will whisk you away,' said Rammy. 'Guys, let's wait and watch, consolidate ourselves, and strike when the iron is hot.'

Anyway, we didn't have too much time to worry about all this as our final Univ exams were just four months away. Remember, we were in the ninth term – just on the threshold of passing out, so we decided to lie low and set our sights on our academic target instead. We had quite a bit on our hands.

Medicine, Surgery, Obstetrics and Gynaecology, Preventive and Social Medicine, ENT, Ophthalmology, plus imagine all the journals and clinics and tutorials, and you could say that even the four-armed Vishnu's hands would've been quite full if he'd decided to try his hand at academic multi-tasking in the final term.

Thankfully, after a week it was announced ('this is just unofficial—totally off the record' were the T.O.'s exact words) that all ninth termers were exempt from the notice issued a week ago, apart from the uniform bit of course. Perhaps they felt that folks of our stature ought not to be rule-provoked too much, especially since we were the senior-most Monarchs in the college who wielded quite a bit of clout at the hostel with the disgruntled student fraternity. We told the T.O., quite clearly and collectively, that we weren't going to wear uniforms and all at the hostel, or when we ventured outside, and he could do whatever he felt like doing. The Warden just kept warning us about it every now and then, whenever he came on his mandatory rounds and spotted us in Bermudas or pyjamas (Sattu even began strutting about in a *lungi* just to rile him, heehee). But the Warden did nothing seriously damaging about it all and Rammy mentioned that the authorities were just waiting for the remainder of Yankee batch to pass out before they started enforcing the new rules with the kind of vehemence you generally associate with sadistic administrators.

But we heard lots of reports of the rooms of our juniors being raided in the middle of the night, with the Warden and the T.O. demanding the removal of sleazy posters of actresses and *Debonair* centrespreads. One report even mentioned some poor junior guy having been caught self-stimulating his joy with a *Playboy* playmate acting as the hormonal catalyst, and the Chief Warden had, on that occasion, confiscated the said magazine and embarrassed the poor junior guy with some pretty shitty talk on 'the art of self-control' and 'the art of channelising one's animal energies into more creative, human pursuits'.

Our immediate juniors, the Zulu batchers, were the worst-affected. Lots of them got fined and reprimanded, and they felt as harassed as slaves at a harem. Everyone felt claustrophobic and suffocated by the stupid killjoy rules that Gen. Raheja had formulated. Even our profs and most of the support staff began complaining (of course in private) of Gen. Raheja's autocratic ways, and his systematic destruction of morale, and his methodical plans to convert a vibrant campus into a dreary concentration camp.

There are only two things students do when they are disgruntled. They protest openly or crib privately. Okay, you can add a third thing: they drink gallons of tea at the new Insti and say that somebody has to sort out the tyrant and wonder who will put his head in the line of fire. But to give credit to Gen. Raheja's administrative skills, he had planted a few moles in the hostel, and he always got a whiff of any proposed act of rebellion, and you usually saw a few vociferous rebels being fined heavily or rusticated mercilessly.

'If this is a taste of things to come, then I don't wish to join the army. What about you?' asked Sattu as Haluji brought us a new experimental concoction of hot chocolate one fine night. Our final exams were just a month away.

'Well, statistically speaking,' said Rammy, 'it's not wise to gauge the entire armed forces by the attitude of one General. One needs a larger statistical sample to arrive at a correct estimate.'

'No, dear, I understand all that,' said Sattu. 'What I mean is, once we join the army, we are trapped for twenty years or thereabouts. Would you like that?'

'We'll know if we like the ocean only when we take the plunge,' I said.

'Ya, but what if you realise you don't like the ocean? And you know, you can't step out of it just because you don't like it,' said Rammy.

'Exactly my point, assuming there's a fifty-fifty chance that we don't like it, there's nothing we can do about it,' said Sattu.

'You're right, Sattu, but if you consider the job security and the standard of living etcetera, then it might turn out to be a good deal,' I said.

'Freedom is top priority, dear, not job security, no doctor can ever starve...' said Sattu.

'Ya, you can't just divorce the army once you marry it,' said Rammy. 'But Sattu, you can always pay out.'

'That's the problem, dear. Mom can only arrange the money after a year or so. She lost some money in the stock market, and an LIC policy matures next year, so she'll come into money only then.' (Sattu had lost his dad and brother in 1982, after some loan sharks pushed them into a Ludhiana well after his dad defaulted on some payments. Thereafter, the loan sharks had bribed the cops to write off the case as suicide, and had vowed to bump off the rest of the defaulting family. He and his mom had escaped to his uncle's place in Delhi, and his mom had promised her God that they both would become vegetarians if they survived the ordeal. Then, she'd begun working as a primary school teacher. Later, she'd disposed of their hosiery business and home at a throwaway price...Sad but true.)

'Oh, okay,' said Rammy, 'do you know that either you have to pay out within four months of passing the finals or join the army if you can't raise the money in time?'

'Ya, I know, so I have decided to flunk a few papers,' said Sattu.

'You can't be serious?' I screamed.

'Of course, dear, I'm serious,' said Sattu.

'You mean, you will deliberately try and...' said Rammy.

'Look, guys, are you *sure* you want to join the army?' asked Sattu. 'Be honest.'

'No, I'm not sure,' said Rammy.

'No, me neither,' I said.

'What's the heated discussion about, dudes?' asked Dusty, plonking himself next to us.

'We're debating the pros and cons about joining the army,' said Sattu.

'Hmmm,' said Dusty, 'lots of pros actually, free rations, cool job, golf and sports facilities, good quarters, steady salary, subsidised canteen facilities, social prestige, post-retirement pension, patriotic satisfaction, and of course the pride of wearing the uniform...'

'Ya, that's okay, dear, but isn't freedom a far greater need of any human being?' argued Sattu.

'Well, depends, one has to sacrifice something for security, I guess,' said Dusty.

'So you've decided to join the army?' asked Rammy.

'Oh, I'd love to, but I can understand what you guys fear – loss of individuality, freedom, liberty, that sort of thing?' observed Dusty.

'Rammy, can you afford to pay out?' asked Sattu.

'Well, actually ditto problem as you. It'll take dad a while to arrange ninety-five grand, that's quite steep given his present financial status—what about you, Hucks?'

'I guess dad can manage it,' I said.

'Rammy dear, it's better not to pass this time, think about it,' said Sattu. 'We'll have more time to decide if we don't…'

'You guys are planning to *fail*?' asked Dusty, clearly perplexed.

'Yup,' said Rammy, 'it's an idea floating around.'

'I can't believe it!' said Dusty.

'Listen, Rammy dear, do you know you can't just write to newspapers once you join the army? And you're doing well writing ads and all. You're so talented, man, I'm telling you, it'll be a sheer waste of your potential. I suggest you seriously consider paying out, dear,' said Sattu.

'Ya, Rammy, with your creative intellect, you'd be a misfit in the army,' I agreed.

'So what about you, Dusty?' asked Rammy, clearly deflecting the convo, 'you think you'll enjoy twenty-something years of a regimented lifestyle?'

'Absolutely,' said Dusty, 'I am looking forward to it, hey guys, I forgot to tell you, I'm getting engaged two months later, I met this superb girl, Manisha, at my cousin's wedding some six months ago, and they have sent a marriage proposal to my dad which we have tentatively accepted…'

'Amazing, dear, so now marriage and responsibility is making you accept lifelong slavery…' said Sattu.

'You can say that, Sattu, her dad's a Brigadier, and they're looking for a *fauji* son-in-law, plus this girl is just *superb*, so once I pass and become a lieutenant or something, my life is set…' said Dusty.

'Is she an Ecstasy?' I asked.

'Better, Hucky, a Football Ecstasy,' said Dusty. 'She was Miss Shimla and all that…'

'Another one bites the dust, and falls prey to lust,' observed Rammy.

◇

Just a week before the final exams, we realised that our Paediatrics and Anaesthesiology journals had not been signed by the profs. When you have too much on your hands, you tend to forget a few minor details. But these were important if you wished to clear your Medicine and Surgery vivas, so when Dusty reminded us about it, we swung into action. We were only planning to flunk a few theories – the easy ones like ENT and Ophthalmology.

'Where were you all these days?' thundered Dr Megha Gupta.

'We were busy studying,' said Sattu.

'Yes, ma'am, sorry for the delay...' I said.

'Better late than never,' philosophised Rammy.

'I'm not going to sign your journals so late,' she said.

'Okay, ma'am, thanks for your help,' said Rammy, and we began exiting the room after he eye-hinted that we follow him.

'Wait,' she shouted as we turned at the doorway.

'Yes, ma'am?' enquired Sattu.

'You people seem to be unbothered that you'll flunk the Medicine viva,' she observed.

'Ma'am, tell you the truth, we're not too eager to even pass this time,' said Rammy. 'We're postponing it actually.'

'What?' she asked, sounding totally surprised. 'You *don't* want to pass?'

'Yes, ma'am,' said Sattu, and explained their plan of extending their hostel stay for a few more months, till they were able to arrange money to pay out.

'What about you?' she asked me.

'I want to pass, ma'am, but it would be fun to hang around for a while. Perhaps I'll clear a few papers and not be too stressed-out about it. I'm actually enjoying being with Ramakrishna and Satinder...' I said.

'I've never come across students like you in the past twenty years,' she said.

'We're all unique concepts ma'am, and perhaps we're only looking for an excuse to flunk, so if you don't sign the journal, we'll surely fail, that's why I said thanks for your help...' said Rammy.

'Okay, enough, I don't want to be burdened with your failure, leave the journals here and collect them tomorrow morning,' she said.

We pulled off the same trick with Lt. Col. Gaurang Malhotra, the Anaesthesiology prof, and got away with it.

Rita had gone back to Germany 'to earn a living', according to Sylvia. We decided to hang around for a month or so before our results were declared. Maria was back and they gave us Rita's room. Ya, Sattu had also joined us and was quite eager to meet Zeno. These girls were really lucky – they worked back home for close to six months and they could afford to trek back and forth. The living standard of someone working as a waiter or waitress in Europe was far better than someone working as a manager in India.

Maria had got a used Grundig colour TV and a Technics VCR from England, so we saw lots of movies. The girls wished to learn Hindi, so we rented loads of drab and mushy Hindi stuff, and we kept translating the dialogues for them. But a few words like *suhaag*, *mangalsutra*, *raakhi*, *sindoor* and *aarti* defied translation; I mean, we could explain the meaning and all, but you just can't explain the *significance* of these to people who were constantly asking why these were given so much importance in almost every Hindi movie ('as if your very life depended on it'). No, they weren't poking fun at our traditions (so don't plan to lynch them or something, saying they have hurt your religious sentiments and all). They were just wondering if we as a people were heavily dependent on traditional symbols to

(a) add some meaning to our tired lives or (b) feel secure or (c) escape the reality of our individual consciousness or (d) all of the afore-mentioned. They were trying to understand the Indian mind and Rammy said that the Indian mind is 'a collective tangle that has got trapped in a space-time warp'. What he meant was that we were all living in the past.

◇

Zeno had returned from a brief lecture tour to Hong Kong and we were all eager to meet him. He seemed *more enlightened* (if at all you could become that) than before and, quite uncharacteristically, invited us all to his room for a 'group discussion'. He usually preferred one-on-ones, but we were glad that he wished to meet our entire gang together. Perhaps he wished to analyse the interplay of our emotions.

This was the first time Sattu was meeting him. (Sattu later said that 'Zeno was a raft powered by clarity which was floating majestically and blissfully on the tumultuous sea of life'. Like they say, you never get a second chance to make a first impression, and Zeno definitely seemed to have impressed Sattu, though I was sure Zeno didn't feel the need for any compliments from anyone.)

We had all gathered in Zeno's room and I saw that now even the bookshelf had been removed. I said perhaps Zeno felt he'd done enough of reading, but Sylvia explained that they had created a new study room for him just behind the cafeteria.

'So,' asked Zeno of me, 'how's your tennis-meditation going on?'

'Of late, I didn't find much time for that, Zeno, we've been too busy with our exams.'

'Aha, time is never enough,' he said, 'have you all ever wondered what is time – Rama, you remember you asked me about it last time?'

'Yes, Zeno,' said Rammy, 'Sattu here, and I, we keep discussing the nature of time and all...'

'Can you understand the concept of time through discussions?' wondered Zeno.

'Well, sir, no,' said Sattu, 'but I guess that's the best we can do.'

'Not at all, there's one more thing you can do. Thoughts, if you realise, take time to happen. You think a thought within a certain span of time. So, you can say that thoughts and time are part of the same dimension. And, timelessness is beyond time, beyond thoughts, beyond ideas, concepts and ratiocination. One can only understand time from the realm of timelessness,' explained Zeno.

'You mean from the state of *Samadhi*?' asked Rammy. 'Like what Swami Vivekananda experienced, *Nirvikalp Samadhi*...'

'I don't like to use grandiose terms, but yes, you can call it our *natural state* if you like,' said Zeno.

'This natural state is lying hidden in all of us till it manifests...' said Sylvia.

'The only thing that happens naturally to me is worries,' said Maria.

'Absolutely,' said Zeno, 'as long as we are trapped in the world of thoughts—everything is just thoughts—we can't sense or feel anything else. But our natural state is beyond that. And, that's what one should aim to attain before we depart from the world stage.'

'What happens after that, sir?' asked Sattu.

'Again, that's a thought,' said Zeno, 'what happens *after* you reach the *thoughtless* natural state can't be inferred through thoughts – it's a state of *supreme being*, or more rightly, the state of *non-being*, what Buddha calls *anatta*.'

'Have you reached that stage, Zeno?' asked Rammy.

'What do you *think*?' retorted Zeno, and we all laughed. 'Well, no person who's attained *anatta* or who has tasted it will ever tell you that he's tasted it. Because there is *nobody* left to taste it. It is attained by the *non-person* actually. When you are *not*, you truly *are* for the first time. This will seem contradictory to you because the mind can't assimilate esoteric truths. But to inspire you that it's possible to attain that state—I was also in the same boat as all you people here—the *non-I* in me did reach it.'

'Is it possible to reach it without doing anything, sir?' asked Sattu.

'Call me Zeno. Of course, it's possible – in fact, it's *only* possible without doing anything. *Doing* is of the ego. *Non-doing* is egolessness. But you can't reach it directly. When *doing* gets tired, exhausted, fatigued, when the ego gives up, *then* it will begin happening. But you'll have to tire it out. You'll have to begin with meditation and reach *non-doing*. If you're lazy right from the beginning, then it can't happen.'

'But why should one try to attain that state, Zeno?' I asked.

'Because that's the answer to all your problems, all your miseries, and all your troubles. Because you can—only a human being can. Birds, animals, insects, they can't even try to attain it. But you and I can—that's why we should try to reach it. Plus it's Supreme Peace, Supreme Joy, Supreme Bliss. There is nothing greater than It – there cannot be. Does that satisfy you?'

'A bit,' I said.

'Zeno, we wish to discuss something practical with you. We're all confused whether we should join the army – I mean Sattu is clear that he doesn't want to, but we both are confused,' said Rammy, pointing at me.

'Well,' said Zeno, 'everything is choice. Life throws up different opportunities and it's up to you to make that choice. Do whatever will make you happy. If you join the army and regret it later, there's no way out, is there? And if you don't join the army and regret it later, you can always do something else. Sylvi tells me you are maturing as a writer. Who knows, maybe being a doctor is not your calling. If I were you, I wouldn't join the army. Anyway, the decision should be solely yours. Never let someone else take a decision for you.'

'Exactly what I've been telling them, Zeno, that there will be more freedom, more choice. As for me, I feel one shouldn't walk into a one-way street,' said Sattu.

The final MBBS results were declared on Wednesday evening. Thankfully, we had failed. Rammy had flunked in Surgery theory. Sattu had failed in Medicine and Ophthalmology theory. I had 'plugged' both in Medicine theory and viva; plus Surgery theory. So, we were Maharajas now – the guys who lag behind the regular batch by two terms. We guys were in fact happy with our results and Sattu said that now our destiny was in our hands and we were playing with it at will.

But Dusty was devastated. He had flunked Surgery theory again. He lamented that his dad was pretty angry with him as his prospective Brigadier father-in-law was quite eager to get Manisha married off to Dusty as soon as he passed out. You could say Dusty was totally besotted with this girl and he showed me a snap of Manisha snuggled up with her Labrador. I must say, she was quite a bomb actually, so his attraction was understandable. He even slept with her snap and a greeting card she had recently sent permanently tucked under his pillow. (I wondered if I was rather heartless for I never used to preserve Ranju's letters or greeting cards—incidentally she was in Udhampur now—and I used to discard them after a day or two. Or perhaps Ranju and I had taken each other for granted and we were done with the puppy-love stage and all? And you don't expect mature lovers to keep mushy stuff tucked under their pillows, do you?)

Also, Dusty was quite sad that Mangy and Chopsy had cleared before he could. Mangy joined the navy; Chopsy, the air force. They bumped into Rammy and me at the new Insti and offered to treat us to an exotic dinner, but Rammy shooed them away, and I politely declined their offer.

'It is always better to make a clean break and to make your dislike clear, rather than be wishy-washy about things. It keeps life simple, uncluttered and uncomplicated. Life is too short to carry a long memory of anything, including earlier friendships,' Rammy explained after a while, when I mentioned that perhaps he was being too harsh with Mangy and Chopsy.

17

The Bulldozer, the Shock, the Rumblings

Then. August through early December 1990.

WE NOW HAD A NEW RESIDENT WARDEN. HE WAS QUITE A terror actually, and we called him 'Bulldozer' for the way he used to run into unsuspecting students in the corridor and find fault with everything from their uniforms to the manner in which they walked. Gen. Raheja undoubtedly loved him for obvious reasons, but we liked him as much as a mango tree fancied termites. 'I am Colonel Ranjit Kalra,' he'd said, introducing himself at his maiden speech at the hostel two days ago, 'and I'm a bit of a no-nonsense person...' (*A bit?* Was he kidding? Surely the 'bit' ran into a cool million tonnes, if you want a conservative estimate.)

Now, Lt. Col. Kalra had a problem with everything. He was miffed about the pigeonhole hosting graffiti; about the Yankee Maharajas playing blaring music in their rooms (he even said we should be listening to *ghazals* and not to Led Zep, can you imagine?); about our chin-wagging sessions at the new Insti late in the nights; and about generally everything that made hostel life fun.

So when a few Zulu batchers saw Lt. Col. Kalra talking to the waiters in the mess kitchen and giving them a dressing down, they

268 ♦ Campus Cola

quickly scurried away from the danger zone, throwing a mournful look at the half-finished breakfast on their plates. The Bulldozer began approaching our table with an army jawan in tow. It was close to 10 a.m., one hour past the official mess timings and all that crap. Rammy, Sattu and I stayed put.

'Just ignore him when he reaches our table,' said Sattu. 'And Rammy dear, you do the talking and *bajao* this guy's trip, okay?'

'Okay,' said Rammy, not looking up from his plate.

'What are you people *doing*?' asked the Bulldozer.

None of us replied or looked up. We continued wolfing down our omelettes and toast. Sattu of course was having tomato-onion chutney with *utthappams*, since he wasn't even an 'eggetarian', as you know. Sattu took a fuck-you sip from his glass of milk and said 'aaaaahhhh' rather deliberately, exaggeratedly, and hyper-contentedly.

'Hello!' shouted the Bulldozer. 'Are you guys deaf? *I asked you what you people are doing?*'

'Are you blind, sir?' asked Rammy, 'can't you see we are enjoying a lavish breakfast of half-cooked masala omelettes and burnt toasts?'

'How dare you talk like that…?' thundered the Bulldozer.

'Count your lucky stars that I'm even talking, sir,' said Rammy.

'Don't you even have the basic courtesy to get up or greet a senior when he approaches your table?' enquired the Bulldozer.

'Firstly, this is students' mess, not a concentration camp. Secondly, there's a simple rule in the mess – you don't get up for anybody, all rules of seniority are invalid here. Thirdly, we wouldn't even get up for God, so stop disturbing us, sir,' said Rammy.

'Don't you have classes?' asked the Bulldozer.

'We're Maharajas, we don't need to go to stupid classes for stupid attendance,' said Sattu, without looking up from his fork-pierced piece of onion utthappam. His tone clearly meant 'fuck off or get bashed up'. Rammy gestured with his hands, asking Sattu to remain silent, and Rammy's eyes said, 'Let me screw this guy peacefully, don't spoil my show with any verbal or physical violence from your side'.

'What do you mean Maharajas? What's Maharajas?' asked the Bulldozer.

'Maharajas are elite students who have failed twice in the Univ exams, sir,' I explained. I guess we were playing the good-cop-bad-cop thing with him, so I was being more genteel than Rammy or Sattu.

'That's nothing to be proud of,' said the Bulldozer.

'Pride is an individual choice, sir. Some are proud to be ass-lickers, and some are proud to be ass-kickers,' retorted Rammy.

'So you think you people can dine in the mess at any time?' asked the Bulldozer.

'We don't eat breakfast when the clock tells us to. We eat breakfast when our endocrine system tells us to,' said Rammy.

'The army doesn't function by your endocrine system, what's the time now?' asked the Bulldozer.

'I don't know, as you can see none of us feels the need to wear a watch,' said Rammy.

'It's 10:15 a.m.,' informed the Bulldozer angrily.

'Why don't you sit down, sir, so we can discuss this peacefully...' I offered.

'No, thanks,' said the Bulldozer gruffly.

'But why are you angry, sir? Is it about the timings?' I asked, pretending virgin innocence.

'Yes, you can't dine after 9 a.m. I shouldn't see anyone in the mess after 9 a.m.,' said the Bulldozer.

'Oh,' said Rammy, 'so all this brouhaha is about mess timings? So what exactly *is* the official timings?'

'7 a.m. to 9 a.m., that's all,' said the Bulldozer. 'The mess doors will be shut at 9 a.m. sharp, I've given strict instructions.'

'Aha,' said Rammy, 'okay, so technically I can enter the mess at 8:45 a.m.?'

'I don't care when you enter the mess – you should be out by 9 a.m.,' said the Bulldozer.

'Okay, let's imagine this scenario...' said Rammy.

'What scenario?' asked the Bulldozer.

'We enter the mess at 8:45. And, we decide to place an order for masala omelettes or egg bhurjis or dosas, depending on our mood and our hunger levels. Now, as you must have observed, perhaps at the kitchen in your home or the one here, it takes nearly ten minutes to cook an omelette, if at all it is cooked in the first place...'

'What are you getting at?' asked the Bulldozer.

'Sir, hear him out, patience is a virtue, he might have a point, and in a democratic nation, we ought to listen to the other party...' I mediated.

'The army isn't a democracy,' said the Bulldozer.

'We aren't in the army yet. In fact, we aren't joining the army,' said Sattu.

'Forget all that, as I said, technically we can enter the mess at 8:45 a.m.? Yes or no?' asked Rammy.

'Well...what do you mean...?' wondered the Bulldozer.

'Can I enter the mess at 8:45 a.m.?' repeated Rammy.

'Yes, you can,' said the Bulldozer.

'So imagine this scenario, sir,' began Rammy. 'We enter the mess at 8:45 a.m. We place our order at 8:46 a.m. after carefully weighing our options. It takes ten minutes to make omelettes and dosas. So, now we have reached 8:56 a.m. It takes at least two minutes for the waiter to deliver it at our table. Now we have reached 8:58 a.m. And, since it normally takes thirty minutes to eat our breakfast, because one proverb says "eat less, chew more", and Sattu does more chewing than most of us because he takes proverbs rather seriously, we have already reached 9:28 a.m. Then we need to have tea, and we usually drink two glasses of it since it's all free, and it takes twenty minutes to drink two glasses of tea, so we have reached 9:48 a.m...'

'Enough of this total nonsense! I'm not here to listen to your stupid arguments, you'll leave the mess at 9 a.m. sharp!' screamed the Bulldozer.

'Without finishing breakfast?' asked Rammy. 'Listen, you can regulate *when* I enter the mess, but you can't regulate my *speed* of eating...'

'I don't care whether you finish or don't finish, I shouldn't see you people in the mess after 9 a.m., that's all...' said the Bulldozer.

'Don't come to the mess, and you won't see us...' said Sattu.

'I don't take orders from you...' said the Bulldozer.

'And we don't take orders from *anyone* in the mess,' said Rammy, 'don't you have anything better to do than terrorise students having breakfast? We come late so our juniors won't get delayed for their morning classes. So, we're in fact doing a favour by coming late to the mess. Do something useful, sir, something more productive...'

'Ya, go and clean the bathrooms, ppllleeeaaasssee, and that's a request, not an order, the bathrooms are so dirty,' said Sattu.

'Okay, enough, now you people get up!' shouted the Bulldozer.

'Stop being a whippersnapper, sir,' said Rammy.

'What...what-snapper?' asked the Bulldozer.

'Whippersnapper. It means an insignificant person who's trying to act important,' explained Rammy.

'How dare you! Just get out of the mess right now!' screamed the Bulldozer.

'Fuck off!' said Sattu.

'Fuck off!' said Rammy.

'You guys will regret this! I'm going to the Dean...' warned the Bulldozer.

'Go complain to the President of India for all we care – we are going to lodge an official complaint against you with the Commandant and the Ministry guys, Rammy's uncle is an Undersecretary there...' lied Sattu.

'Ya, and you can kiss your ACR goodbye,' said Rammy. (ACR = Annual Confidential Report. It's the army equivalent of your annual report card – only it's infinitely more powerful since it decides whether you'll be promoted or not. Have a bad ACR and you'll be posted to the boondocks.)

So the Bulldozer scurried off and never troubled us again. Of course, he never complained about the spat we had to the Dean, so I guess Sattu's threat had worked, heehee. Or perhaps he was ashamed to admit that he'd received a sound drubbing from us.

Our final exams were scheduled for the second week of October, and Rammy and Sattu hadn't been able to arrange the money to pay out, so your guess is as good as mine on what they planned to do in the exams. I wasn't too eager to clear either as I was having the time of my life. Someone even said that we had removed the letter 's' from hostel and were milking the college for all it was worth. As you know, Maharajas never needed to attend classes and could just chill, so you could say that we were having a whale of a lazy time at the 'hotel'.

Well, not too lazy if you took into consideration our creative pursuits at Lighthouse Communications. One of Rammy's ads came quite close to winning an award at the Bangalore Ad Club and Verry offered him a full-time position as a Senior Copywriter. He didn't take up the offer of course but I was sure he was toying with the idea rather seriously. Sattu said that Rammy could afford to pay a good chunk of the bond amount with his own money if he worked in advertising for one or two years and joined one of the biggies.

We were in the middle of September and, as usual, the ninth term regulars—this time it was the Zulu batchers who were facing the heat—were pretty worried about the detention list that was about to be put up soon. And, since the change of guard had so vociferously hinted at 'enforcing the kind of discipline the armed forces expects' (remember Gen. Raheja's grisly warning in the auditorium?), the collective trembling was registering an alarming 8.5 on the Richter Scale. The detention list was put up at the pigeonhole on a Thursday evening. The corridor was so crowded that you'd have felt you had walked into a Kumbh Mela. We had to literally battle our way and pull rank to take a look at the list. Dusty was detained! Hello, no Maharaja *had ever been* detained, and Dusty couldn't believe his eyes (neither could we) and he kept staring at the detention list like you would at a death warrant. This was definitely a first at Defcoms. Maj. Gen. Yogesh Chandra Raheja was surely one helluva sadist. Rammy and I tried consoling poor Dusty that we all would just be spending some more time together, but he kept lamenting that his folks would cut a sorry figure in front of 'Miss Shimla's Brigadier dad'.

Rammy said that Manisha could wait a few more months to marry him if she liked him so much, and Dusty whined that an astrologer had asked her dad to get her married off within the next three months, so Dusty was pretty sad and depressed that Miss Shimla would soon slip out of his romantic grasp. Did you ever feel like wringing the neck of some powerful law-maker who changes the course of your destiny with just a single signature on an official document? That's how we collectively felt, and if wishes could be translated into reality, then you and I would have been gleefully reading Gen. Raheja's obituary in the newspaper the next morning. But then, you know that life doesn't give a damn about our wishes, so there was nothing much we could do save moan and groan and curse the system over a few glasses of Haluji's kerosene-flavoured tea. Haluji offered to lace a cup of tea with some deadly poison and serve it to Gen. Raheja (I gathered that the General had rubbed him the wrong way and given him a tongue-lashing when he came on his official let-me-see-things-for-myself-and-screw-your-trip rounds) and Sattu said that he'd heard of a black magic woman at Hennur who might be a better bet and a safer option.

The results were declared in the first week of December. Thankfully, we all had flunked again. We decided to celebrate by heading off to Leopard Spot. We spent the entire night there and all three of us were thoroughly sozzled and nursing wicked hangovers by daybreak.

Dusty was not with us and had left for Madras to meet an uncle of his. We returned to the hostel at 7 a.m. and asked Haluji to make some anti-hangover nimbu-paani. We slept the entire day and I was in no mood to wake up to the hurried raps on my door in the evening.

'Hucky sir! Hucky sir! Open the door fast!' screamed a shrill voice that I couldn't quite recognise. When I opened the door I saw it was an Alpha 2 batcher whose name I couldn't recall either.

'What happened? Why are you...?' I asked, irked by the intrusion.

'Sorry sir! Bad news sir!' he screamed.

'What happened...?'

'Sir, Dusty sir...Dusty sir...is dead, sir...he committed suicide...I'm just coming from the T.O.'s office...'

'*What? Are you mad? What are you talki...*'

'No, sir, it's true, sir, they discovered his body...his body at Bellandur Lake in the afternoon and...and...you better come with me to the T.O.'s office, sir...'

I was in a daze. Was this really happening? Dusty dead? Why did it remind me of Alistair MacLean's *The Way to Dusty Death*? I shrugged off the analogy. I wished this Alpha 2 batcher (oh ya, I remembered his name, Neeraj-something) was joking. But he wouldn't dare. I wished to wake up Rammy and Sattu but decided against it before I confirmed the tragic news.

The T.O. confirmed the news. He said that the post-mortem had revealed that Dusty had consumed Tik-20 about twenty hours ago and his body had been found floating in Bellandur Lake by some fishing enthusiast early in the morning.

Shit! It was indeed true. So, Dusty didn't go to Madras? He had planned to go to the realm of no return? I felt guilty and nauseated that we hadn't taken good care of him. Darn, how was I going to break the news to Rammy? He'd be devastated. He'd always had a soft corner for Dusty. I still couldn't believe it. I could still hear

Dusty screaming 'Tora! Tora! Tora!' The bad smell of foreboding that usually originated from somewhere within my head began spreading like diffusing gas once again. I could barely stand. The T.O. signalled to Neeraj to hold me. Someone gave me water. I sat in a chair with my twirling head buried in my palms. How will we face Dusty's folks? What will we tell them if they asked whether his close friends were so blind that they couldn't perceive his obvious depression? And what if they wondered how could we become doctors if we missed clear clinical signs and symptoms of acute depression in our final year? 'Ya, he was sad, but we never thought it would be so serious, we are sorry,' we would say to them, and sound like miserable quacks. Holy scum, we had lost Solly to drugs; and Dusty to depression. Will someone please assassinate this Gen. Raheja? Will someone please give me the local contract killer's phone number? I was a mad mix of sadness, guilt, anger, and thoughts of revenge and retribution. Neeraj took me back to the hostel.

A huge crowd had gathered at the new Insti. Rammy and Sattu must have heard the news, for they were sitting slumped on the stairs. All eyes were on us. We were the only four Yankee Maharajas at the hostel – make that only three since Dusty was no more. We didn't speak. We sat in silence for a long while, too shocked and too stunned to say anything. A few Zulu Monarchs were shouting slogans against Gen. Raheja. Many of them said that we all should boycott the condolence meeting organised by the authorities. Nearly all said that nobody would go for classes. All eyes continued to scan us. But we had withdrawn into a shell. Haluji brought some tea and quietly placed the glasses next to us. The glasses remained untouched. The tea remained un-sipped. Nobody disturbed us. An hour passed. Rammy was the first to get up. I guess he just wanted to go back to his room. Sattu followed him. I was too choked and angry to speak – or to move. You know, raw emotions function like invisible nooses that tighten around your larynx, and then a few invisible ropes (perhaps distant cousins of the nooses?) slowly wind around the rest of you and freeze your body into a state of complete paralysis. If you've never experienced that, then either (a) you've never been in love or (b) you've never lived through the death of a loved one. A few tragic lines of Alfred Tennyson played themselves in my mind: I hold it true whatever befall/I feel it when I sorrow most/'Tis better to have loved and lost/Than to have never loved at all. The invisible nooses and ropes don't paralyse thoughts. In fact, they somehow catalyse them into a mad frenzy and torture you more than Gen. Raheja ever could. Neeraj came and sat next to me.

Someone suggested I eat something and signalled to Haluji to get some butter bun for me. I declined it, gesturing with my hands to Haluji that I was feeling too nauseated to have anything. Neeraj said everyone was with us and that all the students were quite angry with Gen. Raheja for having detained Dusty – which, according to those expressing their solidarity, was the sole reason that had driven him to this extreme irreversible decision. One Zulu batcher said 'this mad Hitler has to be sorted out before he claims more lives.' I looked up at the sky. The shimmering diamonds reminded me of Ranju and our nights at the Commy Garden and how Dusty used to chuck the Frisbee so expertly and how he had won a bet with Ranju when she challenged him once to make the Frisbee touch the building's dome…

The authorities had sealed Dusty's room and they said they hadn't discovered any suicide note. Perhaps it was a cover-up. Perhaps they were trying to save Gen. Raheja's ass. No, no, it was certainly a cover-up. Dusty would have *definitely* left a suicide note. He was kind of meticulous when it came to correspondence. In fact, he would have addressed it to Rammy. It would have read something like this:

Dear Rammy, I am sorry to be taking this extreme step. But I must. I just received a message that Miss Shimla is engaged to an IAF fighter pilot. I can't take the pain anymore. How I wish I hadn't been detained. How I wish Raheja had never

been born. Tora! Tora! Tora! Attack him with all your might
after I am gone. Bye. P.S. Tell Raheja I'll be waiting for him
in hell. To throw him live into a burning oil-well.

The loonies must have destroyed that note. Ya, the great cover-up
had begun; and they will muckrake issues and say Dusty was a drug
addict or a jilted lover or a manic depressive, and file a report, and
coolly secrete the file into a dusty office shelf (pun not intended).
Not a word will be mentioned about Draconian policies and Raheja's
Hitlergiri and other awkward truths. Dusty will just become another
forgotten Defcoms Graduate Number who '...couldn't cope with
academic pressure; and to prevent such unfortunate incidents from
recurring, we are making it mandatory for all cadets to undergo
psychiatric evaluation once every month, and are also appointing Col.
Sudhakar Pundir, Head – Dept Of Psychiatry, as the Cadet Guidance
Officer; and henceforth the CGO will be directly responsible for
monitoring, reporting and normalising academically and/or socially-
deviant behavioural patterns in cadets'. They might as well appoint a
Pass-The-Buck-To-Him Officer. But that would be too honest a thing
to do. So then, next time a cadet, sorry student (how infectious can
official jargon get!) commits suicide, you know who's going to shoulder
the blame: the CGO and CGO alone. And, what will the CGO do
to lighten his burden? He'll file another report that will go into the
same dusty office shelf, and it will say: 'Despite regular guidance,
counselling, and sustained medication, the subject failed to respond
to treatment or recover fully due to an uncontrollable predilection for
raw self-destruction; so the Commandant is hereby appointing Col.
Vasant K. Tarneja as Hyper-deviant Cadet Counselling Officer and
henceforth the HDCCO will be solely responsible for those cadets
classified as "too far gone" in psychiatric parlance...'

Sleep had vanished from my system and I went to Rammy's
room to check on him. He had fixed his usual card on his door
that said: 'Do not disturb unless (a) World War III has begun and

we are winning (b) You are pregnant with Superman's love child (c) Your pet tigress is demanding Monaco biscuits (d) Your pet Monaco biscuits are demanding a tigress.' Sattu too had locked himself in his room and a similar sign was fixed on his door. By similar I mean Sattu's sign meant quite the same, though not in as many words, and it just said : 'EFF OFF.' Word economy was Sattu's forte since he was quite a to-the-point kind of guy and all.

A few Zulu and Alpha 2 batchers were discussing the immediate future, and wondering if it could be punctuated with a vociferous protest, and their scattered rumblings of dissent could be heard throughout the hostel. I don't know why, but I drove all alone to Bellandur Lake (perhaps it was my way of bidding a final goodbye to Dusty?) and returned at 4 a.m.

The zoo was unusually crowded for this time of the day. I parked my bike and a few animals gheraoed me and began firing their salvos. I was feeling so muzzy that I couldn't recall their names. No, that wasn't the real reason. I was feeling so low that I had scored some LSD at 2 a.m. from a contact I had, and this time around everyone was transformed into some birds and animals.

Perhaps there is a subconscious bird or animal buried deep within all of us and LSD reveals it to the rare few who have the good sense to trip on it?

'Where were you, Hucky?' yelled a Zulu gorilla.

'Sir, we've been looking for you for so long…' said an Alpha 2 swan.

'What? What happened?' I asked. What was I – a cat? Ya, my voice was more of a meow now, but perhaps that was only because I had lost all strength? Normally, I sounded like a hippo in labour.

'Actually, sir,' said a Bravo 2 deer, 'we all have decided to protest, and we are definitely boycotting the condolence meeting in the morning, and we are waiting for your approval…'

'Okay,' I said.

But why were the animals telling me all this? Was I the king of the jungle or something? Or the crown prince?

'But the strike isn't happening. Everyone's just wondering if a strike is possible...' said an Alpha 2 goat.

'So?' I asked.

'So we need a rallying point...we need someone to lead us...' said a Bravo 2 horse.

Now why did animals need a rallying point? Where was I? Stuck in George Orwell's *Animal Farm*?

What was going on? When did these animals attend an English speaking class? Who am I? Why am I feeling like drinking milk all of a sudden?

When I came to, I was sprawled on the steps of the new Insti. Haluji was throwing some water on my face. I shook my head and sat up. Shit. That was quite a weird hit. But I guess I needed it. The sun began peeping from the horizon. Haluji brought me a glass of ginger tea. A few juniors came and sat next to me.

'Sir, you were pretty smashed when we left...' said one.

'Ya. Anyway, wassup, what's the latest?'

'You have to ask Rammy sir to make a strike happen. Both Zulus and Alphas—in fact all batches—are saying they will do anything he says...' said another.

'Okay, I'll talk to him, actually we haven't spoken ever since the...'

'We understand, sir, it takes time to recover from such a deep shock.'

Rammy had locked himself in his room and I gathered that he hadn't stepped out. Rammy used to make tea, coffee, and Maggi in his room, in case you are wondering how he managed to survive without food and beverages for so long, especially since he was addicted to tea.

Sattu too had withdrawn into his shell. (He could starve though. He hadn't eaten for three days during the 1982 escape to Delhi, and he'd said that he wouldn't forget that experience even after death. Plus he wasn't addicted to any beverages.) I was a bit recharged and all—LSD zindabad!—and raring to go. I mean, I wished to do something concrete and shaft General Raheja's trip. But it was Rammy who was the kingpin. All the guys were rooting for him and everything would hinge on him. What should I do? Plan A: Go and rap on his door and run the risk of getting a tongue-lashing from him. I was used to it anyway (he had berated me so many times for disturbing his solitude). Plan B: Wait for him at the new Insti. I plumped for Plan A and decided to try my luck at the door carrying the creative 'do not disturb' card.

I knocked softly on the door.

'Who's it?' screamed Rammy, 'can't you read English?'

'Arre, it's me, Hucky, c'mon yaar...'

'Buzz off, Hucks, leave me alone...'

'Hey, we need to talk, man...'

'No, not right now, maybe later...'

Plan C: Wait for 'later' to present itself. Was there any other option? Patience and hope were the only options in the face of stubbornness.

Dusty's parents arrived late in the evening to claim his body. I know that sounds pretty gross, but is there a politically correct way of expressing such things? Sattu and I met Dusty's folks and they were both quite stoic about it. Rammy didn't meet them and I felt that he was somehow blaming himself for Dusty's death since he prided himself on understanding people's minds and behavioural psychology and that kind of crap. Sattu cried, and I was sure that his emotional breakdown made Dusty's parents feel more horrible, so I hastily whisked him away. They left the following evening, after a hastily-arranged funeral. I promised them that Dusty's death would be avenged as I saw them off at the railway station, but neither of them said anything. Perhaps silence *was* consent?

Most of the Zulu regulars had passed out, but all the Zulu Monarchs were still with us and baying for Gen. Raheja's blood. Some of them had also been detained along with Dusty, so they were pretty eager to work out some action plan to kick administrative ass.

They kept wondering why Rammy had become such an introverted recluse and I dodged their questions by hiding behind morose, tongue-tied expressions. What could I do if Rammy was still behaving like a hermit? Even Sattu seemed to have taken after him. I knew that both were stubborn as mules and would only follow their inner steely voices, not external emotional pleas.

Time was running out though.

The students were pottering around like worker ants pulling a grain of sugar in different directions. Some wished to throw a Molotov cocktail into Gen. Raheja's car; some wanted to break into his office and trash it; some chalked out mad schemes that ranged from kidnapping and extortion to decapitation.

Something had to be done before the collective anger got replaced by collective apathy.

But what could I do? Contact Master Nevero telepathically?

C'mon, Rammy, battles aren't won by the swiftest or the strongest, but by the smartest!

Wars aren't won by brute brawn, but by bright brains—and only you have it!

Was he listening to my mind-waves? Perhaps deep in meditation, like Master Theron receives Mandrake's thought-bytes?—if Lee Falk and Indrajal Comics were to be believed!

18

The Mother of All Strikes

Then. 7 December through 13 December 1990.

$\mathcal{I}$ CAN NEVER FORGET THAT DAY. LET'S CALL IT DAY ONE OF our protest. We boycotted the condolence meeting organised by the authorities and all guys and girls unanimously bunked classes. We were dissenting in disparate groups and everything was as disorganised as you could imagine. As you know, we didn't have a General Secretary now, so there was actually nobody to rally around.

There was lots of poster-designing and slogan-mongering happening though. I was sure the authorities weren't taking us too seriously and had definitely decided not to dignify our weak protest with a kneejerk response. Perhaps Gen. Raheja had asked the other top brass to just ignore us, saying that 'all this childish dissent would fizzle out in a while'.

It would have; but for Rammy.

Neeraj said Rammy had booked a train ticket to Bombay (his banker dad had been transferred from Delhi to Bombay recently) and I felt as if a sledgehammer had connected with my chest. No, I shouted to myself, no, this couldn't be true, and ran towards Rammy's room. This time around I knocked much harder on his door but he didn't respond. I went around to his window (thankfully, he always liked to stay on the ground floor).

'Hey, listen. Is it true that you are going home?' I shouted into the tightly-shut, heavily-curtained window.

'Ya, buzz off!' said Rammy.

'But you can't desert us like this, man! We need you, dude! You got to do something for Dusty, or his soul will never forgive you and...'

'Buzz off, Hucky. Nothing can be done. You think our guys have the balls? Remember how the previous strike ended up being a damp squib?'

'We will not give up this time, Rammy, we will fight till we win – c'mon, dude, at least open the door, *pleaaassse...*'

The room smelled of tea and Maggi masala and the kind of mugginess that gathers in rooms that have remained shut for a long while.

'Shit, man, at least open the windows, you've made this a cave,' I said, throwing the window open.

'What's your problem?'

'Okay, listen, all the guys and girls want you to be at the forefront and lead us...'

'Lead you to what?'

'C'mon, we *have to* protest more *unitedly* and more strongly. *We have* to be heard, we have to create some noise, and you know that only you can do it...'

'Hucks, your intentions are very noble, but I just don't have the energy for all this...'

'Rammy, you're just bottling up your anger and frustration and sulking in private! It's time to emerge out of your shell and *unleash* yourself...'

'How?'

'*How?* You are the idea guy! You can think up something, I know. Right now, the authorities aren't even taking our weak protest seriously, do something Rammy, *pleeeaaasssse* do something, anything...'

◇

Evening. 7 p.m. Fortunately, Rammy sent a Bravo 2 batcher to get his train ticket cancelled. I was happy. Now that he had agreed to stay back, there was hope for us.

'Okay, Hucks, do you have the Dean's phone number?' asked Rammy.

'You mean his home number? No, but I can get it for you from Neeraj, he must have it, but what do you want his...?'

'Don't ask questions. Just get the number.'

I got the Dean's number and Rammy called him up from a PCO some three km from the hostel. (I'm reproducing the convo he had with Gen. Raheja exactly as Rammy said it had happened. Of course, I was standing next to him at the PCO, but I could hear only one side of the convo, right?)

'It's ringing,' he said. 'Hello...'

'Hello,' said the General.

'Good...good evening...sir...' stuttered Rammy, pretending nervousness, 'am...am I...speaking with...General Raheja, sir?'

'Yes, speaking, who is this?' asked the General gruffly.

'Sir...sorry...sir...to disturb you at home...I can't reveal my name sir...but I'm a Zulu batcher...in fact a Monarch topper...'

'But why are you calling me up at my residence? Meet me at the office tomorrow. And, you are not even telling me your name...'

'Sir...sir...it's a very serious matter, it can't wait, hear me out please...some students from our batch are...are planning a *strike*, sir...and they are threatening to beat me up if I go to classes, sir...and this will...affect my studies, I'm a topper, sir...please stop it, sir...please...'

'Who are they? Tell me their names, this is the army dammit! They just can't go on strike! Tell the bastards I'll come down very heavily on them...'

'Sir, generally everybody...everybody is *for* the strike, sir...please *stop* the strike sir...okay, sir, good night sir, I have to go...some of my batchmates are coming…they might beat me up if…' said Rammy, and hung up abruptly.

'What was all that about, Rammy? I don't get it. Now, he will try to *stop* the strike…'

'Hucks, think, use the little grey cells for once. You said in the morning that most students are wondering *if* a strike is happening, *if* a strike is possible, right?'

'Ya.'

'So now when he sends somebody to *stop it*—and if my surmise is right, he will send Col. Ballal (the Chief Warden and Gen. Raheja's cardinal trouble-shooter)—then the students will be convinced that the strike is definitely happening, because you don't go about *trying to stop things that aren't happening*, right?'

'Point! You got brains, Chanakya, that's why we need you…'

'But remember, Hucks, let's not get into it directly, this guy can get pretty vindictive if all this fizzles out, get someone to put up posters saying you are your own leader, and that sort of thing…'

We grabbed dinner at Southern Lunch Home and headed back to the hostel.

◇

9:15 p.m. Rammy and I saw a huge crowd gathered in Sattu's room—5 Ground 7. As we passed by, we saw Col. Ballal in deep conversation with a few Zulu batchers and Sattu. There was an excited throng of fifty gathered at the window to grab the discussion. The door was jammed by a group of ten. The room held some twenty-odd students. Someone announced our arrival.

'Hey, Rammy,' yelled Sattu, 'come here.'

Rammy and I entered the room as a few guys made space for us.

'Who's this?' asked Col. Ballal, giving Rammy a derisive once-over.

'A Yankee Maharaja, sir,' said Rammy.

'You're from Yankee batch? I've never seen you around…'

'I keep a low profile, sir,' said Rammy.

'So,' said Col. Ballal to Sattu, 'as I was saying discipline is most important…'

Sattu eye-hinted to Rammy to take charge of the conversation; and Rammy didn't disappoint.

'Sir, that reminds me, is it true that you had caught a Bravo 2 batcher in his room, in a rather compromising position…?'

'What do you mean?' thundered Col. Ballal.

'Sir, you caught him self-stimulating his joy with a *Playboy* magazine in his hand, and you confiscated the magazine…'

'Of course, I did,' said Col. Ballal, curving his eyebrows in a weird manner that can only be perfected by army veterans. 'What about it?'

'Is that the right thing to do? To embarrass a person like that…?'

'Listen, young man, what was wrong about my stopping the sin of self-abuse…?'

'Sir, may I ask you a question?'

'What?'

'Have you *never* stimulated yourself during your youth?'

'WHAT? How *dare you* ask me such a question?'

'Sir, let's not worry about my courage quotient. You don't know what I can dare. Have you *never* moaned in solitary pleasure?'

'I'm not going to answer such a stupid…'

'Sir, answer him,' said Sattu menacingly. 'It's not a stupid question. And, even if it is, just say yes or no…'

'Well…see…' began Col. Ballal, 'the reason I stopped him was…'

'Fuck the reason. Answer Rammy's question…' said Sattu.

'Forget it, Sattu, he has already answered it. He didn't say an immediate and vehement no, did he?' observed Rammy, and Col. Ballal's face turned crimson with anger and embarrassment.

'Okay, but this strike thing has to stop,' said Col. Ballal.

'Sir, I'm not done. Plus you caught a Zulu batcher, I think it was Negi, with a girl in his room…' accused Rammy.

'So? What do you think this place is? A whorehouse?' asked Col. Ballal.

'No, sir, but are you against sex? Funny that in a country where everyone is breeding like rabbits, everyone seems to be against such an innocent activity like sex…' said Rammy.

'Well, there is a time and place…' defended Col. Ballal.

'Who decides the time and place, those with power?' asked Rammy,

'Well, I've been given certain responsibilities to manage the hostel by the Dean, and I'm just conforming to the brief given to me.'

'Okay, if you hear *a girl's voice* coming from my room, what will you do – according to this great brief?' asked Rammy,

'I'll throw her out, what else?'

'And, sir, what will you do if you hear *two male voices* coming from my room?' asked Rammy.

'Then what's there to do? That's no problem.'

'Okay, guys,' said Rammy, turning towards the guys standing at the door, and then towards those gathered at the window, 'spread the news. Colonel Ballal is only against *heterosexual relationships*; but not against *homosexual ones*. Congratulations, guys!'

All the guys laughed and clapped rather exaggeratedly. Sattu and I thumped Rammy on his back. Col. Ballal must have wished he could melt away. That one statement skyrocketed Rammy's popularity at the hostel. There was now no doubt in anyone's mind that Rammy was our leader. Rammy would show us the way and we'd just follow. The collective acceptance level of that fact touched stratospheric heights.

'Okay,' said Col. Ballal to Rammy, 'I need to talk to you in private…'

'No, sir, whatever you wish to say, you can say in front of all. Tomorrow, you'll twist my statements…'

'Trust me,' said Col. Ballal, and gently nudged Rammy's elbow, 'let's discuss everything at the canteen…'

'Sure, sir,' said Rammy, and we all trooped down to the new Insti.

'Listen, if you want, you can stop this strike…' whispered Col. Ballal to Rammy, and I barely caught his words as I followed them. The collective din was ear-shattering.

'I know, sir,' said Rammy, 'and that's precisely the reason I won't.'

Col. Ballal and Rammy spoke with each other for close to an hour (we guys were just silent spectators) and Rammy said that the Commandant, Lt. Gen. Manoj Chauhan, should come to the hostel to talk to the students, while also adding that we were boycotting Gen. Raheja and would definitely not talk to him. The mutiny had begun. Col. Ballal left, assuring us that he would convey our wishes to the Commandant, and Rammy predicted that Lt. Gen. Chauhan would never show up.

Day Two. 8:30 a.m.

Nearly hundred students were waiting for Rammy to emerge from his room. Nobody was willing to make the slightest move without Rammy's consent. I waited outside his door like the rest, wondering what he'd have to say. Rammy opened the door after some ten minutes, wrapped just in a towel, and as he was walking to the loo, the Training Officer, Lt. Col. Mishra, parked his scooter next to 5 Ground.

'All of you fuckers! Get lost from here! Get dressed and go to your classes!' he screamed at the students.

All of us looked at Rammy. He didn't say anything. He merely gestured with his hands, asking us to stay put. We didn't move a millimetre. Lt. Col. Mishra resembled a speed-loving express train that had been brought to a cruel, unexpected halt.

'You…you…' he yelled at Rammy, 'you think you are their leader?'

'You tell me. You screamed and they didn't respond. I merely gestured and they listened. So, am I or am I not?' Rammy asked coolly.

'Listen, Ramakrishna, you don't know what we can do to you…'

'What the fuck can you do, Mr Mishra? At the most, you can *expel* me – here, consider *this* my MBBS degree,' fumed Rammy, flashing the newspaper he always carried into the loo to crack the cryptic crosswords, and tore it into bits and threw it away. 'I don't want the fucking MBBS degree from this fucking college, okay? You guys are sadists, so balls to you and to your threats, Mr Mishra. *Now* tell me, what *can you* do to me?'

Rammy was pure fire, and we all were stunned into silence. I had never seen him so angry before, and Lt. Col. Mishra revved up his scooter and departed without saying another word. We were rooted to the spot even after Rammy returned from the loo after ten minutes. Nobody dared to speak. Rammy had made his intentions clear. No longer would we have a hush-hush strike. We were going hammer and tongs after the authorities. Rammy didn't look at any of us; and there was this mad glint in his eyes. He entered his room, got dressed, and came out after five minutes.

'Please ask everyone to gather at the new Insti at 9:10 – including all the girls,' Rammy said to us, and went back into his room.

That was the first instruction he gave as our unanimously-accepted leader. Many such would follow in the days to come. Not a single student would object. Not a doubt would cross anyone's mind. I learned something that day. A leader is not born; not made; not elected. A true leader is *spontaneously requested* by a group to be its collective spirit; its guiding force; its confident anchor. Plus a true leader never speaks too much. Just a word, just a hint, just a look would be enough to take nearly six hundred students in his control. And paradoxically, a true leader doesn't feel the need to control anyone. His followers just flow with him, like driftwoods carried by rivers, secure in the knowledge that the river is moving in the right direction.

9:10 a.m.

We all had gathered at the new Insti. Sattu and I had decided to mingle with the rest and give Rammy the space he needed. Sattu mentioned that Rammy was talking like a man possessed. Ya, Rammy seemed a different person altogether. Plus we knew that he would be taken more seriously if everyone saw that even we were behaving like commoners; and not like his close friends. Nearly five hundred students had gathered at the new Insti when Rammy arrived. He didn't waste much time and quickly began addressing us.

'Dear friends,' he said, in a loud and confident tone that could be heard for at least a mile (true leaders don't need loudspeakers either?), 'the time has come; and the time is now. We *have* to be heard. We have tolerated too much nonsense and harassment for too long. We won't anymore. And, we aren't doing this for Dusty. We are doing this for *ourselves* and for future batches. None should suffer like we have. I have a few *requests* to make. One: our protest will be totally non-violent. I don't want anyone breaking anything anywhere. Remember, we are not against Defcoms. It is the best medical college in the country. We are *against* the people managing—or rather *mismanaging*—Defcoms right now. Two: we will later take a silent procession through the roads; we will only carry placards. Remember, self-restraint is important to drive home the message that we are indeed self-disciplined. Three: I believe in *freedom* and liberty. Anyone who wishes to go to college and attend classes is free to do so. We have to respect individual choices too. And, nobody will forcibly try to stop such students either. Do you agree with what I have just said?'

There were loud cheers and nearly everyone said, 'Ya, ya!'/'Whatever you say, sir!'/'We are with you all the way, sir!'

'Also, remember,' continued Rammy, 'much pressure will be exerted by the authorities to break our resolve. But we won't break, will we?'

'Never, sir, never!' screamed four hundred voices.

'Good,' said Rammy, 'now go back to your rooms, and I want everyone getting into their uniforms and assembling here at 10:30 sharp for the silent procession. All the best, and may God be with all of us!'

9:45 a.m.

Col. Ballal was running all along the hostel corridor and he had two army jawans following close at his heels.

'All of you go to your classes,' screamed Col. Ballal into a megaphone, 'otherwise all of you will be rusticated!'

He kept repeating the same lines for some fifteen minutes and was making a laughing stock of himself. A few guys clicked photographs and it was really funny to see Col. Ballal pacing the corridor and repeating the lines like a king's announcer from the medieval ages. After a while he got into his Fiat and departed from the scene, having failed to create the slightest impression on any student.

10:30 a.m.

'Thank you for assembling in time,' said Rammy to the five hundred students gathered at the new Insti, 'and thank you for your trust in me. Okay, now we will take a silent procession through the roads. I mean, *really silent*. Nobody, I repeat, nobody will shout slogans or raise their voices. Okay?'

'Okay, sir!' all of us shouted enthusiastically.

'We have written everything on placards, and that's enough,' continued Rammy. 'We won't block traffic and be a nuisance to the public. If someone is inadvertently blocked by us, apologise, and quickly move ahead. If anyone violates my request then I will just go home. Understood?'

'Understood, sir!' screamed everyone.

'Okay, let's move,' said Rammy.

Our silent march snaked its way through the campus, and by the time we exited and covered some two km down Hosur Road, we had a posse of twenty cops escorting us, with an inspector walking along with Rammy.

'Good protest, very peaceful, I've never seen students striking so peacefully,' said the inspector to Rammy.

'Thank you, sir,' said Rammy.

We all were carrying posters and placards saying: Mean Dean/4 suicides in 3 years; there shall be no 5th/Hitler Dean: The Worst We Have Seen/Down with 100% attendance/We are doctors, not bonded labour/We are medical students; not the Dean's slaves etcetera.

After about three hours, we returned to the hostel, physically exhausted and psychologically uplifted. We were creating a dent in the establishment and we were voicing our views. We were finally being taken seriously. Or rather, too seriously, as the coming days would show.

Day Three. 8 a.m.

Nikhil Dhingra of Alpha 2 batch, actually Rammy's friend, was another kind of oddball, and he didn't like the idea of a strike. He was the only guy who didn't participate in our protest march the previous day, and had attended classes on both Day One and Day Two, so the entire hostel wanted to bash him up for bucking the trend. Rammy interceded by lying that he had himself sent Dhingra to attend classes to gauge the pulse of the authorities and professors, adding that 'anyone who dares to touch my personal spy will invite my personal wrath', so Dhingra was left to his devices, and nobody creamed him.

When wisdom dawned on Dhingra that he hadn't done the right thing by hurting collective sentiments, he apologised to Rammy for his errant behaviour, and Rammy said rather generously to Dhingra a while later: 'Nikhil, I support anyone who stands by his convictions, in fact I am really proud of your guts to go against us all—plus I have already stated that only those who themselves volunteer to participate in the strike need to do so; all others are assured of my personal protection even if they decide to go against my wishes.'

Thanks to Rammy's non-forceful attitude, everyone felt that nobody was curtailing their freedom or imposing their views on them, so you can say that it was a tremendous psychological ploy to have the general public flowing with the leader's wishes. I thought that Rammy would make a great politician – but then, come to think of it, he was a bit too straightforward and honest to make politics a career option. Though, I must add that he definitely had the makings of a sagacious statesman.

Meanwhile, Shiva, an Alpha 2 batcher, had gathered strategic information that the Health Minister and the Railway Minister were camping at the Circuit House near the Cantonment, and would be inaugurating a railway line to some constituency the next day. This was great news. Now, we could try and meet the chief decision-maker and hope to swing things in our favour. A few Zulu batchers made a neat type-written list of demands and gave it to Rammy. It was decided that Rammy, Sattu, and I would meet the Health Minister. Shiva had some contacts with the local political parties, and said that he had arranged for us to be allowed an audience with the Health Minister at the 'public darbar' between 9 a.m. and 10 a.m. We dolled up hurriedly and rode like Jehu towards the venue.

A Health Minister is no ordinary person. We were thoroughly frisked; our I-cards were checked; and we were asked to wait at the first floor lobby. The Health Minister, accompanied by the Railway Minister, emerged from a room after about half an hour. He was surrounded by nearly fifteen gun-toting black cat commandos. It was all an imposing sight and Rammy whispered to me that 'power is the greatest drug and the biggest addiction known to mankind'. Rammy moved forward with our petition.

'Good morning, sir,' said Rammy, 'we are from Defcoms, and I represent the students...'

'Do you have an appointment?' asked the Health Minister.

'No, sir,' said Rammy.

'Then I can't meet you,' said the Health Minister.

'Sir, this is *ridiculous*, a student has committed suicide because of the stupid policies of one General, and Defcoms comes under the direct purview of the Health Ministry...' yelled Rammy.

Since Rammy was speaking in a loud tone and rather excitedly moving towards the Health Minister, a few black cats raised their weapons and surrounded him.

'Okay, *shoot me*, go ahead!' screamed Rammy at them, and Sattu and I looked on, totally stunned.

'Go away!' said the Health Minister.

'One day you'll regret this,' said Rammy, and walked off.

'Are you crazy?' screamed Sattu at Rammy after we exited the Circuit House, 'how can you talk to the Health Minister like that?'

'Appointment? He wants me to fix an appointment when it's a matter of life and death? When he comes begging for votes, then he doesn't seek a prior appointment from me. You guys are mice. Always afraid of powerful people...' said Rammy.

'What do you mean he will regret this?' I asked.

'I meant what I meant, Hucks, forget it,' said Rammy.

11 a.m.

The authorities had put up notices outside all the five messes saying: 'Mess closed indefinitely – By order of the Dean, Defcoms, Bangalore'. The screws were tightening. Haluji would be happy that he'd get to do roaring business. But maybe they would ask him to down the shutters at the canteen too? That wasn't all. They disconnected the water and electric supply at the same time they shut the mess. Gen. Raheja was proving the placards we had made earlier so absolutely right. Mean Dean.

3:10 p.m.

We all gathered at the new Insti wondering what to do. We saw a huge convoy approaching the hostel from the distance. Two jeeps were followed by three Shaktiman trucks full of army jawans. A jeep belonging to the Military Police brought up the rear.

Rammy went and stood in front of the convoy and we all cheered. He shushed us and challenged the Major commanding the first jeep to run over him or take a detour. The convoy took a detour.

'We have been given simple instructions to seal all your hostel rooms within the next one hour. Collect all your essentials and vacate the hostel,' shouted the Major into the megaphone.

'What do we do now, Rammy?' I asked.

'Ask everyone to collect their clothes and money etcetera—don't forget your bank passbooks—and assemble here in half an hour,' said Rammy.

'But where will we stay…?' asked Sattu.

'First things first,' said Rammy, 'I have a plan.'

3:55 p.m.

'Okay, friends, this is crunch time. We can tremble and crumble; or we can create more rumble,' said Rammy, 'what do you guys want?'

'Rumble! Rumble!' The collective chorus reverberated enough to rattle Haluji's tea glasses.

'Great. Since we need a place to stay, the Cantonment Gurudwara has agreed to accommodate us. If the girls find it tough, they can take the next train back home,' said Rammy.

5:40 p.m.

We all had checked in at the Gurudwara. They were kind enough to allot us a huge hall on the first floor and a separate accommodation for the girls. They even hastily whistled up *rotis*, *daal*, and *subji* at the *langar* when they found out that many of us hadn't grabbed lunch since our mess and wet canteen were shut down.

Day Four. 10 a.m.

A few girls had left for their homes; and the rest were planning to. Rammy asked them not to return till the authorities had acceded to our demands. Nearly everyone had gathered around Rammy. A few were playing chess or Scrabble; or had curled up with their novels. (Cards were a strict no-no, we'd been told.)

'What now?' asked Sattu of Rammy.

'Let's see how things unfold in this grand design of God...' said Rammy.

'Sir,' enquired Neeraj, 'I've heard you and Sattu sir discussing that all this is a grand design – couldn't our existence be mere chance, and maybe there's no God...?'

'How can it be mere chance?' said Rammy. 'It's an *intelligent design*. From just a sperm and an ovum, we have grown into a complex trillion-celled organism. Look at our brain, eyes, ears, nose, tongue, blood, nerves, digestive system – we are a bio-engineering miracle. Look at the sheer diversity of plants and animals. How can a genetic code happen by chance? There *has* to be a programmer. That's why I like the Hindu concept of a Creator, not because I'm a fanatic, but because I'm a scientific person. And what amazes me most is that we carry the same electrons and protons as a rose or a chair. In fact, everything in existence is made up of the *same* electrons and protons but everything is so unique. That's the miracle.'

'But sir,' said Neeraj, 'all this still doesn't prove that it *didn't* happen by chance...'

'I agree it doesn't,' said Rammy, 'but understand one thing. Any system tends towards disorder unless order is restored every now and then by an external agency. And, if you say all this is a mere accident, then you are saying that chaos and disorder *create* order. That's like saying that the car accident will, one day, evolve into a car. That's absurd. Car accidents will begin to happen *after* cars are created; not vice versa. Likewise, disorder will follow order; not vice versa. Maybe accidents are a matter of chance, or perhaps even accidents are not accidents, and happen only to reflect the underlying order that much more. And, why would chance or chaos, even if we accept your argument to be true, try to create order within a system? Chaos will create more chaos; not an infallible genetic code. The human body is enough proof that someone designed it meticulously, intelligently and carefully. Chance or disorder is just another synonym for recklessness. So, why would *reckless disorder* take the pains to create such an orderly universe? And if you say that reckless disorder somehow moved towards order, it's still only a theory, a hypothesis. It can't be proven. And Neeraj, tell me, if you ask five hundred persons to assemble at the parade ground, and don't give them any instructions, what are the chances of them standing in a single file or in an orderly manner in columns of ten?'

'None, sir,' said Neeraj.

'Exactly, so disorder is the natural state of affairs, but *order* has to be *created*. And I tell you Neeraj, science itself is enough proof that there exists someone or something or some-xyz power that has designed all this. You can call It the Greatest of Designers if you will. Like Einstein said, He doesn't play dice with the world. Einstein simply meant that this God is an *engineer* of orderly systems...' said Rammy.

'Then why is this God invisible?' asked Shiva.

We were all listening to Rammy with rapt attention. Somehow we all sensed that this was the last time we were listening to him. The strike might not produce a favourable result, but everyone was just thankful that we were spending so much quality time with Rammy. He had become quite a recluse in the recent past and you could call yourself lucky if he spoke with you for more than ten minutes.

'Whys can't be answered, Shiva. When you answer one why, you merely postpone the question. It provides no real answers actually. A child can ask, "Why is a leaf green?" You can say because of chlorophyll. Then the child can ask, "Why does chlorophyll impart green colour to leaves and not blue?" So there are no real answers. The best answer is: this is how things *are*, this is the nature of things, the *suchness* of things. I like the Zen way actually. So, when you ask, "Why is God invisible?", the only real answer is, *that* is the nature of God, the *suchness* of God. If He were visible, we wouldn't call him God. We would call him Sattu or Neeraj," said Rammy.

'But, sir, since God is All-powerful, He should be able to make himself visible too…' observed Shiva.

'True. Maybe He is not really invisible; maybe we haven't developed the vision to see Him. Just like you need a microscope to see bacteria, maybe we need a Godoscope to see God. For instance, we can only hear sounds between twenty hertz and twenty thousand hertz. Now, that doesn't mean that frequencies *below* twenty hertz or those *above* twenty thousand hertz don't exist. It just means that *our* sense of hearing is limited. And, how can we see an unlimited God with limited senses?' observed Rammy.

'Then how to enlarge our senses?' asked Neeraj.

'I don't think we can do that without God's help. This is called grace; and this Godoscope could be deep meditation or *bhakti* or whatever,' said Rammy.

'I feel there's no God-shod,' said Dungu, a Zulu batcher.

'Dungu, as I said, your feelings are limited too. We are limited in everything: sight frequencies, touch frequencies, thought frequencies.

Perhaps right now we are sitting on the railway track of another dimension and trains are passing right through us, but just because they are beyond or below our touch frequencies, just like sound, we don't perceive them. That doesn't mean dimensions we can't see or feel don't exist. We were, are, and will always be limited, for a very simple reason. If you became The Unlimited, then there would be nobody *except You*. There would be just One, One Conscious Entity – You. Since we're limited, we've so many individuals, so much diversity. If we became Unlimited then we would encompass everything in existence, like our body encompasses all our cells. Perhaps all of us are God's cells or God's protons or electrons or whatever. And, how can a cell see the body, Dungu? The body can see the cell; but the cell can never see the body. Or perhaps God is kind. And, He has left a way for us to see or hear or talk to Him; only we haven't discovered it yet.

'Mystics claim to have spoken to God or claim to be God, and are usually idolised or dismissed as madmen. If a cell claims it is one with the body, it is both right and wrong. The other cells will call it mad and say there is nothing called the body, while living in the body itself. Also, understand one thing. The *Unlimited* has neither beginning nor end. Anything with a beginning cannot be Unlimited because it *has to have* an end – so it can be gigantic, mammoth, and these are relative terms. For instance, an ant will say an elephant is infinite. A microbe will say an ant is infinite; but God is not a relative term. God stands alone. In fact, God is the loneliest person in the universe. He can never communicate what He really *is* to *anyone*, just like we can never tell how very intelligent we are to an ant. Try doing that and the ant will ask, "Can you guys dig a hole through a wall and get a grain of sugar?", and we will say no, and the ant will dismiss us as unintelligent, and rightly so, for that is the ant's idea of intelligence. Intelligence itself has no absolute values; it's relative. For a cobbler, a tea-seller is doing an unintelligent task; for a surgeon, a cobbler is doing an unintelligent task. But *intelligence*, let me tell you, is the very *stuff that existence is made up of*,' explained Rammy.

'Then what is intelligence?' I asked.

'Consciousness *is* intelligence, Hucks. They are inseparable. Do you think bacteria aren't intelligent just because they can't take the Defcoms' IQ test? Do you think a crow isn't intelligent just because it can't theorise about relativity? You might be good at talking; I might be good at writing, so we have *different intelligences*, but we both are intelligent. Nobody can say I am more intelligent than you. Not Einstein, not Edison, not God. In fact, if someone says he's more intelligent than you, then he's the greatest fool. Only three scenarios are possible. One, he and you are equally intelligent, so he is wrong. Or he is of lesser intelligence, and his claim is wrong. Or he is of greater intelligence, but how can or why will a greater intelligence try to prove that it's more intelligent to a lower intelligence? – since the lower intelligence hasn't evolved enough to understand greater intelligence, just like the ant-and-us analogy, so he's wrong in saying so,' said Rammy.

'So we are as intelligent as God?' asked Sattu.

'No. Again, when we use the word "as", we are comparing. Intelligence can't be compared. Every atom, every electron, every proton, every rock, living beings, plants, animals, anything in existence, is uniquely intelligent in its own way. In fact, physicists say even the electron is conscious and changes its behaviour if it senses that it's being observed. Perhaps even space-time is conscious and intelligent,' said Rammy.

'But what is God's trip, sir?' asked Prateek, a Charlie 2 batcher.

'Fun. *Unlimited* fun. What else can be His trip? Everything leads to boredom, Prateek, sooner or later. But fun and laughter are beyond boredom. Every time we're having fun and we're laughing, we are exactly in the same position as God,' said Rammy.

'But this God, He's having fun at our expense, man...' I said.

'Ya, true, just like your liver cell is complaining that you are drinking alcohol at *its* expense. What's fun for you is sheer misery for your liver cell which has to work overtime and remain paranoid about developing a fatty liver or eventual cirrhosis. But do you realise that the liver is not in pain when that happens? *You* are in pain; and an intelligent God will not inflict pain upon Himself...' said Rammy.

'But you just said that everything is conscious, then the liver cell, since it's conscious, will feel pain...' observed Neeraj.

'Good point, Neeraj. But do you realise that you and I feel pain because of the pain centre, the thalamus in our brain? The nerve pathways transmit this pain from the liver cell to the brain and then we consciously perceive it. The liver cell consciousness is not concerned about the thalamus at all; our consciousness is. So, the liver cell is oblivious to pain – of course also to pleasure. I was just saying it in a lighter vein – no, the liver cell is *never* going to complain about your drinking habits. Perhaps it's even totally oblivious to your existence, just like we are generally oblivious to God's existence,' said Rammy.

'But where is all this heading to...?' asked Sattu.

'You mean *existence*?' asked Rammy.

'Ya.'

'Nowhere. There can be no goals for the Unlimited. Because goals exist only for finite concepts, for limited ideas. We are a limited body-mind-combo idea. We can have goals. For instance, we can have a goal that we have to reach our room within the next fifteen minutes. How? Because we *are here* and we are *not there* in the room right now. So, we have a goal. But the Unlimited is here, there, and everywhere, at the same time or at the same timelessness, it really has nowhere to go, so there can be no goals for God. A goal implies a future we have not yet reached. But for God, for the Unlimited, the Always, there's no past, present, and future – it's all one gigantic unlimited here-now. It's just Unlimited Inexhaustible

Energy playing Unlimited Inexhaustible Games, what Hindus call divine *leela*, mere play...' explained Rammy.

'Mind-boggling. How can someone exist everywhere at the same time...?' wondered Shiva.

'No, it's simple to understand. I can in fact prove it to you theoretically,' said Rammy.

'How?' asked Shiva.

'Okay, what's the concept of God according to most people, I mean generally what powers are attributed to God?' asked Rammy.

'You mean He's Omniscient, Omnipresent and Omnipotent – that kind of thing?' asked Shiva.

'Exactly!' said Rammy. 'Okay, assuming God comes before us right now—it's possible, it's not lack of ability but lack of desire that prevents Him from meeting us—and if you ask Him, "God, can you tell me what will happen after five minutes?", would He be able to tell you or not?'

'Of course, He's Omniscient, All-knowledge, so He has to have knowledge of the future too...' said Shiva.

'Great. And, since He's also Omnipresent, that means He is present in the past, present, and future, at the same time...?' guided Rammy.

'Ya, I guess so...' said Shiva.

'So, in a sense, the future has *already happened*, and we'll get to know it later, whereas God is already *present* in it?' observed Rammy.

'Ya...' said Shiva.

'And what about the past? Has it gone out of existence or is it hidden there at the same time, just like the future is...?' asked Rammy.

'Man, the past is past, it's gone, man...' I said.

'Gone out of *our* line of vision, accepted, but has it gone *out of existence?*' asked Rammy.

'Of course,' said Sattu, 'it is gone...'

'And if it has gone out of existence, where exactly has it gone to, Sattu? How can anything go *out of* existence? And how can all the energy comprising the past just vanish? We know energy can neither be created nor destroyed. The previous second – where did it go to? As I am talking, I am moving into the future. Where did the previous sentence of mine go to? Did it go outside existence? No, it will continue to reverberate in existence eternally. Nothing goes anywhere, Sattu. Everything is just one, solid, here-now, *cosmic present* from God's vision. But things come for a brief while in our line of vision, and we call it present, things slide past our line of vision, we call it past, things will come into our line of vision later, and we call it future, because we all have *limited vision*, but for an omnipresent God with *Unlimited Vision*, the past and present and future *co-exist* at the same time or timelessness, according to our own definition of God...' observed Rammy.

'Who taught you all this man?' I asked, thoroughly amazed. Rammy was making more sense than even Zeno.

'Self-inference, or maybe God is planting some ideas in my head...' said Rammy, rather modestly.

'But if we are just parts and parcels of God, then isn't it His duty to reveal Himself to us...?' observed Neeraj.

'Is your liver cell Neeraj or a part of Neeraj?' asked Rammy.

'Part of...' said Neeraj.

'Yup, if we're talking *only* about the physical form. Is a drop a part of the ocean or the ocean itself?' asked Rammy.

'Part of...' said Neeraj.

'Physically, yes, it is just a part ...' said Sattu.

'But in its basic essence, a drop *is* the *ocean*...' said Rammy.

'What about size?' asked Shiva.

'I just said so, apart from physical parameters—and size is a physical parameter—a drop is *exactly* the ocean in its basic essence, don't you agree?' said Rammy.

'I have to...it will have the same salinity and properties as the ocean...' said Shiva.

'Now when we say God, we are talking something very very subtle; subtler than space-time, subtler than emotions, subtler than even abstract truths like purity, truth, nobility etcetera. And, how can a gross mind understand the subtle essence behind all that is? This has been a problem throughout history and it's not going to change. It's in-built in nature. If a drop says it *is* the ocean and starts dancing and singing, then all the billions of drops surrounding it will say that there is nothing called the ocean; or even if a few believers accept the concept of the ocean, they'll say that a drop is infinitely different and distant from the ocean. Whereas the drop that knows, knows it knows, and knows it so deeply that it cannot convey it to the billions of drops glorifying their superficial concepts...' said Rammy.

'Ya, just like some enlightened beings say they are God...' said Prateek.

'True, now take a man who says, "I am God." The people-drops around him will say he is insane or place him on a pedestal, which are both the same thing. It means you are different from us, dude, but the man who has touched those heights knows that the billion people-drops around him are no different from him or from God who is the subtle ocean surrounding us always,' said Rammy.

'It can even be called megalomania, dear,' said Sattu.

'I am coming to that. Or you have more stupid people like modern-day psychiatrists who'll say that he suffers from megalomania and they'll incarcerate him and treat him and try to cure him, when in fact it is *they* who require the cure. People are stupid. Many say I want to meet God, speak with God, talk to God, but nobody says *I want to be God*. I don't mean that in an egoistic sense, as a power trip. I mean that in a *wanting-to-know* sense. And, how can you understand something without *being* it? I know myself, I understand myself because I am me; and you know yourself and understand yourself because you are you. *Being is knowing*. And, the enlightened person who has become God and knows at the same time that he is not God will either be dismissed as insane or worshipped. Both things are essentially the same, as I said,' explained Rammy.

'Sir, many say that God reveals Himself only to those who worship Him…' said Shiva.

'No, nobody needs to worship anyone. We have to become so worthy in our own eyes that we become our own object of worship, our own God, our own idol, our own hero. But ignorant people will keep visiting places of worship, not knowing that these superficial acts of social grace, conformity and sentimental journeying will not help them an iota in realising the True Essence of Reality. It is so illogical to walk towards the divine. If we thirst earnestly, the divine will rush towards us. So, the sincere seeker patiently waits for all such places of worship to come to him, with all their pristine divinity in tow. And, they do!' said Rammy, rather excitedly.

'So you are saying you are God, sir…' said Neeraj.

'In essence yes, and so are you, only you haven't realised it yet…' said Rammy.

'And at the same time you aren't God – physical parameters and all…' observed Sattu.

'Absolutely. Even if we evolve for billions and billions to-the-power-of-infinity years, we can't be God in a *physical* sense, but we already are in an *existential* sense. This is as difficult as understanding that something is black and white at the same time – without being grey. This will defy logic. Normally a is not b; and b is not c; but in the realm of spirituality, a is both b and c; and *not b* and *not c* simultaneously. In fact, a is a and *not a* at the same time. The mind can't conceive it – call it para-logical or paradoxical or supra-logical, whatever, that's the True Nature of Reality. Lord Chaitanya called it unthinkable, inconceivable difference and non-difference simultaneously, *achintya bheda abheda tattva*…' explained Rammy.

'When did you feel all this and the presence of God?' I asked.

'What is there to feel? Who is there to feel it? Can you feel the space-time around you with your fingers?' wondered Rammy.

'C'mon, space-time can't be *felt as a tactile sensation...*' I said.

'Exactly. We just discussed that God is more subtle than space-time. So, if even something as tangible as space, which is there all around us, can't be felt as we normally feel things, then how can we feel God?' said Rammy.

'No, I mean when did you *realise* all this...?' I paraphrased my question.

'Let's just say it happened one night...' said Rammy.

'Tell me about it...' I said.

'Maybe some other time...' said Rammy, becoming thoughtful.

'Does it happen only in solitude...?' wondered Neeraj.

'As I told you, God is the loneliest being in the universe, with hardly a handful who understand Him; and He meets you when you have the courage to be most alone. I don't mean physically, anyone can achieve that, I mean alone without thoughts, ideas, notions, theories, in a state of innocent not-knowing, not-being; it is then that He arrives. You don't have to call Him. When the cup is empty, the tea rushes in...' said Rammy.

'How to empty it?' asked Shiva.

'You can't. The very effort of *trying* to empty the cup will fill it up with *effort-energy*. When you give up, or rather, when a deep giving-up happens, it's always a happening, it can't be manipulated, then the cup is empty...' smiled Rammy.

'Till then one has to just wait...?' I asked.

'Yes, wait. That's all one can do. As they say, everything comes to the man who patiently waits in his supreme aloneness...' said Rammy.

'Even physically it's not possible, I'm not able to be alone for a single moment, Rammy sir, why is that?' asked Prateek.

'Because you're afraid of facing yourself and your reality. Past guilt, regrets, present complexes, problems, and future worries make you uncomfortable with yourself. But try to maintain solitude because nothing great was ever achieved by groups. It's always the alone person who achieved anything noteworthy. If you can't be alone for most part of the day, then you can never realise your true potential or essence...' observed Rammy.

'Reminds me of a quote of Francis Bacon...' said Neeraj.

'Tell me,' said Rammy.

'Anyone who delights in solitude is either a wild beast or a god.'

'So true,' said Rammy.

Day Five. 4 p.m.

The authorities pulled strings (so what was new?) and the Gurudwara Committee guys said rather regretfully and guiltily that we would have to vacate the premises and find alternative accommodation for ourselves. Even Rammy was stumped for a while.

'Folks,' said Rammy, 'we have only one choice now – the railway station.'

'Why the railway station?' asked Sattu.

'Because you have mobile loos coming every ten minutes, plus folks can depart for home anytime,' explained Rammy.

'Shucks, so the strike is as good as over?' I asked morosely.

'No, we'll continue hounding them through the press,' said Rammy.

We all camped at the railway station in the evening. The girls were asked to head back home. Half the guys also took off with them. Rammy said that he had already sent a few scathing articles to the newspapers since he had good contacts in *The Bangalore Herald* and *The National Chronicle*. But what good would that do except elicit a bit of a tired applause from us?

We were all feeling pretty low. Gen. Raheja had systematically frustrated our moves. He had hit us where it hurt the most. He had exposed the fact that we were a weak rebellious bunch that could get scattered for want of accommodation.

We couldn't blame Rammy, could we? He had tried his best, but even he was no match for the power politics and meticulous machinations of our top brass. I looked at him sprawled on a bedspread, with his head propped against a pillow, reading Michael Crichton's *The Andromeda Strain*. Did nothing faze him? One man with courage is a majority. I had read that somewhere. So very true. One man pitted against the strong, well-oiled government machinery. One man against the powers-that-be. One man against injustice. There was no way he would win; and there was no way he would give up. Rammy was the kind of person who believed in fighting to the finish if you began a fight in the first place. As he had said earlier, 'winning isn't as important as fighting for one's rights'. Well, it was all pretty cool to read that in books by idealistic philosophers, but it wasn't easy putting idealism into practice. God save us. How long could we stay at a railway station anyway?

Day Six. 5 a.m.

'Rammy sir! Rammy sir!' shouted Neeraj, and shook Rammy excitedly, 'wake up, sir, your article has come!'

Rammy's article had appeared in the editorial page of *The Bangalore Herald*. It was titled *Dragons at the helm*. Here's the gist:

'...Defcoms cannot be equated with NDA, and hence can (and never should) become an academy. For the simple reason that in NDA the emphasis is on physical training—and rightly so—because you want the fighting units of your armed forces to be manned by officers who can run at least a half-marathon without suffering a cardiac arrest; whereas at Defcoms, the emphasis has to be on intellectual training because you want to rely on your doctor's brain, not brawn.

'What matters most? A doctor who can run a marathon or an intravenous drip when you need it? I'm not saying your doctor needn't be fit. But Defcoms thinks that doctors are being trained to take part in the Decathlon in the coming Olympics. This is where I beg to differ. And, why do they insist on 100% attendance is a query that defies my intelligence and my sense of reasoning – perhaps because both got barbecued in the compulsory parade they made me do yesterday?

'When there is an exam system to deem me pass or fail, why do you detain me from appearing for exams if I don't meet your stringent attendance norms? What if I maintain 0% attendance and still top my exams? Many do. Many have the ability to, if only you'll allow them to. But you detain students from taking the exams (just to boost your ego?) and the weak ones commit suicide; and the strong ones commit the greater crime of getting angry.

'Okay, let's say I am even cool with the 100% attendance norm. Then just scrap exams. Tell me: Here buddy, take your MBBS degree, you have maintained 100% attendance, there's no need for you to clear University exams and all, just by virtue of 100% attendance, we declare you a doctor. C'mon, give me a break. A confident institution, a confident professor shouldn't *force* you to attend his classes, but in fact should *magnetically pull you* since he's so very good and interesting.

'But since most professors are dull and drab, and will continue to be dull and drab, I guess the dull and drab attendance norms are here to stay...'

Day Seven. 10 a.m.

Nearly everyone had left for their homes the previous day. In fact, Rammy had insisted that everyone leave. The authorities had wired everyone's parents and threatened them with dire consequences if 'their wards didn't withdraw from this strike', so all parents had hastily summoned their 'wards' to 'just come home and not participate in collective insubordination'. We were just six people left at the station. Rammy was reading *And Then There Were None* by Agatha Christie. How very apt.

'So what now?' asked Sattu.

'Hucks, what do you say? Shall we go and check if the Zeno girls will take us in?' asked Rammy.

We asked the other three guys to leave. And Rammy, Sattu, and I checked in at New Nirvana by afternoon the next day. The girls were happy to shelter us – bless their souls.

19

The Aftermath, the Case, the Houdini, the End

Then. 17 December 1990 through 30 January 1991.

NEW NIRVANA WAS NOW FULL OF FOREIGNERS. THE ENTIRE area seemed to have been taken over by Europeans and Americans. Rammy said this was the only way we could experience another country and culture without applying for a visa, and Rita said he should check out the 'more international Goa'. The girls were extremely happy that Rammy had stood his ground and kept saying that following one's heart and doing one's thing was a very Zen way of living.

Sattu and I went to the hostel to check things out after some ten days. The gates were locked and we weren't allowed to enter. Even the breach in the wall that led from Ugly block to the proximal raydi was plugged. The sentries informed us that all rooms carried seals anyway and the hostel and college were as deserted as a ghost town. Good. At least that would make Gen. Raheja squirm with discomfort as the Hellmints would accuse him of (a) grossly mismanaging the situation and (b) failing to understand students' psychology and (c) using a sledgehammer where a mere fly-swatter would have sufficed. They would make him feel uncomfortable and rib him with typical bureaucratic queries and he'd be at the receiving end for once. Perhaps he'd already received a dressing down from the Ministry and he could kiss his promotion a sweet goodbye. It made me feel good – to think that his lifelong dream of becoming a Lieutenant General would remain just that: a pipe dream. The guy should be posted to the Gobi Desert or Siberia, I thought. But then, why spoil the Mongolian-cum-Chinese desert or the desolate Russian expanse? I'm an environmentalist; and folks like Gen. Raheja would be an environmental disaster wherever they go. Perhaps we can deport him permanently to a space station? Or build him a dacha on the moon? Will someone powerful please do something to make this powerful tyrant's life really *really* miserable? *Please.*

The hostel reopened after about twenty days and the student community began trickling in. The seals were removed and the rooms breathed their first breath of fresh air in days. A huge notice was impaled at the pigeonhole. It was perfectly understandable and predictable. We were all instructed to appear for the mandatory Court of Inquiry (COI) that followed any ruckus. What we had got into was The Mother of all Ruckuses anyway. (Is ruckuses the plural of ruckus, I thought, and made a mental note to ask Rammy about it.) Rammy had refused to come to the hostel and had asked us to find out what was going on. The COI was a joke (at least for us two) and Sattu and I had lots of fun filling in the questionnaire. The authorities even coached the students on what to fill out in the questionnaire, so they could submit it to the Hellmints and settle for a fall guy to take all the blame. The darned wily let's-save-our-ass foxes. Actually you couldn't blame the students as they had been promised immunity if they toed the official line that 'Ramakrishna Iyer somehow brainwashed all our usually disciplined and happy cadets; so we have to come down heavily on him and have decided to exonerate his juniors who just got misguided by him.'

Q 1. Who were the leaders? Or was there just one leader?

My answer: Phantom, Mandrake, Bahadur, Spiderman, Superman, Flash Gordon, Batman, Tintin, Obelix, Hardy Boys, and many others.

Sattu's answer: The leaders were people who were more honest and principled than those mismanaging Defcoms; and they descended on rainbow chariots from their abodes in heaven; and they said their names are Lord Yama and Senor Chitragupta, adding that they will be waiting to transport the sadistic authorities at Defcoms to a luxurious spa called hell in the coming months.

Most students' answer: Ramakrishna Iyer.

Q 2. What was the motive of the leader(s)?

My answer: To lead. (Your IQ is in single digit or what?)

Sattu's answer: To see you make an ass of yourself.

Most students' answer: To disrupt our academic routine and campus harmony.

Q 3. Did you participate voluntarily or were you forced?

My answer: Did you borrow your brains from a millipede or from an amoeba?

Sattu's answer: I was forced to participate by Gen. Raheja's Hitlerish attitude and dictatorial policies and consummate idiocy.

Most students' answer: We were emotionally blackmailed and intellectually brainwashed by Ramakrishna Iyer.

Q 4. Do you apologise for your act of gross insubordination?

My answer: I apologise for having the intelligence and the balls to protest against spineless tyrants like Gen. Raheja.

Sattu's answer: Kiss my ass (you are good at it anyway), then I'll think if I want to apologise.

Most students' answer: I apologise profoundly and regret and realise my mistake.

Q 5. Do you promise not to participate in any future mutiny?

My answer: Vande Mataram! Quit Defcoms! *Inquilab Zindabad!*

Sattu's answer: Do you promise to rejoin the zoo you escaped from?

Most students' answer: I promise and wish to be forgiven for my immature act.

Two days later another predictable notice was impaled at the pigeonhole. Neither Sattu nor I felt any anger now. We were in fact happy and proud of our efforts. Haluji and a few of our professors were extremely delighted with our stance and asked us to convey their regards to Rammy. We were prepared for anything now and had decided to take all academic blows squarely on our chin. Sattu said life was a marathon and not a hundred-metre dash, adding that eventually we will outshine all the spineless tyrants. We looked at the notice and laughed. Perhaps it was exactly what we had always wanted anyway.

OFFICE OF THE DEAN, DEFCOMS, BANGALORE
The following cadets are hereby expelled from the college and the hostel for a period of one year w.e.f. 9 January 1991, due to gross insubordination and for misguiding the cadet fraternity. They will vacate their hostel rooms at 0800 HRS

on 9 January 1991 and report to the Dean on 8 January 1992 at 0900 HRS. They can appear for their final University examination only after the expulsion period. They are also declared NSL (Non-Service Liability) cadets due to poor academic performance.

1. Cadet Ramakrishna Iyer (DGN 3017)
2. Cadet Hari Iyengar   (DGN 3016)
3. Cadet Satinder Singh   (DGN 3110)

NSL meant that you couldn't join the armed forces and that suited us just fine. Of course, we would have to wait for one more year to pass out and we didn't care a damn anymore. Ya, we had failed miserably as far as the strike was concerned, but we had created enough noise and were content to be three irritant thorns in the flesh of the Draconian administration.

Rammy said that we should challenge the decision regarding expulsion (not NSL), so we moved the High Court a week later. A division bench sat to hear our case, and dismissed it in under three minutes. Both the judges said they won't interfere in Defence-related matters. Waste of time and money.

I suggested we go to Delhi; talk to a few Hellmints; and have them reverse the decision. Rammy and Sattu agreed and we did the rounds of the North Block and the South Block and the Secretariat. We literally ran from pillar to post. No result. They heard us patiently and said that nothing could be done. More waste of more time and more money.

But there was good welcome news too. Gen. Raheja had been shunted out. 'Retiring early for personal reasons' was the official line. It did make us feel immensely satisfied.

◇

Then. August 1994 through September 1995.

I was missing Rammy like hell, but he had done a Houdini and one couldn't find fault with his perfect disappearing act, considering that I couldn't trace him for the past three years. Sattu and Shaky were the only other Yankees at the wedding. (Ya, Sattu and I had finally passed out in July 1992 and we had paid the bond amount. Rammy dropped out, and never got the MBBS degree, exactly as he had wildly vowed to Lt. Col. Mishra many moons ago.) Sattu was 'post-graduating' in Ophthalmology. I had given up all dreams of practising as a doctor as I'd discovered that Medicine wasn't my calling. Late realisation, I accept, dude, but better late than never. I was working as a Creative Supervisor at an ad agency in Bombay and had even won a few awards for creativity and all. So, you could say I was finally successful at something, hah! Ranju was looking plumper and lovelier. Alka had pulled down a bit. We had two weddings in Ahmedabad: a Tamil-style and a Punjabi-style to-do; and two grand receptions in Delhi and Bombay. Sattu joked that I could get nailed for bigamy – or even polygamy. We went on our honeymoon to Singapore, now that Ranju could travel abroad without seeking permission since she had quit the armed forces (remember, she had only joined as a Short Service Commissioned officer?).

After we returned, she checked in at my pad in Andheri, and life was one long love song. We had a pretty cool routine. Mornings, I'd drop off Ranju at KEM hospital (she was chasing a postgraduate degree in ENT now) and drive down to my agency at Colaba. In the evenings I'd pick her up and we'd always eat strawberry and cream on Marine Drive. Later, we'd take a long walk on Juhu beach and pick up a take-away dinner or eat outside. Ranju didn't fancy cooking and I liked the arrangement. After hostel life, restaurant food was pure heaven, dude. On the few occasions she tried her hand at whistling up daal and rice, either the rice got burnt or the daal remained horribly undercooked. Once, even the pressure cooker's lid took off like a rocket towards the ceiling and created a yellowish-white fresco that I had to clean with a mop for close to half an hour. After that incident I banned Ranju from the kitchen and she was pretty happy about it. I could make Maggi, whistle up omelettes and beat-coffee, and I must say that my culinary skills were improving by the day. We were planning additions to our family after a year or two, so we were the perfect DINKY (Double Income No Kids Yet) couple. We never had any arguments; never fought; and never got on each other's nerves – can you believe that? I couldn't. But then, that's how it was. Two lovers who had learned to provide space to each other and who understood each other as much as they understood themselves. Life was beautiful…

Then came 11 September 1995 – wish it hadn't. It should rate as the most horrible day of my life. I got up early and went to Juhu beach for a jog. Then I prepared a hurried breakfast of cheese omelettes and toast and flew to my agency in my Fiat. Just another day in my life – but it wasn't. Ranju had gone to Poona to visit her cousins, along with her maternal uncle who'd come from US. They had driven down in Ranju's Maruti about two days ago and were expected to return in the afternoon. They didn't return. Well, not alive at least. I got the news as I was trying to write some copy for a new Talcum account we were pitching for. They both had died after an oil tanker had spun out of control on the Bombay-Poona highway and destroyed my life forever. A police inspector called me up (Ranju always carried a diary with everyone's contact numbers) and probingly enquired about the Maruti's registration number etcetera… I was too shocked to feel any pain; or too pained to feel any shock. Whichever. I just froze when he began describing her clothes and jewellery, and the receiver slipped out of my hands. I didn't cry. I just couldn't. I was a living corpse for some two months and had to be medicated heavily to be pulled out of the vortex of depression. (I don't claim to have recovered fully even now. I guess I never can. I am not ashamed to admit that depression is a constant thread in my life, the grammar of my mind, and the language of my soul. But one has to live with it – perhaps I'm used to depression so much that happiness and bliss would be unbearable. So be it. It's a temporary life, after all. Nothing lasts forever. This too shall pass, as Rammy would have said.)

Well, I had understood a few things. Life is a river that doesn't ask the raft if it likes the flow. Life doesn't give a flying fuck about our desires. Life is too stubborn, too self-willed, and much too *Draconian* for our liking. (Have we heard that word before?) Pity, we can't protest against Life though.

Well then, that was *then*. And, many thanks for walking down the staircase of time with me. It's time to clamber up and taste the *now*.

20

The Vodka, the Journey, God, the Games

Now. 18 through 19 December 2008.

$\mathcal{P}$ADDY (MY NEPHEW, REMEMBER? YA, THE ONE I AM SHACKING up with?) has flown off to Delhi to convince his dad that 'Neelu will make a wonderful daughter-in-law and would do the family proud'. His dad calls me up and is wondering 'how can a Neelu Motiani, a Sindhi girl, a meat-eater, do any Tam-Brahm family proud?' I have no answer to that.

Okay, first let me take you through the Tam-Brahm procedure if at all you wish to know how traditional Tam-Brahms get married the traditional Tam-Brahm way. Just sample the following steps:

1. Tam-Brahm families are proud only of slavish sons and daughters who, if they wish to marry, will first consult their parents, then an astrologer uncle, then their respective birth charts – and precisely in that order.
2. If all seven (that is two sets of parents, two birth charts, and one astrologer uncle) agree, then you are allowed to see the would-be spouse's photograph. (And that's a quantum leap in evolution

compared to the times when a groom saw the bride only *after* the marriage.)

3. Then we do a background check from the Tam-Brahm grapevine. (And we usually drop the girl immediately if anyone says 'we saw the girl *talking* to a guy at the market some seven years ago' or even if someone says 'we saw the girl *looking* at a guy at the market some five years ago'.)

4. If the background check throws up a favourable result, then we fix a post-*rahu*-kaal appointment to meet the girl at her house.

5. Then we allow the boy and girl to steal a few coy glances at each other, while the boy's folks are busy digging into semolina halwa (piping hot *sooji* pudding) and marinated potato/plantain/brinjal fritters.

6. Then, if the boy's parents take a fancy to the girl because (a) she just touched their feet or (b) she just sang an old Carnatic classic or (c) the girl's parents are delightfully subservient; then we do a further background check on the girl's parents, brothers, sisters, brother's wife, sister's hubby etcetera.

7. Then we wonder why one of the girl's brothers is still a bachelor, and we drop the girl if we don't get a satisfactory answer. ('He doesn't want to marry' is not a satisfactory answer and is as acceptable as 'He's a trained, professional, serial rapist'.)

8. Then we do more background checks on the girl's cousins, and generally check the entire family tree, and get DNA samples (since you are metaphorically drawing blood anyway) to look for genetic abnormalities.

9. Then we run all the prospective in-laws through the FBI database if you have the right contacts.

10. Then, if the boy's parents are satisfied, we go back to astrologer uncle who'll look for the right *muhurat* and somehow fix thirty-two compatibility signs and charge a bomb to do some *havan* and 'mitigate evil' in their birth charts – mostly all three together.

11. Then, and only then (that is if astrologer uncle waves the green flag) do we reach the final titration point of how much dowry the girl's side can fork up.

12. Then, if we are satisfied with the girl's parents' financial ability, we take a collective decision on whether boy and girl can marry and live happily ever after, never mind whether boy likes girl or vice versa.

Now that we have run through most of it, I am sure you can understand Paddy's dad's ire and frustration.

'That's how it happened during our times, Hari,' Paddy's dad screams into the phone, 'and how very successful our marriages have been.'

'Yes, sir,' I say, wondering if the success rate of any Tam-Brahm marriage is directly proportional to a woman's cowardice quotient which prevents her from walking out when she wants to. (High CQ is the secret behind long and—not necessarily—happy marriages.)

'How wonderful were those times, Hari, when sons used to listen to fathers. And, how very irritatingly and individualistically intelligent today's boys and girls try to be,' he continues.

'Yes, sir, you are right, sir, absolutely, sir,' I lie.

'How can Paddy just bypass such a carefully-thought-out, scientific process of getting married…?'

'Yes, sir, correct, sir…'

'How can he use his own brain when his parents, who are his best well-wishers, are carrying two experienced brains…?'

'Yes, sir, how can he? I'm shocked, sir, to tell you the truth…'

'Which good son has ever used his own brain, tell me…?'

'Right, sir, a good son will never do something so primitive, sir…'

'How understanding you are, Hari, so you better convince this mad man, he's returning in the evening, that if he even thinks of this Neelu-Sindhi-Shindi-Girl, then I'm going to disown him, and completely cut off all financial support, okay?'

'Okay, sir, I'll try sir…'

'No trying-shying, just do it, okay?'

'Okay, sir.'

'I'll call you tomorrow night, and you better have some good news.'

'I will, sir.'

'Okay, bye.'

'Bye, sir.'

I want to tell him that I have troubles of my own right now, and that I'm also madly in love (though sadly one-sided) with a Parsi girl called Tanu, so I don't give a rat's ass about the fact that Paddy is planning to clearly breach Tam-Brahm tradition and rigid protocol, but you don't go about rubbing a multi-millionaire the wrong way, especially when you are planning to touch him for some monetary help in the coming months.

Normally, I don't like an afternoon siesta. But after my brain-crunching convo with Paddy's dad, I desperately feel the need for one. I switch on the AC and pull the blanket over my head. I definitely need to sleep off the stupid convo and its mind-numbing after-effects. How can people be so unreasonable? Shouldn't love be the highest value? What's wrong with marrying the person you love? Shouldn't one be applauded for that actually? I toss and turn.

Paddy returns early in the evening and slumps on his bed. I wake up. He declines coffee, and I know that he's feeling really low. (If Paddy declines coffee or Maggi or French fries, it's a clear signal that his mood has plumbed the depths.) I decide against broaching the subject and wait for him to recover from his obviously acrimonious nerve-wracking meeting with his dad.

One hour later. Paddy is still lying down on his bed, blankly staring at the ceiling. There's no expression on his face – neither sadness nor anger nor worry. I am worried, yes, but I don't wish to disturb him. I get back to my game on Yahoo! Chess. I am winning, but I'm not happy. My mind is on Paddy.

Two hours later. I whistle up a dinner of egg bhurji and butter toast. Paddy nibbles a bit and sets aside his plate. He fixes himself a drink—vodka and Miranda—and sinks into the massage chair next to the living room balcony. He's in no mood to talk, so I step out to take a walk. Actually, I wish to leave him alone for a while – aloneness and unintrusive companionship and empty space are great healers.

Thirty minutes later I return to the apartment and let myself in. Another glass of vodka is sitting on the window sill. I can say it's his second peg as he's added a bit of tomato puree into it. That's Paddy's drink routine: the first peg with Miranda; the second with Miranda *and* tomato puree. I am tempted. I take a few sips. It tastes tangier than usual. I drink half of it. Paddy emerges from the loo.

'What the fuck are you doing, you idiot!' he screams, seeing me with the glass, and violently pulls it away from my hand.

I am surprised. Normally, Paddy is so very generous, always sharing everything with me – except his Reebok T-shirt of course. But I am happy that he's finally emerged out of his vow of silence.

'What? Chill, dude, just felt like taking a few sips, funny that you're so possessive about vodka...'

'Shut up! Fuck you! You've no idea what you've just had!' he screams, and gulps the rest of the almost Bloody Mary.

'Hey, you'll scald your throat...'

'Does it matter, now that we're both going to die?' asks Paddy.

'Are you mad? What are you rambling...?'

'Look,' says Paddy, showing me a small white tablet. 'This contains some fast-acting cyanide and digitalis and some other deadly stuff. I'm tired of life, dude. Dad has blocked all my money and savings. I got this from Delhi, from a contact in Pahar Ganj, saying I wanted it for my dog suffering from some terminal illness...'

'Ya, ya, good joke...'

'You don't believe me, do you? Just see what happens to you. You are right, like you've mentioned on so many days, life just sucks, man, and I can't take it anymore. I just hate life and all the fuck-all traditions, so I made myself a death cocktail, and I went into the loo for a last-minute talk with the bathroom mirror...'

'Balls! You expect me to buy your nonsense story?'

'Okay, you'll know in two minutes. Just wait.'

I begin to feel dizzy. My chest feels a tightness first and then an excruciating pain. I go and lie down. Paddy does the same.

'Dude, I'm not joking. We're both gonna die. But you'll be first. I'm sorry you drank the stuff, but there's nothing we can do about it now.'

'Aaarrgghh...how...could you...do...somethring soo... strupid...'

I hear my voice tapering off and find myself losing consciousness. No, I don't see any tunnel with light at the end and all. I just don't see or feel anything.

We are lying down in a lush orangish-green meadow. I see a steady rain of multi-coloured light falling all around us – only we aren't getting wet. Everything is so psychedelic that I wonder if we've popped some LSD. It's neither day nor night nor evening. The sky is a deep yellowish-red and the stars are shimmering with some pretty crazy colours I've never seen before (no, not even in an Asian Paints or Nerolac catalogue). A few cows are grazing in the distance; and a few peacocks are preening. Surreal, definitely surreal.

'Holy cow, where are we, man?' asks Paddy.

'Search me,' I say.

'This place is beautiful, dude, how very groovy and sublime! Just look at all the colours, dude, it's like Van Gogh and Dali are collaborating and creating a magical realm on the canvas of existence ...!' screams Paddy.

'Now stop writing an essay, and just shut up. Let's enjoy the view in silence,' I say, and get up.

The first thing I feel is weightlessness. The second thing I notice is that I'm wearing a yellowish robe – the kind *sanyasis* wear. The third thing I sense is that there's no feeling of time. Perhaps Paddy is feeling much the same, for he's smiling and dancing like a mad man.

'Wherever we are, this place just rocks, dude, this place just rocks!' he says excitedly.

I can't deny that. As I'm looking around, I see a boy (who's definitely not more than sixteen-years-old) walking up to us. He's dressed exactly like us.

'Hello,' says the boy, 'so how are you?'

'Great, just great,' I say, 'but could you please tell us *where* we are?'

'You'll soon know,' he says. 'Come with me.'

We follow him and it would be wrong to say that we are walking. To say we are floating is closer to the truth. He takes us to a small lake and I am quite surprised to see that the water isn't blue – it's actually light red in colour, as if someone has thrown lots of vermilion powder into it. A few swans of varied colours adorn it, along with lilies and lotuses. The ambience is so very peaceful, tranquil and soothing that you'd have loved to stay there forever. A huge round table made of antique wood is fixed at the lake bed, surrounded by a few bamboo chairs that carry rather wide armrests.

'Please sit at the table,' says the boy and we sit down. The bamboo chair is softer than a silk cushion. Surprising.

'What the hell is going on, dude?' asks Paddy, and I don't reply because I have no idea what the hell is going on.

'What's your name?' I ask the boy.

'Gautam,' he says, sinking into a chair opposite mine, and his eyes look as if they are gazing into the distance but not looking at anything in particular. He's so still and serene, and everything about him is so full of grace.

I wonder if he's a statue brought to life. I feel my eyes closing and I am engulfed by waves upon waves of bliss.

'Hello,' says another voice, 'so we got company?'

I open my eyes to see two other boys sitting in the chairs. They all are spitting images of each other and I wonder if they are triplets. Paddy is sitting with his eyes closed, and I wonder if Gautam has sent him deep into meditation. Boy # 2 taps Paddy on the forehead and Paddy comes to with a jerk. Then I see that Boy # 3 is playing with a small ball that's neither solid nor liquid nor gaseous. It's as big as a tennis ball and looks like the kind of spheroidal holograms you see in sci-fi movies. The ball looks as if it has a life of its own. He's tossing it in the air, watching it bounce off the ground, letting it twirl around his fingertips, smiling as it runs along his hands and neck, and tossing it in the air again. *Air*? There is no air! Funny I didn't notice it before. I am not breathing. Nobody's breathing.

'Who are you?' asks Paddy of Boy # 2.

'You can call me Naren,' he says.

'Where are we?' I ask, looking at all three of them.

'You are in *Timelessness*, the last frontier of the spiritual worlds,' says Boy # 3.

'Huh?' I say, 'you mean we're in an astral dimension?'

'Beyond,' says Boy # 3, 'you are in fact beyond even the *Causal Dimension*. It all begins and ends here. This is my *Supra Causal Supreme Abode*.'

'What's your name?' I ask.

'Call me Govinda,' he says.

'But...but...where is God?' I ask. 'I thought *God* was the last frontier, the Primal Cause of all that is and...'

'I *am* God,' says Govinda.

Paddy is tongue-tied and speechless. So am I.

'Well,' says Gautam, 'so now that you'll be here for quite a while and since you're beginning to like it – I assume you're liking it...?'

'Ya, ya,' says Paddy, recovering his lost composure, 'this place just rocks, dude, it just rocks, but I always thought that God would be an old man with a long beard and all...'

'Yes, most people think that,' says Govinda.

'How come all of you people look alike? Frankly, I thought you were triplets,' I say.

'In a way, we are the same. You must have heard psychologists saying that a husband and wife who are compatible and think alike begin resembling each other in later years. It's much the same with us. We are all tuned into the same Eternal Truth – Govinda,' explains Naren.

'Yes, I've heard that husband-wife thing before, when I was on Planet Earth – by the way how far is Planet Earth from here?' I ask.

Govinda throws me the hologram-ball and I catch it in my hands. It feels like gelatine and is as light as a feather and quite smooth. I try pressing it but can't. You can't compress it – to that extent it behaves like a solid. I toss it at an angle like I've seen Govinda doing and it returns like a boomerang. I throw it away horizontally and it comes back. Same result. I hold it again in my hands and see that the hologram is changing colours.

'How far is Planet Earth? You are holding it, my dear,' says Govinda.

'You mean *this is* Planet Earth?' I ask, looking disbelievingly at the hologram-ball.

'This is not Planet Earth. This is the *entire material creation*, comprising billions of universes and billions of galaxies and billions of stars – Planet Earth is a very small planet within it...' says Govinda.

'Are you crazy?' screams Paddy. 'How can this be the *entire material creation*, dude? Material creation is so vast, so infinite...'

'What's infinite?' asks Gautam. 'For an ant, an elephant is infinite. For bacteria, ants are infinite. Infinity is a relative term, it has no absolute values...'

'I've heard that before from Rammy. Are you *really* God?' I ask Govinda. 'Or are you guys pulling a fast one on us?'

As soon as I ask the question the hologram-ball goes back to Govinda. He touches a part of it with his fingertip and a huge room swims into view. *It's our room in Thane. Paddy and I (well, Paddy's body and my body, how very weird that sounds!) are lying spread-eagled on the bed, with their mouths and eyes wide open.*

'Shit, that's us, dude, that's us!' screams Paddy.

'As you can see,' explains Govinda, 'everyone dies while exhaling; nobody can die while inhaling, that's why your mouths, or rather your body's mouths, are open. That's your physical body. Your *supra-causal body* is here.'

'Swing it around to the Ajanta Quartz clock on the West wall,' I say. I wish to check the time in *that dimension.*

2:40 a.m. The second hand is moving. That dimension is full-on.

'Hey!' I say, 'just five hours have passed since we died there...' And then it all comes back to me. *The Bloody Mary laced with deadly poison. Paddy's violent yank. The slipping into unconsciousness...* 'Fuck you, Paddy, do you recall? You made a *death cocktail*?'

Paddy looks guiltily at me and I know that he remembers it too.

'Forgetfulness and remembrance are in Govinda's hands, he's explained it in the *Gita*, so now you're able to remember what happened because he wants you to...' says Naren.

'You mean Govinda is *Krishna*?' I ask.

'You still have doubts?' asks Gautam.

I look at Govinda and he's smiling.

'So, now that you know who I am, where would you like to be? Here or there?' asks Govinda.

'Here,' says Paddy, 'it's so beautiful and...'

'There,' I say, 'I want to go back there...'

'You nut,' says Paddy, '*you want to get back into that stupid ball...*?'

'Yes, Paddy,' I say.

'But why?' asks Naren.

'Naren, it's blissful here, but I'd say it's a li'l too *blissful* for my liking. I'd like to get back to that dimension where everything is so *blissfully miserable*, if you know what I mean. Here everything is *miserably blissful*. Plus I'm not going to leave my mom all alone out there…' I say.

'I accept,' says Govinda to me. 'One has to get used to bliss, you have to develop a taste for it. That takes time. And, I'm impressed with your love for your mom.'

I nod understandingly. Paddy shakes his head vigorously.

'You go back. I'm not leaving,' says Paddy to me.

'That's not possible,' says Gautam, 'your destinies are interlinked. Plus, Paddy, you are here because of Hucky, not the other way round. So, either both of you stay here or both of you head back.'

'Okay, I'll be fair,' says Govinda, 'you both can play three different games, and the winner decides where you guys will be, okay?'

I nod yes. Paddy doesn't say anything.

'Okay,' says Govinda, 'Hucky, you choose the first game.'

'Chess,' I say.

'I accept defeat,' says Paddy.

'So soon? Without even trying?' Govinda asks him. 'You never know.'

'Okay, let's play,' says Paddy.

A small hologram chessboard appears on the table and I get to play black. Paddy plays d4. I reply with d5. He knows that I am generally unbeatable with a King's pawn opening, so he's trying the Queen's pawn opening. After twenty-seven moves, Paddy resigns after I devastate his king-side with a brilliant knight sacrifice. It's mate in three. Absolutely unavoidable.

'Great,' says Govinda, 'Paddy, you choose the next game.'

'Snakes and ladders,' says Paddy.

Gautam and Naren laugh.

'You leave it to chance, huhn,' says Naren, 'next you'll convert this place into a casino.'

A snakes-and-ladder hologram board appears on the table along with a hologram dice. I cavort with lots of snakes. Paddy coolly and steadily climbs the destiny-ladder. Ultimately, Paddy wins and is jumping like a mad man again.

'Okay, last and decisive game,' says Govinda. 'What game, Hucky?'

'You decide,' I say, 'I leave it to you, Govinda. It wouldn't be fair if I choose two games and Paddy gets to choose only one.'

'Good, I always like those with a sense of fair play,' says Govinda smilingly. 'Fine, we'll test your intelligence, are you both okay with that?'

'Cool,' says Paddy.

'Ya, sure,' I say.

A series of hologram letters appear on the table.

O T T F F S S E N T _

'What's the next letter in this series?' asks Govinda.

'Someone *sent* something?' asks Paddy.

'No hints. It's fairly simple. Count on your intelligence,' says Govinda.

We think and run our fingers through our hair and rack our brains, but the answer eludes us.

I think more: What did Govinda say? No hints, he said. But Govinda is a wily guy – no wonder he's God. (When was the last time you heard that a simpleton has become God?) Did he give us a hint when he said *no hints*? Did he mean *know hints*? Possible. It's fairly simple, he said. What's simple? Elementary? Elementary school? Something to do with school? *Count on your intelligence.* Did that hold some clue? *Oh yes! I got it! That was the hint! Count! Omygod! So simple and so superb!*

'E,' I scream.

'Sure?' asks Govinda.

'Of course, I *counted* on my intelligence,' I say smilingly.

Paddy has still not got it. He looks quizzically at Govinda.

'Okay, explain,' says Govinda to me.

'It's fairly simple. We learnt it in kindergarten, Paddy,' I say.

'Huhn? Alphabet?' asks Paddy.

'Close, numbers,' I say.

'Numbers?' he asks.

'Yes, say the first ten integers after zero...'

'One, two, three...'

'There, you got it,' I say. 'O for One, T for Two, T for Three and so on...'

'Oh no, man, how could I have missed it?' screams Paddy.

'Happens,' I say.

'Okay, now that you are heading back,' says Gautam, 'do you wish to remember meeting us all or do you wish to forget it?'

'Since Govinda is God, he knows best – let him decide what's best for us,' I say.

'Okay,' says Govinda, 'Maybe Hucky will remember all this as a dream? Maybe Paddy will recall nothing or recall a different series of events? Maybe Hucky will be confused? I won't tell you exactly what I have decided. Anyway, you're going to live through it. Now, you both prepare to leave...'

'Before I leave, I have a few questions. May I?' I ask Govinda.

'Be my guest,' he says.

'What's *life*, Govinda?'

'You already know the answer. Sattu and Rammy were discussing it at the new Insti one night.'

'Huhn?'

'Remember Rammy said God is just an acronym for...'

'Ya, Greatest of Designers...'

'True, but he mentioned another at the end...' hinted Govinda.

'Hmmm...Greatest of Directors...?'

'Exactly...'

'So life's a movie?'

'Absolutely. What else could it be?'

'And we have no choice in the matter? We're just given whatever role you decide?'

'Actually, I don't decide. We have something called the Laws of Nature which take care of that. Be good, Hucky, and don't worry too much about philosophy. Sometimes, I do edit a few things here and there, but I generally make it a point not to interfere. Have faith in yourself and in the powers of goodness. Maybe you will meet Rammy later in life...'

'But, Govinda, you have the power to do anything, absolutely anything, you are God, dude, so why don't you make everyone blissful and happy and peaceful *right now*?' wonders Paddy.

'Nothing comes free, Paddy, they have to earn it. Even Naren and Gautam had to earn it when they visited Planet Earth...'

'They are from Earth?' I ask. 'I thought they have always been here...'

'No Hucky, I'm the only one who's always here – the rest have to journey...'

'But Naren and Gautam, where were they, what were they?' I ask.

'Know any enlightened persons, Hucky?' asks Govinda, and Naren and Gautam are smiling naughtily.

'Oh, shucks! You mean Gautam is Gautama Siddhartha, the *Buddha*...?' I scream.

Gautam nods.

'...and Naren...Naren is definitely Narendranath Dutta aka Swami Vivekananda!'

Naren smiles.

'Omygod, how could I have missed it, your names sounded familiar but I just couldn't place it,' I say, and bow to express my respect and love for them.

'No, Hucky, no,' says Gautam. 'Love knows no superiority, don't bow.'

'Yes, Hucky,' says Naren, 'we don't even bow before Govinda. For Love stands tall and stands as an equal.'

'Farewell, Hucky and Paddy. See you later. All will be well. My blessings are with you. Hopefully, next time around, you'll like to stay here much longer,' says Govinda.

I hug them all and become misty-eyed. It's tough to leave God, but leave I must. Perhaps I love mom more than I love God. So be it. (Dad had kicked the bucket some five years ago, and I was her only emotional anchor left.)

Gautam asks us to close our eyes, and I can feel his fingertip on my forehead and...

◇

'Fuck, man, what an experience!' I scream, and try to wake up Paddy, but he continues to snore deeply.

'Hey, wake up, you nut, wake up!' I shake him violently.

'What...the hell, man? Seeing...nightmares again?' he mumbles.

'Dude, wake up, we had the *most crazy* experience...'

'Not crazier than my meeting with my dad, what's it? Why are you waking me up, dude?' he asks tiredly.

'Listen, do you remember that I'd stepped out for a walk three hours after you returned and you had made this death cocktail and you'd mixed some cyanide-cum-digitalis pill in it and how I had it accidentally and you screamed at me and we both died...?'

'Dude, you are hallucinating. When I returned, you were fast asleep. We never spoke, and in fact you've been asleep for the past nine hours...'

'No, no, after you returned, you were lying on bed, totally blank and all and you even made this death cocktail that I accidentally had and...'

'Fuck you, did you see a dream or something? Why will I attempt suicide, dude? You the suicidal type…'

'Arre, don't you recall yanking the glass from my hand…?'

'Nonsense, you've been dreaming, dude, as I said you were fast asleep when I returned, in fact I let myself in, and I didn't wish to wake you up…'

'Hell, no, everything's so confusing…ya, Govinda said that I'd be confused if all this was a dream…in the dream…' I say.

'Now who's Govinda?'

'He's *GOD*, man! Don't you remember we went to the *supra causal dimension* and we met Buddha and Vivekananda and Krishna, and you wanted to stay back and I wanted to head back and we played games…?'

'Dude, you are hallucinating and confusing dreams with reality. I think it's time to meet your Tardeo shrink again. This time, you've gone totally crazy…'

Shit, man, was I really dreaming from the time he returned to the apartment…? Have I really been asleep since then…? Didn't I make dinner…? Didn't I take a walk and accidentally have the death cocktail…?

Perhaps Paddy was right. I'd been fast asleep when he'd returned to the apartment, as he says. Why would Paddy lie? But it all seemed so real, buddy. It was all more real than life itself. Holy cow, I met Krishna and Buddha and Vivekananda! I can't believe it! So what if it was in a dream? Perhaps life itself is a dream seen from some other dimension. And, when we wake up there, perhaps we are lying down in a lush orangish-green meadow and seeing a rain of multi-coloured light falling all around us – only we aren't getting wet because we are in *Timelessness* where raindrops are actually lightdrops…

Time? What time is it? 3:25 a.m.

'Here, have a coffee, dude, it'll make you feel better…' says Paddy, and settles next to me with his cup.

'Gosh, it was so blissful, Paddy…in that dimension…'

'Forget it, dude. *This* is reality. *Here* and *now*. Even I get some pretty crazy dreams at times, but I don't attach too much importance to them...'

He's right. I should live in the *here* and the *now*. I should forget the past. Okay, not forget, that's impossible unless you suffer from total amnesia, but throw it all into a remote memory attic where we dump all our hope-it-hadn't-happened-that-way scenes? Anyway, fuck it.

Epilogue

Now. 0340 HRS. 19 December 2008.

$\mathcal{M}$Y CELL RINGS. I INSTINCTIVELY SURVEY THE AJANTA QUARTZ clock hanging on the wall. Paddy throws a queer look at me wondering who is buzzing me so late in the night – or call it so early in the morning if you will. I look at the screen disinterestedly. The number seems familiar. Tanu?

Tanu! My heart misses a few beats. I gather myself.

'Hello,' I say, taking the call and pretending to sound gruff and trying to hide my eagerness to hear her voice.

'Hiiiii! How's you?' she shrieks.

'Great,' I lie. 'Just great, wassup? Trying to check if I'm still alive?'

'Was just thinking of you, Hucky – hope I didn't wake you up from your beauty sleep or something.'

'Not at all. Anyway, what's happening?'

'Why are you sounding so distant, honneeeey?'

Honey? Did I get that right or is my semi-asleep brain hearing things?

'What did you just say?' I ask.

'Honnneeeey,' she says, knowing well that I am thirsting to hear that again. 'I just asked why you are sounding sooo cold and distant...'

'Helllooo! What do you expect me to do? You dump me for a bum and expect me to sound cordial and sweety-sweety, hahn? I'm not a saint, girl!'

'Hey, c'mon, I'm just a li'l immature girl – you the mature one, you should've handled me better.'

'Aha, so the fault's mine!'

'Yes,' she giggles.

I am savouring the giggle and it's making my entire body shiver and igniting my loins and curving my face into a billion smiles.

'Say something,' she says.

'Something,' I say as I angrily remember all the heartaches I have endured because of her.

'Hey, c'mon, that's all in the past…'

'Ya,' I say. 'Anyway, why have you called? I'm trying to forget us.'

'Liar.'

'Listen girl, enough is enough.'

'But I love you, na!' she says, giggling again.

'Tanu,' I say, in the deepest tone possible. 'I've had enough of your nonsense.'

Paddy sits up, eagerly absorbing the tiff, and tosses a gesture-request that asks me to put my cell on speaker. I refuse. He sidles closer.

'Really? So you don't love me?'

'No!'

'Not even if I say sorry and that I wish to kiss and make up?'

She is trying to woo me back! Or is it the other way round? My entire body is grinning. My voice is pretending anger.

'So you can dump me again?'

'Fucker! Now you listen! I made a mistake, people make mistakes okay, and that's that – you don't have to stretch it like a rubber band. FUCK YOU!'

She hangs up. Paddy raises his eyebrows cattily. He's heard that. I am breathing like a steam locomotive. *Shit! Have I blown it again?*

'Dude,' says Paddy. 'You look the *khichdi*-picture of happiness and fear. Don't worry, she'll call again. YOU DON'T CALL BACK, OKAY?'

I don't. Five minutes ride a snail. Seems like five hours. My heart-thumps are shaking the bed. My mind weighs a few tonnes. Then the cell rings again. I take the call and say nothing.

'You and your mega ego!' she says.

'There's not much of it left after what you did to me,' I say. I have her by her ovaries and I'm making the most of it.

'Okay, listen,' she says commandingly. 'We are meeting soon, okay?'

'Really?' I ask snarkily.

'Yes, you meet me at McDonald's, Lokhandwala, sometime in the morning.'

She wants to meet me! She loves me! She needs me! I am a boy again.

'Okay, if that's what you want – but evening, four-ish or five-ish, I need to sleep...' I say snootily.

'Okay, but you'll be there, na? Promise?'

'Promise.'

'Love you, honey!'

'Bye – and gimme a call around two, so we can coordinate...'

'Okay, will, bye. Sweet dreams.'

She hangs up.

'Dude, it's sinful to look so happy,' says Paddy.

'Shut up,' I say, beaming like blooming sunrise.

◇

Now. 1658 HRS. 19 December 2008.

I am late. Deliberately. (I'd promised to meet her around 4 p.m. It's close to 5 p.m. now. Serves her right. Did I tell you I'm a bit vindictive? Well, now you know.) She's sitting sipping a milkshake at the far right corner. Chocolate. Her favourite. We've spent so much time there. In that very corner. Nostalgia is a lump in my throat and a vacuum in my knees.

She looks up and smiles.

'Hi, sorry, got stuck in traffic,' I lie.

'Really? You wanted to make me wait deliberately.'

'So, what's the story?'

'What story?'

'Why – you and that bum of yours…'

'Oh, forget him yaar, I just got carried away…'

'Into his bed?'

'Shut up! We just kissed. Twice. No sex.'

'So you're still the pure *Sati-Savitri* types, hahn?'

'Hucky, we're meeting after *such* a long time – you know I've been missing you like crazy. I love you only, honest. And, stop being so *sarky-sarky*.'

'Okay, so what's the plan, girl?'

'I want us to be together again.'

'And you promise not to leave me and…'

'I told you na – ya ya I promise…'

She paws me. I let her. We get as cosy as is socially acceptable – which is pretty cosy as Bombay is a cool city for lovers.

'So what were you doing all these days?' she asks.

'Writing a book.'

'About what?'

'My life at Defcoms.'

'You think it will sell?'

'Maybe, maybe not. It's fun writing though.'

'Hucky, let's begin a fresh musical chapter.'

'Hey, that sounds nice – maybe I'll call my book that. *A Fresh Musical Chapter*. That has a buoyant ring to it!'

'Promise me you will title it that otherwise it means you don't love me anymore!'

'Hey, I can't promise. It all depends on the publisher and my editor. We authors are just small fry, we don't call the shots. I will suggest the title to them though…'

'Do that and your book will sell like hot cakes.'

'Toblerone in your mouth…'

'I want more than that in my mouth…'

'Shut up, baby, don't make me horny now, people are watching.'

'Let them.'

Ya, let them. Life is beautiful again. The French fries are crunchier. The chocolate milkshake is tastier. And, Tanu is lovelier than ever.

I wish to gather Life in my arms and give it a grateful smooch on its cheeks, but how the hell do you go about doing that to Life? Any ideas?

Glossary

Aarti	Idol-worshipping by lighting oil lamps and camphor
Achintya bheda abheda tattva	Inconceivable difference and oneness of Creator and Creation, a philosophy of Chaitanya Mahaprabhu
Adda	Meeting place / Gangster's den
Agarbatti	Incense stick
A.K. Hangal	A Hindi film actor of yesteryears, renowned for on-screen laments
Aloo	Potato
Aloo chaat	Spicy, fried potato cubes seasoned with tangy chutney
Aloo gobi	Potato and cauliflower curry
Aloo parantha	Thick, unleavened, whole wheat flatbread with potato filling
Anatta	Non-being, non-I, non-mine; a term used by Buddha
Asanas	Postures in the Hindu system of yoga
Athithi devo bhava	Guest is God, a popular sentiment in India
Bachao	Save / Save me / Save them; an SOS cry for help
Back-roll(ed)	A ragging technique at Defcoms entailing bowing on the ground, curving your body into a foetal position, and rolling backwards
Bahut	Lots of

Bajao (this guy's trip)	Screw
Band bajao	Ruin someone's happiness / Play a band
Band baj gayee, man!	We are screwed, dude!
Behenji	A woman who's not stylish / Elder sister
Bhaisaheb	A man who's not modern / Elder brother / Bro-in-law
Bhaiyya	A man who's not classy / Brother
Bhajans	Devotional songs
Bhakti	Devotion / Reverential love
Bhatura(s)	Thick, fluffed, deep-fried leavened white flour flatbread
Bhature	Plural for bhatura
Bhav	Slang: Self-centred, cocky importance
Bhel puri	Puffed rice flavoured with spices and sweet tamarind chutney
Bindaas	Slang: Gay abandon / Unconventional / Happy-go-lucky
Biryani	Rice cooked with spices, vegetables, mutton etc
Biryani and raita	(See Biryani); Raita = Churned spicy yoghurt
Brahma	The Creator of our Universe in the Hindu pantheon
Buddha	Founder of Buddhism, aka Gautama Siddhartha
Butter chicken	Buttered chicken curry
Butter naan(s)	Thick, buttered leavened white flour flatbread
Carnatic	South Indian classical music
Cashews	Defcoms-speak for cash
Chaat	Spicy snack mix of various types
Chacha	Your dad's younger bro / Any uncle
Chaitanya	A famous Krishna devotee of yesteryears
Chakra	Discus / Wheel
Chambal Chali Chaloo Chokri	Chambal-towards moves cunning girl, a fictitious erotic Hindi movie

Chambal valley	An area notorious for dacoits
Chanakya	A movie hall in New Delhi/An epithet for any brilliant strategist/A hyper-intelligent kingmaker in ancient India
Chitragupta	Chief Data Officer of Yama, the God of Death, who records all your earthly actions to dish out suitable rewards or punishments after death
Chole	Chickpea curry, usually a side dish with bhatura
Chup kar yaar	Shut up, pal
CQ	Cowardice Quotient (a neologism)
Daal	Spicy stew made from any of various pulses or lentils
Darshan(s)	Appearance of an enlightened master for communion
Desi	Regional/National
Desi ghee	(See Desi); Ghee = clarified butter
Despo	Slang: Desperate, sly, skirt-chaser/Acronym: Dumb English-speaking Prowling Organism (new coinage)
Devdas	Epithet for a jilted man pining for his lost lover
Dhaba	A roadside restaurant, usually on highways
Dhammapada	A Buddhist scripture
Dishum-dishum	Slang: Fisticuffs
Distal raydi	A roadside tuckshop which is afar
Dosa	Thin, salty pancake made from a batter of rice and black gram
Egg bhurji	Scrambled eggs cooked dry with spices, onions and tomatoes
Egg curry	Boiled eggs in spicy gravy
Eggetarian	Vegetarians who eat eggs though
Ekdum	Slang: Totally/Absolutely
Fauji	Of or related to the armed forces
FIR	First Information Report, lodged at police stations

Fish koliwada	A flavoursome fried fish appetiser
Frog leap	A ragging technique at Defcoms entailing sitting on your haunches, balancing yourself on your palms, and leaping forwards
Front-roll(ed)	A ragging technique at Defcoms entailing bowing on the ground, curving yourself into a foetal position, and rolling forwards
Funda	Slang: Fundamentals / Concept
Gaajar halwa	Carrot pudding
Gandhiji's three monkeys	Three monkey statues that represent the dictum: See no evil, hear no evil, speak no evil
Ganja	Marijuana: the dried leaves of hemp plant smoked or chewed to give a high / Bald / Baldie
Gautama Siddhartha	A prince who became the Buddha
GB Road	A notorious red light area in New Delhi
Ghazal(s)	Arabic and Persian poetry, also sung as Hindi melodies
Gherao(ed)	To enclose someone or some place within a human circle
Gita	Bhagavad Gita, The Song of God, a Hindu holy scripture detailing how the Supreme Personality of Godhead, Krishna, convinces Arjuna, to fight a righteous war, while also explaining the basic purpose and essence of life, some 5000 years ago.
Gol gappa	(See Paani puri)
Govinda	Another name for the Supreme Personality of Godhead, Krishna
Guru dakshina	A fee or gift given to a teacher by a grateful student
Gurudwara	A Sikh temple
Gyan	Knowledge

Halwa	Pudding
Hanuman Chalisa	Forty sacred verses by Saint Tulsidas, praising Hanuman, Rama's trusted confidant and foremost devotee from the venerable Hindu holy epic, Ramayana
Havan	A holy sacrificial fire lit for religious purposes
Heer	The lady love of Ranjha (Heer-Ranjha were diehard lovers akin to Juliet-Romeo during yesteryears)
Hijra	Eunuch
Hinglish	Slang: A lingo amalgamating Hindi and English words
Hitlergiri	Autocratic behaviour reminiscent of Adolf Hitler
Idli	A steamed salty patty made from a batter of rice and black gram
Inquilab Zindabad!	Long live revolution!
Jai Hind	Victory to India / Hail India
Janam-janam-ka-rishta	A relationship lasting many births
Jawan	Army soldier / Tyro youth
Kabaadi-wallah	Junk dealer
Kama Sutra	Sage Vatsyayana's sex treatise
Kebab	Marinated meat cubes skewered and barbecued
Kebab-mein-haddi	Literally means a bone (haddi) in meat (kebab); Refers derogatorily to an uninvited intruder or a thorn-in-the-flesh kind of person
Keshto Mukherjee	A Hindi film comedian of yesteryears, renowned for his unique imitation of the comic drunkard
Khichdi	A hotchpotch / Also a rice dish cooked with pulses or lentils
Khukhri	A curved sharp Nepalese dagger
Kompootur	Computer
Krishna	The Supreme Personality of Godhead

	from whom everything orginates; while others maintain that He's an avatar of Vishnu
Kulcha(s)	Thick, leavened baked white flour flatbread (non-fried variant of bhatura)
Kulfi	Frozen milk-based dessert, the Indian version of ice cream
Kumbh Mela	A humungous congregation of sages and spiritual seekers, occurring once every 3, 6, 12 or 144 years
Kumbhakarna	A warrior from the Hindu holy epic, The Ramayana, who slept for six months, and remained awake for six months
Kurta-pyjama	A flaring tunic and loose pajamas worn by men
Langar	A community kitchen in Sikh temples aka Gurudwaras, where everyone is served free food
Lao Tzu	An enlightened master from ancient China; Taoist
Lassi	Sweetened churned homemade yoghurt, sometimes salty
Leela	Play, usually refers to divine play
Lungi	Cylindrical colourful one-piece lower garment for men
Maal	Slang: Sexy babe/Marijuana/Item/Goods
Machchar(s)	Mosquito
Maida	Super-refined soft wheat flour aka white flour or all-purpose flour
Maida parantha(s)	White flour flatbread
Mangalsutra	Auspicious necklace worn by married ladies
Mantra	Commonly repeated word or phrase/Sacred verbal formula repeated in prayer, meditation or incantation
Mar gaye yaar	We are doomed/We are done for
Masala	Spice or condiment

Masala Dosa	Dry, spicy mashed potatoes wrapped, Frankie-like, in Dosa
Masala vada	Deep-fried patty made from coarse batter of various pulses
MCQs	Multiple Choice Questions, an objective examination method
Meena Kumari	A breathtaking Hindi film heroine of yesteryears, renowned as the 'Tragedy Queen' for her melancholy roles
Mess bandh bilkul induffinitully	Mess closed totally indefinitely
MLA	Member of the Legislative Assembly
Mooli parantha	Thick, unleavened whole wheat flatbread hosting radish filling
Muhurat	Auspicious time for an event or commencement of an activity
Mutton biryani	A spicy rice dish hosting mutton
Mutton rogan josh	An aromatic Kashmiri mutton dish
Naan	Thick leavened white flour flatbread
Natak	Drama / Unnecessary melodrama or hysteria
NCC	National Cadet Corps
NDA	National Defence Academy, close to Pune, in Khadakwasla
Nimbu-paani	Homemade lemonade
Nirvikalp Samadhi	Thoughtless, timeless, trance-like state
NRI	Non-Resident Indian
Ooi maa / Oooi maaa	Slang: Oh mummy! / A girlish exclamatory intensifier
OPD	Out Patients Department
Paani puri	Spicy water (paani) placed in puffed pastry-balls (puri), along with mashed potatoes and sweet tamarind juice / Aka Gol gappa
Pakoras	Fritters
Paneer	Cottage cheese
Paneer butter masala	Buttered cottage cheese in spicy gravy
Paneer parantha(s)	Thick, unleavened whole wheat flatbread hosting cottage cheese filling

Parantha	Thick, unleavened whole wheat flatbread, with or without filling
Patao	Slang: Seduce / Attract / Influence
Pav	Small rectangular bun, an inexpensive Indian bread
Pile on	Slang: Freeloader
PMS	Pre-menstrual syndrome, characterised by unease and irritability
PoK	Pakistan-occupied Kashmir: an integral part of India illegally and forcibly occupied by Pakistan
Post-rahu-kaal	After an inauspicious time (See Rahu-kaal)
Proximal raydi	A roadside tuckshop close to Defcoms boys' hostel
Public darbar	An area where ministers meet the public to address grievances
Pucca	Definitely / Solid / Matured / Ripened / Concrete construction
Pulao	Rice cooked with vegetables and spices
₹	New symbol for the Indian currency, Rupee. Ideally, we should have carried 'Rs' (the old abbreviation for rupees), since our story is based in a bygone era, but we are, quite anachronistically, carrying this new symbol as a tribute to India's economic might and growing supremacy.
Raakhi	A sacred wrist-band tied by sisters on brothers
Raavanammy	(Ravana, the enemy of Rama in the Hindu holy epic, Ramayana, had ten heads, and in our story, since Rammy is considered a guy with extra brains, Solly is punning to jocularly punctuate Rammy's genius.)
Rahu-kaal	An inauspicious time created daily by the demon, Rahu

Rajma chawal	Red kidney beans (rajma) cooked in a spicy gravy, and mixed with rice (chawal)
Ramsay Brothers	Hindi filmmakers noted for their horror movies
Ranjha	The male lover of Heer (Heer-Ranjha were diehard lovers akin to Juliet-Romeo during yesteryears)
Rasam	Extremely thin, spicy soup made by South Indians
Rashtrapati Bhavan	The official residence of the President of India
Raydi	A seedy roadside tuckshop
Roomali roti	Literally means 'handkerchief bread'; An extremely thin white flour flatbread (roti) folded like a handkerchief (roomal)
Roti	Thin, unleavened whole wheat flatbread, aka chapaati
Saala/Saalay	Brother-in-law; Also used as an intensifier to convey everything from friendliness to enmity, and can thus mean idiot/ bloody/bro/dude/wow!/fantastic or a million other things
Saala chor!	Bloody thief!
Saalay grud	Bloody moron
Saala lag gayee	Bro, we are screwed
Saamp hain saalay!	They are snakes!
Saas-bahu	Mother-in-law and daughter-in-law combo
Saas-bahu serials	Indian TV soaps
Sadhus	Renunciant monks
Sai Baba	One of the most worshipped saints of India
Salwar-kameez	Loose pajamas-like lower garment and flaring, tunic-like upper garment worn by Indian ladies
Sambar rice	Spicy pigeon pea stew hosting vegetables, and mixed with rice
Samosa(s)	Deep-fried pastry pyramid case hosting

	a filling of spicy mashed potatoes (sometimes meat)
Sanyasis	Renunciant monks
Sarpanch	Village chieftain
Sati-Savitri type(s)	A pure, chaste, loyal kind of woman devoted to her husband
Shabbaash	Appreciative, congratulatory, spirited expression meaning Bravo!/Excellent!/Fantastic!/You rock!/Proud of you!
Shabbaash mere laal	Well said, my dear/Well done, my dear
Sheek kebab(s)	Spicy minced meat thinly skewered and barbecued
Shikakai shampoo	'Fruit for hair', a herbal hair wash
Shiva	The Destroyer of our Universe in the Hindu pantheon
Shree 420	An untrustworthy person: culled from Section 420 of the Indian Penal Code dealing with cheating
Sindoor	An auspicious vermilion mark applied by a married woman in her parting
Sirshasana	A yogic posture entailing standing on your head
	weapon
Subji	Curry/Any vegetable
Sudharshan Chakra	Lord Vishnu's golden, serrated, discus
Suhaag	An auspicious term for a husband
Sundal	Spicy, steam-cooked chickpea snack seasoned with grated coconut
Swami Vivekananda	(See Vivekananda)
Tamasha	Frivolous drama/brouhaha/street play
Tam-Brahm	Slang: Tamil Brahmin
Tandoor	A clay oven powered by burning coal
Tandoori chicken	Marinated spicy chicken cooked on a tandoor
Thoda	Little bit
Tik-20	An organophosphorous poison and insecticide, commonly used by suicide victims

Un-pataoable	Impossible to seduce (a slang neologism)
Upma	Spicy salty dish made from semolina or vermicelli
USMLE	United States Medical Licensing Examination
Utthappam	Thick salty pancake made from a batter of rice and black gram
Vada sambar	Vada = Deep-fried spicy patty made from a batter of black gram, and dunked in Sambar
Vande Mataram!	I bow to thee, Mother!
Veena	A stringed instrument, used for playing classical Carnatic songs
Vishnu	The Preserver of our Universe in the Hindu pantheon
Vivekananda	One of India's most famous yogis
Yaar	Friend; also an intensifier in convos
Yaaron	Friends
Yama	The God of Death, the overlord of hell
Yamadhoots	Yama's assistants who escort sinners to hell after death

www.ingramcontent.com/pod-product-compliance
Lightning Source LLC
Chambersburg PA
CBHW022002050726
47499CB00002BA/271